THE VISION OF CALDARIA

Ashley —
Thank you for reading my
book! I hope you enjoy
the world of the Caldar.
Best wishes —
Juli Faye

By Julia Faye

THE CALDARIA TRILOGY
The Vision of Caldaria
The Quest for Caldaria
The Waking of Caldaria

The Vision of Caldaria

Book 1 in the Caldaria Trilogy

By Julia Faye

THE VISION OF CALDARIA

Publishing History
First Paperback Edition published 2009
Second Edition published 2015

Published by Julia Faye Slade via CreateSpace
Orange, California

Copyright © 2015 by Julia Faye Slade
Map by Kelsea Schmidt

ISBN 978-1449914134

For Andrew

Chapter 1

The walls were lined with the tapestries and portraits of all those who came before her, but Myla only glanced at them with a passing interest. She was supposed to be there. She was worthy of this place. It was her home.

She walked down the marble spiral staircase with no exact purpose or meaning. It didn't matter where she ended up because she already knew that he would be there for her wherever she was. He always appeared, and she was always glad and thankful to see him.

She wandered into the grand throne room to be greeted by a large crowd. She knew each person there and they were all happy to see her. She looked around through the masses of people, searching for him, but she could not find him. The room waited silently for her cue, but she did not give them one. She simply kept searching for him. He was supposed to be there... Where was he?

Myla woke up with a sharp pain in her neck. She had rolled over into an unnatural position on the uneven ground. These hunting trips were never very comfortable, but that wasn't what they were about. She was there to learn something; though it was hard to say what lately.

She poked her head out of her small tent to see the silent forest. As far as she could tell, Zira and Neph were fast asleep in their individual tents, blissfully unaware of the world around them. She wondered if they dreamed, and if their dreams haunted them as well.

Myla knew that the day ahead was probably an intense one, but she didn't feel like sleeping again, at least not so soon.

Instead, she grabbed her hunting knife, climbed out of her tent, and tiptoed out of the camp circle towards the woods. She appreciated the forest in the middle of the night. The trees danced in the wind playfully as they enjoyed time undisturbed by humankind. These trees were more alive and aware than most. The Caldar were always at peace with the forest, but even Myla knew that this was not their home. They were the guests of the trees, and she needed to remember to not take that fact so lightly.

"I'm pretty sure that you're supposed to be sleeping right now," whispered a voice from behind her.

Myla turned around to see Neph, who had apparently followed Myla without her knowledge. Only he was skilled enough to tread that lightly.

"Are you standing in for Malachi on this trip?" she asked him with a smile.

Neph shrugged.

"While I'm pretty sure your grandfather would have an issue with your decision to wander off alone, I don't have the power to fail you on your hunting lessons," he answered.

"Malachi wouldn't fail me," she answered. "I passed all the hunting lessons a long time ago."

"You and me both," said Neph. "The joys of keeping up pretenses."

Myla smiled for a second before quickly turning towards the woods. She had heard a sound, and instantly everything else faded away. The sound was faint, but it was definitely there. Something was out there… She could feel it.

She didn't have to look. She could feel its presence and knew what it was. She immediately grabbed her knife and threw it into the woods. She could hear the slight thump as the deer hit the ground. It was only then that she turned back towards Neph.

"You disgust me; you know that?" he said with a small laugh.

8

"You're just jealous that you didn't hear it first," she answered before sprinting towards the deer.

With Neph's help, they carried the body back to the camp. Zira was awake when they arrived, indicating that they hadn't been as silent as either had hoped. She glared at them as she came out of her tent, visibly still sleepy.

"You know it's the middle of the night, right?" she asked.

"It'll be morning soon," answered Myla.

"And thanks to your best nocturnal friend here, we'll have plenty of food tomorrow," added Neph.

Zira looked over to Myla and then at the deer, whose presence she only just registered. She looked back at Myla.

"Did the deer wake you up?" she asked, confused.

"I woke me up," answered Myla. "The deer just was running on a similar schedule."

"Poor deer," said Zira rather sullenly.

Neph and Zira were both too awake to sleep at this point, so they reluctantly helped Myla prepare the deer. They kept their annoyed expressions to a minimum, and based on years of friendship, Myla knew that they were both secretly having a good time. Zira and Neph were her closest friends among the Caldar and the first friends she made after joining them from Mertana. Myla had been raised by Tarrans, a people who lacked the Caldar's magical gifts. It was only when she was ten years old that she had returned to her people.

The next day was a long one. That wasn't uncommon for a hunting trip, but this day felt even longer. Myla knew their lack of sleep had something to do with it, and she felt bad that Zira and Neph were struggling to get through the day, but she didn't know what she could do about it now.

Myla and Neph weren't really supposed to go on these trips anymore. They both were attending it now to support Zira and get away from the village for a while. It was normal for Caldar to go on one of these trips to complete a series of tasks when they were nineteen years old, as Zira was doing. It was an initiation into adulthood for the Caldar. However, Neph and Myla had both completed their trips when they were just seventeen. Myla, in particular, didn't like to call attention to that fact because she didn't like to be viewed as different as much as was feasibly possible.

Myla loved the forest. She could still remember the feeling from the first day she entered it. She had wondered why no one ever came there. It was mesmerizing. The trees themselves were enough to preoccupy her thoughts for hours. They were so full of life. She had never known that trees could actually appear to be happy before. Everything in the forest was brighter, like it hadn't yet been touched by the human world. It was untainted.

Growing up with the Tarrans in Mertana was different. The land was cold and hard, and the trees were sparse. The buildings were made of stone and brick, and the dusty streets made everything a little more muted. At least that's how she remembered it. It had been nine years since she left that place, and she never had a desire to return. Of course, life wasn't always easy among the Caldar, even with the presence of their magical gifts. Belonging to the Caldar community was difficult as she still often felt like an outsider looking in, but she felt more at home with them than she ever had with the Tarrans.

"What do you think?"

Myla paused and looked to her. Zira had asked her a question and she hadn't been paying attention. Was she really that tired?

"I'm so sorry, Zira," she answered. "I must have drifted off there. What did you say?"

Neph laughed.

"You can kill a deer in the middle of the night without even looking, but now in broad daylight, you can't follow a conversation?" he asked.

Myla smiled and shrugged. She didn't really have a response to that.

"I asked if you wanted to head down to the waterfall," said Zira. "We can have lunch there."

"That sounds great," answered Myla.

"I hate that you both have already finished these tests," mentioned Zira. "It's weird that you two are out here for fun."

"Why do you say that?" asked Neph, seeming amused.

"I love the forest, but five days out here without my bed does not sound like fun to me," she answered.

"You could have taken the test a year ago, you know," said Myla. "Then you would already be done."

"I don't need to be special," said Zira. "I put these tests off for as long as possible."

Neph laughed in his usual carefree way, but Myla was a little more cautious. She always sensed Zira's frustration that she was consistently behind Myla and Neph on training, but Myla never felt that this frustration was justified. Zira was commonly considered to be one of the more talented younger adults in the village, but Myla knew that Zira didn't view it that way. Neph never seemed to mind that Myla was always ahead of him, but then again, he was always ahead of everyone else. Myla didn't know how to handle it, and she knew that bringing it up to Zira was the last thing she should do. As a result, she always stayed silent when Zira made comments about not being as advanced as the other two. She never knew what to say.

"I have no desire to be special," said Myla after a bit of a pause. "Just a desire to get the annoying tasks over and done with."

Zira gave her a pained look.

11

"And yet here you are, tagging along on one of these tasks for fun."

Myla shrugged.

"I guess it's different when you aren't the one who is being evaluated," she answered.

Zira just smiled and shook her head.

The rest of the day was uneventful. Zira completed her required tasks with ease, and thanks to the deer, the three friends ate well that evening. Exhausted from their early rising, they didn't waste any time at getting to sleep.

It was well into the night when Myla awoke with a shudder. It took her a moment to realize that it was plenty warm and that there hadn't been a breeze. Again, she shivered, but it wasn't due to cold. Myla lay there confused, wondering what was causing her to shiver. If it wasn't cold, what was going on?

Then a distinct feeling came over her, and it was one she couldn't shake. There was something, or someone, outside the tent. It didn't feel like a deer, or any other animal she knew. There was something there, however, and it was almost as if it was calling to her. Myla wasn't used to doubting her senses, but with this, she was starting to. What was going on with her?

Neph and Zira were fast asleep and she had no desire to wake them, certainly not for something that was probably all in her head. Quietly she pulled herself to her feet and climbed out of the tent. She let out a breath in relief when she saw nothing, but yet again, she shuddered. Something was out there. It was something that she couldn't see.

Once again she shivered, but this time she almost felt a breeze. It wasn't from the wind, however. It was from something else. There was something else out there calling to her and she didn't know what it was. Without thinking, she plunged into the woods, following a whisper in the wind that she couldn't trace. She didn't think as she moved forward, mesmerized by whatever was calling to her. She was scared, but she couldn't turn away. There was something out there. Something was trying to reach her.

"Myla?"

She jumped much more visibly than she would have liked when Zira called her name. Quickly she turned around. The whisper was gone. She wasn't shivering anymore.

"What are you doing out here?" asked Zira.

Myla looked behind her and then back at Zira. She didn't know what to say.

"I'm not sure," she answered. "I heard something."

"You don't look very well," said Zira. "Your skin is very pale."

Myla refocused and suddenly felt very stupid. She wasn't sure what had happened or why she was out in the woods. Had she really managed to scare herself?

"I think I had a dream and mistook it for reality," she eventually said. "Let's go back to the camp. Just ignore me."

Zira nodded her head and patted Myla on the shoulder as they turned back to the camp. Myla could tell from the look on her face that Zira wasn't going to completely drop what happened. She was concerned, but she was not going to say anything right now.

The next morning Zira acted like nothing had happened, but Myla knew better than to think that it was the last that she would hear of it. Despite their very different childhoods, Zira understood Myla far better than anyone else, and even though Myla was commonly considered to be the stronger Caldar, it was Zira who had always looked out for her friend. Zira's life had been much less complicated than Myla's. Zira had grown up in a normal Caldar family. Myla had been raised first by her Tarran father in Mertana and then by the old innkeeper Misha, a man who was hardly kind to her. To add to that, Caldar were considered more folklore than fact in Mertana. Everyone knew that the Caldar existed, but they never acknowledged that existence. The Caldar gifts made them uncomfortable, and as a result, Myla had always made the people of Mertana uncomfortable.

In Mertana, secrets held everything together. Many had lived their lives spinning lies into the world and others, such as Myla, found themselves caught in their web. Many times as a child, Myla had been told that the Caldar were not real, but she knew the truth. She knew because she was one of them. She wasn't sure if anyone had told her. All that she was sure of was the memory of a soft voice, whispering to her the secrets of her past.

Myla had tried her best to forget the events of her childhood. Most of the time, she succeeded. It was only times such as this, when she was out in the forest, that she found herself thinking about her past life. Being away from the distractions of the village tended to bring out unwanted thoughts.

Maybe that was all that had happened to her the night before. There was nothing out there except the trees and the wind. Myla had simply just let the quiet of the night get to her. There was nothing there. There had to have been nothing there.

And yet she was scared. Something had scared her the night before and it was something that she could not understand. She wanted to put it behind her and forget it ever happened, but she couldn't. She couldn't because she was still scared and she knew that Zira could tell.

They returned to the village with little discussion. It didn't take Neph long to realize that something had happened the night before. He was patient however and had learned long before that Zira would fill him in on the events after Myla wasn't around. Myla tried to not let that knowledge get to her. She figured that soon enough, those two would move on from the event and it would be like nothing happened.

14

It was nice to be home. The Caldar village was built far differently than Mertana's cold brick and stone houses. Each house and building was interconnected in a web of meandering paths and bridges, all spinning out from the trees. The houses weren't just built; they had actually been grown from the trees, in a combination of Caldar magic and the will of the trees themselves. The entire village was alive.

Myla didn't hesitate at returning to the small house that she shared with her mother, Malika. It was a small home, but much more of one than the creaky old attic she was relegated to when she lived with Misha. She hated that place and tried to not think about it, but for some reason, Mertana was weighing heavily on her mind still.

Malika wasn't home at the moment, something which Myla was grateful for. She didn't really want to talk to anyone. Instead, she quickly put her bag in her room, then went to the shelf and grabbed a book to read. The local fiction wasn't anything exciting, but she appreciated the escape that it brought. She nestled into the large cushioned chair in the main room and started to read.

About an hour passed before she heard a knock on the door. It was Malachi, and he had a look of concern on his face. It was clear that he had figured out that something had happened. Just what she needed! Myla had never had a great relationship with her grandfather, or her mother for that matter, and she didn't always appreciate their cryptic meddling. They had kept many things from her early on in her days in the village. She had been there for weeks before she even found out that Malika was her mother! Malachi always seemed to think he knew what was best for Myla, and in Myla's experience, it usually made things worse.

"I understand you had an interesting adventure in the forest," he said as stepped inside the house, clearly skipping the pleasantries.

"It's nice to see you too," said Myla somewhat sarcastically. "And the hunting trip was pretty uneventful. Zira passed all of the tests with ease."

"So what happened to you last night?" he asked. "I understand you had a scare."

She couldn't believe it. Zira had actually told Malachi! How could she do that what she knew that he was the last person Myla would want to talk to about it? Myla was already embarrassed enough.

"There was no scare," answered Myla. "I thought I heard something and then I didn't. Did you come all the way over here to rub it in?"

Malachi shook his head. He was stern but never cruel. She knew that.

"I just wanted to make sure that there was no chance you actually did hear something," he said.

There was concern in his voice. Why was there concern in his voice? This was a nonevent.

"There was nothing out there, Malachi," she answered. "Just the wind."

And yet, somehow she felt like she was lying.

After she convinced her grandfather to leave, she went looking for Zira. Myla found her at Neph's house. Zira and Neph looked like they were expecting Myla as soon as she walked in the door. The guilt on their faces was apparent.

"Look, before you say anything, we didn't tell him," said Neph.

"I didn't even tell you!" answered Myla, flabbergasted and embarrassed.

"I told him," said Zira sheepishly. "Neph, that is. But I didn't tell Malachi! He overheard us."

"We were at Eli's café," explained Neph. "We had no idea he was there and listening. He confronted us about it and then immediately left."

"What did you tell him when he confronted you?" asked Myla.

"Just that you thought you had heard something but didn't," said Zira. "And that it was no big deal. He didn't seem to believe me though. I don't know why."

"Why do you think he cares?" asked Neph.

It was a legitimate question.

"I have no idea," answered Myla. "He probably just needs something new to hold over me and blow out of proportion."

None of them completely bought that answer as it was rather odd that Malachi cared so much. His reaction was just strange. There was something he wasn't telling her, and Myla didn't like being left in the dark.

"I think you need to just let it go," said Neph, with a smile. "Malachi is going to be paranoid about you. He's your grandfather. It's his job."

Myla nodded her head in defeat. She appreciated her friends. They always were able to put things into perspective for her.

"We should do something tonight," said Zira, changing the subject. "I passed my tests and want to celebrate."

"I heard that Allasta is having people over to her place," suggested Neph.

"Allasta? Really, Neph?" asked Zira, clearly annoyed.

"I really don't understand what your problem is with her," he answered.

Myla laughed slightly at her friends. This wasn't a new argument.

"Well, I would love to hang out, but I have dinner with my mother tonight," she said. "You two have fun."

Myla hoped that was going to be the last she would hear about her scare in the woods, but it wasn't. Malika brought it up to her again during dinner that night. Apparently Malachi had mentioned it to her. Like him, she seemed concerned that it was a bigger deal than it was, and it had Myla second-guessing herself even more. Yes, she had thought she had heard something, but clearly there had been nothing there. There had to have been nothing there.

But why were they so concerned? She couldn't help but feel there was something the two of them weren't telling her. It wouldn't be the first time. Keeping secrets was their specialty. There were so many things that Myla didn't know about her past, so many things that Malika and Malachi never told her. Her father was a Tarran from Mertana, yet somehow he had a child with a Caldar. Such an action would have violated the laws of both peoples. On top of that, Myla was allowed to live with her father in Mertana instead of the Caldar village. It wasn't until she had called for them that she was taken to live with her people. It never made any sense to her.

Uncharacteristically, she decided to leave her questions for another day. Some doors were too painful to open, and she had a feeling that this may be one of them. Instead, she did what she always did in her nineteen years of life: pretend that she was normal, that she lived a normal life, and that her confusions she may have had were all in her head. Malachi and Malika would get over this. There was nothing in the forest.

There had to have been nothing in the forest.

The next day, Myla wandered into an area of the village that she knew to be uninhabited. It was a common place for her to wander because she could actually be alone there. Everything in the area looked well taken care of, but there were no houses in sight. No one else was around. Myla walked along the path as it

18

meandered away from the village. Finally, she reached the end. There was a single room house growing out of a solitary tree. Many times she had been down this road before, and every time the room was locked. This time was different however, because to her amazement, the door was open. Myla cautiously walked towards it, unsure if she should enter. The air around her became very cold as she approached the door. She hesitated, wondering if this was a bad idea, but her curiosity got the best of her and she went inside.

The room was just an empty small circle. There were writings etched into the wooden walls in a script that she didn't recognize. In the center of the room, there was a small round stone platform. She didn't know what it was, but she hesitantly stepped onto it.

Suddenly, everything changed around her. She found herself inside a white crystal city, and in front of her stood a magnificent fountain, with the statue of a king in the center. She moved towards it. She had been here before. Across from her stood a man. She recognized him and then realized that she knew him. He was the man in her dream. He beckoned to her, but before she could do anything, she felt a hand rest gently on her shoulder and saw the city melt away around her. She was back in the small round room. She turned around and saw Malachi in front of her. Myla looked at him, and immediately knew that she wasn't supposed to have seen what she saw. He didn't seem upset though.

"There are some things that you cannot yet understand," he said firmly. "However, I suspect in time you will."

"What is that supposed to mean?" she asked, annoyed at his cryptic tendencies.

He simply stared back at her.

"What is this place, Malachi?" she asked. "What is it you are keeping from me?"

He still didn't answer her and just held up his hand, motioning for the door. Reluctantly, she walked outside of the room. Malachi followed her out and locked the door.

"I wasn't just hearing things in the woods, was I?" she asked him. "There was something out there."

"We should head back to the village," said Malachi, evading her question.

Once again, he was leaving her in the dark.

Chapter 2

When Myla first met Zira's family, they were a little intimidating. They weren't unfriendly or overly proper; it was actually the complete opposite. They were so friendly that Myla didn't really know what to do with herself. How was she supposed to behave? Everything was so new to her then that she didn't know what was acceptable or inappropriate to discuss. This resulted in Myla being unusually quiet, even for her. Luckily, though, no one in Zira's family seemed to notice, and over time, she had developed friendships with all of them, even if those friendships tended towards the superficial. Myla never completely let her guard down in front of anyone, including Zira and Neph.

Zira's mother, Nora, was not a tall woman, but if someone wasn't paying close attention, they might find themselves thinking so. Her presence dominated the room. Her voice was twice as loud as any other person present, and when she laughed (which was a frequent occurrence), everyone could hear. She consistently had a smile on her face and loved to tease Zechariah, her much more serious husband. Nora's behavior was on the more unusual side, but Myla found it comforting. Malika wasn't like that. Though she was definitely friendly around Myla, she never seemed entirely at ease. Of course, Myla was never completely comfortable around her either. It wasn't because she didn't want to trust Malika; it was because she knew that she couldn't trust her.

"Now, what would you like to drink?" Nora asked her.

"I will be fine with anything," answered Myla. "Thank you."

Myla's reply was hesitant and cold. She had been so distracted by what she had seen in that room before that she had difficulty focusing. Did Nora notice? The smile on her face faded for a second, but it quickly returned to its normal place, especially when the twins started laughing at a story Zechariah was telling on the other side of the room. If Myla's distraction was apparent, it was quickly passed over.

As they sat down, Myla's hunger allowed her to refocus on the situation at hand. Myla loved it when she could join Zira's family for dinner. The food they served was not that much different than what she had eaten as a child in Mertana, and she appreciated their family's togetherness, even if she didn't belong.

It was comfortable there, yet always a little unnerving. Everyone smiled and laughed, and they seemed to genuinely care for those around them, even Myla. She had always had a hard time believing that others cared for her, even Malachi and Malika, who were her family. She knew it wasn't a healthy way to view others, but it was always the way she had. At this table though, she still struggled with her preconceptions. She still could not comprehend why these people would be so warm and welcoming to her. In her mind, she was always the stupid strange girl from Mertana. It didn't matter how many years passed.

Myla looked up from the piece of bread that she had been fixating on. She had so many questions and was suffering from a drought of answers. How did one silly incident in the woods set her on such a confusing path? Why couldn't she just be normal, like everyone else? Myla knew, even as the question entered her mind that she could never be normal because she wasn't normal. She was different, and maybe not simply in the sense that she was one of the more talented Caldar; she felt it extended beyond that. She didn't have a normal childhood because she wasn't a normal child. There had always been something different about her: something that set her apart from everyone else, even here among the Caldar. Malachi knew that.

He knew when she entered that room and saw the vision of that city, of that fountain, of that man. What was that place?

"Now, Myla, tell me. How are your lessons going?"

Zechariah was speaking to her. She was too fixated in her own mind and it was becoming apparent to everyone else.

"I'm not really taking any lessons right now," answered Myla, quickly recovering. "Malachi has been working with Neph and I on some specialized training. We've finished all the normal exams."

"It's impressive," he responded. "Especially when you consider all of the schooling that you missed when you were a child."

With those words, Nora started to get rather emotional, which was normal for her when Myla's Mertana upbringing was mentioned. Myla got the strong feeling that if there hadn't been a table between them, Nora would have given her a hug. Zechariah quickly put his arm around Nora's shoulders.

"You have to understand," he explained. "Many of us were very worried about you being raised so far away."

Zechariah seemed rather embarrassed by Nora's reaction, and Myla was about to dismiss it, per the usual, but for some reason, tonight she didn't.

"Why is that?" she asked. "I never completely understood it. As far as you all knew, I was with my father."

"Well, yes, but you see…" He paused as he searched for the right words. "No Caldar child had ever been raised outside the presence of our people… well, except for one other."

"Who?" asked Zira suddenly.

Zira's question eased Myla because with just those few sentences, her curiosity had become uncontrollable. Nora stared at her husband as if he had just committed the greatest sin. He looked back at her awkwardly.

23

"I probably shouldn't say," he said slowly. "In fact, I have said too much already."

Myla wanted to continue the conversation, but she knew that whatever subject had been breached tonight needed to be handled gently. She would find the answers in time. Zira, however, didn't look so content with the ending of that discussion, but with a loud sigh, she willingly relented and asked no further questions.

Instead of letting the previous conversation hinder the meal, Myla decided to use it as a launching point, so she started telling them of Mertana and some of her experiences there. She told them about how the other children there would give her a hard time, in particular this one girl Serena who had made it a point to antagonize her. She also told them about the inn, and about Misha. She skipped over much of Misha's cruelty, however. They didn't need to know about how nasty the old man was who raised her. They were very amused at how the inn was run and how odd some of the people who stayed there were. To them, the idea of people commonly traveling from town to town was completely bizarre. A Caldar village would never have a building designated to providing places for travelers to stay. They were far too protective for that. They didn't even have separate names for the various Caldar villages, since they didn't have any need to distinguish one from another. With the exception of only a few, such as Zira's family once did, nobody ever left the village. It was a very independent society.

"Why did you live at the inn?" asked Zechariah.

"I didn't really have anywhere else to stay," answered Myla, not thinking much about the question.

"Well, surely your father had some sort of place for you to live," said Nora, slightly confused.

"He did," explained Myla. "We lived in a shack outside of the inn, so when he died, the innkeeper, Misha, took me in."

24

Nora and Zechariah looked completely shocked. The both turned to each other before turning back to Myla.

"Your father," Zechariah asked. "He is dead?"

"Yes," answered a confused Myla. "He died when I was seven. You didn't know?"

"None of us knew," said Nora quietly. "Did you tell Malachi or Malika?"

"Yes, of course," she answered, completely bewildered. "I would have assumed that they would have told you as well."

"She told me too," Zira pointed out. "Why is that so shocking? Wasn't he some sort of drunk?"

With that, the conversation reached a halt. An awkward silence followed as everyone ate their food, not really knowing what to say. Finally Nora found the courage to ask one last question.

"How did he die?" she quietly asked.

"He was found dead on the street one morning," said Myla. "People figured he drank too much."

At this, Nora turned and whispered something to Zechariah. He nodded and excused himself from the table, stating that he had to get some work done. Neither Myla nor Zira believed him.

Dinner didn't last too long after that. Nora was quiet as she quickly finished her food. Myla tried asking her a question about how she made the food, but it seemed that Nora did not even want to entertain entirely off-topic questions. She only answered with a simple: "it's not that hard... I'm sure you will learn at some point." She then picked up her plate and cleared off the table leaving only Myla's and Zira's plates.

"I better go check on the twins," Nora said softly. "I don't want to leave them alone for too long."

"Can we help in anyway?" asked Myla.

"No, no. I can handle it just fine," assured Nora. "You two enjoy yourselves."

Nora quickly made her way out of the room. Myla and Zira were both relieved to see her go, since they were desperate to talk about what had just occurred. Once the door shut behind Nora, Zira immediately turned to Myla.

"What just happened?" she asked.

"I have no idea," answered Myla. "How could they not have known that my father was dead?"

"You never told them apparently."

"But then why would they have joined Malachi and rescued me from Mertana if they thought that my father was still alive?" asked Myla.

"Maybe guilt for letting you live there in the first place?" Zira suggested.

Myla shrugged at the possibility, but thinking of this made her think of many other things about her past she didn't want to.

"I wonder if I wasn't supposed to live at all," she said abruptly.

Once the words left Myla's mouth, she knew that they were true.

"What do you mean?" asked Zira, looking rather appalled.

"Maybe no one here wanted me," she said. "You're probably right. It was only guilt that made them come and get me finally."

"That's rather morbid, don't you think?" pointed out Zira.

"But it's probably the truth," said Myla.

"Why would they not want you to be here?" asked Zira. "You have to be one of the most naturally talented Caldar here."

"Yeah, but I'm not pure," Myla pointed out.

26

She hated to think that such a factor could be an issue, but she had to wonder.

"That shouldn't make a difference," assured Zira. "If they didn't want you, it was because of something else."

"Maybe I'm diseased."

"Now you tell me," said Zira with a smile. "Oh well... You probably already infected me. Just don't touch my food."

Myla laughed at that. Zira was good at making her feel more relaxed. She didn't like the thought of being unwanted. She had no way of knowing if that was still the case, but she was pretty convinced that, at one point in time, she was not welcome in the village.

She didn't want to dwell on it, however, so she decided to change the conversation to the other little gem that Zira's parents had given them in their conversation.

"So what did your father mean when he said that someone else had been raised by Tarrans?" asked Myla.

"That someone else had been raised by Tarrans," answered Zira with a smile.

"You know what I mean... Do you have any idea who?" asked Myla.

"Not a clue, and I would give up searching for an answer if I were you," answered Zira.

"Why?" asked Myla.

"You know why. Everyone here is secretive," explained Zira. "People are very cautious in what they tell each other. It's like every person is hiding some crime and one slip could cost them their life."

Myla was surprised to hear Zira say that. It was something she had been aware of since she had first arrived in the village nine years ago, but it never crossed her mind that Zira might feel the same way.

"Why do you think that is?" asked Myla.

"I've never understood it," said Zira. "I think a lot of the behavior is just inherited. It could even go back to Caldaria for all I know."

It was very rare to hear someone speak about Caldaria. All Myla knew of the city was from what she read in a book from the Mertana library, and she couldn't know how accurate that was. She didn't even know how the Tarrans had such a book. It was that book that gave her the instructions on how to call the Caldar when she was ten years old.

"What does Caldaria have to do with it?" asked Myla. "Wasn't that a thousand years ago?"

"Yeah," answered Zira. "But I think there is still a lot of hope that we will someday return home, and those who have lost hope are too ashamed to admit it."

"Wouldn't the city be in ruins now anyway?"

"You would think, huh?" agreed Zira. "I think a lot of it is the dream of ruling the world again and not having to hide. Everyone here is so paranoid that someday we will be destroyed by a Tarran army that has finally braved the forest."

Myla was surprised by Zira's comment. She knew her friend was intelligent and had an interest in history, but it never occurred to her that Zira thought about these things as well.

"Haven't you ever wondered about how you came to be?" asked Zira.

Myla wasn't quite sure where Zira was going with this. Of course the question had crossed her mind before, but she had always been more curious about why she had left in her father's care.

"As in how did my parents ever even interact?" she clarified.

"Yeah," answered Zira. "There are strict rules against interacting with the Tarrans. How Malika is still accepted by everyone makes it even weirder."

"Maybe that's why she didn't raise me at first. She wanted to spare her name," Myla suggested.

"Maybe, but everyone knew about you anyway," argued Zira. "It was a source of shame for the village that you weren't with us."

Zira was being surprisingly frank. Myla began to wonder why she hadn't talked to her about this before.

"Why aren't the Caldar allowed to interact with the Tarrans?" asked Myla. "Do you think there has always been such a separation?"

"I've actually been reading up on this a lot lately," answered Zira. "Supposedly, there didn't used to be a separation at all. Some children were born with the gifts and others weren't."

"So then why are all Caldar children born with the Caldar gifts and all Tarran children are born without?" asked Myla.

"I guess being gifted became a source of pride for people," answered Zira. "They would only marry others with the gifts. If they had children without them, it would be quite shameful. However, over time a whole hierarchy developed, and that was rarely an issue."

"How long ago was this?"

"I guess it was already pretty segregated by the time of Sherah."

"Who?" asked Myla, confused.

"The first of the two sorcerers," answered Zira, simply.

She seemed puzzled by Myla's question.

"There were two sorcerers?" asked Myla, very confused.

"Yes!" answered Zira, clearly shocked by Myla's lack of knowledge. "Sherah almost conquered Caldaria fifteen hundred years ago. It's because of him that the second sorcerer existed. How do you not know this?"

"Raised in Mertana until I was ten, remember? It's not a surprise I missed some details."

"There was this fountain in Caldaria," answered Zira. "Sherah placed a spell on it saying that his successor would drink from it and inherit all of his powers."

"And five hundred years later..." Myla continued.

"The sorcerer that destroyed our world did," finished Zira. "The king during the time of Sherah also cast a spell saying that the second sorcerer wouldn't rule forever. I guess that's the case, since we are all still here."

"That was definitely not in the book I found in Mertana," said Myla.

"I guess the Tarrans wouldn't have that detailed of information," suggested Zira

"The way to call you all was in that book," noted Myla, thinking back to the evening when the letters rearranged themselves to give her the instructions she needed to reach her people. "I think it was written by a Caldar."

"Really?" asked Zira. "That's weird."

She was definitely confused. Myla was glad someone else was as in the dark as she was.

"Especially considering that the Caldar aren't supposed to interact with the Tarrans," added Myla.

"You should ask Malachi about that book," suggested Zira. "I bet he would know about it."

"Yeah, but would he tell me?" asked Myla.

Zira laughed. It was clear she realized it was a stupid suggestion. Why some random book in a town nowhere near them would have a purpose made little sense, but that wouldn't stop Malachi from being cryptic. And if it had a purpose, Malachi wasn't about to share it with them.

"Did the second sorcerer have a name?" asked Myla.

Zira shook her head.

"No one knew who he was," she said. "He was just some Caldar that drank from the fountain."

"There weren't any records of him?"

"No, it was actually a big mystery, since all of the known Caldar were accounted for," explained Zira. "He must have been extremely gifted though, so he couldn't have been a Tarran."

"What do you think happened to him?" asked Myla.

"No idea," answered Zira. "It's not like anyone has been back to the city since the banishing."

"Which is weird, don't you think? It's been a thousand years. He's dead and the city is probably in ruins," said Myla. "So why haven't we returned, at least to check it out?"

"Maybe the fear of his descendants?" suggested Zira. "He could have followers that still dwell there."

"Doesn't that seem a little strange?"

Zira didn't answer, and she didn't have to. There had been enough strangeness for them to dwell on that day.

Myla didn't want to sleep that night. Something seemed unsettled. Lying in bed, she couldn't feel comfortable. Every time she started to fall asleep, she felt a sudden chill, as if a breeze was flowing in through the window. Why couldn't she just close her eyes and sleep? It was frustrating. She knew she needed rest, but she had an unusual amount of energy. Eventually, she gave up trying, and slowly crept out of bed.

Outside, she sat down leaning against a tree with her feet dangling off the edge of a wooden bridge. She loved looking out on the village at night. Amidst the silence, the trees seemed to dance in the moonlight. This night was exceptionally beautiful as the sky was unusually clear. Myla looked up at the half moon and tried to lose herself in the fairy tales and fantasy worlds that she had once created as a little girl. When she first came to this village, she thought she had finally found them, but this world was no fairy tale.

"Trying to run away?"

It was Malika. Apparently, Myla wasn't the only one lacking sleep.

"Would I be sitting here if I were?" asked Myla

"Maybe you haven't figured out where you are going," answered Malika with a smile.

"Perhaps, but why would I leave?" Myla pointed out.

"I can't think of a good reason," answered Malika. "Why aren't you asleep?"

Was Malika suddenly trying to become a concerned parent? It felt strange and out of place.

"I couldn't sleep," said Myla.

"And coming out here is helping that how?" asked Malika

"I like to look at the village at night. It's peaceful."

It was only half an answer, but it worked for the time being.

"I used to come out here and dream of running away," said Malika softly. "I was about the same age as you are right now."

Was Malika providing clues to her past? Myla felt a sudden burst of hope at the thought, but masked her excitement.

"Why?" she asked.

"I wanted to see the rest of the world," explained Malika. "This village was all I knew. I dreamt of finding something better."

"Did you?" asked Myla.

"Run away?" asked Malika, seeming a bit surprised by the question.

"Find something better," clarified Myla.

32

"I don't think there is anything better," answered Malika. "I think that this village is the best place we've got."

"There used to be some place better once, right?" asked Myla.

"That place was destroyed a long time ago."

"Do you know that?"

"Yes, I do," answered Malika.

The next morning, Myla decided to skip her lessons with Malachi and Neph. They would be fine without her and she had more important things on her mind. She didn't know what she had heard in the forest the other night, or what she saw in that secret room, but she knew that they were connected somehow, and she knew that Malachi and Malika had more answers than she did. If life were simple, they would have just told her what was going on, but life apparently wasn't that simple. Myla wanted answers, and her instincts told her that they weren't here in the village.

She didn't know why she left the village or why she decided to head northeast. Caldaria was to the northeast, but there was no way that she could get there on foot in a day. Part of her felt like she should just try to walk there, just to the edge of the forest to see, but she knew that wasn't where she was headed. Something was in the forest. There was something there that she needed to see, and for some reason that she couldn't quite pinpoint, this felt like this was the right way.

At first, the path she took out of the village seemed normal, just rather neglected. This wasn't the way that students or hunters ever went, but there was a small trail. The blue sky filtered in through the green trees and the forest was quite beautiful, if also a bit quiet. Myla enjoyed discovering this part of the woods that she had never seen before.

After a while though, the trees became more twisted and tangled around her. They were no longer the same vibrant green as they were before. Instead, the branches and leaves were now almost black. The sun was still out, but it suddenly became darker as the trees covered most of the sky. It made her uneasy as she felt more and more out of place.

This is how so many Tarrans get lost in the woods, she thought to herself. *The trees consume them.*

She couldn't tell if the sun had set. It was becoming darker. How long had she been walking? Without the sun, she couldn't be sure. It seemed like hours, but she knew better than to judge based on her feelings. Something was too mysterious about this area that she had journeyed into. She wasn't sure about anything.

Myla didn't know why she kept moving along that path. She couldn't imagine what was down there, but something was calling to her there. It was the same feeling as before, and it was only growing. Somebody was there. She could feel them. She was tracking somebody. She was tracking a person.

Suddenly she realized that she was walking faster. Her heart began to beat quickly as she could feel herself getting closer. Someone was right there in front of her; she could feel it so strongly. A presence had never been so dominant before. She needed to find them.

Now she was almost sprinting as she tore the branches away from in front of her. The trees seemed to be attacking her, but she needed to keep moving forward. Someone was there. She had to reach them. They were calling to her.

Myla...

It was a voice inside her head, pounding through her. Who was there? Who was calling to her? She needed to know as she raced down the path. Why were the trees trying to stop her?

Myla...

She had reached a dead end. There was nowhere left to move. The path was completely stopped by the trees, and she

34

couldn't tell where the presence was. It was all around her. She turned around to head in the other direction, but the trees had moved into her way. She was trapped. She couldn't find her way out. She couldn't see.

Someone's hand was on her shoulder.

She jumped and turned around to find large shadowy figure looming before her. Two piercing eyes glowed through a twisted body of smoke and darkness. Evil was what she saw before her, pure and unholy. In her petrified state, she couldn't think past the phantom presence before her.

Myla...

She felt its presence all around her and moving through her. Her fear was overwhelming. What was this? What was she seeing? She had to push past her fright if she wanted to survive.

Then she saw a face. This was the person she was following. She could see it now. She could see him.

"Myla," he said in a quiet voice that was closer to a hiss.

"Who are you?"

Her voice didn't betray her fear. Somehow, it remained more confident than she was.

"Don't you know?" he asked, as he circled around her.

"No... Why would I?"

"It flows through you," he answered. "It's in your veins."

"What are you talking about?" she asked, as her voice cracked just a little in fear.

"Your destiny."

The words pierced through her like a knife.

"I don't understand," she said.

All she wanted to do was leave, but her feet wouldn't move.

"But you do. You've always understood."

"You're him... Aren't you?" she asked.

35

Could it be?

"Now you are beginning to understand," he whispered.

"You didn't die."

The thought was too awful to consider.

"Even the Caldar don't know everything about our world," he answered.

"Why are you here?" she asked

Myla was beginning to be terrified at an entirely different level.

"Don't you know?" he asked in return.

"Why would I?"

"You've seen me before," he said.

It couldn't be, could it?

"That's impossible," she argued.

"It flows through my veins as well," he said.

"What are you saying?" she asked, her fear too strong.

What was he talking about? Why was he talking to her? She wasn't special. She was anything but!

"You and I: we are the same," he answered, his voice cold as stone.

"You're a liar!" she shouted.

How could he say that? Why was he talking to her like this? Why did he even know who she was?

Somebody was shouting her name. He heard it too. His eyes glowed red as he circled back towards her.

"Aren't you tired of secrets, Myla?" he quickly questioned.

"What do you mean?" she asked.

Even though Myla was hoping that whoever was out there would find her, her curiosity was growing.

"Ask your precious leader, Malachi," he said. "Ask him for the truth. He can't keep you from me forever."

36

With that, the trees blasted away from the path next to them, and he quickly dissolved into the air, disappearing from sight.

Malachi and Zechariah ran over to where Myla was as she collapsed onto the ground in shock. Together they picked her up and quickly raced out of the woods.

*　　　*　　　*

"What did he do to her?"

"I'm not sure. I think she is fine."

"Fine isn't good enough! That is my daughter passed out over there!"

"And it is my granddaughter. You must control yourself. You don't want to wake her."

"How did he find her?"

"It's beyond my comprehension. We have no way of knowing how long he was waiting out in those woods."

"He shouldn't even know she is alive. We should have never brought her here."

"At least here we can protect her."

"And what a good job we have been doing!"

"We knew the risk when we brought her home."

"I just didn't think he would ever find her..."

Myla could hear Malika and Malachi talking, but she didn't want to open her eyes just yet. Never before had she heard them speak so honestly. She was angry with them. They knew she was in some sort of danger, and they never even told her.

Who was that man? That creature or ghost or whatever he was: could he really have been Sherah's heir? Could the second sorcerer still be alive? It was unbelievable. Her entire sense of comfort vanished in those few moments. She would

37

have traded anything to be back in Mertana, where at least she once knew she was safe.

What did he want with her? Why was she important? It didn't make any sense. She was no one. There was nothing worthy of his attention in her. Yet somehow he knew her name. He called her 'Myla'.

"What do you think he told her?"

Malika's voice quivered as she spoke.

"Whatever he said, it was too much," answered Malachi. "We can't let her know anymore."

"So then, what do we do?"

That was Zechariah's voice. Myla hadn't realized he was in the room.

"We make up an excuse, a story, something," answered Malachi, his voice dripping with stress.

"She'll know we're lying. She's way too smart for that."

This was just more evidence to their secrets. Myla was so angry with them, so she did the only thing that she could think of doing. She sat up.

"I want the truth, and I want it now," she said, much more sternly than she had anticipated.

"It was just an old rival getting even with me through you. It's none of your concern," mumbled Malachi.

Myla was furious. Even Malika and Zechariah looked annoyed at his cover.

"Don't give me any of your excuses," insisted Myla, angrily. "I'll find out the truth somehow anyway, so you can at least make sure I listen to you when I do. You can't keep hiding things from me! If there is some thousand-year-old sorcerer after me, and you knew about it, how could you not tell me about it?"

Malachi stared at the enraged young woman in front him in disbelief. Suddenly, he seemed very old, as if he was holding too much and his arms were about to break.

"I should never have brought you here," he said quietly, as he fought back the tears in his eyes. "I wanted to know my granddaughter. I didn't want you to live alone with that horrible Tarran. I wanted you to be with your own kind, where you could really live. But I messed up. I've given you right to him."

Malachi lost his balance and fell down onto the chair next to him, sobbing into his hand. At first Myla wondered if it was all another act, but started to believe that it was genuine.

"What's going on?" she asked him, much more gently.

"The second sorcerer: he's not dead, and Caldaria is not destroyed," answered Malachi softly.

"How is that possible?" asked Myla.

"He found a way to extend his lifetime," answered Malachi. "He was incredibly powerful."

"And you knew about this?"

"Every leader of the village has been informed of this fact. Zechariah and Malika have been my sole confidants up till this point."

Myla took a moment to take in what he just said before speaking again.

"So why did he come after me?" asked Myla.

"Most Caldarian children are told that fifteen hundred years ago, the Caldarian king fought against curse of the fountain saying that the second sorcerer would not rule forever," explained Malachi. "This, however, is not the case. The king couldn't guarantee the end of the sorcerer's rule. Instead, he predicted that another would rise: someone that would bring balance. This person would be the sorcerer's equal. The sorcerer has spent the past thousand years searching for this person in hope to recruit them to his cause."

"What does this have to do with me?" asked Myla, unwilling to let her mind wander too far.

"The first sorcerer, Sherah: he didn't just want to destroy Caldaria," continued Malachi. "He wanted ridicule the Caldar by letting them be conquered in the most humiliating way possible, by someone who wasn't even a pure Caldar. This was the part of the curse that no one ever knew. The second sorcerer was only half Caldar. His mother was a Tarran. Somehow, though, he had the most powerful Caldar gifts of his time despite his Tarran blood, but no one knew this until after he drank from the fountain. Do you understand what I am saying, Myla?"

She shook her head; though she wasn't as far from comprehension as she would have liked.

"The one that will bring balance has to be the second sorcerer's equal, Tarran heritage and all."

Myla looked up at the three people in front of her in complete disbelief. Malachi leaned over and rested his hand on her overwhelmed shoulder and looked at her with the most honest eyes she had ever seen in her nineteen years.

"Myla, in the thousand years since that sorcerer took power, there has been just one person born from a Caldar and a Tarran."

Chapter 3

Escape wasn't out of the question, as a small window in the cell was just out of his reach. He wondered if he could climb up the wall. The uneven and broken stone provided some footing, but once he got out of the building, where would he go? Amos knew his father, and no matter how he looked at it, there wasn't any way around it. He knew that if he stayed, he would surely be killed, but if he escaped, he had a chance. Yes, he would probably die of hunger and cold in the woods. However, at least with that option, there remained some amount of hope for him. He had to climb up that wall.

It was more difficult than he originally expected. The cut in his leg was growing more painful with each second passing, and the stone kept crumbling in his hands, but Amos kept moving. Seven feet remained and the pain was getting worse. As he paused to catch his breath, he found himself looking down below. The ground was swimming around him, detached from any single spot. The dizziness seemed unbearable, but he took a deep breath and kept moving. Four feet were left to go, and he could see the window nearing. However, as he gripped for the next stone, it crumbled to pieces in his hand. Before he had time to think, he was back down on the ground on his back, with his leg throbbing in pain.

They were coming. He could hear their footsteps echo down the hall. He knew that he needed to get out of that room, so he forced himself up from the cold stone floor and began to climb up the wall again at an even quicker pace than before. With six feet left to go, he could hear them standing at the door. His father was whispering to a companion as he fumbled with the lock on the door. Amos couldn't let the knowledge of their presence slow him, so he quickly gripped the next stone and continued his climb. With three feet left to go, Amos stretched out his arm and reached for the window. He heard the lock begin to turn just as he pulled himself up to look outside. The room that they had locked him in was partly underground, so it wasn't that far of a drop. He heard the door open behind him as he jumped out of the window and ran into the wilderness.

Amos ran as best he could with the pain in his leg. He wiped the tears away from his face as he heard his father yelling behind him. He wouldn't stop; even when he thought that he could no longer breathe, he would keep running. Running was all that he had left, and it was all that he had to distract himself from the shame. His mother had warned him, but he hadn't wanted to believe her. He didn't think that it was possible that his father would betray him in such a manner. At least, it had never seemed possible before. Amos never was able to let go of the hope, or the need rather, that his father would love him. He knew that his father had always been ashamed of him, but he had hoped that deep down, his father would not completely forsake him. Apparently though, the shame won over his father in the end.

Amos was a scandal and an insult to his heritage. He was the son of a Caldar who had never displayed the gifts. For him to carry on the family line would dishonor his father and everyone else in his family line. Amos knew that at some point, he would have to demonstrate his powers or be shunned from the family, but he was only twelve years old and had hoped that he had more time. He did not anticipate his younger brother having such great power so early in his childhood.

That was when his mother had first warned him. His father would want the younger child to be the heir and not him. He should have run away that day. Amos wanted, however, so much to trust his father that he had stayed, despite the man's blatant rejection of him. And now, he was running towards the forest with blood dripping down his leg and nowhere to go.

Where was the nearest town? Amos tried to remember his geography, but he couldn't seem to think of anything that his mother had taught him. When his father wasn't home, she had spoken to him secretly about the outside world to prepare him for this likely fate. It was only in those brief moments that Amos learned of the world around him, as he was rarely allowed to leave the house for fear that it might be discovered that he was a Tarran and one of the many ungifted souls. It was a fall from privilege and a black spot on a prestigious family.

The night wind pressed against him as he shivered in his stride. By the time he reached the edge of the forest, he was growing weary and hungry. As the hours passed, the pain in his leg persisted, and he wondered if any glass from the vase remained in it. When he was sure that no one had followed him and that he was alone, he sat down against one of the larger trunks in a tree grove. He placed his hand over the cut. He smiled as he felt warmth flowing into his leg and the pain slowly subsided.

For that was his great dilemma: Amos knew that he was gifted, even if his father didn't. He hated the societal games and class segregation, and he chose to not be involved. Amos didn't want his father's name and status. He didn't want to have to have to flatter his way through life. It was such a fraudulent existence and a waste of time. Amos knew that he was destined for greater things, so instead, he secretly nurtured his gifts, expanding them in ways that he knew weren't taught in the normal world. He had always planned to leave his family and give his birthright to his younger brother. Only fear and a lingering desire to belong made him stay as long as he did.

Amos breathed as the last bit of pain left his leg. Exhausted, he couldn't find the energy to resume his journey and quickly fell asleep. That night, he dreamt of a magnificent city, a place he could call home. He was happy there and at peace, and for once, he wasn't alone. She was there with him, by his side.

He didn't know her, and yet somehow he knew her better than anyone. Who was she?

The next morning, he woke up startled by the sun's height in the sky. He looked to the west towards his home in Nyela, and he knew he couldn't go back that direction. He had to keep venturing into the forest, which didn't seem to be such a bad prospect. The trees were stunning and so full of life, and early on, he came across a small stream where he could fill up on water. Many of the trees had fruit in them so he wasn't short on food. Part of him contemplated just living out the remainder of his days here in the forest, but he knew that was something he couldn't do. He had to keep moving on.

Unfortunately, Amos had no way to carry water with him, but he guessed that water would be plentiful in the forest. As time moved on, however, he realized that this was not the case. By that night, he had yet to come across another water source. The next day was the same. No water was to be found. That evening, thirst started to overwhelm him. Unfortunately, he certainly couldn't see any stream or water source in sight, and Amos was too tired to search for one, as the events of the previous few days still weighed heavily on him. Instead, his thoughts became fewer and more scattered while he drifted off to sleep.

Amos woke up with a sharp coarse pain in his throat. He needed water. How long had he slept? The sun was just above the horizon through the trees. Quickly he jumped to his feet and continued his journey through the forest, hoping to find a water source soon. He was so very thirsty.

What was actually only a few hours seemed like an eternity to Amos, as the pain in his throat was growing worse with each step that he took. Finally, he came to a clearing and started to regain hope. Up far ahead, he could see a city, glimmering white against the morning sky. Putting aside his thirst, he ran toward it. He knew a place like that would have

44

water. If he had stopped to remember his lessons, he would have known what city this was, and he would have known what lay inside it. Amos, though, was not concerned about such things. He needed water and that was all that he cared about.

He sprinted to the gate as the towering white structure loomed before him. He threw himself against it, and the doors opened quite easily. He didn't even pause to take in this incredible sight, and instead, he jogged down the passageway before him. It opened to a square filled with people. Some of them were buying food while others were chatting with one another, but Amos didn't notice them. He also didn't notice how they stared at him when he walked to the magnificent fountain with clear sparkling water in the center of the square. And Amos didn't notice the terrified looks on their faces when he knelt down and drank.

Chapter 4

"No, you need to put your left foot forward... Like this. Are you watching?"

It didn't seem to be that difficult of a task, but little Kalina could not understand it. Myla was growing impatient. Working with the children was not her expertise. She couldn't understand the way they would think. She was quickly becoming one of the most skilled Caldar in the village, if not the most, yet one simple child could cause her such frustration.

"Okay, Kalina. I am going to walk it through with you. We will do each step together. Do you understand?"

The child nodded her head.

"Okay, the right foot steps forward, then your left hand moves out like this, and your left foot follows. Do you get it now?"

Kalina nodded her head unconvincingly. It was going to be a long afternoon. It always bothered Myla, teaching warrior tactics to such a young child. She was aware that they needed to know how to defend themselves, but something about it still seemed odd. Kalina was only ten years old. When Myla was her age, she was in Mertana, where the adults still tried to convince her that the Caldar didn't exist. Warrior tactics were far from her mind. Most Caldar children just thought these lessons were fun, but Myla felt like she was breaking their innocence too young. She didn't want them to have to think about defending themselves so early.

"Myla, I can't do it."

Kalina was very frustrated. Myla smiled and knelt down to her eye level.

"You know Kalina, when I first started learning this stuff, I couldn't do it either," she said kindly.

Kalina's eyes widened.

"Seriously?" she asked.

"Yes, and I was older than you," assured Myla. "But you know what?"

"What?"

"I figured it out, and I know you can too."

Kalina smiled up at Myla. She sighed heavily and began to practice again. Eventually, after the afternoon was spent, Kalina finished the task. Afterwards, Myla walked Kalina home and then headed back to her small one room house. It felt good to be home as it had been a very tiring day. Myla liked her small place. Telling Malika that she was moving out had been difficult, but it had been a year and she was growing accustomed to it. It was just been too difficult to keep living with Malika after the truth came out. The betrayal still stung. How her mother and grandfather could justify keeping such a secret from her was beyond her comprehension. She knew it was their intention to keep her safe, but it was stupid none the same. She didn't cut either of them out of her life, but she couldn't keep living with her mother after that.

It helped that her new house was near many of the other Caldar her age that were also studying the higher gifts. This area of the village was almost always full of life. There was always something happening. Tonight was no different. She could hear the laughter coming from Neph's place, but she didn't feel like stopping by. Instead, she fell down onto her bed in exhaustion. All she wanted to do was sleep.

One year had passed since her encounter with the second sorcerer, and for the most part, life had returned to normal. He had made no more attempts to come after her, and for her part, she had remained close to the village. She never told Zira and

Neph what had happened. Zira still had questions and was frustrated by Myla's insistence to drop the subject, but she eventually did. Part of Myla wanted to share with them what she had learned, but doing so would set her apart again and she liked the feeling of belonging, even if it was false.

Now she was a student of the higher gifts, though mostly in name. She spent the majority of her time teaching the other students. It didn't bother her as much as it used to. When it first became apparent that her unparalleled gifts extended far beyond her fellow students, Myla became intimidated. She didn't want to be special or unique in any way. She was partly worried that the other students would begin to detest her for her talents. Luckily she was so clueless in so many other ways that they didn't let it get to them. Many, for the longest time, still felt sorry for her for having to live in Mertana.

That wasn't the only reason she didn't want those gifts. That fateful day a year ago still haunted her every step. She didn't want to be the one who would equal the sorcerer; she wanted to forget the whole ordeal and pretend that there wasn't an evil being outside of the village set on finding and most likely killing her. Every time she excelled in another area, it was another stone being tossed against her.

"Myla, you have to come quick; you're missing everything!"

Zira had neglected to knock on her door before entering. That was so frustrating. Myla didn't want to move. Though as she thought about it, maybe she hadn't shut the door when she entered the room after all.

"Zira, go away," she said shortly. "I'm trying to sleep."

"It's not even dinner time so that answer is just not going to work," answered Zira, determined.

"What is so exciting that I have to come now?" asked Myla, her curiosity peeking.

"Neph was practicing levitating objects, but he somehow managed to levitate himself!"

That was all that Myla needed to hear. She jumped off her bed and ran with Zira out the door. Sure enough – Neph had actually managed to levitate himself. He didn't have much control over it though and was bouncing around his ceiling aimlessly with four other students sitting on the floor in fits of laughter. Self-levitation was a rare art. Only a few Caldar in history had managed it, and each time it ended disaster. Levitation simply required too much power to perform it on oneself. They didn't even try to teach students how to self-levitate anymore, since no one could ever do it. Myla was both slightly worried and impressed by Neph's accomplishment, however stupid it may have been.

"Hey, Myla!" shouted Neph, with a huge grin on his face. "How's it going?"

"Good," laughed Myla. "How about yourself?"

"I've been a little preoccupied," he answered, trying to look serious. "I've been examining the higher arts, in more ways than one. Ouch!"

Neph had just crashed his head into the doorframe. He started to laugh, until he realized that his body was being pulled outside of his house. Suddenly, everybody jumped up and started to try to pull him back inside, but the levitation was too strong. They couldn't hold onto him, and he was moving outside despite their efforts. Soon enough, Neph was floating up into the sky above the village.

"Myla, do something quick!" Zira shouted.

Myla had never dealt with self-levitation before, and there was no known procedure to control it. In the past, people just had to wait for it to wear off. Neph, however, was floating above the village so they didn't have that luxury. She had to do something.

49

Her hand was throbbing. She could feel the magic pulsing through her veins. There was a way to stop him. She knew she could do it, but she had no idea how. Instinctively, she reached her hand up and a blinding blue light streamed out of her hand. The strength of it lit up the entire village and threw her fellow students to the ground. Then it stopped, and Neph was falling. Thankfully he landed safely on one of the branches of a neighboring tree.

The other students stared at Myla. They knew she had powerful gifts, but nobody had ever seen anybody do that before. Myla didn't even know what she had done. Nothing she had studied ever involved a blinding blue light. Everyone in the village must have seen it. This was going to take some explaining.

Malachi had entered the vicinity. Myla didn't even want to think about how he got there so quickly. He immediately walked over to Neph, who appeared to be unconscious. Malachi rested his hand on Neph's forehead and beckoned over a few of the older Caldar. They lifted up the young man and carried him out of the area. Malachi then walked over to Myla and the other students.

"Is Neph going to be okay?" asked a stuttering Zira.

"He should be fine," answered Malachi. "Luckily he didn't float off too far. I have to say that I am disappointed in you all. I thought you would have known better than to experiment with self-levitation."

The five other students nodded their heads, acknowledging their mistake. Myla, however, looked away, lost in thought and anxiety about the blue light that had just come from her hand. What was that and how far away could it be seen?

"Myla, could I speak with you in private for a moment?" Malachi politely asked, as if no one had just seen the phenomenon she caused.

Myla nodded her head, and they walked away from the group. Myla followed her grandfather as he led her away from the center of the village. At first, she was confused by their trajectory, since it was neither towards Myla's home nor his; however she soon realized where they were heading, to a place she hadn't seen for a year.

Malachi led her down the narrow wooden pathway to the small round room. She didn't ask why they were going there, assuming that it would be apparent at some point in the near future. It was odd to her, realizing that she had forgotten this place. She never figured out what it was for. It wasn't like her to abandon a mystery.

Then she remembered why she let it be: he was there. He was inside it, in that city from a dream that Myla had tried so hard to forget. It was beautiful at first, but those dreams only served as a reminder to her of what her life had in store. They never went away. There were a countless number of nights that Myla danced along those crystal floors with a man she preferred to forget. It was him. She knew it. She recognized him. The sorcerer in the woods; it was always him.

Myla found herself hesitating as they reached the door to the room. She didn't want to go in. Malachi turned to her and laid his hand on her shoulder, smiling at her kindly. He then walked ahead of her and into the room. Myla suddenly felt foolish. There was no reason for her to fear this room. The sorcerer wasn't actually in there. She was stronger than this. She quickly found the courage she needed and followed Malachi into the room.

Again, she was in the small round room. As she walked inside she could feel the wooden floorboards bend under feet. She wondered if anyone had entered this room since she was here last. The writing on the wall didn't seem so cryptic anymore. It was the ancient script of the Caldar. She had studied it in her classes on the higher gifts. In the center of the room was

51

the tiny round platform that she had stepped on before. Malachi was standing on the opposite side.

"Why are we here?" she asked, more boldly than she was anticipating.

"To discover the repercussions of your actions," he answered.

"Are you saying that I shouldn't have helped Neph?"

"No, you quite possibly could have saved his life," he answered. "At what cost, though, is the question."

"What do you mean?" she asked.

"Exactly what you know I mean," he answered. "How far do you think that blue light was visible?"

"I don't know."

"Myla, it projected at least a mile above your head, which means it could have been visible in Mertana..."

"Or Caldaria," she added.

"Up until this point, we have used our gifts to make this village blurred from his vision," Malachi explained. "This is why he has only been able to reach the outskirts. Now though..."

"I've given him a direct route to us," she finished for him. "What was that light?"

"I was going to ask you the same question. In my many years, I have never seen nor heard of anything like it."

"So why are we here?" she asked.

"Every village was built with a room such as this after Caldaria was abandoned."

"What is it for?"

"It serves as a telescope, a map of the world around us," he explained.

Malachi waved his hand over the platform, and soon the room began to transform around them. They were flying above the forest with Mertana far off in the distance. Myla wanted to look closer at it, but Malachi turned her away towards the other side of the woods. It was an image Myla never expected to see. Rolling black fog covered the land right up to the edge of the forest, and the sky above it was black with lightning and thunderstorms. Myla turned to Malachi in shock, as he reached out and pulled them closer in.

They were traveling solely above the clouds now. It was chilly to the point that Myla could actually feel the icy rain drops on her face. A dark shape was ahead of them, looming on the horizon. She knew instantly that it was Caldaria, dark yet magnificent in its towering shape. Suddenly Malachi grabbed her arm and turned her around. She could see the forest. A blue pillar of light just shot up from the top of the trees. The wind picked up and the clouds above the city behind them began to turn. Malachi then waved his arm and everything began to fade away. They were back in the warm small round wooden room.

"It was visible," Myla realized. "He saw it."

"It appears that way," answered Malachi.

"This room: it can show you the past?"

"And the future, though it gets more inaccurate the further away from the present you are in either direction."

"So what do I do now?" asked Myla.

"You head back to the village, go on with your life, and hope nothing comes of this."

Myla didn't like Malachi's advice, but at the moment it seemed like all she could do. She returned to Neph's house to find him having a grand time telling everyone of his great adventure above the village. Nobody had ever seen it from the above before, so naturally everyone was very fascinated by it, except of course for Myla.

"Myla, how could you?" asked Neph, trying to keep a straight face. "I finally accomplished a magical feat that you hadn't, and then you had to go top me with your crazy blue light antics."

"I'm sorry, Neph," answered Myla, smiling. "I'll try to be completely invisible during your next brilliant psychotic accomplishment."

"As long as you're not using magic to become so, that's good," he approved.

"So Neph, tell us again what the village looked like from above," asked Allasta, one of the other students who was a bit too obvious in her affection for Neph. She had been attached to him since they were both orphaned as small children due to a terrible accident. Neph, however, never seemed to notice her affection.

"Well, it was... a big circle," answered Neph to an overly-fascinated Allasta.

"Your descriptive abilities are awe-inspiring," said Zira, looking rather disgusted by the change of pace in the conversation.

"Well, you know what was interesting..." responded Neph. "There was a clearing about two hundred feet out from the village. I never knew it existed."

"Where?" asked both Zira and Myla, almost simultaneously.

"The opposite side from the school, east of that old library."

"What's the big deal about a clearing?" asked Allasta.

"Wait... That's impossible," said Myla, thinking back to her view from above the village. "There's no clearing there."

"How would you know?" asked Allasta.

"Well," Myla hesitated, not wanting to mention the secret room. "Malachi showed me an aerial map of the village once. It wasn't on it."

"Maybe the map lied," suggested Zira.

"Why would a map lie?" asked Neph.

"I don't think this was a type of map that could lie," answered Myla.

"Maybe the clearing is protected by some sort of magic," said Zira. "And it's only visible to the human eye."

"Why would nobody have heard of it though?" asked Allasta, who could always be counted on for an obvious question.

"That area of the woods is forbidden, considered dangerous," answered Neph. "You know that."

"Yeah, but I can't believe that no one has gone back there before," she said.

"Well, maybe that's where we got all of those horror stories, Allasta," said a rather annoyed Zira.

"You know, in Mertana, everyone was afraid of this entire forest and nobody ever entered it," commented Myla.

"With good reason though," said Zira. "The trees are not exactly welcoming to Tarrans. Unless they are accompanied by a Caldar, that is."

"How do we know it's the trees that stops them?" asked Neph. "It's not as if anyone ever found the bodies."

Myla shuddered at that thought.

"Good point," answered Zira, unaffected. "It makes me very curious about what the forest is hiding."

"It's a clearing," said Allasta, rather frustrated. "How is that a big deal?"

"Well, if it is the trees," said Myla, ignoring Allasta. "The trees in the forbidden part may not be too welcoming to us either."

"Us?" asked Allasta. "You act as if we are going to go back there."

"Of course we are," answered Neph. "We just have to figure out when."

"Are you serious?" said Allasta, looking quite skeptical. "We could die!"

"It'll be fine," answered Neph. "We've got Myla, remember? If anything attacks us, she can just shine her scary blue light at them."

Allasta eventually relented and agreed to join the other three in their expedition, to the slight disappointment of Zira. Myla was relieved, since she knew she could better prevent Allasta from talking about it if she was actually involved. Myla suspected that she would be able to get permission to explore those woods despite their forbidden status, but she didn't want to talk to Malachi about their plans. Myla had never fully regained trust in Malachi and Malika. At times she found it a cruel twist of fate that they, along with Zechariah, were her only confidants about the sorcerer and the true nature of Caldaria. She didn't want anyone else to know about her, so she would find herself cutting Malika and Malachi out of other parts of her life to compensate for it. She didn't know why she found it necessary to do that, but she did feel safer that way.

Safety was what she most often strove for. For every move she made, she had thought out all of the possibilities. She didn't want to be surprised. She wanted to be in control. Sometimes she took risks, but she knew the chances when she took them. She was successful in this philosophy too, until Neph decided to perform a self-levitation and a blue light shot of her hand. Now her safety was compromised and her philosophy was changing. The risks of her searching for that clearing were boundless, but she was feeling bold. If her security was already lost, she might as well find out what, if anything, was going on.

The four friends decided to put off exploring the clearing until the end of the week. There was too much commotion over Myla and Neph's magical displays to disappear unnoticed anytime before then. They devoted the rest of the week to their studies and teaching, mentioning no word of their intended plans. Not even Malachi seemed to suspect anything, to the surprise of everyone but Myla. She had known for a long time how to shield her thoughts from the old man, whose unusual perception had convinced many of the other students that he had telepathic abilities.

The night of their intended excursion, the four students retired quietly to their respective homes. Myla entered her small one room house and collapsed face down onto her bed as if nothing else was planned for the rest of the night. In many ways, she wished that she could just spend the rest of the night lying right there. She rolled over onto her back and looked at her ceiling, the wooden planks cracked from old age. Why did she have to be so curious? Why couldn't she just leave well enough alone? She never entirely trusted her surroundings. There was always a mystery she had to unlock. She wouldn't be Myla if she acted otherwise.

She looked out her tiny round window. Light from the village danced into her room. The area was still unsettled. It would be a while before they could venture into the forest. She closed her eyes hoping to escape from the inevitable future. Why did she have drag herself into this? She wanted a peaceful life, without harm or risk, and this wasn't the best way to accomplish that. Of course, nothing could happen. As Allasta was so quick to point out, it was just a clearing. There was no reason to jump to conclusions.

However, she knew that it wasn't just a clearing. Nothing was protected by magic just because, even if it seemed entirely inconsequential. Something was being hidden in that place, and Myla desperately wanted to know what. Besides, she was twenty years old and wanted to challenge the norm somehow. What was so wrong with a little adventure?

Now, though, she was exhausted and suddenly felt the overwhelming urge to sleep. Hesitantly, she closed her eyes as she lay there and soon enough, she drifted off into another dream filled sleep.

"Myla!" whispered Zira. "Can you hear me?"

Myla looked over to the window. Her three friends were peering in, eagerly waiting for her.

"Is it time already?"

She hadn't realized she had been asleep so long. She had been so entranced in her dream.

"Yes, it's time," Zira answered, rather frustrated. "Now, hurry up!"

Myla grabbed a sweater that was randomly hanging off the back of her chair and hurried outside. The cool crisp air bounced off of her back as she faced her three companions, who were shivering as they waited in anticipation.

"Take your time," commented Neph, slightly sarcastically.

"How long were you guys trying to wake me up?" asked Myla, feeling rather guilty.

"Too long," answered Allasta, showing that she meant it more than she should have.

"I'm sorry. I didn't realize I had fallen asleep."

"You know that's usually how it works, right?" asked Neph, while maintaining a serious face.

Myla rolled her eyes as Zira tried to stifle her laughter, and the four friends left to begin their investigation.

They didn't speak very much on their way to the woods. Their aim to remain unnoticed took precedence and all of them felt a little intimidated by the unknown waiting for them. The trip to the other side of the village never had seemed longer. Each step seemed to take forever. Eventually, they departed from the main part of town and headed along the long windy dirt road to the old library.

The library was the most neglected part of the village, with only the possible exception of the secret map room. For years, the local children spread rumors that it was haunted, and the adults almost never found the need for it. So rarely was it touched in fact that Myla was not even sure if it still contained anything. Several hundred years previously, the Caldar still studied their history in hope of returning home. Now most Caldar had given up hope, and as a result their history remained unstudied.

"Let's go inside," requested Allasta, as they walked up to the building.

Zira turned to her completely bewildered. Allasta just shrugged.

"I always wanted to know if it was haunted," she explained, attempting to respond to Zira's disbelief.

"Since when did you grow some courage?" Zira asked, not even trying to shield her disdain for Allasta.

"Neph, you want to look inside right?" asked Allasta, pulling on his arm.

He looked over at Zira, who subsequently rolled her eyes.

"Maybe we should leave that for another trip," he answered, clearly trying to please Zira.

"How about we check it out on the way back?" asked Myla, somewhat intrigued. "I'd like to see this clearing first if that's ok."

"Sounds like a plan to me," responded Zira, who then proceeded to walk towards the woods behind the building.

The others didn't hesitate to follow Zira into the forest, though it was clear that all of them were a little more nervous than she was.

The trees were immediately thick. It was as if they were trying to form a wall discouraging anyone from venturing in at all. It was a good deal of work, but the four eventually were able to squeeze themselves through. It didn't let up at all, however, and they were soon finding themselves high above the ground in an effort to make it through the density of the trees.

Myla wondered if the trees were positioning themselves in this manner to prevent them from coming in. She wouldn't have been surprised if that were the case so she decided to lean over and place the palm of her hand on one of the trees in an effort to communicate to it. She could feel heat flowing through her hand and into the tree. It worked, the trees suddenly shifted, and the four friends fell to the ground. The trees had parted and now they could walk straight through.

At first, Myla was disheartened. No clearing seemed to be in sight. Perhaps it was all a mistake, and Neph wasn't seeing clearly that evening. It was perfectly possible considering that he was under the influence of a very powerful spell. This entire adventure could have been a waste of time.

Myla's thoughts were misguided, however, because soon enough they could see the trees thinning ahead of them. The four friends paused, waiting for one of them to venture in ahead. It didn't take Myla long to realize that the other three were looking to her. She took a deep breath and stepped out in front. The other three followed cautiously behind her as she headed through the last remaining trees.

What lay before them initially appeared to be a barren wasteland. Nothing living was visible. The ground seemed burnt, while dead branches and rocks lay scattered along the ground. Neph walked up to one of the larger rocks and knelt down.

"Hey you guys come look at this," said Neph. "I think there's something written on it."

Myla and Zira both walked over to where he was kneeling.

"What kind of writing is that?" asked Zira, staring at the symbols on the rock.

"It's Tarran," answered Myla, solemnly.

"What does it say?" asked Neph.

"It's a warning," Myla answered. "This place is where all the Tarrans are sent when they wander into the woods."

Allasta screamed. The other three immediately turned towards her. She had frozen still next to a large branch. They ran towards her. Neph reached her first and gasped. The branch was no branch; it was a bone.

"Well," said Neph slowly. "I think we know what happens to all the Tarrans that reach here."

"Not all of them," said an unfamiliar voice.

The four friends jumped and turned around. In front of them stood a young man about the same age as them. Myla recognized him almost immediately.

"Would you four be able to tell me where I am?" he asked.

"Who are you and how did you get here?" asked Zira, not one to be tactful.

"Shouldn't I ask you the same?" he responded.

He was bolder than Myla had realized.

"We're from this forest," answered Neph. "You're a Tarran, aren't you?"

"Of course!" he answered with surprise at the question. "Then you four... you're actually Caldar?"

"Of course!" responded Zira, mimicking his surprise. "Where are you from?

"A town called Mertana," he answered, appearing overwhelmed. "To be honest, I doubted your existence."

"Well, now you know better," said Zira, sounding slightly insulted.

"I'm sorry. My name is Paul. I wandered here in search of the residents of the forest, to find out the source of the blue light."

"Yeah, that blue light was a mistake of mine," said Myla quickly. "The girl frightened there on the ground is Allasta, and this is Neph and Zira. My name is Melina."

Myla held out her hand to shake Paul's as Neph, Allasta and Zira all shot her bewildered looks.

"Do you think you would be able to help me out of here?" Paul asked Myla, oblivious to the confusion of the other three. "I could use a place to crash for the night, and I'd love to meet your people."

"There's a question," said Neph. "Can we help him, *Melina*?"

"Of course, we can," she answered, ignoring Neph's obvious emphasis on her name. "Just follow us back to the village."

Chapter 5

Paul was very thankful when the four strangers appeared in the clearing where he was staying. He wasn't sure if he would have survived if they hadn't found him. Getting lost in the forest wasn't his first plan of action, and that clearing was definitely terrifying.

When the blue light first shot into the air, Paul didn't think much of it. It was a random blue light. It was strange, yes, but it was a known fact that people occupied the forest, and what they did with their time was none of his business.

That was his philosophy at least until he realized that following that blue light was the perfect excuse for him to get away from Mertana. It was not as if there was anything wrong with Mertana in itself;he just hated being there in every way imaginable. He never fit in. He spent his whole life in that town, and yet he always felt like an outsider. He did a very good job of faking his belonging, but in reality there had been only one person there that he thought might have been able to understand him, and she had skipped town when they were ten.

It happened that Paul was out to dinner with an old friend that fateful evening when the blue light hit, and she wasn't particularly happy either.

"You're going to die alone," Serena said in a matter of fact tone.

"I'm twenty years old!" responded Paul, disgusted at her accusation.

It was always known that Serena wished to marry Paul, but this was knowledge that he chose to ignore.

"Your inability to commit is a clear sign of the future," she responded, as she reached for another bite of her food.

Paul just stared at her. He was so tired of her lecturing him. He didn't have an inability to commit. He just didn't want to commit to her.

"Are you even listening to me?"

Serena didn't seem to appreciate his lack of response.

"Yes, I am listening," he said cautiously, using his last ounce of patience. "I just didn't have anything to say."

Serena scoffed at this remark and continued to eat her food with a disgusted look on her face. Paul knew that he was in trouble with her, but he really didn't care. He was tired of her always assuming that there was more going on between the two of them than there was.

Instead of satisfying her with an apology, or at least another comment, he grabbed his fork and picked up a piece of potato. The food never reached his mouth, however, for at that moment, several people outside of the restaurant started to yell. Paul dropped his fork and ran to the window. As he looked outside, he saw a stunning blue stream of light pillaring up from the forest.

"What in the name of heaven is that?" breathed a man's voice behind him.

Paul looked around and realized that the entire restaurant's population had gathered around him at the window. Paul looked at the man who must have spoken.

"We have no way of knowing," he responded before quickly looking back at the light to make sure he missed nothing.

"It's a sign."

A clear voice echoed from the back of the room. Paul turned around and let all the other people push around him to peer out the window. The innkeeper, Misha, was sitting in a chair, glaring at him.

"A sign of what?" Paul hesitantly asked, unsure if he should humor the man.

"Them: the Caldar," he spoke slowly, as if only realizing his thoughts as he relayed them. "They took her. They will come back for more."

Misha's voice was cold and deadening. Paul tried not to let it touch him, as he looked at the skinny old man staring back at him with his long bony fingers closed tightly together. It was a known fact that Misha carried lingering guilt about Myla's kidnapping. When she willingly let herself be taken, her treatment at the inn was the first thing called into question.

"If that is the case, then what can we do about it?" Paul asked, hoping Misha wouldn't start a scene.

"Go find them and bring her back. Let them know that we won't let them treat us like this," Misha responded abruptly.

With that the old man got up out of his chair and exited the room.

Paul laughed to himself at Misha's suggestion. The mere concept of such an expedition was ridiculous, especially considering that they had no way of knowing whether or not the people in the forest, whoever they were, would be coming after them again anyway.

Misha, however, was not the only one who shared such fears. It didn't take Paul long to realize that Mayor Dansten was standing behind him, and considering Misha's words much more carefully. He placed his round hand on Paul's shoulder.

"Son, I think we should call a town meeting," Dansten said, trying to not sound afraid. "Something must be done to prevent a catastrophe."

Paul immediately knew that things were going to get ridiculous, and sure enough, they did. The town meeting was far from calm, let alone reasonable.

"You can't be serious," he said to the larger group.

"They could be on their way here right now!" answered one of the older women at the meeting.

"We have no way of knowing what that blue light meant."

"Which is why we have to assume the worst," said Dansten.

"That it is a call to battle? Have we ever seen that before?"

"No, which is why we must assume that this will be at an even larger scale. We must do something."

"So going and asking them to be nice is the best idea we can come up with?" asked Paul.

"We have no other alternative."

"Yes we do: doing nothing."

Paul couldn't believe the reaction of the townspeople. He had no idea that so many of them were so paranoid. No matter how hard he tried, none of them seemed able to see how ridiculous this plan was. To even think of sending someone into the forest to try to bargain with the people in the forest was suicide. They were only sending that person to their death, for no good reason too.

"So who is going to take on this great mission?" asked Dansten.

As soon as the words left the mayor's mouth, the entire room fell silent. Not one person seemed ready to take on such a burden.

"Are you sure this is what the people of Mertana wish?"

Paul couldn't believe he was asking such a question.

"This is what the people have decided," answered Dansten.

"Then I shall take on the burden, as pointless as I find it," answered Paul to the shock of Dansten.

"Why would you do this, if you see no reason?" He asked.

66

"If it helps the people of Mertana sleep at night then I shall do my part."

It wasn't as noble of a step as it seemed. Paul had simply realized at that moment that he had nothing in common with these people he lived with. In a lot of ways, it was a culmination of events, capped off by that particular night. He always knew that he didn't belong and wanted more. He was even in some ways jealous of Myla. At least she had been able to leave, even if it may have ruined her life in the process. He had no way of knowing, but he didn't want to be in Mertana anymore. This expedition might not have been the ideal way of leaving, but at least he was getting out.

Paul took his time in walking home that evening. Many people in Mertana wanted him to leave that night. Luckily, Dansten thought it would be better if he had a full night of sleep first. Anyway, he still needed to tell his parents, which was a task he was not looking forward to.

How were they going to react? Would they be supportive? Or would they see right through him and know that this was simply an excuse to leave? If so, would they take that personally? Paul liked his parents, but he didn't see himself living the rest of his life with them. He never quite fit with them in the same way that he never fit with the rest of the town. He was ready to leave.

*   *   *

"Melina?" Neph asked Myla quietly, slightly disgusted at her deception.

"It's a name," she responded, hoping to sound more amused than anything else.

"Not your name," he answered. "Now, what are we going to do when Malachi gets here and refers to you as Myla?"

"One of you just will have to call me Melina before he gets that chance."

Myla was beginning to think her deception was a lost cause, but she didn't want Paul to know who she was. She wasn't even sure why.

"And afterward? When he runs into the other townspeople?" asked Neph, rightfully skeptical.

"I think it's time I get a nickname. How does Mel sound to you?"

"We'll have to spread the word disturbingly fast."

Myla could tell that Neph was starting to see a possibility in this.

"I'll need your help," she said.

"And why should I help you?" he asked,

Even as he said it, both of them knew that he would.

"Because you're my friend, and I need you to trust me."

The two of them walked into the other room where Zira and Allasta were preparing food for Paul. Bringing him back to Neph's home was quite the process, since he had clearly grown weak from hunger.

"Sorry for leaving there," Neph said in the direction of Zira and Allasta. "Mel and I were trying to figure out how to explain this to Malachi."

Both Zira and Allasta nodded and smiled, indicating that they caught the nickname.

"So how are we going to explain this to Malachi?" asked Zira, suddenly realizing that this may be an issue.

"You will simply tell him," boomed a voice at the door.

Malachi walked in from the shadows.

"Now who will have the honor?" he asked.

"Melina can," said Neph quickly, pointing to Myla.

Malachi didn't even flinch at the name change and looked in her direction.

"There's a clearing in the woods," she said, more confidently than she would have expected.

"The trees have many secrets, Melina," he responded, surprisingly smoothly.

"Did you know about this?" she asked.

"I was aware."

He didn't even seem apologetic as he spoke directly to her.

"And you failed to inform us of it?" she asked.

Myla didn't want to appear angry, but it bothered her that he was so willing to keep secrets from her.

"Like how you failed to inform me of your expedition?" Malachi asked in return.

"We wouldn't have had an expedition if you had told us that it was there to begin with," answered Myla.

His logic was flawed, but Myla suspected that he knew this.

"And then you wouldn't have found your friend now, would you have?"

Again his logic was flawed, but Myla could only roll her eyes.

"Why do you allow such a clearing to exist?" Zira had finally spoken up, and Myla welcomed her input.

"Why wouldn't I?" he answered, clearly a bit surprised by her question. "It keeps us safe."

"At the expense of the lives of many Tarrans," Zira responded.

Her disgust at Malachi's words seeped out of her.

"Yet, apparently not all," Malachi answered completely ignoring Zira's frustration.

The others followed his gaze towards the young man sitting in the corner.

"Don't all stare at once now," said Paul, not particularly enjoying the attention.

"When did you arrive in the clearing, boy?" Malachi asked in a not very respectful tone.

"Four days ago, and my name is Paul," he answered defiantly.

"How did you survive that long?" chimed in Allasta, to the surprise of all the others since she had stayed silent for the most part since the clearing.

"I had food and water with me to last three nights. Those trees around the clearing; they close around you. I never thought they would open up again."

Myla looked to the floor. It must have been her magic that reopened the trees. If she hadn't gone there, he would have died in that place.

"In the past, the trees have just continued closing in on any Tarran that entered," Malachi said unemotionally, as all the others winced at the thought. "I am surprised that they didn't with you."

"To that, I have no explanation," responded Paul. "But I am glad they didn't."

"Well then, I have one last question for you," continued Malachi. "Why did you come here?"

"To find out the meaning of the blue light and to beg for peace if it is a sign of your impending attack," said Paul, completely monotone.

At this, Neph bust up laughing. The other three girls tried to hide their giggles. Malachi, however, did not find Paul's assumption so funny.

"I can assure that the blue light was simply an accident of Melina's and nothing more," he replied calmly. "Is there anything else you came for?"

"Actually, yes," Paul responded, hesitantly. "About a decade ago, a girl was kidnapped from our town. I was hoping to find her and bring her home."

"And what was her name?"

"Myla."

Myla hoped her lack of breath was not too apparent. She shot the others glances and was relieved to see their faces not showing too great of a reaction at Paul's mention of her name.

"I am sorry, Paul," answered Malachi. "But there is no one in this village who goes by that name."

Myla didn't know why she chose to not give Paul her real name. She never believed he was a bad guy, despite not being his biggest fan when they were kids. She certainly never would have guessed that he would have come to find her, especially after ten years. It was an instinct that caused her to give a false name: a security measure that only she would ever think of doing. She wanted to get an idea of who he had become before revealing her true identity. And now with his goal of bringing her back apparent, her desire to keep it a secret was even greater.

As she walked Paul to Malachi's house where he would be staying, Myla stayed mostly silent. She wondered if Paul recognized her. She did look remarkably different. The light hair she once had was now a dark brown and her clothing actually fit her properly. Her round face had thinned and she was a good deal taller. She wasn't the most beautiful girl in the village by far (that title would probably go to Allasta or even Zira), but she certainly wasn't the mess that she once had been.

"This Malachi, he is the leader of your people?"

Paul's voice caught her off guard. Myla hadn't realized how lost in thought she was.

"Yes, more or less," she answered. "He is the leader of the elders, who govern the people."

71

"And what is your role?" he asked.

His voice was softer than it was at Neph's. He wasn't interrogating. He was making conversation.

"I am a student of the higher gifts," she answered.

"Which means?"

"I am still very young," she answered with a smile.

"Now that I can understand," responded Paul, giving away a small laugh in his voice.

He paused in his steps, and walked to edge of the wooden path. He looked out into the village lit up by singular pieces of candlelight. As he leaned over the railing, he quietly took in a breath.

"I like it here," he said, looking back at Myla.

"You've barely been here," she responded, playing dumb but knowing exactly what he was going through.

"I know," he answered. "It's so calm here. It's very different. Mertana is very... tense."

He looked towards Myla, wondering if she had any idea of what he was saying.

"There are struggles in any place in the world, Paul," she said. "The trick is finding the place where you can handle them the best."

Paul nodded his head in agreement and the two continued to walk towards Malachi's. Paul kept looking around, trying to absorb everything that he could, and Myla tried to make it not too apparent that she was watching him. He kept looking towards her as if to say something, but then he would pause and keep silent.

Malachi had a room already prepared for Paul when they reached his home. Malachi himself did not even stay around to see if everything with Paul was okay. He had already retired to his own room and was most likely fast asleep, if the man ever did sleep. Myla sometimes wasn't sure. She did, however, suddenly realize how exhausted Paul actually was as he sat down on the bed. She decided to make her way out the door.

"Thank you for escorting me here, Miss Melina," he said, as she was just about to leave.

"Oh, no problem," she answered, turning around. "And just call me 'Mel'."

"'Mel' it is then."

"If you don't mind me asking," she added, hoping to not overstay her welcome too much. "How long do you intend on staying here?"

"Well, I guess whatever the time limit is," he answered, clearly not having thought that far ahead.

"Well, the time limit may be forever," she warned, hoping to not sound too negative. "The Caldar are very cautious about visitors, especially visitors that later leave."

"You sound as if you are not one of them," he pointed out to Myla's sudden panic.

"I don't share the same fear about visitors," she responded. "But you must remember that I am not the norm."

Myla turned around and headed back to her own small house. She wouldn't worry about Paul or her hidden identity till the morning. When and how he would find the truth about her was in the future and not of her present concern.

Neph, Zira and Allasta were more impressive than Myla had anticipated. By the morning, the entire village knew to refer to Myla as 'Mel'. She didn't know how they set it up so fast and suspected that some sort of magic was in the works, but she didn't dare to ask, at least not at first. Mind manipulation by magic was strictly against the Caldarian code, and Myla didn't want to get them in trouble.

Her morning started out pretty typically. She kept pretty silent, choosing to eat breakfast alone at the café near her house. Normally she would have met up with Zira and Neph. It was an off day from teaching so it made it a bit more difficult for her to find a reason to avoid dealing with Paul. She figured that if she put off seeing him enough, the chances of him figuring out who she was lessened. Keeping her identity a secret was not going to be easy, even with everyone calling her 'Mel'. Especially since she didn't really know why she was keeping it hidden.

What if she just told him who she was? Would that really be a big deal? Sure, he might try to convince her to return to Mertana, but she could tell him that she was happy here, and it wouldn't be an issue. Unless of course, he thought she was brainwashed and decided to bring her back despite her protests. It wasn't as if the Caldar and the Tarran were actually going to believe each other. They might just use the situation to hate each other. By keeping her identity a secret, she might just be saving the two peoples from an all-out war.

Myla laughed at herself silently as the thought crossed her mind. She was being ridiculous. She didn't want to deal with Paul trying to take her back to Mertana, but she also knew that that was mostly an excuse. She didn't want to have to deal with the girl she used to be in Mertana: the girl that everyone picked on. A stigma came with the name Myla, and as silly as it was, she preferred to avoid it. Getting the entire village to call her Mel was actually a better concept to her.

And it seemed safer. She always had to have a backup defense. She couldn't let anyone know too much about her. Paul knew her when she was in Mertana. That was knowledge that nobody else had. She felt safer if he stayed in that Mertana world and didn't cross over.

Changing her name didn't seem like such a bad idea for other reasons besides Paul as well. Melina didn't have the other stigma that Myla liked to avoid. There was no evil sorcerer after Melina. He didn't have that name. Though it wasn't a sure defense, an extra confusion factor couldn't hurt.

She was over-thinking this. She needed to just move on and deal with what was ahead. Right now, that involved handling the Paul situation. She didn't know how the Caldar would receive him. They didn't like the Tarrans at all, yet the trees spared him. Why did they spare him?

"Um Mel, would you like me to take that for you?"

Eli was talking to her. She was so lost in thought that she hadn't realized that she had finished her food, but sure enough, her plate was empty.

"Oh thanks, Eli," she responded. "How is your morning going?"

"Okay, I guess," he smiled. "How's our visitor adjusting?"

He knew about Paul. It really didn't take long for gossip to spread.

"That is a question I do not know the answer to. I was just thinking that I would go find out."

"You should… being from the same place and all."

He paused as if he had just mentioned something forbidden.

"Not to imply that you aren't from here first," he explained. "You're Caldar through and through."

Myla smiled.

"Don't worry, no offense was taken," she said calmly.

With that Eli thanked her and took away her plate.

Myla immediately got up and walked towards Malachi's house. Eli was innocent in his words, but he did alert her to one thing: Paul's presence here was going to draw parallels to her past in the Caldar's mind. She wasn't prepared to feel like an outsider again, and she could only hope the other Caldar wouldn't feel like she was one. It was time that she went to talk to Malachi to find out how long their guest would be staying.

She hurried down the path towards his house. Once she reached it, she didn't pause to think and just walked right in. To her surprise the entire elder council was sitting inside in a circle with Paul standing outside of it by the wall closest to the door. The elders were in a heated discussion, with their voices the closest to being raised as Myla had ever heard them. Paul turned towards her when he saw her and gave her a look that told her he was very thankful to see her.

"They don't know what to do with me," he whispered, with a very worried tone.

"What have they suggested?" she quietly asked, hoping to not disrupt the elders, who were already having difficulty understanding each other due to the consistent interruptions occurring.

"Mostly keeping me here or sending me back. Only Malachi has suggested that I make up my own mind."

"Sometimes the man is quite intelligent," she answered, though Myla wasn't sure if Paul could hear her over Anala yelling at Zechariah who was sitting next to her.

"Don't you realize that this boy could disrupt the last bit of security our village has?" Anala yelled, with her round face turning bright red. "We don't involve the Tarrans in our lives and they don't involve us in theirs. It's safer that way. If we let him go back, he could tell the whole Tarran world of our location!"

"And if we force him to stay here, he shall only corrupt the purity of our existence," answered Zechariah. "Hasn't that occurred to you?"

"Well then, what do you suggest?" Anala responded. "We let the trees have him?"

"The trees will be having nobody," Malachi's voice boomed over the council, silencing everyone. "Besides, they don't seem to want him. Slightly odd, wouldn't you say Melina?"

Myla jumped. She didn't expect to be involved in this conversation.

"Yes, considering that they kill all Tarrans who come close," she answered, wondering what Malachi was getting at.

Then it hit her.

"Which means he is not a Tarran," she added.

The entire council, excluding Malachi, gasped. Myla couldn't blame them. Why didn't she see this before? Paul was different. He even told her that the night before. He didn't belong in Mertana.

"What do you mean I am not a Tarran?" Paul asked, extremely confused.

All the council members nodded their heads in agreement.

"Only a Caldar could enter this village," she responded simply.

That's all she could say. She couldn't explain it herself.

"Tell me, boy," Malachi asked. "Do you know your parents?"

"Yes," he responded, and then he paused. "Actually no... I don't. My parents who raised me... They say they are my aunt and uncle."

Paul looked ashamed to admit this. Myla wondered if he ever had before.

"Zechariah, you know who this boy is," Malachi continued, without much regard for Paul's response.

"I didn't think it was possible," Zechariah said softly. "Do you think it could be him?"

"I am quite positive," Malachi answered. "He is a Caldar. I can see it in him."

Everyone turned and stared at Zechariah. No one had expected this twist of circumstances.

"My sister, Sarah," Zechariah said slowly. "She was still with child when her husband died. She told everyone that the baby was stillborn, but only years later when she passed away herself did we find out that she gave the baby away to a Tarran couple. We never could find the child."

Myla looked over at Paul. His face looked stunned. She wondered if he was really registering what they were saying. She noticed his black hair and his features. She wouldn't have seen it otherwise, but he did have a certain resemblance to Zira. She looked over at the others in the room. She hadn't been the only one staring at Paul. Every single elder had turned their heads toward the young man – all of them except Zechariah. He had his head towards the ground, with his face distraught. Myla looked towards Malachi. He seemed to have no sympathy for the current situation. She knew he wasn't heartless, but he often wasn't sensitive either. This silence was going on too long.

"Well, if Paul might be a Caldar, then clearly we must have him stay here until we know for sure."

She spoke clearly in an authoritative voice. She knew she wasn't an elder and probably shouldn't have even been in the room, but someone had to take initiative.

"Unless, of course, he wants to leave," she continued. "Then we have no choice, but to let him. We do not keep prisoners here."

She didn't expect her comments to be welcomed, so it surprised her when the elders all nodded their heads in agreement. The revelation of Paul's origins must have eased their concerns. The elders had a tendency to trust Myla more than they should, simply because of her exceptionally strong gifts. Myla knew that it probably wasn't wise, but at the moment she was grateful for it.

Slowly one by one, each of the elders stood up and headed out of the room. Nothing more was to be said. Silently, they all filtered through the door leaving Myla, Paul, Malachi and Zechariah alone in the room. The air was thick with awkwardness, so much that Myla started to leave, but Malachi called her back.

"Melina," he said calmly. "I would like it if you would be in charge in introducing our new resident to the ways of the Caldar. Make sure he is aware of anything that might set him off guard or catch him by surprise. He will also need some training in the Caldar gifts as well. He could still become very skilled. Oh, and you should probably arrange for him to have his own place to live at some point, since it isn't practical for him to stay with me."

"What if he wants to return to Mertana?" she asked, hoping to not be saying something too obvious.

"Does he?" Malachi responded.

"You could always ask since he is right here," interrupted Paul rather shortly.

Apparently he had snapped out of his momentary state of shock.

"Of course, I meant no insult. What would you like to do, Paul?" asked Malachi, being more polite than normal.

"I think I would like to stay, at least for a while. If I am who you say I am, I think I would like to know my people."

"Then you shall. Melina, please show Paul around the village."

With that queue, Myla and Paul exited the room leaving Malachi and Zechariah alone. She didn't know what they were about to discuss, and though she was quite curious, she was also very thankful to be out of that room.

Paul walked to the edge of the path outside of the room. He grabbed onto the railing and hung his head. Slowly he breathed in and out, staring at the ground. Myla stood there silently, unsure if he was going to ever move. She knew the shock of the revelation must be difficult for him, but she didn't know how to help him recover. There was nothing she could say to make this easier.

Eventually, Paul lifted up his head and began to look around the village. He leaned against the railing, as he comprehended the world around him. Gradually he turned around to Myla, who was trying hard not to stare.

"Mel," he said softly. "Do you think I could really be a Caldar?"

"I think it's a distinct possibility," she said, trying to not sound so sure. "Malachi seemed pretty convinced, and he isn't easily convinced of anything."

"And what do you think?" he asked, seeing right through her cover.

"You don't act entirely like a Tarran," she said quietly, unsure of if she should be saying anything. "You seem to fit here."

"What makes you say that?" he asked.

"This place is thick with magic, but you don't seem to be bothered by it."

She recalled her first trip into the forest, where she herself wondered if a Tarran could survive in such dense magic.

"It was a bit overwhelming at first, but I like the feel of it," he answered then paused as if he just found some energy that he didn't know he had.

He looked at Myla and smiled.

"Well, Malachi told you to show me around the place," he said. "Were you planning on it or what?"

Myla laughed and began to show him around. It was a bit difficult, because where she started exploring the city when she was ten was probably not the typical route. That time she focused on where she was not supposed to go, and that's not what she wanted to encourage Paul to do. Instead she chose to start out with the market square. He had seen it the night before briefly when they took him to Neph's, but it wasn't in full life then. Myla was pleased to find that everyone did in fact call her Mel. What did they do to inform the whole village of the change?

She showed Paul the little stands that surrounded the market square and got him to try some of the various fruits and berries that would be impossible to find in Mertana. She was amused at Paul's reaction, because he couldn't seem to get over how much more flavorful they were. He also loved chatting with the fruit stand owners. He always had a new question to ask each one, and they all seemed eager to answer. He enjoyed telling Myla about life in Mertana and how different it was there. She liked to hear his opinions of the place. They actually weren't that different from her own.

"It's so much less friendly there," he kept saying after each of the fruit stand owners welcomed him to the village.

Myla laughed at his reaction, knowing that the villagers wouldn't have been so kind if they hadn't already heard that Paul was a Caldar.

"How is Mertana not friendly?" she asked, pretending to not know.

"They don't like people who aren't like them," he answered between bites of a large red fruit resembling a giant strawberry.

"What makes you think it's different here?" she asked. "They weren't being all that nice to you when they thought you were a Tarran."

"Yes, but now everyone is friendly," he answered. "In Mertana, they will exclude people who are from the town."

"Really?" asked Myla, trying to act surprised.

81

She knew that she was one of the people he was referring to.

"Oh, yeah," he explained. "When I was a child there was this one girl that was always harassed, and not just by the other children, but by the adults too. She was the one I was hoping to find. I wish I knew what happened to her. I can only hope she came to a village as nice as this one. She always believed she might have been a Caldar."

Myla felt her face turning bright red. She hoped Paul didn't notice. It was weird seeing him talk about her. She never thought her disappearance would have been a big deal to anyone, certainly not to him.

"Did you ever tease her?" she asked, hoping to sound ignorant of the events.

"No," he said slowly, looking slightly guilty. "But I didn't exactly stick up for her either."

"I wonder how the Tarrans would react to a Caldar going there."

Paul laughed at that thought.

"Well, many of us were convinced the Caldar were just a myth," he said. "So they would probably freak out and run for their lives."

"Even if the Caldar just said 'hello'?" she asked, smiling at his reaction.

"I guess they wouldn't be too scared of you. You don't seem too dangerous," he said smiling. "They'd probably think you were really interesting, once they got used to the concept of you."

At that, Myla started to laugh. The idea of the people in Mertana thinking of her as interesting was very amusing, especially considering that she was probably one of the most dangerous Caldar alive. However, Paul didn't need to know that.

Myla took Paul all around the village after that. She showed him the farmlands and the places the children liked to play. She also showed where the school would meet and where the majority of people their age lived. The entire time she talked to him about life with the Caldar and answered the numerous questions he had. At first she was very worried about him finding out who she was, but eventually she forgot about it. She enjoyed talking to him. He was actually more interesting than she ever would have suspected. Maybe he really was a Caldar.

After she showed him around, they walked over to Lena's so that he could try some of her amazing pastries. Neph, Zira and Allasta were there, sitting at a round table looking outside. Zira and Allasta seemed to be arguing over something. This was no surprise to Myla, since the two girls never seemed to get along. Neph was laughing at them, so she figured it wasn't too serious. As Myla and Paul walked up behind them, the three didn't seem to notice.

"I tell you I saw it," Allasta was saying, clearly frustrated.

"You didn't see anything," argued a frustrated Zira. "Now would you stop trying to get attention."

"I did!" Allasta said, rather loudly. "It was big and orange... and black!"

"Would you be quiet?" hissed Zira. "You're making a scene. You were dreaming – face it!"

"You're just jealous because I saw it first."

"Because I didn't see a big orange and black ball of energy outside of Mel's door?" asked Zira, trying to contain her laughter.

Myla, however, froze at those words.

"That's ridiculous, Allasta," Zira continued. "It clearly was a dream."

A big orange and black ball of energy? Outside of her door? Was Allasta dreaming? Paul looked like he was about to say something to announce their presence, but Myla quickly grabbed his arm to hold him back. He turned to her confused, and she motioned to him to stay silent. She wanted to hear the rest of this uncensored.

"Why are you so quick to assume that it was a dream?" asked Allasta, beginning to sound hurt.

"Because why would a big orange and black energy thing be outside of her door?" asked Zira, visibly trying to not laugh as she said it.

"Because she is special," said Allasta, as if that answer was obvious. "We have always known she was special. What if some evil thing knows she is special too? There are things in this world that we do not understand. The least we could do is warn her."

"And scare her over something that may not even be real?" asked Zira. "No, thanks. She's got enough to deal with."

Up to this point, Neph had stayed completely out of the conversation, but now he turned toward Zira.

"But Zira, what if it's true?" he asked, laying his hand on her shoulder. "Don't we owe it to her to warn her?"

"You don't really think something could be after her do you?" Zira asked, looking back at him.

"I think we should at least let her decide that for herself," he said softly, being unusually kind to Zira.

Paul looked over to Myla. He clearly wanted to make their presence known. His face indicated that he was at least concerned with what they were saying. She nodded her head, and he immediately turned and said "Hey guys what's up?" His tone made it very obvious that they had been listening.

"Um hi!" said Zira, looking very awkward. "How are you?"

"I'm good," he said, sounding purposefully fake. "Now, why don't you tell Mel what's up so that she doesn't have to stand behind you listening anymore?"

Myla wanted to sink in her shoes. She took comfort in the fact that other three looked even worse. She actually appreciated Paul, sticking up for her like that. Zira was the first to speak.

"I'm sorry, Mel," she said, sounding really guilty. "I just didn't want to worry you unnecessarily. I'm sure it was nothing."

"It was a big orange and black ball of energy," interjected Allasta. "Like fire or something. It was right outside your door. Just sitting there. I couldn't sleep so I walked outside to get a breath of fresh air and there it was, right across the way from me in front of your door."

"She was probably dreaming," said Zira, clearly still frustrated with Allasta.

"Even dreams can have meaning," said Myla softly.

What did it mean?

"Was there anything else?" she asked.

"No, it disappeared within seconds so I went back to bed," Allasta answered. "I probably should've gotten somebody then. I don't know why I didn't."

"Because you were asleep," said Zira, under her breath.

"I was not asleep!" answered Allasta, raising her voice.

"It doesn't matter if she was asleep or not," said Myla, abruptly. "It is still good to know, and thank you for informing me."

With that, the conversation ended. Allasta made some comment about needing to do something and excused herself from the table. Myla and Paul then sat down to join Neph and Zira, both of whom apologized to Myla for discussing it behind her back and considering not telling her. Myla told them to not worry about it. She knew that they didn't mean any harm and

85

only had her best interest in mind. They had no way of knowing Myla's actual situation. She had never told anyone of the sorcerer and the fate that lay before her. She certainly wasn't going to start now.

Zira and Neph were very interested in talking with Paul and finding out about how he was adjusting. They had already heard about the possibility of Paul being a Caldar, and they still couldn't believe it. They kept asking him whether or not he had ever noticed that he could do special things or that he was different in anyway. Paul answered that he always felt a bit different but never noticed any unique abilities. This disheartened Myla, since she had noticed her gifts at a very young age. It was just another example of how unusually powerful she was in her gifts, which which was not something she wanted.

It was a weird situation sitting next to Paul and listening to him talk about the Caldar. He was such an image from her past. She couldn't quite comprehend the idea of him in her life now, yet there he was, associating with her and her friends. This was the same person that would only associate with Serena and the other Tarran children who were mean to her. She knew that they had both grown up since then, but those feelings of rejection still echoed within her. She should have been angry with him, but instead she was helping him, being his friend.

And now here he was, talking with her and her friends. They were her friends. This was her life. He didn't belong. He belonged in Mertana, a place that was supposed to remain buried in the back of her memory. If she couldn't hide from Mertana, what could she hide from? What could she keep separated from her life? She'll never be able to fully run away. Someone will always find her.

What was it that Allasta saw outside of her door?

Paul was talking to her. Why did she have to not be paying attention? What did he say? Something about Zira and

86

him possibly being cousins. She gave him an odd look and then confessed to not be listening. He gave her an odd look back before repeating himself. That jogged his memory. That was a look of recognition he gave her. She had always gotten lost in her thoughts as a child. Did he know? No, the moment of recognition had passed. He continued on with the conversation as if nothing had happened. She just needed to remember to pay attention.

"So *Mel*," said Neph, having fun emphasizing her new name. "I hear you get to be in charge of showing our new resident around. Makes things a bit more complicated for you, huh?"

"I can manage," Myla answered, not wishing to entertain Neph's endless ability at teasing.

"When are you going to start training him, do you think?" asked Zira.

"I was thinking right after this actually," answered Myla. "We do have to find out if he is one of us after all."

"What do you think they will do to him if he turns out to be a Tarran?" asked Zira.

"I don't know," answered Myla. "Hopefully just the death sentence."

"Well, torture would be a bit over the top," answered Zira.

"Yet so much more fun," chimed in Neph.

"I hope you all are joking," said Paul, clearly amused, but slightly worried.

After they finished eating at Lena's, Neph and Zira departed, leaving Myla to train Paul. She didn't really know how to start, but she figured heading over to the school grounds was a good idea. It was an off day so they were completely empty, leaving them at peace to learn. Myla wasn't sure what to teach him first, so she figured the best place to start was what she first learned, with freezing an object in the air.

She started out by tossing a leaf and stopping it herself. She had grown so powerful that she didn't need to say anything or make any movements to stop the leaf. All she had to do was think the object still. When the leaf stopped, Paul stared at her in disbelief. She had forgotten that something so simple could have taken him off guard. She had just defied his knowledge of the world.

"I didn't think that was possible," he said quietly.

"It is," she answered. "And if you are really a Caldar, you should be able to do it pretty soon yourself."

She showed him how she first learned to stop the leaf, by reaching out and yelling stop. She then tossed the leaf into the air and let him try. The leaf fluttered gently to the ground.

"Well, it didn't work," he said, sounding disappointed. "Though I can't see why it would. If it was that simple, I probably would have done something like that long ago."

"Well, it isn't simply reaching out your hand and yelling," she answered.

How did she figure out how to do it?

"You have to believe you can," Myla explained. "You have to will it to stop."

Paul gave her a look of skepticism, but tried again. For a second time, the leaf fluttered to the ground. Paul breathed a heavy sigh.

"I don't think I can do this, Mel," he said.

"Keep trying," she answered. "Nobody said you would get this right away."

Myla then went and sat on a log to the side. She watched as Paul threw the leaf up in the air and watched it slowly flutter down. After nearly a dozen times, he came and sat down next to Myla, looking defeated.

"You don't believe you can do this, do you?" she asked, feeling his frustration.

"No, I don't," he answered. "And I don't see how I can change that."

"Well, maybe we should change our plan of action then," she suggested, trying to sound optimistic. "Let's see if we can do this together."

Next Myla tossed a leaf sitting next to them up into the air and stopped it. She then grabbed his hand and reached it out towards the leaf.

"Now let's see if you can hold it there with me," she said.

He looked at her not really understanding what she was aiming to do.

"How do I do that?" he asked.

"Believe you are the one holding it up," she answered simply.

Paul gave her another odd look, but then turned around and started to stare at the leaf, with both his arm and Myla's pointed towards the frozen leaf. His face became determined, and when Myla realized he was ready, she withdrew her arm from his and rested her hand on his shoulder.

"You're doing it yourself now," she said smiling. The leaf was still perfectly frozen.

"What?" he asked, and the leaf fell to the ground.

"You were holding it up on your own at the end there," she answered. "It seems that you can do it."

"That's amazing," he said, looking overwhelmed.

"Yet very real. Now let's see if you can stop the leaf yourself this time."

Paul stopped the leaf on his very first try after that. Myla was surprised to discover that once Paul developed the confidence to use his gifts, he was actually very talented. By the end of the afternoon, he was not only stopping various objects in the air, but he was moving them around as well. Myla didn't know if Paul was learning too late to ever study the higher gifts, but it wouldn't take him too long to be quite proficient as a Caldar.

Which meant that he was there to stay. Myla wouldn't be saying goodbye to her Mertana past anytime soon. Paul would find out her true identity at some point, and she would have to deal with the consequences. Where and when this would occur were the only questions that remained.

Chapter 6

Paul's adjustment to Caldar life was surprisingly easy. He didn't expect that when he first found out that he was going to be a resident of the village. He thought that he might start to miss Mertana and the ways that he was so familiar with, but as each day passed, Mertana quickly slipped from the front of his mind. He didn't know if he would ever return to the town of his past, but as time went on he realized that he probably wouldn't want to.

The Caldar people were exceptionally friendly, despite Mel's hesitation. At first, he figured that she must have been a bit paranoid, because everyone seemed so warm and welcoming. She was so secretive. Every day he spent with her, he felt like she was hiding something. After a while though, he realized that she wasn't the only one. All of the council members, Malachi in particular, were hiding something, something much larger than whatever Mel and her friends seemed to be hiding.

He liked it there, despite the secrets. He liked learning how to use his Caldar gifts. He wished he wasn't so far behind everyone else, though Mel was a good teacher. Their warrior tactics were fascinating. He also enjoyed the tracking and some of the simpler things used in everyday life, such as moving the trees. One thing in particular that he enjoyed was the art of healing, and it didn't take Mel long to point out that he had exceptionally strong gifts in that area. In the month of intensive training he had been under since he got there, he had already skipped along to some of the more advanced healing methods. Mel thought it would only be a matter of months before he could start learning the higher gifts in healing.

Zechariah took Paul into their family pretty quickly. He and Zira went over there for dinner all the time. It was a nice family. Nora was very sweet and would always make the best food for him. Judah and Esther were good children, and Paul would often play games with them outside.

He was also making friends outside of the people that he was related to. He would hang out with Neph a lot of the time and actually ended up moving into his spare room. It allowed him to interact with the others his age better. He found he could relate to Neph better than he could to his friends back in Mertana.

Then there was Mel. She quickly became his closest friend there, which was probably because of all the time they had to spend together. He knew that she kept secrets from him, but it didn't really matter because out of all the people in the village, he trusted her the most. Yes, she was the strongest Caldar in the village. (It really surprised him when he realized how superior to the others she was.) However that wasn't why he trusted her so much. He knew that; he just wondered if she did.

For the time being though, he chose to ignore his feelings for Mel. There was too much else for him to deal with. He still had so much to learn and needed her as his teacher. His life was very hectic as it was. He devoted each full day to his studies, with Mel instructing him the majority of the time, and Zira and Neph helping when Mel worked on her own studies.

Today was a day where Paul was really feeling the weight of everything he had to learn. He had spent the entire morning with Zira trying to master one of the most elementary defense moves, and he was still unable to properly blend in with the oak tree he was using. How these Caldar could completely blend into tree was beyond him, but apparently it was possible. He, however, was having a difficult time believing it.

"Let's take a break, Paul," said Zira, clearly as frustrated as he was. "You're going to set the tree on fire before you blend in with it."

"What an encouraging teacher you are, Zira," Paul answered, trying to hide his own frustration.

"My point was that you need a break," she explained. "How about we walk over to Eli's café to get some food?"

Paul reluctantly agreed.

"Why do you think I am having such a difficult time?" he asked her, as they started for the café.

"Your mind seems to have been elsewhere all morning," she answered smiling. "You should try to stop thinking about Mel."

Ouch. How long had she been holding back that one? Well, at least one person could see right through him. He decided it was best to play oblivious to her stab.

"That's funny," he responded, trying to sound surprised. "I was actually just thinking about that big orange and black ball of energy outside her door the night I arrived."

He hadn't been thinking about that in particular, but the thought did cross his mind.

"We should really develop a nickname for that," Zira noted. "The big orange and black ball of energy just takes way too long to say."

"I was wondering what you actually thought it was," he asked, ignoring his cousin's sarcasm.

Zira looked at him, surprised.

"What I said before, a dream of Allasta's," she answered, seeming quite confused by his question.

"And to think I thought you just didn't like Allasta," he said, keeping his most innocent voice.

"Well, she is kind of annoying."

"And she likes Neph."

Zira hit him in the arm.

"Seriously, though," Paul continued, ignoring her violent reaction. "Do you think it was a dream?"

"Honestly, Mel has always acted as if she was hiding from something and couldn't let the rest of us in on it. She used to always wonder about Caldaria and the old sorcerers – you've heard of them, right?"

Paul nodded his head.

"Well, Mel had a lot of doubts about what we've heard from the elders," Zira continued. "She had good arguments too. Anyway, about a year ago she got lost and hurt in the woods. They told us she fell down and hit her head on a log. No one ever even explained why she was out there."

"But?" Paul asked.

"She never mentioned Caldaria again. It's really not like her to abandon a mystery. She has to solve everything. It's why she's the best."

"So what are you saying?"

"She didn't necessarily buy the idea that Caldaria was destroyed," said Zira.

"And ever since then, you haven't either," finished Paul.

"No one has been back since. How can we really know?"

"Do you think she stumbled onto evidence of that? Something that freaked her out enough to never bring it up again?"

"I don't know," said Zira. "But whatever that thing was outside of Mel's door was connected. I think she knows the truth, and they want to make sure she stays silent."

"Why do you say that?"

"Because whoever sent that thing would have made it much less visible if they were just going to spy on her," she continued. "They were threatening her."

"But only Allasta saw it, and that could have been a dream," said Paul.

Then he realized what she was saying.

"You saw it too."

"It's been there more than once," she answered sadly.

"Why didn't you say anything?" he asked.

"Because she already knows it's there. I can see it clearly in her. She's my closest friend. I know when something is bothering her. Plus, I was also worried that someone might blame you."

"It is odd how it first happened the night I arrived," commented Paul.

"Yes, but that wasn't the only unusual thing that happened that night," added Zira. "That was the first time in a year that Mel wandered outside of the known parts of the woods."

*   *   *

Myla...

The voice rang through her ears. She sat up quickly. Her pulse was racing with sweat dripping down her neck. She pressed her hand to her forehead. She was dreaming again. She didn't have to worry. She was safe, for now.

Her dreams had only become that vivid in the past month. Perhaps it was her fear of being watched and that he may be after her. It probably was all in her head and she had nothing to fear. Sadly though, she knew that wasn't true. He was after her. The blue light gave her location away. It was only a matter of time before he came for her.

Myla pulled herself out of bed and walked outside. Cautiously, she looked around for any anomalies, but none were to be found. She wasn't dreaming anymore. He would have already left if he had been here. She tried not to think of his presence. She could still feel it around her. He had been here, standing at this door, just moments before. She could feel it.

She sat down at the edge of the wooden path and dangled her feet over the edge. He had been there many nights since the blue light. She began noticing it after Allasta spotted that fire-like thing outside her door. Many nights she stepped outside of her little house to face what was there, and each time she only found the remnant of him. Simply another reminder that she was being watched, and that there was nothing she could do about it.

"You know if I had ghosts visit my room at night, I would tell somebody."

Paul had walked up behind her. She chose to not really acknowledge his presence as he came up and sat down next to her.

"I saw it tonight," he said softly. "Zira's seen it too."

"I guess that makes me the odd one out," she answered, trying to smile.

"Well, I wouldn't be too sure about that," he said trying to return a smile. "I don't think Neph has ever seen it."

Myla didn't respond. She simply leaned on the railing and looked out into the village through the poles.

"Why haven't you said anything?" he asked, clearly concerned.

Myla looked over at him. Why hadn't she said anything? And now why was she considering talking to this person that she had only known for a month?

"There are some situations that words cannot help," she answered.

She was tired. The dream was still very present in her mind, but it was fading. She wanted it to go away. She wanted peace. She wanted to sleep. Paul, sensing her exhaustion, put his arm around her. She leaned into him and rested her head on his shoulder. Why she trusted him now she did not know, but her eyes slowly began to close as she rested there in his arms.

Myla awoke from a dreamless sleep in her own bed the next morning. She rolled over and looked outside. The sun didn't seem too high in the sky. She had plenty of time before she had to meet Paul for his first lesson. She must have fallen asleep right there the night before. He probably had to carry her to bed. Myla buried herself under her covers in embarrassment. What a moment of weakness for him to have seen! How was she supposed to be the strongest of the Caldar if she couldn't handle those situations? How could she have confided in him about what was going on?

Because he already knew. He saw the shape outside of her door. Zira apparently had as well. How much did Zira already know? Myla wasn't ready to confide in anybody about her situation, but if she had to pick someone, Zira, Paul or Neph would be preferable to Malachi or Malika, that was for sure. She might even take Allasta over those two. She never did gain trust in them.

Myla peered out from under her covers. It was probably time for her to get up for the day. Breakfast at Eli's sounded like a good idea, so she jumped out of bed and quickly bathed and got dressed. On her way out the door, she caught her face in the mirror. She was relieved to see that she didn't look as tired as she was expecting. She didn't need any more people asking how she slept than was necessary.

Eli's café was pretty crowded when Myla arrived. It was a peak hour for the Caldar to have breakfast so Myla had to wait in line for a seat. She looked into the café to see if anyone she knew was inside. Sure enough, Zira and Neph were there at a table on the other side of the room. Myla didn't want to go bug them, because she always sensed there was more between them than either would admit. However, Neph saw her and began to wave her over. She quickly bypassed the line and made her way over to the two.

"How's it going?" asked Neph in a cheery voice.

97

"Not bad," she answered, smiling at Neph's consistently positive attitude. "How are you two?"

"Pretty good," they both answered simultaneously, cracking each other up.

"How did you sleep last night?" Zira asked.

There was that question Myla was hoping to avoid.

"Pretty well," Myla answered, suddenly very preoccupied with the cup of tea she was just served.

"Really?" asked Zira, clearly knowing more than Myla realized. "Because I ran into Paul this morning."

"You did?" Myla asked softly.

"You know, Mel," Neph asked, trying to sound very serious. "If I had a big orange and black energy ball infestation, I would have it checked."

"Okay, we seriously need another name for that," insisted Zira.

"I'm sorry I didn't tell you guys," said Myla, appreciating their humor.

"And I'm sorry I never said I knew what was going on," said Zira. "I kept hoping you would come to me about it."

"And I'm sorry that I am such a heavy sleeper that I didn't know what was going on," added Neph, keeping a smile. "Now tell the truth, Myla…"

"Mel!" squeaked Zira.

"Whoops, sorry," said Neph, looking sheepish. "Now tell us the truth, Mel: do you know what it is?"

"Yes, I think I do," Myla responded. "But I can't tell you here. I think we should put off this conversation till we are at a more discrete spot."

"As long as it still happens," answered Zira.

Zira's sincerity was clear, and maybe Myla was ready to confide in her friends. Having help may not be such a bad thing. She would consider it, but now was not the time.

"So onto a different subject," continued Myla, presenting a huge smile. "I never asked... How did you guys get everyone to start calling me 'Mel'?"

At this, Zira and Neph both started laughing.

"We did it the old fashioned way," Neph laughed. "The two of us, along with Allasta, stuck notes under everyone's doors."

"Notes saying what?" asked Myla, suddenly very worried.

"Just that you had a traumatizing memory from your Mertana past come to surface and now the sound of your actual name caused you to have a seizure," explained Zira.

"And if everyone would be so kind as to call you 'Mel' from now on even if you weren't around for fear that you might be set off convulsing again if you overheard," added Neph.

"Oh and then the three of us made sure to go up to every person on the street and ask them if they heard about *Mel* the next morning," finished Zira. "I can't believe it worked."

"A feat of brilliance I should say," commended Neph.

Myla just stared at them in disbelief.

"Well, I guess I did give you an impossible task, and you didn't do anything too illegal," she said slowly. "But I would have appreciated something a little less unflattering."

Then she started to laugh.

"Though that is really funny," she added.

Neph and Zira were glad to find out that they weren't in too much trouble for their prank/favor. They were quick to point out to Myla that whenever she did decide to tell Paul the truth about her identity, everyone would also find out that she actually wasn't traumatized.

"So can I ask you something now that we are on the subject?" asked Zira, clearly knowing she was about to step out of her bounds. "How well did you know him in Mertana?"

99

"Not too well, but I definitely knew him," Myla said slowly. "Life in Mertana was... hard... The people there... They didn't really accept me. I guess he is part of some traumatizing memories that I choose to not relive. It's been weird having him here."

"But now you are friends," said Zira. "I'm sure he won't let his opinion of you as a ten-year old get in the way of that."

"And so what do I do? Tell him that I have been lying to him all this time?" Myla asked.

"He's going to find out at some point," noted Neph.

"Even so, I don't think I am ready to tell him yet," responded Myla. "I know sometimes my cautious attitude doesn't make sense, but it's how I handle things."

"We know that, Mel, and we trust your judgment," assured Zira. "We will support you no matter what."

Paul was already there when Myla showed up to his lesson. She was prepared to deal with him asking her questions about the night before and if she was all right, but he didn't say anything more than a "how are you?" Myla appreciated his willingness to not bring it up. Instead, he got right to his lessons and worked as hard as ever. He did seem more caring in the way he spoke to and treated Myla. He was worried. She noticed it, but took the opportunity he gave her to ignore it.

Myla was probably giving him too difficult of exercises. She realized this, but he was handling them well, and she didn't want to appear weak in any way. Each time she felt herself about to yawn, she gave him something else to do. Why did she have to act like that? He didn't deserve it. He wouldn't judge her for being tired or weak. She wasn't behaving rationally. She knew it, but she wasn't about to change it either.

By the end of the lesson, Paul was panting for air. He sat down on the ground and leaned against the log. He stretched out

100

and let out a huge yawn. Of course he would be sleepy too. Why didn't she think of that?

"Had some extra energy to let out there?" he asked in between breaths.

Why did he always have to speak so candidly?

"What? Was that too difficult?" she asked, trying to play naive.

He didn't buy it.

"I already know you are a way stronger Caldar than me," he said. "You had nothing to prove."

Myla just stared at him. She felt herself getting angry.

"You know," he continued, standing up and facing her. "Even the strongest Caldar is allowed to feel weak every once in a while."

With that he walked over and started to pick up his stuff. Myla just stood still, fuming inside. His blatant honesty was too much for her to handle at the moment. She felt her eyes tearing up. She needed to get out of there, so she did the only thing she could think of doing. She turned around and left. It probably wasn't such a smart move. Why did she have to act like such a jackass? Now he really would think that she was weak.

Myla headed back to her small house and plopped down in a chair. She looked towards the food she had in her cupboard. Rice and bread – what a diet she had going. She needed to go to the market square and get some fruit for lunch, but she didn't have the energy at the moment, so bread would have to do. She got up and walked to the cupboard and pulled out the loaf. She then returned to her chair and began pulling off small bits and eating them.

Myla...

Myla jumped up in her chair. The voice sent chills down her spine. She looked around the room. No one was in sight. She pinched herself. She was definitely awake. His presence, she could feel it. He was there.

She ran to her door and tried to open it, but it wouldn't move. She turned around and each of the window shutters began to slam shut on their own. Where was he?

Myla...

There it was again, yet no one was visible in the room. She had to know what she was up against, so she lifted up her hand and a pale blue light came spiraling from it. She circled it around the room and in it appeared a shimmering black shape huddled in the corner of the room. Once the light shone on it, it lunged toward her. She jumped out of the way, but was not nearly quick enough. She felt a sharp piercing pain in her arm as she pulled away from the dark shape. She then realized that she no longer needed a light to see it. In front of her stood a ghostly man. It was the being she met in the forest a year before, only more defined.

Myla gasped as he peered at her with his sickly black eyes. Suddenly, she was taking every effort to not pass out at his presence. The pain in her arm was increasing. What did he want with her? Was this her end?

"Who are you?" she stammered out finally.

"You know the answer to that," he said in a deep, almost human voice. "I am the great ruler of Caldaria."

"Do you have a name?" she asked.

What was she doing? Making conversation?

"Such an interesting question for someone who has tried so hard to avoid me," answered his cold dead voice. "My name is Amos, if you desire to know it so much."

"Well then Amos, if you are the great ruler of Caldaria," she asked, gaining more confidence than she ever realized she had. "What are you doing here? Don't you have governing to tend to?"

"What a bold girl you are," he noted, seeming somewhat curious. "This may change in time."

"What do you want with me?" she asked, trying not to shiver so visibly.

He walked up to her to the point that he was almost touching her and looked her straight in the eye.

"To know you," he responded simply.

Then he disappeared, her windows reopened, and his presence was gone.

Myla stood there shaking, staring straight in front of her. Blood dripped down her arm into a pool on the floor. She knew she had to move and get help fast, but she couldn't bring herself to start stop shaking let alone start walking. Who could she talk to? Who could heal this wound that she could trust?

*   *   *

Zira was having lunch with Neph and Paul when Myla burst in on them at the boy's house. She didn't say anything, just stumbled in and fell on the floor shaking with her arm bleeding profusely. Paul saw her arm and immediately ran to grab his healing materials. Meanwhile, Zira and Neph lifted her onto the couch, as she mumbled incoherently. Zira knelt down by her face and looked at her in the eyes.

"Mel, are you okay?" Zira asked her.

"Myla," she responded.

Zira and Neph looked at each other worried.

"He knew my name," she continued, shaking. "He called me Myla."

Paul knelt down beside them hesitantly and started to clean up her arm. He didn't say anything, but the expression on his face said everything.

103

"Myla, he hissed it at me, Zira. Just like he did a year ago. He'll never leave me alone."

Myla started to cry.

"Don't worry, Myla," Zira said softly. "You're safe now. We're taking care of you."

Myla drifted off to sleep as Paul finished healing her arm. Zira looked over. The arm was as good as new. Paul was talented with healing. He didn't stick around after that though. He immediately got up and walked out of the room. Zira wondered about how much damage those few simple words would cause.

* * *

It was evening by the time Myla opened her eyes again. Neph was sitting over by the fire, clearly waiting for her to wake up. It must have been his shift. Slowly she sat up and pulled the blanket that she was under around her shoulders. She cycled through the past events in her mind. Amos. That was his name. He wants to know her. What did that mean? Myla. She had said her name. In her frenzied state, she had said her name. Paul healed her arm. He must have heard her. The charade was over.

Neph noticed her sitting up and immediately called into the other room saying that she was awake. Pretty soon, Zira ran in and brought her some tea, then sat down beside her.

"Here, drink this," she said softly. "It needs to steep a little, but Paul said it should help with the arm and with the shock. How are you feeling?"

"I'm okay," she said quietly. "Sorry to burst in on you guys like that."

"I can't believe you are apologizing," said Neph, who had pulled his chair over to where she was sitting.

Paul walked into the doorway, but stood silently over there keeping his distance.

"What happened?" asked Zira.

"I am getting stalked by a thousand year old sorcerer," Myla said simply, managing a small laugh, before she looked down and continued talking, not meeting anyone in the eye.

"When Sherah's curse was placed, the king declared that another person would rise up and equal the second sorcerer. He believes I am that person."

All three stared at her in shock. No one appeared to know what to say. Finally, Zira found the strength.

"How long have you known this?" she asked.

Myla stared down into her cup of tea.

"Since the incident in the woods over a year ago," she answered. "His presence sent me off track and he started hissing at me, whispering *Myla* into my head."

Paul winced at that and leaned his back against the side of the doorframe so he didn't have to face the others.

"Malachi filled me in after they rescued me that night," she continued. "I've been living with that knowledge ever since."

"Why didn't you ever tell me?" asked Zira, completely stunned.

"Malachi told me not to, and I didn't want people to think I was special or different. I wanted to be normal."

Myla looked over at Paul, but couldn't read his reaction. Zira and Neph saw her looking over and decided it would probably be a good idea to excuse themselves, leaving Myla alone in the room with Paul. Several minutes went by without either of them saying anything. Finally, Paul looked over and faced her. His face looked crushed.

"How's the arm doing?" he asked, clearly wishing he could be sympathetic.

"Good," she answered. "Thank you."

"Okay then," he responded shortly and then started to walk out of the room.

"Wait, Paul!" she called after him. "Can we at least talk about this?"

He turned around and looked at her hopelessly.

"About what?" he asked. "About how you not only lied to me for the past month, but you managed to get the entire village to as well? You know I came here looking for you. This entire time I thought you had been killed or worse."

"I didn't want you to discount me right away. I know it wasn't right of me, but it's what I did."

"To think that's what you have always thought of me," he said, trying to not look her in the eye. "And I thought... I thought..."

"You thought what?"

He stared at her.

"I thought it was obvious."

He didn't say anymore. Instead, he turned around and left the room. Myla fell down on the couch, trying to hold back tears. Guilt had overwritten fear, and it finally got the best of her as she sobbed into her pillow. Zira came in and pulled the blanket back over her, letting Myla cry herself back to sleep.

Teaching Paul the next day was one of the more awkward experiences in her life. He didn't say one word to her that didn't pertain specifically to what they were doing. The entire time, he avoided looking at her. Myla thought it was pretty immature, but at the same time she did see where he was coming from. She was the one who had the entire village lie to him because she didn't want to deal with her past. If the silent treatment was what she was getting for it, then she would have to accept it. She did earn it.

At the end of the lesson, Paul immediately took off, not giving her a chance to even try to apologize. Oh well. She had bigger things to worry about. What to do about Amos was her new focus. She was meeting Zira and Neph for lunch to discuss that very question and needed to start heading over to Eli's.

Neph and Zira were already at the café when Myla arrived. They seemed to be deep into a conversation already. Myla was tempted to eavesdrop, but at the moment she figured she shouldn't risk getting into any more trouble with her friends than she was. Alienating Zira and Neph on top of Paul didn't seem like a good idea. Instead, Myla walked straight up to them and said hello.

"Hey, Myla!" Zira exclaimed, seeming relieved. "How are you doing?"

"Fine," she answered. "What's going on?"

"We think Malachi knows of your encounter last night." Neph sounded worried.

"What? Why?" asked Myla, rather alarmed herself.

She hadn't decided whether or not to tell Malachi or Malika of her new trouble and she didn't like the idea of them knowing out of her control.

"Because he brought it up to me this morning," answered Neph. "I swear, Mel. I don't know how he found out."

"What did he say?"

"That he appreciated us watching over you, and that in the future, we should probably notify him of any encounters with the sorcerer."

"Well, that means he knows," Myla said quietly.

How did he find out? Now she would have to go talk to him herself. So much for being in control of the situation...

"Maybe it's better this way," suggested Zira in an uplifting voice. "He is by far the most knowledgeable Caldar in this situation. He could be able to help."

107

"And keep as much from me as possible the entire time he does," Myla added, trying to not sound too frustrated.

"Is your entire family based on keeping as much from each other as possible?" Neph asked, clearly a bit amused.

"I don't know if we could even qualify as a family. That would require some legitimate interaction."

"You interact more than you admit," pointed out Zira.

She was right, but it often didn't feel that way to Myla.

"So how did class go this morning?" asked Neph, trying to tactfully change the subject. Of course, bringing up Paul was probably not too tactful.

"He didn't say one word to me that he didn't have to."

Myla tried to not sound too upset, but it was evident in her voice.

"He'll get over it," Zira said hopefully. "He has to. It's only a matter of time."

That evening Myla made her way over to Malachi's house. She heard raised voices inside. It sounded like Malika was there and the two were arguing. Myla decided to humor herself and pretend that it wasn't about her. She went ahead and opened the door to find Malika and Malachi standing in the center of the room facing each other. Malika had tears streaming down her face and Malachi had turned an interesting color of red.

"Myla, shut the door," said Malachi firmly.

"Don't talk to my daughter that way," ordered Malika. "She's an adult now. It's time you started treating her like one."

Was Malika really saying that? This was a surprise. Myla was used to her being Malachi's main supporter.

"If she were truly an adult," Malachi responded firmly. "She would have brought this issue to my attention sooner."

"Maybe she would have if you had treated her like one," Malika bit back. Myla was impressed.

"And how have I not treated her well?" Malachi asked.

"By consistently hiding pertinent information from her at every turn," Malika answered furiously.

Myla knew she probably should have been more concerned, but she actually found this display quite amusing. It was nice seeing that Malika wasn't as bad as she had thought.

"It still would have been nice if we had dealt with this situation without anybody getting hurt," answered Malachi, clearly frustrated with the turn this conversation had taken.

"Oh, don't worry about me," answered Myla, rather sarcastically. "I am fine."

"Thanks to Paul," pointed out Malika.

"How long have you been dealing with Sherah's heir, Myla?" Malachi asked, ignoring the amused look on Myla's face.

"About a month," she answered, trying to conceal a smile. "Is that bad?"

"You will not make fun of this serious situation!" bellowed Malachi.

That only angered Myla.

"Excuse me?" she responded loudly. "This is my serious situation. As I recall, I am the one in danger here, and if I choose to not take you seriously, that is my own prerogative."

Malachi and Malika both looked at her silently. It had been a long time since they had seen this side of Myla.

"I hate to break it to you, Malachi, but Malika is right," she continued. "How can you expect me to fill you in on every little detail, if you don't return me the same courtesy? I acknowledge that I am in a risky situation and your help would be useful, but I would prefer to take a chance rather than trust someone who would rather risk letting me fall into a situation blindly, than actually fill me in with the information he has!"

Malachi backed up and sat down in a chair against the wall. He held his hand to his head and looked over at the two ladies in the room, both completely furious.

"I've messed up," he said softly, his voice sounding weak and broken. "I just wanted to protect you..."

"You can't protect me," Myla responded gently. "This is my issue, my destiny. Amos is coming after me no matter what. I will have to face him again. There's no hiding from it."

"Amos?" Malachi asked, confused.

"Sherah's heir – that's his name," she answered.

"You spoke with him?" he asked.

"Yes."

"Paul didn't tell us that," Malika explained.

"Paul told you about this?" asked Myla. "That's how you heard?"

What a low move on his part... Now Myla was angry with him.

"Yes, he mentioned it to us this morning," she answered.

Why hadn't Myla guessed that? Of course it would have been Paul. She was glad to find out, but she couldn't deal with that right now. She turned towards her grandfather.

"Malachi, you must tell me all that you know about my predicament."

"He may not want to kill you," he said quietly.

This was something Myla had already figured out.

"So what does he want with me?"

"He may try to see if you will rule with him instead of against him. Over the years the Caldar have suspected that Sherah's heir will never be truly satisfied until the entire world is conquered. Caldaria is not enough."

"So he wants my help?" she asked, surprised by this revelation.

110

It made sense, though she wondered why she never thought of it before.

"If it's possible," said Malachi. "If it becomes too evident that you will never help him, he will kill you."

"Should I expect him to return soon?" asked Myla.

"No, I would think not. You are not advanced enough yet. He most likely came because of the blue light. He probably learned in your encounter that you are not quite ready to help him. He will return one day though. It is only a matter of time."

"Then let us use our time well," stated Myla strongly. "I need to know everything there is to know about fighting the forces of evil. If I am to face him again, I want to be prepared."

"There is much for you to learn," said Malachi, sounding doubtful.

"I will pass off my training of Paul to Zira. She is perfectly qualified."

Training Paul was not something she would really miss at the moment anyway.

"Very well then. We shall begin tomorrow," decided Malachi. "In the meantime, I suggest you return to your own house. You cannot appear as if you are in danger. The other Caldar cannot know. We do not need a panic."

"I agree," responded Myla. "I shall let Zira know that she is training Paul from now on."

Myla stopped by Zira's on the way back to her own house. Zira agreed to take on Paul's lessons, but did express concern that Myla and Paul would never resolve their issues if she weren't training him. Myla acknowledged the possibility, but argued that it wasn't their main concern. She didn't let Zira know that it was Paul that leaked the situation to Malachi and Malika. That was something she wanted to handle on her own when the time came.

Once she left Zira's, Myla made her way back to her own little house. As she opened the door she realized that it was the first time she had entered it since her encounter with Amos. She looked to the floor. It had been freshly mopped. Zira or Neph must have come in and cleaned it up while she was gone. She paused at the doorway, making sure she sensed no presence in the room. It was empty. There was no one inside.

Slowly Myla walked inside the room. The bread she had out on the table had been put away neatly in her cupboard. She slowly reached up and grabbed herself a huge chunk. She ate it as she looked around the room. This place would be her prison. He could always find her there, and she would never be able to leave. No longer was this village her place of refuge. She would never be safe again. Of course, if Amos did intend to conquer the world, she would never be safe anywhere. All she could do was hope that when the time came, she would have the strength to save her people.

Sadly though, she knew that this would never be. Myla was powerful, but she would never match the power of the sorcerers. Her people were lost. She would be their failure, not their savior. She wept to think that their innocent lives were in her completely incapable hands.

Myla, however, couldn't worry herself with this now. Exhaustion had once again come over her. She collapsed on her bed, without the energy to even change her clothes. She pulled her covers over her eyes and fell into a long dreamless sleep.

The next day, the map room was the last place Myla wanted to be. That room was thick with Amos' presence. However, when Malachi came and found her that morning for her training, he immediately brought her there. He said it was remote from the rest of the village, so that they could speak in secret. Myla also suspected that there was more to the room than a map of the past and future. She didn't dare ask Malachi however. Though she felt she had gained some ground with him the previous day, she did not want to push her luck.

Malachi didn't speak as they approached the door to that dreaded room. Myla peered into his face trying to find some indication of what was in store, but his face showed no emotion. As usual, he was stone to the rest of the world. So few times had Myla seen him portray his feelings. Seeing such a display the day before meant nothing right now.

As Malachi lead her into the room, Myla immediately started to feel for Amos' presence. She felt nothing. Malachi walked to the opposite wooden wall and pressed his hand against it. Quietly, Myla waited on the opposite side, wondering what Malachi was thinking. Why hadn't he said anything? And why was he standing over there with his hand like that?

Suddenly, Myla heard a small crack. She looked over to Malachi. Coming out from his hand a tiny line had developed all the way to the ceiling. After a small pause, another line appeared. Then another. Soon cracks were coming out from his hand and stretching to all the walls surrounding them. The room was going to collapse.

"What are you doing?" Myla shouted, but Malachi gave no response. He was deeply intense in his magic. Myla wasn't sure if she could trust him? What was he trying to do? Was he trying to kill her in here, to perhaps save the village from the doom her presence would bring?

Light was shining in through the millions of cracks surrounding them. Myla shouted at Malachi again, but to no avail. She ran to the door behind her, but it was shut fast. She couldn't get out of the room. Perhaps Malachi was trying to kill her. Maybe that was why he gave in to her demands so easily. Maybe he feared that she would betray the rest of the village and bring death to them all. She ran to him and tried to pull his hand back. He wouldn't move.

Crack...One of the wooden boards above had split into. A large piece of wood began to fall down onto the ground. This would be her end. Falling to the ground in a collapsed map room where no one in the village would find her. How appropriate it was that this would be her demise. No fancy epic story – just a girl who fell to her death when an old shack collapsed in on her. She had to do something. She had to stop him. She had to end this psychotic venture.

"*Stop!*" she shouted, stretching out both her arms.

Then to her surprise, it worked.

She looked up ahead of her. A falling board was stopped midair. All of the cracking had ceased. The building stood, frozen around her. That destruction of the building wasn't the only thing that had stopped however. Malachi was frozen as well. His eyes didn't even blink. Somehow in a powerful fear, she had not only stopped the building from collapsing, but she had stopped Malachi, the most powerful Caldar in the village as well.

Cautiously she walked towards him. There he stood, with his hand stretched out against the wall. His eyes cold, staring. She tapped him on the shoulder. He didn't respond. How was this possible?

She quickly turned around and ran out the door. It was then that she realized the true extent of her mistake. Leaves were frozen midair around her. She had stopped things outside the map room as well. What had she done?

Myla slowly walked toward the village, hoping with each step she would find one sign of life. Her hopes however, were to no avail. With each step she took, she saw more signs of everything around her, frozen in place. She could only hope that once she reached the rest of the village, she would discover the effects of her feat had not spread that far. She knew, however, that this would not be the case.

The wooden path made no noise as she ran along boards leading to the village. Normally, the trees would move towards her as she ran, but they made no motion. Soon the path split into two different directions, and she was at the border of the village. She took the way toward the market square and without the sound of her feet hitting the ground, she raced toward any hope of life.

Her hope was wasted, however, because as she expected, everyone in the village was frozen still. A small boy stood still with an apple placed firmly between his lips. A small shop owner stood with his hands in the air trying to bargain with a client. Not one person moved. How was this possible?

Every time, she had frozen an object midair, she was able to unfreeze it simply by no longer concentrating. How was this different? Hadn't she just done the same thing, only at a larger scale?

Myla made her way down to the ground level and sat down on a log. She tapped her fingers against the wood as she lost herself in thought. How was it that she had frozen all of these people? How far did the extent of this reach? Then she realized it: what made this situation different. Her fingers made no noise as she tapped the log she rested on. She hadn't just stopped everything from moving. She had stopped time.

Stopping singular objects was only part of a much larger gift, only no one had ever discovered the extent of it before. That's why the object would always fall to the ground if she had stopped concentrating. She had only gone part way. The natural instinct would be to bounce back to normal if she hadn't completed the job.

This time, however, she had completed the job. Time was stopped still. But now, how could she turn it back? To reverse this magic, it would require the same amount of force, a level of power she only reached when her life was on the line.

Could she turn time back on without being in imminent danger? Was this even a possibility?

And what about Malachi? He was still in the map room, bringing the building down around him. She was safe but he was not. Perhaps he deserved to fall to his doom in that room. He did try to kill her. Yet then again, if he was, it was probably only to save the village. Maybe he wasn't even trying to kill her. Maybe this was his twisted way of getting her to use the kind of power that she didn't know she had.

Of course, nobody could have known she had that power. Nobody had ever accomplished such a feat. Nowhere in any history book was it ever recorded of someone stopping time. It was considered impossible. Malachi could have never expected such a reaction.

The history books didn't record Amos' existence either though. They had a habit of leaving out those details that no one knew about. Malachi seemed to always know about them though, and maybe he did know about this. Myla had no choice but to trust that his attempted murder was actually one larger lesson. And if that was the case, she had to figure out how to restart time and save him as well.

Chapter 7

Zira had an angry and puzzled look on her face. It was clear that she was mid-speech. Paul didn't look much happier. His face was flushed red and his mouth was open as if he was about to shout. Myla felt a twinge of guilt when she saw them like this. They had no way of knowing that she could see this. What were they talking about? Was it her? She couldn't distract herself with that. That wasn't why she was here. She came to the school to get help, and that was all she could focus on.

Myla pulled Zira's arm. It moved with her, but once she let go, it returned to its position midair. It was another symptom of time's strange behavior. It didn't like to be messed with. Myla, however, had to mess with it. It was her only hope. She had to somehow wake up Zira.

If she could only partly stop time in order to stop a leaf in the air, couldn't the reverse happen? Couldn't she partly wake up Zira? Then again, she would have to concentrate the entire time on keeping her awake if that theory was correct, so perhaps it wouldn't be the wisest idea.

Unless of course, Zira could somehow keep herself in time on her own. Zira was a more powerful Caldar than she gave herself credit for. The ability to separate herself from Myla's magic was not far from her. She could probably manage it.

Myla figured that she had no choice but to just try it out and see. She stared at Zira. "Move," she whispered softly. Zira remained like stone. "Move," Myla said a little bit louder. Her voice created a gust of wind blowing Zira's hair back. Zira, however, didn't stir. "Move." This time Myla's voice was firm and solid, and suddenly Zira was yelling at a still frozen Paul.

"How can you even think…"

Zira's voice trailed off as she realized that Paul had stopped moving. She looked to the side and jumped back in shock as she saw Myla standing right next to her.

"What the…" said a very disturbed Zira.

"I have a little problem," said Myla sheepishly, working hard to not lose concentration.

"Um Myla, I'm looking at a leaf next to your head that isn't going anywhere. One of us definitely has a problem. I am just hoping it is you."

"I froze time," said Myla.

"No kidding," answered Zira, trying to not look too overwhelmed by the situation. "I didn't think that was possible."

"Neither did I, but apparently it is."

Myla was getting tired from focusing on keeping Zira awake.

"Well, what can I do?"

Leave it to Zira to not ask any more questions. Myla knew that Zira got tired of always having to ask how.

"Help me keep you awake," answered Myla. "It's the same way we'd keep a leaf still in the air but in reverse."

Zira immediately nodded her head and Myla felt the weight lift off her shoulders. She was good.

"Now what can I do?" asked Zira, still very perplexed.

"Help me get Malachi out of a room that is about to collapse."

"Why didn't you just wake up him?"

"Because he is the one making it collapse," Myla responded.

Zira seemed taken aback by that.

"Mel, can I ask you a very simple question?"

Zira actually seemed quite amused.

"Sure."

"Why?" asked Zira, holding back a smile.

"Why is he trying to make the room collapse or why should we try to get him out of there?" asked Myla in return.

At that Zira laughed.

"Both I guess," she answered.

"I don't know why he is making the room collapse, but I was in it when he was trying. I stopped time because it was the only way to get out. I don't however want to start time up again with him still in there."

"Myla?"

"Yes?"

"Couldn't you give it at least a week before something else had to happen?" Zira asked. "I mean this is just tiring."

"No kidding," answered Myla, appreciating Zira's humor.

"So what'd you do to piss off Malachi?"

"That's what I would like to know."

Malachi proved a little harder to move than Myla had anticipated. At first they just tried lifting him straight up but he wouldn't budge. Next they tried pulling him away from the wall but again they couldn't move him. They then tried one of them pushing him and the other pulling him. Again their efforts were to no avail.

"How much does this man eat?" Zira finally asked, dropping to the floor exhausted.

"He must be connected to the wall with the magic he was using," Myla said, quite perplexed.

"Since when was magic glue?" asked Zira, clearly frustrated.

"Well, it has certainly stuck time," answered Myla.

"So I guess we better figure out how to break whatever this is holding him to the wall. I recommend an ax."

That made Myla laugh. How did she get herself into this situation where she is working so hard to save the man that just tried to kill her? Did he try to kill her? She couldn't distract herself with those questions. Now she needed to know how to end this magic.

The blue light... The blue light was able to free Neph from whatever was carrying him into the air. She could use it to free Malachi. Myla searched for whatever was in her that brought out that light, but she couldn't find it. Over and over again she tried to shoot out the blue light from her hand, but nothing would appear.

"Are you even trying?" asked Zira, clearly doubting Myla's effort.

"Nothing is happening," said Myla, very confused.

What was wrong with her?

"Maybe you need to start time before you can use your gifts."

"Zira, try to blend into the wall behind you."

Zira immediately stood up and tried but to no avail. She couldn't match the wood. She tried again before collapsed down on the ground frustrated. Without time, they could do nothing.

"You know I have always respected Malachi in a weird way," continued Zira. "But I honestly don't think he thought this one through. There are a lot easier ways to off somebody that doesn't involve freezing time or taking yourself down in the process."

"I think he may have been trying to teach me something," Myla said softly.

"Teach you what? How to freeze time? Again, he could have done that in a way that would have involved not killing himself in the process."

120

"Well, I am not going to restart time until I figure out how to save him and maybe he knew that," said Myla defensively.

"I think we should wake him up and see what happens. He might stop once he realizes you're not in the room," suggested Zira.

"Look around Zira. This room is going to collapse once I restart time. There is nothing left to hold it up."

Zira stood up and started to try to pry Malachi's fingers off the wall. They wouldn't move. They were tightly fastened to the wood. Zira sighed and leaned against the wall before jumping away worried she might make it collapse.

"So we can't pull him away from the wall," Zira said, trying to get the situation straight.

"Right."

"And we can't break this magic," she added.

"Right."

"So it's probably safe to say that the only magic we can use is to actually mess with time itself, right?"

"I would guess so."

"So then let's mess with time," Zira said plainly.

Myla suddenly realized what she was suggesting.

"Going backwards in time is impossible," Myla pointed out.

"Up till this very moment, we thought stopping time was impossible," Zira returned.

"I don't think I am that powerful Zira," Myla said, clearly worried.

Could anyone be that powerful?

"If anyone is, it's you," responded Zira, almost as if she was reading Myla's thoughts.

"How would I even go about it?" asked Myla, skeptically.

"I don't know. Think it."

Myla laughed to herself about the simplicity of Zira's answer. She knew that if it were possible there would be nothing else involved in the procedure, but how to think it was another problem. This is why the Caldar went through training. They couldn't just automatically use their brains to make things happen. It was a mental step-by-step process, and now Zira was asking Myla to skip a step.

Myla tried to open her mind and move time backwards. She wasn't far off before when she stopped time. It could very well be possible to move it backwards, but how? Jumbled thoughts filled her brain. She couldn't concentrate. She couldn't see it. She didn't know how.

Myla sat down on the floor hopeless. She hung her head in her hands, searching her brain for some sort of answer. She didn't have it in her. She was too exhausted. Stopping time had taken away too much energy out of her. Without the specific knowledge of what she was doing there was no way she could turn back time.

Myla's mind raced over the events that had taken place between her stopping time and to her sitting on the floor. She couldn't get a handle on it. Everything was out of order. Despite her best efforts to replay the previous events in her mind, she couldn't. All she could come across was random images. Without time, the before and after was lost within her head, and without any conception of before and after, she couldn't figure out how to accomplish her task.

The sound of tapping on the wood – missing. The market square – filled with frozen people. A little boy with an apple, mid-bite... Zira standing frozen, with a look of complete anger on her face... The images raced through her mind. Zira was angry. She was angry with Paul.

"Zira?" asked Myla softly.

Zira, who was sitting on the floor staring at the wall, leaned back on her hands and looked to Myla.

"What?" she asked, not sure whether to be hopeful.

"What were you arguing with Paul about?"

Myla didn't know if she was crossing a boundary, but she decided to take a chance and ask anyway.

"How did you know I was arguing with Paul?" asked Zira, clearly quite taken aback by the question.

"Your faces: they were angry," Myla answered.

"He showed up today in a really bad mood. He wasn't happy that I was teaching him, and he wouldn't let me help him."

That was the key. Myla thought back to that first day with Paul when she helped him freeze a leaf in the air.

"Zira, I think I need your help. I can't do this alone."

How much did her voice betray her fatigue?

"Mel, I don't know how to even begin to mess with time," said Zira, clearly nervous.

"You are keeping yourself awake, and that's more than you realize. I can't do it alone. I need your help. I need your strength."

Zira leaned over and grabbed Myla's hand. Nodding, the two closed their eyes. Myla could feel energy flowing through Zira's hand into hers. Suddenly she could think again. It started out smaller with her head clearing of any confusion. Then she started focusing in. She was watching the previous events in her head, of her and Malachi in the room. She knew how to control it. She could rewind it.

Myla opened her eyes to see herself in the room, running backwards from the door to the beginning of the cracking to Malachi placing his hand on the wall. They were entering the room. The two were now outside. Myla looked over at Zira, and then at herself. They were transparent, almost like ghosts. Once

Myla let go, time would go on just as before, but would she remember? Had she just led herself into an unstoppable loop that would never be solved? She had no way of knowing, but it was worth a try. Myla squeezed Zira's hand and then let go...

Malachi didn't speak as they approached the door to that dreaded room. Myla peered into his face trying to find some indication of what was in store, but his face showed no emotion. As usual, he was stone to the rest of the world. So few times had Myla seen him portray his feelings. Simply because she had seen such a display the day before meant nothing right now.

Except it did, because she had been here before and she knew there was going to be another display. Myla stopped in her steps. Malachi was opening the door before her. She didn't move. He held it open waiting for her, but she couldn't follow. He was going to try to kill her. He was going to bring down the map room.

Myla didn't let herself think before she acted. She could feel it flowing through her. Her hand was throbbing yet again. Suddenly a blue light shot out of her hand and lifted Malachi away from the door and up against the outside of the map room. Pinned against the wall, she held the old man. Twisting around he tried to release himself from her grasp. She circled the ground around him pondering her next move.

"Myla, let me down," Malachi said, clearly surprised by this action. "What are you doing?"

"I was just about to ask you the same question," responded Myla.

She was fuming. How could he act innocent? If he was surprised by her actions, then he may have actually been trying to kill her and not teaching her how to alter time.

"Myla, if you try to make me tell you your lesson before I can actually teach it to you, we won't get anywhere," said her grandfather, clearly uncomfortable.

124

Was he trying to teach her?

"Tell me what you were planning," she demanded.

For the second time in two days Myla was controlling this relationship. There was nothing he could do. She was in charge. She had the power. Malachi could do nothing.

"There is an old legend among the Caldar," croaked Malachi.

He seemed to be in a lot of pain, but that didn't sway Myla. She had no way of knowing if his presentation was only a farce.

"It is said that if a Caldar is so focused within their magic, they can actually alter the fabric of time," he continued. "There is nothing limiting the Caldar from doing it; it's just that no Caldar has ever been so powerful. I believe that you are that powerful, and that if you were put in the situation where your life depended on it, you would in fact somehow manage to use time to save yourself."

"And this was what you were doing?" she asked, very relieved to hear this from him.

"Was? I hadn't even managed to yet..."

Malachi's voice trailed off. He looked at her puzzled.

"You already have altered time, haven't you?" he asked. "Amazing..."

"Glad you are fascinated. I take it we are done with this lesson for the day?"

Myla didn't appreciate his scientific attitude.

"I guess we are," he answered.

"Good."

With that Myla dropped Malachi on the ground and turned around. She didn't even look to see if he stood back up. She headed back to the village far too disgusted to spend any more time with him. She was also quite exhausted and wanted to rest. She made a straight line for her own small little house, where after today, didn't seem so frightening.

Myla wouldn't have an easy time resting however, for a very angry Paul greeted her outside her door. Myla glanced at him briefly and headed inside, not really considering him. She was too tired and frustrated to deal with his issues. She figured it had to do with his fight with Zira, but she really didn't care.

He, however, wasn't going to let her ignore him. After she walked into her house and headed straight to her cupboard for some bread, he made his way in after her. He stood by the door, his face clearly angry. She grabbed the loaf and sat down at the table, waiting for him to speak.

"So you're ignoring me now?" asked Paul.

Myla slowly chewed on a piece of bread and stared at him.

"Well great, Mel," he said. "You can add that to lying to me, and then running away from the problem."

Paul turned around and started to walk out the door, but he had caught on to something in Myla and she suddenly felt compelled to speak.

"Running away?" she asked, sounding more amused than she intended, though the situation did seem a bit absurd at the moment.

He turned around and looked at her.

"How else do you explain your choice to hand off all of your classes with me to Zira?" Paul asked. "That's sacrificing my future. I may not particularly be happy with you at the moment, but I still know that you are the best teacher in this village."

"I heard Malachi is pretty good," responded Myla sarcastically and not sympathetically. "You should take classes from him. It's a whole lot of fun."

"Well, there's an idea," Paul responded. "Now why didn't you set me up to learn from him?"

"Well, you're in such good contact with him lately, I figured you could handle it yourself," said Myla, disgusted by Paul's self-centered attitude.

"What are you saying?" he asked.

"You know exactly what I am saying," Myla answered. "You went and told Malika and Malachi about my encounter with Amos. Now that is what I consider untrustworthy."

Paul looked shell-shocked, as well as hurt. Clearly he hadn't expected Myla to be so upset about that.

"I was worried about you," he said. "Well, don't you fret. I won't make that mistake again. You don't even ever have to see me again since now I have such a great teacher in Zira."

His voice seeped with sarcasm.

"You got something against Zira?" asked Myla, getting a little defensive of her friend who just came through for her. "She's ten times the Caldar you'll ever be and then some. As for Malachi? He's already busy teaching me."

"Teaching you?"

Paul didn't seem to buy that idea.

"Yes, believe it or not, I still have things to learn too, and considering recent events, we decided that I should start a slightly more accelerated program. Unfortunately that doesn't leave me time to teach you. Sorry to put out your day."

Myla got up from her table, turned her back to Paul and placed the remainder of the bread in the cupboard. She then turned around with her arms crossed and stared at Paul. Paul didn't seem to have a response. Both of them knew he had nothing left to say, but they still looked at each other for a bit, waiting for either one to say anything. Eventually, after what seemed to be much longer than it actually was, Paul turned around and left the house. Myla immediately felt guilty. She thought about running after him, but something held her back. Pride maybe? Or maybe she just knew he would never forgive her.

Chapter 8

Myla's lessons with Malachi took a very different format after that first day. He no longer had the nerve to pull such a dangerous stunt and treated her very cautiously. It bothered Myla some that she had managed to make her grandfather scared of her, but she also didn't want to have him take such a risk ever again. If it cost her some sort of valuable lesson then so be it. She didn't want to die before Amos ever managed to get to her.

Zira and Myla decided that keeping their adventure a secret was the best plan of action. Myla always suspected that Zira confessed it to Neph in the months that passed, but she didn't really care. Neph was the least of her worries. Neph was one of the few people she felt she could trust.

She couldn't trust Malachi – that was for sure. How was she supposed to rely so heavily on one man for her help, one man who had attempted to kill her? She comforted herself with the knowledge that a lesson was involved in the attempted murder, but the fact that he was willing to take such a risk unsettled her. She couldn't trust him. She knew he knew that she had altered time, but she resolved to never tell him how, or that she had needed Zira's help to complete the task.

Not being able to trust Malachi was nothing new to Myla however. It was losing Paul as a friend that was hard. She didn't realize how much she had grown to rely on him in that one month of friendship. The following four months, the situation was awkward at best. They typically avoided each other at all costs. They never once said 'hello' when they accidentally ran into each other, or both were hanging out with Neph and Zira at the same time. Whenever Myla went over to Neph's place, Paul would stay in his room. It pained her to be in the situation. She felt guilty, but she didn't know what to do about it. She didn't know if he would ever forgive her. And why should he? She lied to him and then brushed him off as if nothing happened.

"Myla, would you like something more to eat?" asked Malika.

Myla had grown accustomed to having dinner over there weekly. It was a new tradition, one Myla adopted after witnessing Malika standing up to Malachi.

"Oh no, I am good, thank you," responded Myla. "It was very good."

"I'm glad you liked it," smiled Malika. "It's a recipe I learned in Mertana."

Myla almost choked on the water she was drinking. Malika had never once in the past ten years mentioned having been in Mertana. It was something Myla had assumed, but up till this moment never known.

"You were in Mertana?" Myla asked.

How far could she push this?

"Of course," Malika responded, suddenly looking very preoccupied with her leftover food. "I met your father there."

Did she really just say that?

"Why haven't you ever talked about this before?"

Myla debated asking the question, but she couldn't decide what information was actually more important.

"You never asked," Malika answered with a smile.

She couldn't be serious, could she?

"You have always known that I have always had great curiosity about that," responded Myla.

She wasn't going to let her mother get away with that.

"Well, I guess I didn't think you were ready..." Malika's voice trailed off as she stared into an empty bowl.

"For ten years? And somehow my willingness to eat Mertana food has changed your mind?"

130

Myla's voice was soft. She didn't want to end the conversation.

"All right, so I guess I avoided the subject," answered Malika sheepishly.

"Ten years doesn't qualify as avoidance. Ten years is called blatantly ignoring."

Again Myla's voice remained soft for she wasn't angry. She smiled at Malika, who smiled in return.

"What was he like, my father?" Myla asked.

"He was sweet, very caring," answered Malika.

Myla had a hard time picturing this. So many of her memories of her father were clouded by drunken rages and idiotic behavior patterns. It was strange seeing Malika speak of him so differently.

As Malika continued on describing a man Myla never knew, she listened in fascination. What changed in this person that caused him to collapse in such a way? She remained surprised by Malika's speech, until she began to describe his laughter. Myla had forgotten her father's laughter. His warm hearty laugh used to comfort her as a child. There were many nights where she woke up scared and was only able to sleep from the sound of his laughter telling her that all was safe and that he was there. There were good times with her father, but somehow over all of these years, she had only remembered the negative ones.

"How did you meet him?" Myla asked.

"I disobeyed a law that was never to be broken," Malika answered quietly.

Myla looked at her, wondering if she could dare another question.

"Why did you leave me with him?"

"I had to pay the price."

With that, Malika ended the conversation and began to clear the table. Myla watched her closely. Her eyes were filled with tears. She was crying.

Myla stood up and started to help Malika with the dishes. In silence, the two cleaned. At the end Malika mumbled a 'thank you' to Myla and headed to her bedroom. Myla stood alone in Malika's empty kitchen. She found herself wiping down the table with a rag unwilling to leave. Malika had just opened up in a way that Myla had never seen before. She was taken aback by her sudden willingness, but Myla, as always, couldn't leave well enough alone. She pushed Malika beyond her limit and now she may never find out the truth about her past.

Myla had never really thought about the fact that Malika had a relationship with her father. Never seeing them together or even at the same point in her life solidified the separation in her mind. It was strange for Myla realizing that at one point, the two may have been a happy couple. When Myla first came to live with the Caldar, her mind was preoccupied with the mystery of her past, but ever since her first encounter with Amos, it had taken a low priority in her life.

Eventually Myla made her way out of Malika's house. The air chilled her face as she stepped out the door. Myla shivered and started to briskly walk back to her house. The village seemed very empty where she was, which is why she was surprised when she passed Paul, jogging by her in the opposite direction. She turned her face habitually. The two of them almost never acknowledged each other's presence. Paul, however, legitimately didn't seem to notice she was there. Where could he be heading in such a hurry? Myla didn't even stop to reconsider. She quickly turned around and followed his path, using every bit of her Caldar power to not be seen.

She found herself following Paul quite the distance through the night. Quickly he ran through the village and outside towards the woods. Myla tracked his steps silently, wondering what he could be running to. She felt a small chill of fear as she followed Paul into the woods, wondering if this was a smart idea. Eventually she saw light ahead and followed him toward a group of people. In front of her stood Malachi and Zechariah. The young girl Kalina, her student, lay still on the floor.

Paul ran over to her and knelt down. Myla stayed back, blending in with the trees. She could only sense the presence of three other people there in the woods. She couldn't find Kalina. Myla leaned back into the tree, fighting back tears as Paul tried to do something to save the poor girl's life. She knew it was hopeless. She wished she hadn't seen it. She slowly sank down onto the ground and buried her head in her hands. How could this have happened? What happened?

Myla looked up. Paul was sitting down, sobbing into his hand. They had given up. The girl was dead. There was nothing they could do about it. Myla looked through the trees, stunned by what was before her. She couldn't help but stare, until she caught Malachi's glance towards her. He knew she was there. Of course he did – why wouldn't he? Myla stood up and turned around to leave. She knew Malachi wouldn't make her presence known, but she didn't want to risk Paul finding out she had followed him.

Tears streamed down her face as Myla ran back to her house. She wanted to wish the evening away, as if nothing had ever happened. She wanted to just wake up and have the assurance that it was just a dream, but she couldn't because the child was dead, and Myla couldn't help but know that somehow this involved her. The past four months had been silent for her. Amos had made no visits to her or made his presence known in any way. Now, however, an innocent child was dead, a child that only ever wanted to be a good student and a skilled Caldar. She wouldn't have that opportunity anymore, and Myla couldn't help but guess why.

133

Myla crawled into bed that night, but she didn't sleep well. Not because of dreams or a presence in the room, but because she knew that the next morning she would have to face the truth: what she saw in the woods was real and Kalina was dead. Fear rushed over her. She had no way of knowing if this would happen again. Every time she tried to close her eyes, she woke herself up again because she couldn't bear to see the image that her mind would show her: the image of that child, lying there on the ground. The guilt was too much to take. Somehow, she knew this was her fault. This had happened because of her.

The next morning, Myla made her way down to Eli's in hope that she would find out that she had been mistaken the night before. Unfortunately that was not the case. Everyone in the café looked teary eyed. No one was spared. Myla kept her head down, hoping to avoid eye contact with everyone. She knew the situation, but she didn't want everyone to know how much she knew and that she had actually been there the night before. Slowly she glanced over the tables. Zira, Neph and Paul were sitting at one. Though the conversation was very quiet, Myla could tell that it was intense. Paul, however, spotted Myla and excused himself from the table. He brushed by Myla as he made his way out of the café. She tried not to think about it as she proceeded to sit down at the table.

"What happened?" asked Myla quietly.

Zira's eyes started to fill with tears. Myla could tell they had both been crying earlier.

"Well, the official story is that Kalina ate some of those poisoned red berries while she was practicing for a tracking exam later this week," said Neph in a very disgusted tone.

"*That* sounds likely," said Myla, very sarcastically. "She was almost eleven and had been told to not eat those berries for her entire life... What's the real story?"

"Paul just told us that last night he was called into the woods to try to save her," continued Neph, much more seriously

134

and quieter. "She was just laying on the ground out there – where they never have tracking exams. He couldn't find anything wrong with her. She was just dead, for no reason. He's pretty convinced that there was some sort of higher magic involved."

"Does he know you're telling me this?" asked Myla, wishing that she didn't have to hear it secondhand.

"He actually asked that we tell you," answered Zira. "He may not be your friend, but he knows when you should know something."

"Well, did he say anything else?" Myla asked.

"Just that he overheard Malachi and Zechariah whispering as they carried her body back to the village," said Neph. "She wasn't practicing for anything. Her parents don't know what really happened to her either though. They are just as confused as everyone else."

"Do they believe the official story?" asked Myla.

"Probably not, but the entire situation has shocked them so much that I don't think they are close to any other explanation," said Neph.

"Myla, do you think this could be... his work?" asked Zira hesitantly.

"Quite possibly," answered Myla. "Though I think if he was trying to threaten me somehow, he would let me know the conditions first."

"Mel, maybe this is his way of showing you that he means business, so when he does confront you again, you'll do what he says," suggested Neph.

Myla stared straight ahead.

"That is one scary possibility," she said softly.

"At the same time, we can't rule out the possibility that this isn't related to him at all," said Zira.

135

"Which would mean there's a killer among us," pointed out Myla. "What can we do about that?"

"Hopefully find some clue as to who it is," said Neph. "And hope they don't strike again."

Myla couldn't decide which possibility was worse, a killer in the village or Amos finally exercising his power. With one, she could trust that whoever it was was less powerful than Amos, but if it was Amos, she at least would know whom to expect. There was no good way to look at this, and the concept of the entire village not even knowing that anything was going on left Myla uneasy. She knew that mass panic would be a bad thing, but at the same time, some sort of warning to the Caldar to watch their backs wouldn't be a stupid idea. She knew this was probably yet another one of Malachi's secrets, but she wasn't entirely comfortable with it. She needed to know more than just what Zira and Neph were able to tell her. She needed to know exactly what happened. Part of her knew that Paul would be her best resource in that quest, but he still wasn't speaking to her. She would have to interrogate Malachi, her least desirable confidant.

Once she finished eating, she made her way quickly over to Malachi's house. She wondered if she would be able to speak to him alone, or if she would find the entire council at each other's throats. Myla felt a lump in her stomach as she turned onto the path towards Malachi's house. She wanted to solve this mystery, but she still couldn't believe that a little girl was dead. She didn't want to be in a room of people reminding her of it either.

She didn't have a choice, however, since as she opened the door, her fears were realized. The entire council of elders was inside the room, clearly upset and arguing with each other over the situation. Paul stood to the side. Myla suddenly flashed back to the first morning Paul arrived in the village. He was nice to her then and found reason to talk to her. This time however, he acknowledged her presence, but quickly turned back toward the elders. How did he get to be a part of this situation, but no one had involved her at all? Myla knew that he was the best expert of what exactly killed Kalina – or the lack of anything that killed her. He probably was there to testify, but Myla felt very left out.

Though then again, there she was, inside the room, and not one person even flinched at her arrival. They expected her to be there. They assumed her presence was allowed. Malachi looked over to her but quickly resumed mediating the conversation. He had assumed that she would have showed up anyway. It was a bad tactic, but that morning, that day, Myla wasn't going to get upset. Too much had happened for her to be self-centered.

"You're telling me that you don't even know how she died?"

Anala had turned from the rest of the group and started yelling at Paul. His face flushed red.

"It was not work of berries I can tell you that," he answered, clearly trying hard to not let her get to him. "There was no sign of anything. It had to have been some form of higher magic."

"Do you have any idea of what type?" asked Zechariah calmly.

"It was nothing that I had ever seen before," answered Paul.

"Chances are, whoever performed this task was an extremely skilled Caldar," interjected Malachi. "Only a select few in this village could have accomplished such a feat... perhaps only the people here in this room, not including Paul of course."

A few of the elders shot Myla a glance at that. She shrugged. If they actually weren't aware of how powerful she was, it was about time they knew.

"Taking life completely from a person, while possible, is not exactly a trick they teach in class," said Myla.

The elders listened without hesitation.

"And it seems whoever did this, did it perfectly on the first try," she added.

"This is very true," said Malachi, nodding his head acknowledging that he understood what she was implying.

"Tell me," Myla asked. "Where was Kalina last seen alive?"

"She was playing with one of her friends, Sari, on the school grounds," said Malachi. "Sari said she simply disappeared – vanished into thin air. The child was shocked and ran to find an adult. After hours of searching we found her body in the woods, unharmed, yet she was dead."

"Is this all you know?" asked Myla.

Would Malachi tell her the truth?

"Yes," he answered, convincingly enough.

"Well, then we must prepare ourselves for the idea that there may be a killer among us or nearby," said Myla, addressing the entire council. "This death was no accident."

"What do you suggest we do?" asked Anala. "We cannot risk frightening the Caldar."

"What means will we go to in order to protect the Caldar people from unwanted hardship?" said Myla. "Very well then. Keep the same excuse. Nonetheless, I strongly recommend an investigation to find out who did this. Every member of the council should be questioned, though I obviously hope the killer is not in this room."

Every member of the council voiced their agreement. Malachi, however, seemed puzzled by Myla's response.

"Who, may I inquire, do you suggest that we have perform these interrogations?" he asked. "The very person we choose could be the guilty party."

"How about Paul?" suggested Myla. "He is already well informed of the incident, yet we know he could not have accomplished such a feat. Also I suggest any other Caldar who is not on the council yet still may be able to perform such magic be questioned as well. The council may decide how to handle the situation."

"If we hold these interrogations, people will suspect the situation may be more than we have told them," pointed out Zechariah.

"That they will suspect anyway," responded Myla. "The child was far too intelligent to eat poisoned berries."

"We must prepare ourselves for the fact that the nature of her death will not remain a secret," continued Paul, to the surprise of Myla. "The best thing we can do is to find out as much as possible so that we can prevent something like this from happening again."

Everyone again nodded their heads in agreement. With that, they began to clear the room, leaving Myla inside with Paul, Malachi and Zechariah. Myla was taken aback by Paul coming to her aid. Apparently he wasn't so angry with her that he could no longer see reason. She doubted he would become friends with her again, but it was still nice to see.

"Tell me, Myla," asked Malachi. "Why do you suggest hunting for a killer when you know perfectly well who committed this crime?"

"Because people are going to find out she was murdered either way," answered Myla. "And a regular Caldar murderer is a lot less mass hysteria-inducing than the second sorcerer who once conquered Caldaria. Anyway, we can't know for sure it was him so we might as well eliminate all the other possibilities."

"What do you think the chances are that it wasn't him?" asked Zechariah, looking almost hopeful.

"Unfortunately slim to none, but I still assume nothing," answered Myla.

"It's ironic, isn't it?" asked Paul, his voice cracking with anger to the surprise of Myla. "That your mess is now causing the rest of us trouble as you just sit there doing nothing."

"Excuse me?" asked Myla, shocked at his response.

Was he really getting angry at her? Did he not know how guilty she felt already?

"Well, I was just wondering how long this was going to go," he continued, getting more riled up by the second. "With him killing off each of us, and you just sitting there being valiant by doing nothing."

"One person has died! How do you know if there will be more? And who said I am going to do nothing? I plan on stopping him, just like everyone else here!"

Myla could feel her eyes filling up with tears, but she did her best to hide them.

"I just don't want to see the rest of the village paying for your problem," he answered bitterly.

"Paul..." said Malachi softly, trying to ease the tension.

"No, let him speak," said Myla angrily. "Let him share his ignorant feelings."

"This is your problem," said Paul. "Why don't you fix it instead of sitting around, waiting for it to reach us?"

"And what do you expect me to do?" asked Myla. "I have no way of finding him! No way of beating him! If it is my fate to match him then so be it. I didn't choose it, and right now I don't control it."

Paul didn't respond. Instead, he got up and left the room. Zechariah followed after him, most likely to try to have some sort of uncle-nephew chat. Myla didn't care. She was so furious

140

at him. Too much had happened. She was too angry – at Paul, at Amos, and at herself. Maybe there was something she could have done. Maybe she could have somehow stopped this. But how? How could she beat a sorcerer that proclaimed victory over the entire Caldar race? What was she supposed to do?

"Is there anyway I could just turn back time and stop this all from happening?" she asked Malachi, hopelessly.

"Do you know how to stop a girl from vanishing into thin air?" he asked, walking over to her and placing his hand on her shoulder. "Moving backwards a few minutes in time is far different than moving back a few hours, or a few days. The further you change time, the further it unravels. Sometimes you just have to face the fact that time plays out the way it does, and there is nothing you can do about it."

"Then why did you even teach me how to change it?" she asked, confused.

"I didn't teach you that, and sometimes, in a very great while, a few seconds is all you need."

When Myla arrived at the house, Malika was sitting on her bed, her eyes swollen from tears. Myla hesitated at the doorframe, wondering if she should enter. She leaned against the wall, waiting for some sign of recognition in her mother, but she received none. Malika just stared, fighting back tears. Then suddenly she lost her hold, and burst out crying causing Myla to run to her aid. Myla silently held her mother for several minutes, though it seemed like hours, as she cried out all the tears she had.

"Malachi came by this morning to let me know," Malika said finally, still choking back tears.

"What did he tell you?" Myla asked, trying to be tactful.

"That this berry story is a cover," she said softly. "That no one knows what really happened to her."

"Are you okay?" asked Myla, though probably too late.

She was so bad at this comforting thing.

"I'll be fine," answered Malika, clearly trying to be brave. "She was such a sweet little girl. She would always say hello to me with the biggest smile. It just makes no sense."

With that Malika, started to cry again. Instead of giving into the tears, however, she stood up and walked into the kitchen. She had a pot of water on the fireplace by the time Myla found the energy to follow in after her.

"Would you like some tea?" Malika asked, never looking over to Myla.

"No, thank you," Myla answered quietly as she sat down at the table.

"I was thinking about Kaelin," Malika said suddenly. "About his death."

Myla hesitated. Who was Kealin? Her father. That was his name. Nobody had ever mentioned his name in Mertana; people were far too sensitive for that.

"People assumed he drank himself to death," Myla answered, hesitant about where Malika was taking this.

"And how do you think he died?"

Malika still didn't look over. Instead she stared at the pot of water, waiting for it to boil.

"He was a drunk, Malika, nothing more, nothing less," Myla said flatly. "He didn't do anything to warrant a more meaningful death."

"Are you so sure?" asked Malika.

Was she sure? Myla wasn't comfortable with the idea of analyzing her father's death. She knew he was at one point involved with the Caldar and possibly a better person than she knew, but she didn't want to think that there could be some larger cause to his death. Yet then again, she didn't know how he died.

"Amos had nothing to do with that," said Myla.

Malika looked right at Myla. Her eyes were clear now. The tears had passed. The woman that stood before Myla was strong.

"I don't think we can afford to make assumptions about anything," said Malika.

"Then why didn't Amos kill me when I was a child?" Myla asked, much more forcefully. "It would have been a lot easier than waiting till now."

"You know just as well as I do that Amos doesn't want you dead," Malika answered.

"So then why didn't he kidnap me?" Myla asked, frustrated by the debate. "I was right there. I probably would have gone willingly. I hated Mertana that much."

Myla was distressed. Why did Malika trying to complicate her father's death? He was actually a drunk. Myla knew this; she saw it in him everyday of those years she lived with him. His death had no meaning. It was just another pointless tragedy in the sad life he led. Maybe Malika still loved him. Maybe she couldn't face the idea that someone she once cared for so dearly ended his life in such an insignificant way. Myla wished she could give her mother a reason for his death, but this was not one she could claim. This conversation was only adding stress to a situation that desperately needed to not get any worse.

"You aren't willing to discuss it, are you?" Malika asked, appearing somewhat surprised at Myla's response. "And I thought you were the resident conspiracy theorist in the village."

"Every conspiracy I've thought up happened to be true," Myla responded. "That doesn't make me a conspiracy theorist. That makes me a really good guesser."

"You don't just guess," Malika responded. "You just know... And I think you know there is more to this than you'd like to admit."

143

Myla then changed the subject to how Kalina's family was coping. Malika was right about the parallels between the girl's death and the death of her father. She couldn't, however, figure out why Amos would have let her be if he was so close to catching her. She had no way of eliminating the possibility that her father did just drink himself to death, so that was what she had to assume. Not everything could be a conspiracy, despite what impressions Malika had of her.

After successfully turning the conversation to meaningless chitchat, Myla excused herself from her mother's house. It wasn't a warm day, but it was eerily sunny for such a sad situation. Myla hesitated at Malika's doorstep. She had nowhere she wanted to go. She probably had lessons with Malachi to tend to, but that would inspire conversations that Myla didn't want to delve into. Too much responsibility for the situation had landed on her shoulders. It was getting too difficult for her to deal with it.

Myla took a deep breath, picked a direction and began to walk. She didn't really know where she was walking but the movement felt good. It was a refreshing change from Malika's small constraining house. Myla wanted to go where no one else would be. She needed to think, on her own, away from the pressures of other people's opinions. Unfortunately, the village was too full in the daylight, sprawling with people trying to go about their daily lives. They were people who wanted answers that Myla couldn't give.

Myla began to walk toward the outskirts of the village. She spotted the neglected dirt road to the old library. That was her destination. No one would be there, and considering the lack of any answers elsewhere, it wouldn't be a bad place to check.

As Myla approached the library, she realized how abandoned it actually was. While most of the buildings in the village were built into the trees, this small one-story building was now on its own. The tree that had once been attached to it had long since died, leaving the grayish remainder of its broken trunk supported only by the building itself. The windows were thick with dust to the point that one could no longer see through them, and most of the windowsills had broken off.

Myla walked up to the porch. Slowly and carefully, she stepped onto the wooden stairs. The wood was rotted through, with holes forming at various places. Myla cautiously stepped on the sturdiest steps and made her way up to the porch. Part of the roof over the porch had collapsed, blocking the door. Myla tried to lift the wood out of the way, but it was too heavy. Unfazed, she reached out her hand and guided the wood out of the way. Some of the trees shifted their branches toward her. They weren't used to very much magic in these parts. Ignoring their movements, Myla made her way inside.

Myla coughed from the dust that filled the air. She brushed away cobwebs that blocked her way as she stepped into the library. Once her view was clear, she held her breath as she saw what was before her. Inside this seemingly small library stood bookcase after bookcase. There was a circular staircase in the center of the very large room allowing her to look up to three stories of bookshelves. Here stood the entire history of the Caldar, abandoned years ago by the very people it documented.

Myla walked toward the closest bookcase and started to scan each book. Topics ranged from the first Caldar to the founding of Caldaria. She moved onto the next bookcase. An entire row was dedicated to the first Caldarian government. Another row was dedicated to the early rulers. Myla looked upon many of the volumes with interest, but this was not what concerned her.

She moved along to a different section. Scanning the books, she found documents on early Caldarian culture. Again she switched sections to where she found common Caldar cooking recipes. This still wasn't what she wanted. Slowly she made her way through bookcase after bookcase, all with fascinating subjects, but not what she was searching for. Finally on the very top floor of the building, in the back corner, she found the bookcase she was looking for: the evil magic, the magic that no Caldar should ever know, the magic that only a sorcerer like Amos would use.

Slowly she reached up and pulled down a volume titled "Advanced Forms of Corrupted Magic: From the Final Years of Caldaria". She dropped her bag next to the small table by the bookcase, sat down and opened up the book to read. She shuddered as a cool breeze hit her when she turned the first page. The most disgusting and depraved uses of the Caldarian gifts lay on the page before her. Inside this book hid many of the once known methods that the sorcerers used to conquer Caldaria. She grew sick to think about how accessible these tactics were.

"Not everyone is allowed access to this part of the library."

Myla jumped up in fright causing the book to crash onto the floor. At the opposite end of the table sat Amos, staring very calmly back at her. He looked human. If one didn't look directly into his eyes, he could pass as a normal person.

For several minutes, the two simply stared at each other. He was so calm and not frightening that Myla didn't know how to react. Instead she chose to stand there, staring and waiting for something to happen.

"Aren't you going to ask me who I am and what I want?" he asked. His voice was human too.

"I know who you are. You don't look that different," she responded confidently.

"I look the exact same. It's you who are different," Amos responded with a sickly smile.

"And how am I different?" she asked, and then paused to rethink her question. "Wait, never mind. I don't want to even know."

146

"Fine then," he answered, unfazed. "Aren't you going to ask me what I want?"

"To know me," she responded defiantly.

Why wasn't she more afraid?

"Aren't you a little busy to talk to me?" she asked. "What with a city to rule and children to kill?"

"Oh, I see you saw my handy work," he responded nonchalantly.

Myla suddenly felt very sick.

"You're such a monster, you know that?" She hoped her tears weren't visible.

"You didn't? I thought that was an established fact," he said with a smile. "That's what all these books say."

"Do they?" asked Myla.

What was this? Small talk?

"About a hundred and thirty-seven of them," he answered, maintaining his smile.

"What a nice accomplishment for you," responded Myla, sarcastically.

"Only my predecessor is in more," he continued. "I hope to someday change that. You could be in as many, if not more, you know."

"Really?" she asked, uninterested.

She didn't want to play his games. She wanted him to go away. His presence only added to the responsibility she carried over Kalina's death.

"You and I, we are the same: two sides of the same coin," he said with a certain charisma in his voice. Was this his new tactic? Win her over since scaring her didn't do the job?

"And your point is?" she asked bluntly.

"No one will ever understand you like I do," he answered.

"And how is that?" she asked.

147

"I understand how it is to always be different, to the point that even your own parents can't help you. I, too, was forced to run away from my home in a desperate and futile attempt to find belonging."

His words stabbed her. She liked to think that he didn't know much about her, but it was becoming more and more apparent that he did.

"There are other people in this world that can relate to that," she answered in a desperate attempt to counteract what he was doing.

"But those other people don't have the power to change the world in a blink of an eye," he answered simply, standing up and walking toward her.

He placed his hand on her shaking arm – in the very place he hurt her those months before.

"Other people can't know that responsibility, that knowledge, and the guilt that can come with a single mistake."

"What do you want?" she asked firmly, trying to not let it show that he was getting to her.

"About time you asked that," he answered smiling.

He stepped closer to her so that just a few inches separated them with his hand still holding on to her arm.

"Come with me, Myla, and leave this world behind you. You'll never have to even think about this place again, and finally, you won't be alone anymore."

With that Myla yanked her arm free of his grasp and stepped away.

"I will never join you," she spat at him. "I will not let a murderer destroy this world."

"Then consider this your final warning," he responded, much firmer than before. "You know what I am capable of doing. Just keep in mind that as each person dies, it is only your stubbornness that is causing their deaths."

Then he disappeared, leaving Myla alone in the room. Slowly, she stumbled to her chair and found some air to breathe. She picked up the book from the ground and placed it in her bag. Suddenly that library didn't seem so appealing of a place to read. She quickly made her way down the stairs and out the door and headed back to the village. She wouldn't tell anyone of her encounter – not this time. She didn't want to give anybody any more reason to hate her. Anyway, she had learned something over the past few months: no one knew anything that she didn't already know. There was no way to stop Amos if he proceeded with his plan, so she might as well not start a panic and add to the disaster that he will inevitably cause.

*　　　*　　　*

"Myla, how am I supposed to learn this if you keep getting lost in thought?" Zira said bluntly.

"Sorry, Zira. I just have a lot on my mind right now," Myla answered.

She wished she could tell Zira what happened, but she knew she couldn't let this slip to anyone.

"Mel, you always have a lot on your mind," Zira responded smiling. "Now will you help me learn this? I am supposed to teach it to Paul this afternoon."

"How did you never learn how to transport things?" Myla asked.

"It never came up," Zira explained defensively. "The need to make an object disappear and reappear in another place isn't a common one."

"Yet it is so useful for cheating," responded Myla smiling. "If you don't know the answer to an exam, you just transport them out of the teacher's hands."

Zira gave her a strange look.

"Lots of Caldar can't pull it off," Zira pointed out. "I still say it would be easier if you just taught Paul yourself."

"I'm sure he would just love that," responded Myla, rolling her eyes.

"You both are twelve, you know that?" Zira asked, clearly annoyed.

"You mean we've only aged two years since we knew each other when we were ten? That's pretty bad."

"Just letting you know how stupid you both are being," responded Zira.

"Thanks for your opinion," answered Myla. "Quite frankly, I would like to improve the situation, but there seems to be no way to do it. He wants nothing to do with me."

"Well, you didn't just lie to him for a month. You got the whole village to lie with you," pointed out Zira. "That's got to hurt, especially when he was clearly falling for you."

"Thanks Zira for making me feel so good about myself," responded Myla.

She didn't want to think about what she did to Paul. She had enough guilt to deal with. It had been two weeks since she had encountered Amos in the library, and every day since then had been torture. She hated waiting for his next move, wondering what he would do next. Would he actually kill someone else? Or was it a meaningless threat designed to get her to turn? Maybe he was preoccupied with switching tactics since that one hadn't worked. Or maybe he was just making her sweat a little.

Zira did eventually learn that trick, but she wasn't confident enough to teach it to someone else so soon. Myla however didn't want to deal with it. Zira was more talented than she realized. Myla knew that and was fine with letting her risk it.

That night Myla went over to Malika's house for dinner. Their meals over the past couple of weeks had mostly been accompanied with small talk and silence. Myla wished that her mother would open up to her more, but she was beginning to realize that she could not expect that. Her disbelief in her mother's views of her father's death had damaged their relationship. It was something, however, that Myla was not willing to back down on. Kealin's death meant nothing. In this case, it was not stubbornness. Myla simply knew what the situation was, and she couldn't let it get any worse.

"This soup is delicious," said Myla politely.

"Thank you," answered Malika. "It's one of Nora's recipes."

"Have you and Nora always been friends?" asked Myla, hoping to start a discussion on something besides the food.

"Since we both were children," responded Malika. "We used to dream of traveling together. I always found it fitting that she and Zechariah ended up traveling and I ended up stuck here."

"Are you really stuck?" Myla asked, amused at her mother's wording.

"I am forbidden to leave."

What? This was a new revelation. How had Myla never heard this before?

"Why?" asked Myla, suddenly extremely curious.

"I ventured into the Tarran world and informed them of our existence," answered Malika simply.

She seemed surprised by Myla's question. How much did she already assume Myla knew?

"Because of my father?"

Was that too bold?

"I thought I loved him," she answered softly

"Did you?" Myla asked, equally as soft.

"Not enough to stay in Mertana," Malika said with a half-smile. "To ask a Caldar to live without magic is an impossible charge."

151

"But you left me with him," Myla pointed out, trying to not sound too accusing.

"We hoped you might be safer," Malika answered, looking very apologetic.

"Why?" asked Myla, but she never got an answer because with those few words, Malika vanished before her eyes leaving Myla alone at the table.

Chapter 9

Myla didn't even give herself a chance to think. She jumped out of her chair and ran out the door. She sprinted toward Neph and Paul's place, choking her tears back. Each step hurt increasingly more. Amos couldn't have killed Malika. This couldn't be another Kalina. He wouldn't actually do that, would he? Was he really that heartless?

After what seemed like forever, Myla reached their house. She frantically knocked on the door. Paul answered it, looking very surprised to see the tear stricken Myla.

"Malika... my mother..." said Myla, gasping for air. "She vanished into thin air... I think he."

That was all she needed to say. Paul immediately turned around and grabbed his healing bag. Neph stood in the back of the room. Paul nodded to him and told him to go get Malachi. Then he turned back around to Myla and grabbed her hand, leading her out the door.

They didn't say anything to each other as they ran toward the woods. They both knew where they were going, and what they expected to find. No one had visited the place where they found Kalina since that night, and both were using every bit of energy they had to not think about the possibility of finding a repeat.

Once they neared the place in the woods they both slowed down to a walk. Paul started shouting out Malika's name, but Myla remained silent. She couldn't feel her mother's presence. Slowly she walked toward the spot that they found Kalina. Up ahead she could see it. Something there. Someone was there. She could see her. It was Malika.

Myla ran to her mother. Her body lay still on the ground, her eyes still open, peering out into the darkness. She immediately knelt over and felt her hand. It was ice cold. Suddenly tears couldn't suffice. As Paul ran over and started to try everything in his power to save her, Myla couldn't breathe. There was no air that could stifle this pain. She knelt down and started sobbing into the ground. Paul eventually put down his bag, leaned over, and closed Malika's eyes. Then he reached over and held the sobbing Myla until Malachi arrived.

Myla didn't see them take her mother away, nor the conversation between the elders that ensued. For once, Myla didn't want to know everything that was going on, for right now, all she wanted to do was run away and pretend that nothing had ever happened.

Paul led Myla back to her small place. They were completely silent in the long walk there. Myla could feel Paul looking at her. He was concerned; he didn't hate her. She knew she needed to tell somebody the truth about what happened. She wanted to tell him, but she didn't know how.

Eventually they reached her small little one room house. To Myla's surprise, he didn't just leave her at the door. He came inside and started to light a fire for her. Myla sat down on her bed and watched him place a log in the fireplace and send a spark to it lighting it on fire. It was amazing how simple the Caldar made some things, as they complicated everything else. Paul turned around and looked at her.

"I'm so sorry, Mel," he said kindly.

Myla looked up at him and knew he was.

"It's all my fault," she said, bursting into tears.

Paul walked over to her and sat down next to her, putting his arm around her.

"It is in no way your fault," he said. "You bear no responsibility for his actions."

"But it is!" she said, trying desperately to stop crying. "Amos, he came to me two weeks ago, right after Kalina died. He told me he would kill someone unless I went with him."

"So what were you supposed to do?" Paul asked, after taking a big breath. "Go with him? Provide the end to the Caldar people?"

"I could have told somebody," she answered. "I could have tried to stop him."

"How?" he asked. "Myla, you aren't responsible for what he has done. All you did was stop a panic."

"Well, there will be one now," she said bluntly.

Paul sat down on the floor leaning his back against the bed.

"You sure do have a thing for keeping secrets, don't you?" he asked with a sigh.

Myla slid off the bed sitting down next to him.

"I'm sorry, Paul," she said softly. "I've been a complete fool."

"We've both been complete fools," he said, grasping her hand. She leaned against him, resting her head on his shoulders.

"Am I going to survive this?" she asked, after a long pause.

"I'm sure you will," he answered softly.

"I wish I knew what to do," she said hopelessly.

"Right now all you can do is wait, and when the time comes, it will come to you," said Paul. "I am confident in that."

"Thank you, Paul," she said, looking up at him. He kissed her forehead.

"Myla, I…" His voice trailed off, but she understood.

"Me too, Paul," she answered. "Me too."

The sun surprised Myla the next morning. She and Paul had fallen asleep right there, leaning against the bed. By the time she woke up, however, Paul was already awake, sitting against the fireplace, clearly waiting for a pot of water to boil.

"Why don't you just make it boil?" she asked, with a raspy voice that was clearly damaged from crying too much the night before.

"I wasn't in a rush," he said, smiling over at her. "I thought you might like some tea before we head over to the council this morning."

"Thanks," she responded. "There's a council this morning?"

"A notice was left under your door," answered Paul, pointing to a small piece of paper on the table. "It mentioned that I should go as well. Don't know what to think of that."

"The shades on the window are open," pointed out Myla, making Paul laugh.

"Actually I just prefer to assume that Malachi knows all," he responded.

Myla smiled at that.

"Malachi doesn't know all," said Myla, managing a laugh. "I know all."

"I'm starting to think so," Paul returned, bringing Myla over some tea. "You better drink that up fast. We have to be at the council pretty soon. I am impressed at your ability to sleep in so late."

"Well, you know, I always get my best sleep sitting on the floor," she answered.

"I'm not one to talk. I just woke up ten minutes ago."

For the first time, the council registered Myla's presence when she and Paul entered the room. Not that it was entirely what Myla wanted to happen, since everyone looked at her and sighed with very worried looks. She didn't want such sympathy. It's not that she wasn't sad. She was devastated – her mother had just died. It's just that she didn't want to be viewed as the victim.

156

She wasn't the victim. This whole thing happened because of her. She wanted no sympathy for it.

Everyone in the council, however, didn't view the situation that way. Each one of them came to her saying things like "how are you doing?" and "I'm so sorry for your loss." Myla was mostly frustrated by it. She didn't want to think about it. She didn't want to believe it was real. She wanted to scream. It wasn't fair. She had wasted so many years avoiding being close to her mother and now she was dead. So many questions remained unanswered, so many details left unknown. Nothing about it seemed right.

"Could we call the council into session?" asked Malachi.

Each council member took their specific seat, and Myla and Paul took their usual places against the wall. Malachi stood in front, seeming unusually strong. He seemed tired yet unfazed. Myla couldn't understand it. He had just lost his daughter.

"Now will you tell us what happened?" asked the consistently vocal Anala.

To this, Zechariah stood up in front. Malachi wasn't going to speak. He was hurting.

"To our understanding, last night Malika disappeared while she was having dinner with her daughter Myla," explained Zechariah. "Myla immediately sought out the help of Paul and the two of them found the body of Malika in the woods, in the very spot Kalina was found two weeks ago."

"Dead? The same way?" asked Anala.

The rest of the council seemed too stunned to voice anything.

"I couldn't find anything wrong with her," answered Paul. "But she was dead, just like Kalina."

"It can be safely assumed that these two events are not unrelated," said Zechariah. "Someone is doing this. Paul, how did the interrogations go?"

157

Paul shot Myla a glance. He had never interrogated her, but they both knew there was no need.

"I found nothing suspicious," he answered confidently.

"Understood," responded Zechariah. "Now naturally the poisoned berries story isn't going to work this time. Does anyone have any suggestions?"

"Massive heart attack," suggested Malachi from the back. "She lived a traumatic life. It wouldn't be entirely unbelievable."

So that is the story that Malachi would leave in his daughter's legacy: to have died from a broken heart. Malika may have suffered from a broken heart, but she was far too strong to have died from it.

The council, on the other hand, thought the story was acceptable, and their conversation gradually switched to the remembrance ceremony. Myla, however, didn't want to listen to it and excused herself from the room. She walked outside and held onto one of the wooden guard railings on the side of the path. The air was refreshing. Despite her best efforts though, it was still too impossible to gather her thoughts.

"Great little cover story they have going there, huh?" Paul had followed her outside.

"Oh, yeah," Myla answered sarcastically. "Just how I always wanted my mother to be remembered."

"It's funny how people favor lies over the unknown," he said as he walked up the railing next to her.

"The truth can be scary," she said simply.

"Or relieving," he added.

"But not in this case," she pointed out. "In this case, the truth is extremely scary."

"But they don't know that," he answered.

To that point Myla conceded, and started to walk along the wooden path beckoning to Paul to join her. The two walked through the village, noting the numerous happy faces that surrounded them. The news hadn't been leaked yet. No one knew that Malika was dead. This was Myla's last chance for some time to walk through the village in peace.

"You never told me about how Mertana changed since I left," she said, after a period of time had passed.

Paul laughed.

"Well, the whole not speaking to you thing probably played a role in that," he said smiling. "Mertana hasn't changed. It's still the same close-minded little town."

"Was there much reaction to my leaving?" she asked.

"Not really," he answered. "Serena and Paige thought it was weird. I know Misha took it hard. He always blamed himself for making you want to run away."

"Really?" asked Myla, surprised at that revelation. "How is he now?"

"Very strange," Paul answered. "The last time I saw him was the night of your blue light. He was at the restaurant where Serena and I were having dinner…"

"You and Serena were having dinner?" asked Myla.

She knew they were once friends, but she hadn't realized that it was that recently.

"Well, we were engaged to be married at one point," said Paul, a bit surprised by Myla's amusement.

Myla started to laugh.

"Seriously?" she asked. "But she is pure evil!"

"She is pure evil?" he asked, laughing. "And not Amos?"

"They're pretty much on the same level," Myla answered.

"Glad to know you view your childhood so fondly," said Paul. "I mean, it's not like anyone ever did anything really mean to you, like stick a roach in your notebook…"

159

"I can't believe you remember that," said Myla to the very amused Paul.

"Well, you were a pretty weird girl – very memorable," he answered.

"Thanks," she said dryly.

"No, I'm serious!" he insisted. "It's surprising you turned out so normal."

"I didn't change, Paul. Your definition did," she answered. "So why didn't you and Serena get married? Just because you showed up here?"

"No, we broke up about a year before that," he answered. "We were always very different people. I could never understand why, until now that is."

"The whole being a Caldar thing might have played a role," Myla noted.

"Yeah, that and her being pure evil," said Paul with a laugh.

It didn't take long for the word of Malika's death to spread throughout the entire village. By the time Myla and Paul made it back to the guys' place to talk with Zira and Neph, everyone they passed glanced at them with sad looks. A few even came up and expressed their sympathies. Myla appreciated their concern, but she wanted to talk to her friends. When they finally arrived, Myla and Paul found Zira and Neph already inside waiting for them.

They didn't initially say anything. Both looked like they had been crying, and Zira immediately jumped up and gave Myla a huge hug. Neph walked over and patted her on the back. The four of them stood there, looking at each other for a prolonged second, then they immediately sat down at the table and chairs. There was information that needed to be shared.

Zira was pretty well informed by Neph of the situation already. Neither of them was surprised at all to learn that Malika

160

was found in the exact same place as Kalina, with no visible cause of death. The news that Amos had visited Myla two weeks before came as more of a shock.

"You mean he actually visited you, and you didn't tell us?" asked Zira, clearly bewildered. "What if this situation was somehow preventable? Maybe Malachi would have known something."

"Known what?" asked Paul. "It's becoming more and more apparent that he doesn't know as much as we originally thought."

"I think if Malachi knew how to prevent the situation he would have already told me in our lessons," added Myla quietly.

"So what are you going to do?" asked Neph, looking more worried than Myla had ever seen him. "Is he just going to keep killing people until you say 'yes'?"

"I don't know," asked a distressed Myla burying her head in her hands. "You guys, I am all out of options here, short of suicide."

"That's not an option," said Paul firmly.

"It will certainly stop him from killing people," answered Myla.

"Yeah? At what cost?" asked Zira, clearly bothered by what Myla was suggesting. "If you kill yourself then there is no hope for the Caldar people. There would be nothing standing in his way."

"Plus, we would really miss you," added Paul, making Myla slightly laugh.

"Are you two talking to each other again?" asked a very confused Neph, causing Zira to bust up laughing.

"Yes," answered both Myla and Paul simultaneously.

"About time," said Neph under his breath.

"So what should I do?" asked Myla.

"There's nothing you can do," answered Zira. "You're just going to have to wait this out like the rest of us. Maybe he'll change tactics when he realizes this won't sway you.

"My presence in this village puts you all in danger," pointed out Myla.

"Yeah, but if you ran away, you might just give him the reaction he was hoping for," answered Neph. "It would weaken you. He is trying to get to you. Don't let him."

"No one should be in this situation," said Myla softly.

"But you are," said Paul. "And quite frankly, I think if someone had to be in this situation, you are the best person for the job."

Myla laid her head in her hands on the table. She was fighting every piece of herself to stay composed. The three of them – Amos could take any of them next. Why could they not see this? Maybe they knew this – in fact she was sure they did. They had to be strong. She, however, wanted desperately to be weak. Why couldn't she just run away? Why did she have to wait around to see who Amos killed next?

Because this village was her greatest form of protection. Myla knew that. She herself was strong, yes, but so much help was provided by the magic in that village. If she was ever going to stop him, she would probably need the help of those who shared in her gifts. As strong as she was, she was only there to provide balance to him. To beat him would require even more.

At noon the next day, they held a remembrance ceremony for Malika. Almost every citizen of the village came to watch as they placed all of the items that she owned in a chest, which they buried underground next to the tree that her home was built on. Then they burned the coffin that held her remains, as each member of the village placed a flower petal into the fire, which glowed a combination of reds, greens and blues. The ceremony was one of the greatest honors bestowed among the

162

Caldar. Myla was surprised. Despite all of Malika's past, she still ended her life as one of the most respected people in the village.

Myla stood by for hours watching the flames, until they had completely died down. Only she and Malachi remained close to the fire, though Myla knew that Paul, Zira and Neph waited behind her in the distance. It was well into the evening when the flames settled and Myla and Malachi stepped away. She walked back to her three friends, who each silently proceeded to give her a hug and she thanked them for staying. They offered to make her dinner, but Myla decided to go home instead. She didn't really want to be around anyone at that time.

Paul walked her back to her home. He hugged her at the door. Myla could feel that he didn't want to let her go, but she went inside alone. The room wasn't well lit since it was quite dark outside by the time she got home. She made her way over to the fireplace and sent a spark flying to it. The room suddenly lit up. Myla turned around to the table and suddenly realized that she was not alone in the room.

"Hello again, Myla," said Amos, who was sitting quite casually in a chair. "How was the funeral?"

"Good – you should have one sometime," answered Myla calmly.

"Aren't we witty?" he noted, clearly somewhat amused.

"Always," she answered, without even hesitating.

"So have you changed your mind?" he asked.

"Yes, actually," she answered. "I have decided that you are an even bigger monster than I originally thought. Keep this up and you might get another page in a book. Not a new book however – you haven't done anything too exciting for that."

"Take a seat," he said, pushing out a chair with his foot and clearly ignoring her previous comment. "I thought you might like to reconsider your stance on our little agreement."

"No need," she answered confidently. "There's nothing to reconsider."

"You mean you'd rather watch every single person you know and love die than join me?" he asked, acting surprised.

"No, I'd rather rid you from this world, but I don't really have that option right now," she answered.

"Interesting," he said slyly. "So how is your boyfriend? Paul – is that his name?"

That made her angry.

"How about a new agreement?" she said, disgusted. "You touch Paul – or anyone else – and I will kill myself."

"Why would I have a problem with that?" he asked, trying to seem amused.

"Because if you wanted me dead, you would have killed me years ago," she answered defiantly. "You can't accomplish all that you want to without me. You need me."

"Are you so sure?" he asked, getting a little angry.

"Quite."

"We shall see," he answered. "You won't kill yourself you know."

"Why do you say that?" she asked, trying to act more confident than Amos – though it wasn't how she felt at all.

"Because," he answered. "It isn't in you. You have to survive no matter what."

"We shall see," she returned. Amos then disappeared, leaving Myla alone in her room.

Myla stood there for several seconds debating what to do. Her first instinct was to run over to the guys' place and see if Paul was okay, but she didn't want to create a scene. It took Amos two weeks last time to kill off Malika anyway. She had no way of knowing if Amos would actually do anything anyway. She very well could have convinced him otherwise. She had no choice but to go to bed and not worry about it for now.

164

Yet the fear was unbearable. What if something had happened? She would kick herself forever if Amos did something and she sat by ignorant of it.

Myla couldn't let herself give in to the fear. She got ready to sleep and climbed into bed. For two hours she lay there staring at the ceiling, but eventually she couldn't take it anymore. She jumped out of bed and ran over to Paul and Neph's house. It was dark inside, indicating for once the two actually went to bed at a reasonable hour – that or something had actually happened. Myla knocked on the door in a hurry, and sure enough, Paul answered the door. He looked at her amused.

"Nice nightgown," he said, smiling.

Myla suddenly felt very stupid. She hadn't even bothered to change clothes. She looked down. Her long nightgown was dirty from sweeping the ground at her feet.

"Don't even say anything," she said, turning around embarrassed.

"I was just paying you a compliment," said Paul trying to stifle his laughter.

"Okay, I am leaving now," said Myla sheepishly, as she started to walk away.

"No, you can't do that," he called after her, still laughing. "I am going to be confused all night if you don't tell me what's up."

Myla turned around and looked at him.

"Amos…" she said unsure of how to continue, but that was all he needed.

"He came to visit you again, didn't he?" Paul asked, much more seriously.

"He's not going to stop," Myla said quietly. "At least, I don't think so."

"No, I was guessing he wouldn't," he answered with a sigh. "Did this just happen?"

165

"Actually it happened a couple of hours ago. I just needed… to tell someone," she said, wondering if he would believe her. He didn't quite seem to.

"Well, there's a first," he said with a smile. "Do you want to come inside?"

"No, I should go back to bed," she answered. "Sorry for waking you up."

"Well, at least let me walk you back," he said, grabbing his coat and closing the door behind him. He handed the coat to Myla. "You might want this. You look a little cold."

Myla laughed. She didn't realize how visibly she was shivering. Paul walked over to her. He put the coat around her and then squeezed her hand. She appreciated him not making too much fun of her.

Myla managed to not say anything to Paul about Amos mentioning him while they were walking back to her place. She didn't know if she should tell Paul, but she did want to warn him. She couldn't decide what to do. Eventually when they reached her door she made up her mind.

"Paul, I need to tell you something," she said, looking up at him. "Amos… he mentioned a next possible victim… It was you."

"Me?" he said, seeming very confused, and then his face grew more aware. He looked up into the sky, clearly trying to not react.

"He didn't give any sort of time frame to this, did he?" he asked.

"No," Myla answered. "Paul, I don't even know if he's planning to go through with it. I'll leave here if that's what you want."

Paul faced her and grabbed both of her hands.

"And what difference does it make if it's me or someone else?" he asked. "Myla, we already decided this. You aren't to leave this village no matter what, okay?"

"I don't want you to die," she said looking at him.

"Well, I don't want to die either," he answered. "But I am willing to take that risk."

He then did something Myla didn't expect. He leaned over and kissed her. Myla didn't know how to react. She had never been kissed before and just a couple days before she and Paul weren't even talking. So much had happened in such a short time. It was too overwhelming. She pulled away from him, and he looked at her bewildered. Then she moved back to him and she buried her head in his arms. He held her for several minutes there. Eventually she stepped away and headed back inside.

Myla went to the schoolyard to meet Malachi for their lessons the next morning, but Malachi never arrived. After twenty minutes of waiting, Myla decided to seek him out so she headed over to his house to find him. When she reached his house, she knocked on his door but received no answer. The curtains in all the windows were closed, so Myla decided to be brave and opened the door.

Inside she found Malachi, sitting in a chair staring at the floor. Myla called his name, but he didn't answer. He only slightly nodded his head. Myla slowly walked up to him and sat down next to him.

"She's gone," he said, his voice cracking. "My only child is gone. Once again, she's left me. And now I am left with my granddaughter who hates me."

"I do not hate you," Myla said firmly.

"You've tried to kill me," he said, looking up at her.

"I did not try to kill you. I only attacked you after you tried to kill me," she pointed out.

"You don't even refer to me as your grandfather," he said. "Why are you even here?"

"Lessons," she answered simply.

She wanted to be sympathetic, but she really didn't know how to with Malachi. She was so used to him being strong.

"Why do you even care?" he asked. "It's not like they do any good."

"I just lost my mother," Myla answered strongly. "I want to do everything in my power to prevent losing anyone else, including you."

"We don't even know if it was Amos who did it," he argued, seeming much stronger.

"Yes, we do," she responded. "And I plan on stopping him before he hits anyone else."

"You are too advanced," Malachi said simply. "These lessons should have ended weeks ago. There's nothing left to teach you."

"Yet I still don't know how to stop him."

Malachi must have been making excuses.

"How did you know to create a blue light to save Neph?" Malachi asked.

"I didn't know," she answered. "It just happened."

"Exactly," he responded. "It's in you, my granddaughter, and when the time comes, you will find it."

These were the words Myla had been hearing from everyone. She hated it. She wanted a real, legitimate solution. She wanted to be able to save the Caldar people. However, as she looked at Malachi, she realized that he did in fact have nothing left to teach her. In her most difficult time, she had no instruction. She would have to solve this one on her own.

Malachi made some sort of excuse and retired to his bedroom, leaving Myla alone. Without anything left to do, she decided to wander the village. She didn't get very far, however, because she ran into Neph within a few minutes of leaving Malachi's house.

Once Myla told Neph that she and Malachi had finished their lessons, he immediately asked her to go help Zira teach Paul in the schoolyard. Apparently Zira had never successfully managed to transport an object since the one time she had with Myla before. Zira and Paul had been hopelessly trying to figure it out ever since then. It wasn't exactly how Myla wanted to spend her morning, but she felt bad for leaving Zira in that situation, so she made her way to the schoolyard.

She arrived to find a surprising scene. Paul was sitting on a log watching Zira and Allasta yell at each other. Paul looked like he was doing everything to stifle his laughter.

"You are doing it wrong," Allasta said loudly. "I am pretty sure you have to put your hand out like this."

"This isn't about hand motions, Allasta," argued Zira. "It all happens in the mind."

Paul beckoned to Myla, and she went and sat down next to him on the log. Zira and Allasta didn't seem to notice.

"What happened?" whispered Myla.

"Zira and I couldn't figure out the transportation thing so Allasta decided to try to give us a hand," he whispered back. "Apparently she doesn't know how to either."

"You know, Zira," Allasta was saying. "You aren't as great as you think. You've only been successful because of Myla."

"I have accomplished plenty more than you on my own, thank you," answered a very angry Zira.

"There's no way you could transport them into a tree could you?" asked Paul to Myla, causing her to bust up laughing.

"Nah, one of them would fall," she answered.

"Is that a problem?" he responded.

"Why aren't you at your lessons?" asked Zira, definitely not amused.

"Malachi declared them complete, so I thought I would come give a hand," she answered.

"It's good you're here," said Allasta. "Could you please tell Zira that you have to move your hand like this to complete a transport?"

"Hands don't make a difference. It's entirely mental," she answered. "But sometimes a hand motion can help you accomplish a mental task."

Allasta didn't seem to approve of that answer and stormed away. Zira glared at Myla and Paul.

"You two aren't as funny as you think you are," Zira said. "But now that you're here, Mel, do you think you could show us how to do this?"

"Sure," she answered, jumping up onto her feet.

Then, suddenly, the log that Paul was still sitting on disappeared right from under him, dropping him to the ground.

"That is a dangerous trick," he said, standing up painfully.

"Where is it?" Zira asked.

Myla pointed across the field to where it was laying.

"The trick is to visualize the object breaking down into smaller parts in your head," explained Myla. "If you try to move the whole thing, you won't be able to, but if you move the millions of tiny individual parts of the object, you find that you can."

Myla then picked up a leaf from the ground and held it in front of Zira. She looked at Myla hesitantly and then stared intently at the leaf. The leaf however, wasn't the thing that disappeared, for as she was staring at it, Paul disappeared instead.

For several seconds Myla and Zira stood there staring at each other. Both of them were speechless.

"Did you do that?" Zira finally asked.

"No..." said Myla hesitantly. "Did you?"

Zira suddenly looked extremely panicked.

"Myla, I couldn't even get the leaf to move," she said.

It only took a split second for the two of them to comprehend what was going on. Then they both turned toward the woods and started sprinting faster than they knew was possible. Myla tried to not think about what was possibly ahead. She wasn't ready to lose another person, certainly not this fast. Why had she challenged Amos? Why had she been so cocky? She had gambled Paul's life away. Paul... Why did it have to be Paul?

His hand was cold when Myla grasped it. There he lay on the ground. Unharmed, yet no longer alive. His face was like stone. No longer animated. He was dead. Zira sat next to her, sobbing on the ground. Myla, however, didn't cry. She couldn't. Inside, she was as dead as he was. All she felt was anger – pure unadulterated anger.

Myla looked up. Allasta was moving towards her. She had seen Paul disappear. Malachi was right behind her. Myla stood up as they knelt around the body. Then she turned around and walked away. She heard them call after her as she left, but she didn't care. She couldn't be there right then. She was far too angry.

Myla swiftly walked back to her house. Once she entered, she immediately went to her bag and pulled out the corrupted magic book she had found in the library. She hadn't opened it since that time in the library, but now she was desperate. She tore threw the pages one by one searching for some method, some means to kill Amos. As each page passed, she realized that there was no way she was going to find a single clue as to how to defeat him, but she kept pressing on still. She wanted to kill him. She wanted to end him. She wanted to make him pay for what he had taken from her.

When she reached the final page, she threw the book against the wall. It broke the binding and pieces of paper scattered throughout the room. Myla, however, didn't care. She wanted revenge. She wanted Paul back.

Myla walked out of her home and started to pace around the village. People were walking about normally, clearly unaware that someone else had just died. They didn't know that the only other Caldar besides Myla to have been raised outside of the village was just killed by an evil sorcerer trying to take over the world. If someone told them that, they would have laughed. They had no idea Amos was still alive. They assumed that he had died a thousand years before, and Caldaria lay in ruins. The entire situation was ridiculous.

She walked down to the market square and started to browse the various fruit stands. It was a distraction at best but an effective one, for the time being. Unfortunately, it didn't last for very long.

"Myla!" shouted Neph. He was on the other side of the square waving at her. The smile on his face indicated that he probably didn't know what happened. He ran over to her.

"Hey," she said quietly.

"Did you make it over to help out Zira and Paul?" he asked.

He seemed so innocent. She hated to break him.

"I was supposed to meet Zira for lunch but she didn't show," he said. "Do have any idea what's up?"

"Paul's dead, Neph," she said bluntly.

Too bluntly, but she was too angry to be nice. He looked at her in disbelief – completely broken. It was as if somebody had just dropped a pile of rocks on his head.

"What?" he said almost inaudibly.

"He disappeared while we were trying to teach him," she explained. "We found him in the woods just moments after."

Myla didn't wait around to talk. She knew Neph wanted more information, but she honestly didn't have it. She didn't want to have to comfort Neph, and she sure didn't want him to comfort her.

This was her fault. More than it was with Malika's death. She had practically told Amos who to kill next. Myla simply could not be there for Neph right now. Instead she turned around and headed back to her house. The daylight was getting to her anyway. It was too cheery for the circumstances.

Myla had a visitor when she returned to her house. Amos was sitting in the same chair at the table. The papers from the book lay neatly in a pile next to him on the table. Myla looked at him, walked right past him and pulled a knife out of a cabinet drawer.

"What is this?" he asked, seeming amused by her actions.

"You fulfilled your part of the bargain, now I am going to fulfill mine," she answered, facing him with the knife pointed straight at her chest.

"You're not going to do that," he said forcefully.

"Watch me," she answered defiantly.

Then she slowly started to dig the knife into her stomach. The pain was numbed from her level of anger though she watched as blood trickled onto her hands.

"Stop!" shouted Amos reaching out his hand.

Myla held the knife still, partially under her skin, and looked at him.

"They're still alive," he said. "I didn't kill them. All three of them are in my possession."

What? Was he serious? Myla pulled the knife away from her stomach. It had barely pierced below her skin. Nothing major was damaged.

"How do I know you are telling me the truth?" she asked, extremely skeptical.

She couldn't possibly dream of getting her hopes up.

Amos motioned to one of the pages from the book. It went flying into Myla's bloody hand. On it told of a tactic, commonly used in Amos' time, where a sorcerer would kidnap a person and leave an exact replica of the body as a decoy. Often the kidnapped people would be used for brainwashing or for information gathering. Myla looked up at Amos.

"Why would you do this?" she asked, still doubting his sincerity.

"I wanted to know more about you," he answered, seeming very practical. "These seemed like an easy start. Your student, your mother, the person you chose to love..."

She hated him.

"Why would you take Kalina over someone closer to me?" she asked.

"I thought that was obvious," Amos explained. "I couldn't make it too clear that I was after you. Especially if I was trying to convince you that I was just killing off the Caldar on a whim. Children are so good at creating a strong emotional response in people."

"I don't believe you," Myla said slowly.

"You have to believe me," he said confidently, standing up and walking closer to her.

"You need me alive," she answered. "That is all you have confirmed to me."

"All right, I confess," he responded. "I do need you alive. But, if I do have those people alive and well, you need to stay alive if you ever plan to rescue them."

Then he walked even closer to her so that he was pressing against the knife that Myla still held in her hand. He was so confident, and he was right to be. Myla didn't know if Malika, Kalina or Paul were still alive, but she wasn't going to try to kill (if that was even possible) her only source of information on the subject. Amos knew he had trumped her. He reached up and brushed his hand through her hair. Myla shivered at his touch.

"Don't worry, *Mel*," he said wryly. "I won't be taking anyone else, for at least some time. You will, however, have to start talking to me if you ever plan on getting the ones I have back."

With that he smiled and disappeared, leaving Myla once again alone in the room.

Chapter 10

The water was unusually refreshing. He couldn't believe how smooth and pure it tasted. Maybe it was the journey and his overwhelming thirst getting to him. Maybe it was just the fountain. Whatever it was, the water was the best water Amos had ever tasted. When he looked up from the fountain, however, he started to get a very different feeling about what he had just done.

A crowd of people stood in front of him, each one of them appearing entirely petrified. Amos immediately glanced behind him but nothing was there. They were staring at him. Maybe he had broken some sort of tradition. It was probably very rude, but the looks on their faces described something more horrid than that. It was just water! If it was that big of a deal, they could have put up a sign or something.

Then Amos looked at the crystal figure in the center of the fountain. It was of a great king, and attached to his robe was a golden plaque saying: "The Forbidden Fountain of Sherah". Suddenly Amos gasped. He knew this fountain and what it represented. It couldn't be…

Amos gradually stepped back from the fountain and off the circular platform that surrounded it. Once he left the platform, however, the statue began to change. The crystal king turned black and then shattered into millions of tiny pieces, crashing down into the fountain. The water then started to bubble and overflowed down the platform and out into the city.

Amos could hear screams all around him. The people were terrified, and they were sure to blame him. He didn't know what fountain it was! It didn't make a difference anyway. He wasn't an evil sorcerer. He had purposefully kept his very strong gifts a secret so that no one would pay attention to him. Why then would he try to conquer the world? He realized that the person they would accuse him of being wasn't him. They would try to kill him! He had to run away.

Amos tore out of the city. The sound of his footsteps on the marble floor was echoed by the pounding of footsteps from the crowd that followed him trying to catch him. He looked back. They were going to kill him. They were going to kill him when he hadn't done anything. He couldn't evade them. They were moving too fast.

He didn't stop to think. He turned around and held out his hands toward the crowd sending a giant wave of blue light causing them all to collapse to the ground. It was something that he had never seen before. He certainly didn't know it was possible until that moment. But the wave of blue light shot out of his hand with such force that it threw him back. He rose to his feet quickly. He paused for a second and stared at the completely still bodies that lay on the ground before him, but he couldn't let it get to him. He couldn't wait around wondering what damage his actions had caused.

Instead, he ran as fast as he could out of the city. He made his way through the large entrance gates and into the field that surrounded it. It seemed so far to the forest, but he couldn't linger so he kept running. No one was following him, but he didn't want to risk them following on horseback. There was no way he could outrun a horse, and he didn't want to use that blue light trick again. Who knew what damage that could have caused! He only hoped that the people were stunned and not killed by his actions.

The forest had never seemed so uninviting. It was chilly and dark, a striking difference from the warmth of the city. Amos didn't remember it being this way, but he brushed the thought aside. Finding shelter was his primary concern now. He was tired from running and scared about the fountain. What had he done?

He remembered his mother telling him stories about that fountain, about how it was cursed. Five hundred years ago, Sherah cursed it indicating that someday someone would drink from it and become his heir. Amos shuddered at the thought. It was completely inconceivable to him that in all those years, no one except him would have tasted the water from that fountain, but the looks on their faces and the shattering of the statue indicated something else.

But Amos was a good person, and he was only twelve years old! He was too young for such a role. Anyway, his age didn't matter. He simply wouldn't follow Sherah. He would rather die than help a sorcerer destroy the world. It was a mistake. Sherah had the wrong person.

He had probably thwarted Sherah's plan. Now, no one could drink from the fountain, and since he wasn't going to do anything bad, his actions may have saved the Caldar world. They shouldn't be trying to kill him. They should be thanking him. He drank from the fountain and didn't turn evil. It was a miracle of good luck.

Amos stumbled over to a tree and sat down leaning his back against the trunk. He suddenly felt very tired and sick. It must have been the stressful situation finally getting to him. He shivered from the cold. Why had the forest grown so chilly? He looked down at his hands. They had turned to a disturbing shade of gray, probably from the cold. At least, he hoped so.

Amos leaned his head back against the tree and looked up to the sky. He couldn't see the stars. The sky was too cloudy. He was shivering uncontrollably now, and definitely didn't feel well. He started to wonder if the water had made him ill. Maybe that was the reaction it would have on a good person. He wouldn't be evil so it would kill him instead. All of his skin was gray now. Something wasn't right. He was not well.

Amos couldn't stay there shivering. He needed to find someplace warm. Painfully, he rose from his seat against the tree and started wandering aimlessly through the woods. Everything seemed so out of focus. He couldn't place where he was and had lost all sense of direction. He stumbled about, bumping into trees and constantly tripping over. Eventually, he saw something. It was a small hill and in it was a cave. Amos plunged towards it. In there, it might be warm. In there, he might be safe.

Unfortunately the cave was damp and cold, but Amos didn't let it stop him. He couldn't see the end of it, so he lifted up his almost lifeless hand and sent out a strong beam of light. The cave was deep, journeying far into the ground. Amos slowly walked inside, hoping to find some sort of place he could find rest.

Eventually he reached a large room. A fire was lit in the center, making the room wonderfully warm. Amos knew the situation was suspicious, but he was so cold and wanted desperately to stop shivering. He stumbled forward and started warming his hands by the fire. The heat felt so nice against his dry deathlike skin.

For several minutes, Amos knelt there warming himself by the fire. Soon enough, however, he felt another presence in the room. He jumped up suddenly and whirled around, but he couldn't see anything. Somebody else was in there. He knew it. He could feel them.

"Hello?" he called out, meekly.

Amos...

He jumped in fright. The voice was in his head, but also in the room.

"Who is there?" he called out again, to no avail. The presence was even stronger, but no one was visible.

Amos...

Again the voice came into his head. Now he was really scared. A stick lay partially in the fire. He pulled it out as if its burning edge would provide some additional form of protection.

He couldn't stop shaking. Suddenly he felt very young, even younger than twelve. Where was this presence? Who was it? And what did they want with him?

"Leave me alone!" he shouted at the top of his lungs.

A black ghostly shape appeared before him. It wasn't solid, but more like a part of the air. Like smoke, it started swirling around him. The flame on his stick instantly went out.

Amos... You will join me...

It hissed in his head. Amos didn't know what to do. What was this?

"Who are you?" he mumbled, his voice consistently cracking from fear.

I am your king. You will bow to me.

"Who are you?" asked Amos, his voice now clear.

Sherah...

Amos collapsed to the floor. It was real. The curse was real. Tears swelled in his eyes as he tried to peer through the black fog that surrounded him.

"I will never join you!" he shouted. "You have the wrong boy. I am a good person!"

Do you really think all those people in the city survived your selfish actions?

Amos felt crushed. He had tried to not think about what he had done. He had put his safety first. He didn't mean to make all those people die.

You are not a good person, Amos, and neither are the Caldar. They hurt the Tarrans. They make them live as outcasts. Perhaps to the Tarrans, I am the good one.

He didn't know what to say. He felt a sudden urge to answer that he agreed, but he couldn't. This was trickery. He had to fight it.

"I will not join you!" he shouted again.

180

Sharp pain started to travel through his body. Soon it was unbearable. He lay there writhing on the ground sobbing uncontrollably.

Join me.

"No," he whispered.

The pain was too great. He couldn't survive it much longer.

Join me.

"No," he mouthed amidst sobs.

He couldn't take it. He had lost.

Join me.

"Okay," he answered, crying. "I'll join you. Just please stop hurting me. I'll join you."

Chapter 11

Allasta wasn't exactly Zira's biggest fan. At times, she came just short of hitting her in frustration. This day, however, Allasta and Zira had to cooperate. For this afternoon, Allasta and Zira had to teach a joint class together, and it was not going to be an enjoyable experience.

Allasta partly assumed that it was Malachi's sense of humor that decided to pair the two of them together. It was a known fact among the village that the two women didn't get along. It became even more evident the day that Paul was killed. When Allasta went and brought Malachi to the woods, Zira was anything but appreciative. Instead of thanking her for being so on top of things, Zira hounded her with questions about how she knew to get Malachi and how did she not just assume that Paul disappeared from one of the transportation attempts. Actually, Allasta had thought that Paul had disappeared from a bad transport. She was hoping to get Zira in trouble for teaching a skill that she didn't have when she ran to get Malachi. Allasta didn't, however, plan on letting Zira know this part of the story.

In fact, Allasta wasn't entirely sure Paul's death wasn't the result of a bad transport on Zira's part. Sure the timing of it was disturbing, with two deaths prior to it, but there were reasons for those deaths. No explanation of Paul's death was ever given. As the rest of the village panicked, Allasta wondered if it really was just an alarming coincidence.

The fact that nobody else died after that was also a good indication that it was all just a coincidence. Four months had passed since Paul's death. If there was a killer on the loose, what had he or she been doing all this time? It's not like the village had any clue as to who this person was or how to stop them. It was the perfect setup. It was completely idiotic to just quit.

Allasta decided to not worry herself with wondering, however. Whatever had happened didn't involve her, and she was thankful for that. Now she had other things to worry about, like figuring out how to teach a class with Zira, a woman who couldn't even transport an object without a fatality.

Zira didn't look exactly happy either as she walked toward Allasta. Of course she wouldn't. She was so selfish. Allasta knew that she threatened Zira's standing. Most people thought Zira was a more talented Caldar than most, but Allasta knew the truth. Zira had been riding on the talent of Myla for too long. She was no more talented than Allasta. People were going to find out soon too. It was only a matter of time. Ever since Paul's death, Myla had grown extremely distant from everybody in the village, including Zira. She still taught classes and mesmerized people with her skills, but she no longer volunteered her presence when she wasn't obliged to. She spent most of her free time (the little that she had) in her house, locked away from the rest of the village, and Zira no longer had the support that she was used to.

"So how are we going to do this?" asked Zira quietly as the students were gathering.

"Teach the class?" Allasta responded. "Well, I figured we would tell them the information."

"Yes, telling a 14-year-old how to become invisible will work fine," Zira answered quite sarcastically. "They don't need to try it out or anything."

"What's the point?" asked Allasta. "Any Caldar can still see you."

"It's not a Caldar that they would be hiding from," answered Zira dryly. "The ability for a Caldar to hide from an animal, or even a Tarran, is very important."

"Why?" asked Allasta. "No Caldar has ever been able to hide for more than a few seconds."

183

"Myla did for ten the first time she tried," pointed out Zira.

"Really?" asked Allasta. "What's her longest time?"

"I don't know," answered Zira. "The story is she never tried again."

"That girl is weird," Allasta said bluntly.

"And more talented than either of us will ever be," noted Zira. "So how are we going to do this?"

"Well, most of the time will be spent personally coaching each child right? So why don't you explain how it's done and then we'll just set them loose."

"I guess that works."

Zira proceeded to call the class together and start to give them a step by step process of how to become invisible. She actually ended with an example, hiding herself for a few seconds. All the students looked impressed, but Allasta wasn't. Zira hadn't shown any truly unique talent by that. Most Caldar could become invisible. Allasta sat down on a nearby tree stump and watched Zira. This class was going to be easy. Zira was completely in control, and Allasta was perfectly fine letting her take on that responsibility. She didn't want to be doing this anyway.

As Zira began to teach one of the students as an example, Allasta leaned forward staring into space, or more specifically at a blade of grass in front of her. Life as a blade of grass must be an entirely boring state of being, just sitting there. She actually felt somewhat bad for it, until it quivered. Allasta stood up straight and looked around. All of the students were sitting still, at least ten yards away. The ground softly shook. It was barely noticeable, but Allasta could feel it. It was becoming consistent, as if twenty horses were heading their way. Allasta looked behind her and stared into the woods. She could hear it now. It was becoming very evident that her estimate was not so far off.

The patter of hooves on the ground was becoming more audible. Zira stopped talking and turned around back to the woods too. Allasta shot her a look of worry, and Zira returned the glance. Quickly, she motioned to the students behind her to break for the village. "An early break" she called it, but the fear in her voice made it clear to each one of them that something was up. They didn't question her; they simply turned around and bolted for the village. Zira, in turn, walked towards Allasta. The two women looked at each other in fear and stared at the woods.

"Do you think we should go find Malachi?" Allasta asked, trying to hide her trembling.

"There's not enough time," answered Zira. "They're here."

As she said it, Allasta realized it was true. In front of them, thirty strange men on horses emerged from the woods. Allasta felt her stomach drop down to her feet, but to her amazement, Zira stepped forward. One of the men, a slightly chubby awkward looking man, dismounted and walked up to her.

"Who are you and why are you here?" Zira asked, her voice clear and strong.

"My name is Dansten," he answered. "I am the mayor of the city of Mertana, and we come to represent the Tarran people."

"What for?" she asked.

"Peace," he responded, as if trying to make their entrance more dramatic than it was. "We are here for peace."

*   *   *

185

Zira was not exactly impressed. This was turning into one rather annoying evening. First, she had to deal with this Dansten character blabbing to her the entire way to the town hall about how "fascinating" everything was in their village. Questions like *"Are these buildings part of the trees? How do you do that?"* or *"Is it true you people can move things entirely with your mind?"* were all that was coming out of his mouth. Once they reached the town hall, she successfully passed him off to Malachi, who then had to endure Dansten's constant questioning. It wasn't that much of a relief since Malachi motioned to her to stay with them, which meant she couldn't duck away to a more secluded location where she wouldn't be asked about how the sky was blue.

Eventually, however, Malachi was able to convince Dansten to talk about the real reason the Tarrans were there. It didn't take Zira long to realize that this was not necessarily an improvement, because then Dansten started spouting out ideological sentences about peace and equality – about how Tarrans and Caldar should end their war and unite as friends.

They were at war? That was news to her. In fact, the only interactions she ever knew they had with the Tarrans were regarding Myla and Paul – and those hardly could be considered actions of war. Myla had mentioned that raiders used to come through Mertana, but she was convinced they were other Tarrans from neighboring villages. They weren't Caldar.

Of course, this Dansten character didn't seem to have the same opinion. According to him, they were actually representing all the known Tarran peoples. He claimed that every village had united under Mertana, declaring it their capital. Zira didn't really believe him, but even the suggestion of a united Tarran people was disturbing enough – and she could tell she wasn't the only one with reservations about the thought. Every member of the council started glancing at each other when Dansten mentioned it.

"How did you manage to unite every community in the Tarran world?" Malachi asked, clearly doubtful of Dansten's claims.

"We sent representatives to every neighboring village we could think of," Dansten replied. "People were very eager to the idea of peace and the end of violence so they joined quickly. From there, our representatives set out to the neighboring villages of those towns."

"And people were just willing to agree to peace without any fight?" asked Anala. "Yet it was your villages that were feuding to begin with. Our village has never attacked yours."

"I beg to differ, ma'am," answered Dansten. "Eleven years ago you kidnapped one of our children. And not even a year ago you sent out the blue light as a sign of war, and then took one of our young men as a sacrifice for peace."

Malachi remained silent, and Anala followed his lead.

"And then of course, there are your most recent actions," continued Dansten. "But I prefer to not discuss such a controversial subject in such large company."

Zira was surprised at this comment, since Dansten had been anything but discreet previously, but Malachi agreed to his request and led him into a back room. Zira didn't follow instead she watched the Tarrans. Most of them looked confused and overwhelmed by where they were. She couldn't blame them; this place was so alien to anything they knew. These men were not warriors. They were clueless volunteers, led here by promises of peace. Peace for a war that Zira didn't think existed.

Of course, just because the Tarrans and the Caldar didn't interact, that didn't mean there wasn't antagonism between them. Caldar children were raised to fear the Tarrans, and this village was designed to keep them out, to make sure no Tarran ever knew the world they did. Malika was forced to give up her child for ten years because of Myla's father being a Tarran. Was this

187

really peace? Maybe these Tarrans had a small point – though only a small one.

"How did they get in here?" Zechariah's voice boomed.

Zira had never once, in her entire life, heard her father yell like that. Though never before had she seen him react to such a dangerous situation.

"That is what we are trying to figure out," answered the ever-calm Malachi.

"The trees should have stopped them," Zechariah snapped back.

"But they didn't," Malachi responded. "Now we must decide what to do about it."

"They cannot stay here," piped up Anala.

"And they shall not," assured Malachi.

"They say they want peace," pointed out Zira.

She didn't know why she spoke. She had never been to one of the council meetings. She figured probably only the elders were supposed to speak, but both she and Allasta were invited and since Allasta wasn't going to say anything, she might as well give it a try.

"Yes, but what does peace mean?" asked Zechariah. "They have never been comfortable with us, with who we are. There is an ulterior motive here; they have no practical reason to make such an offering. At what cost will this *peace* come?"

"So did they just decide to get power hungry and conquer the world, and this little attempt to be friendly is just a less costly way to take us over?" asked Zira, rather amused at the concept.

"Possibly," answered Zechariah, as Zira almost choked on the air she was breathing in.

"For what purpose?" she asked, in disbelief.

"The desire to conquer, Zira, is not entirely unexplored in our history," pointed out Malachi.

At this one of the younger elders, Ratel, became overly agitated.

"Are you telling me that we have thirty men who want to conquer our village sleeping in our town hall right now?" he asked.

"Well, you never seem to use it. You all always seem to gather at Malachi's anyway," pointed out Zira.

At this several of the elders chuckled. Ratel, however, was not so amused.

"Which is where we are right now," he answered. "They could be scouring the city as we sit here debating whether or not to offer them something to drink!"

"They aren't going to scour anything," stated Malachi. "That city hall is well protected by a magic they couldn't possibly comprehend."

"I thought our village was as well," pointed out Zechariah. "Maybe we need consider that they have some sort of help."

With that Zechariah shot both Malachi and Zira glances. Zira was surprised. She knew that Malachi and Zechariah knew that Amos was alive too, but she tended to forget that they were aware that she knew.

"Does it strike anyone else as curious that this would happen only months after three people from our village died from strange deaths?" asked the no-longer-silent Allasta from the back of the room.

How was she the first one of them to connect those dots? She didn't even know the cause of those deaths were unknown.

"So whoever killed those three may have helped the Tarrans enter our village?" asked Anala.

"They *were* killed? We know that?" asked Allasta.

189

So she wasn't that quick. Zira wasn't surprised. Everyone didn't seem too concerned with leaving her in the dark however, and nobody answered her questions.

"Their leader, Dansten, told me tonight that they had a similar situation in their village as well, which is what inspired them to come here," said Malachi.

"So what? They thought we did it?" asked Zira. "How many of their people died?"

"Only one – even if they did think we did it, it wouldn't be enough for them to brave the woods," answered Malachi. "If you don't recall, they blame us for the kidnapping of Myla and Paul as well, but they didn't come visit us for that."

"Do they know about Paul?" she asked.

"That is information I chose to not divulge," answered Malachi. "I haven't told them about Myla being one of us either. I'd prefer to properly warn her about them first."

"She doesn't know they are here?" Zira asked. "How is that possible?"

"She was on that hunting trip with Neph and Jeremiah. They only would have gotten back about an hour ago. She probably went straight to bed," said Allasta.

"One of the Mertana men – 'Misha' he said his name was – he kept asking about her," said Zechariah. "I didn't tell him anything. I pretended I didn't know who she was."

"Misha?" asked Zira. "I've heard of him. He's the man who ran the inn that Myla lived at. Apparently they didn't get along too well."

"Perhaps time has changed his perception of her," Zechariah responded. "He seemed to be greatly worried about her, which is surprising after all this time."

"Well, however he feels, Myla is going to have one hell of a surprise tomorrow morning," answered Zira.

*   *   *

Myla cracked her eyes open. She was awake, but it was still dark outside. She could barely sift through the shapes in front of her. As they became clearer, she saw him, sitting there in her chair staring at her. She sat up and lit up the candle next to her bed. Amos' face was unanimated, as cold as normal. Myla glared at him as she stood up and walked over to her counter.

"You know there is a difference between evil creepy and creepy creepy, and you are beginning to cross that line," she said as she poured herself a glass of water.

"Oh, really?" he asked in that subtle amusement that used to drive her mad.

"Do you normally sit in a chair and watch me as I sleep?" she asked turning around, leaning her back against the counter and facing him.

"Only when I am bored," he answered.

Myla took a sip of water, completely not amused.

"Get a life," she said bluntly.

"Too late," he answered just as bluntly.

"You know it's bad enough that you completely terrorize my days. You don't have to during the night as well," she pointed out, trying to sound more mature than him.

"You were gone today," he answered simply.

"Well, this isn't going to work," she tried to explain. "I can't sleep with you in the room, and if I think you are going to be in the room, I won't sleep on principle."

"Poor Myla," he answered.

"You don't want me to stop sleeping. That has a very simple result: death," she pointed out.

"I severely doubt you would stop sleeping to that point," he answered. "But if you insist, I promise to only bug you while

191

you are awake if you promise to be around while you are awake."

"Glad we had this talk," she answered, walking toward her bed. "Now unless you have something of use to tell me, I am going to go back to bed."

"Nothing of use," he answered, still sitting there.

"This is when you leave," she pointed out.

Surprisingly he did. Myla lay down, burying her head under her covers and tried to go back to sleep, hoping with every fiber in her body that he wouldn't return to sit there, watching her, as she slept the rest of the night away.

*   *   *

Zira woke up earlier than she expected to, probably due to anxiety from the arrival of the Tarrans. She never slept well under stress, and lately it had seemed that there was too much of that in their village. These visitors were just another notch in a long chain of events that Zira could have done without.

She sat up in bed and looked outside her window. The sun was still below the trees. No one was going to be awake yet. There wasn't really a point to getting up but she knew she wasn't going to get back to sleep either. She climbed out of bed, put on some clothes and headed outside. She figured she'd head over to the schoolyard and plan her classes for the day. It was an unusually responsible thing for her to do, but she'd take anything over sitting in bed staring at her ceiling wondering what kind of chaos the day would bring.

The pale sky was still not entirely lit, and the air was still chilly from the night before. Her footsteps were silent as the thick cloth of her shoes hit the ground. Everything was silent. The village was entirely calm. She made her way down to the market square, so she could cut through it to get to the school

192

grounds. As she passed the town hall, however, she heard noises. It was the faint sound of voices at an almost inaudible whisper, but Zira heard it, and she had to check it out.

She first planned on just opening the door, but then she realized that would alert her presence to whoever was talking. As she stood next to the entrance she looked around for another way in. Then she spotted it. She silently jumped up to one of the rafters above the porch, her hand grabbing the top and leaving her there swinging. Back and forth she kept swinging until she swung herself all the way up to the top, where her feet silently hit the roof of the porch. She walked toward the window there, opened the shutters and silently walked into an empty room. The only thing in there was a gigantic wardrobe, probably where the council kept their robes for the town meetings that only really took place once every ten years.

Zira walked toward the door so that she could make her way down to the main room, but she heard footsteps. The voices were coming to her. She started for the window but realized she still wanted to know what they were saying. Instead she saw that there was space under the wardrobe. She dropped to the ground and squeezed under it. She felt herself getting thinner as she did it, but she was hidden by the time that she saw two men open up the door and walk in.

"Why would you think that?" the first man asked.

Zira recognized his voice. It was Dansten. His voice seemed much less confident than before.

"It would be the natural response. This is what we must do," the other man answered, seeming very certain.

"Misha, I just don't know if it will work," Dansten answered.

Misha... What the hell was he doing involved in secret conversations with their leader? He was an inn manager!

"But it must," Misha insisted. "They will turn. They will want to turn. Not all of them enjoy this life."

Zira's heart started to pound. What was she overhearing?

"Who wouldn't love this life?" asked Dansten exasperated. "They have everything they ever needed – and if they wanted anything else, it's theirs at the wave of a hand. We have no bargaining power."

"Not all of them are so privileged," answered Misha calmly. "Yes, some of them have amazing gifts, but not all of them. Some have been left on the sidelines. Those are who we need to convince."

"And do they have any majority?" Dansten asked. "Their government is made up entirely of powerful Caldar."

"That is the very argument we need to make to them. They haven't been properly represented or considered as full people."

Zira could feel the weight of the wardrobe against her back. Was it getting lower?

"There aren't enough of them," Dansten pointed out.

"Are you so sure? I believe there is great unrest in this village. These people aren't happy," answered Misha slyly.

Zira thought she was going to be sick. Who wasn't happy in their village?

"I just don't feel comfortable doing it, that's all," stated Dansten bluntly.

"What is there to feel uncomfortable about?" asked Misha much louder. "We are bringing equality to their people and peace to the world!"

"We are uprooting their government and way of life *without* their permission," argued Dansten. "What gives us that right?"

"They will, by the end," answered Misha. "We will have their support."

194

Zira was starting to feel crushed. The space she was in was getting smaller. She couldn't fit.

"Yeah? And how do we go about getting that?" Dansten asked skeptically.

"We start with those that we already know will turn," answered Misha simply.

"Who?!" asked Dansten. He was almost shouting.

"The man watching the door last night – he actually asked me if there would be room in Mertana for someone like him," answered Misha.

Markus was watching the door. Why would he ask that?

Because he was born without any gifts: the exception to the rule. Are they basing this on him?

"Anybody else?" asked Dansten.

"I believe one of the young women that we first encountered might be easily turned," Misha answered.

The wardrobe was closing in on her. She couldn't breathe.

"Why do you think that?"

"Because of the way she acted. She was very out of the way the entire time as the other woman was given full priority – talking to us, introducing us to Malachi, conversing with the elders. The whole night she stood to the side, seeming truly unhappy."

Allasta... She just hated Zira. She wouldn't turn, would she?

"So two people are the basis of your entire plan?" Dansten asked.

"I've only been here one night, my friend," Misha answered confidently. "I will have plenty more by the end."

"I still don't know if they believed our story," Dansten said softly.

"Of course they did. It made perfect sense."

195

"Except nobody in our village mysteriously died," pointed out Dansten.

Zira was quietly gasping for air. She couldn't stay there much longer.

"But three in theirs did," Misha answered. "That girl told me so. She said there were reasons given, but nobody really believed them."

No air – she was going to faint.

"Which is bizarre, that the story you made up had such significance to them," noted Dansten.

"You see, my friend? Luck is on our side. Now it is getting well into the morning. People will be waking soon."

With that the two men exited the room, barely in time. Zira slid out from under the wardrobe and rolled over on her back gasping for air. Right there, she promised herself that the next time she had to hide to eavesdrop, she would pick a larger space.

Allasta was such a fool. She told them more than they should know, and gave them the confidence to do whatever they were going to do. She probably would support the Tarrans in it too, bringing nothing but trouble.

Zira took in a deep breath and let out a long sigh, knowing that no one would believe her warnings because of whom they were about.

Chapter 12

They were late. It was rude. She didn't appreciate them not taking her seriously, but then again, since when did anyone take her seriously? No, it was yet another example of how everyone in this town favored the Myla-Zira-Neph trio over her. She hated to even think it, but she was kind of happy when Paul died. Before he arrived, she was the fourth member of that little group. She hoped to reclaim her status after he was gone, but she had no such luck. Instead, she was still alone and under-appreciated.

Yet here Allasta was, once again fully deserving of complete involvement and being stood up by Malachi and Zechariah. It was stupid of her to go to them. They were too egotistical from their roles of running the entire village. It would have been smarter to go to Anala or Ratel. They were both vocal members of the council but much more humble. Allasta decided that she didn't want to deal with it anymore. They were ten minutes late and she was bored, so she left Malachi's house and headed to the town hall.

Allasta didn't make it to her destination, however, because she was intercepted on the way, and not by Malachi nor Zechariah whom she hoped to find, but by Misha, that old innkeeper who didn't seem to know how to mind his own business.

"Why hello there, Miss Allasta," he said as he walked up to her with a disturbingly cheery look on his face. "How are you today?"

"Um... fine, why?" she asked, not in the mood for pleasantries.

"Can't a man be polite to a nice lady?"

Okay, he was being too friendly.

197

"What's your game?" she asked, not wanting to waste any time.

"Well, you really get to the point, don't you?" he asked, looking quite amused.

"Look, I have to find Malachi and Zechariah, so if you will excuse me," she said as she turned to walk away, but Misha didn't let her get very far.

"It's tough how none of them really consider you, isn't it?" he called after her.

Allasta turned and looked at him. His words were a bit too close to the heart for her comfort level.

"Sure, they consider me," she answered. "I'm still young, that's all. Anyway this really isn't any of your business, so I am going to leave now."

"They seem to consider Zira."

Okay, now Allasta was angry. What was he trying to do?

"Well, that's different," she argued. "She's Zechariah's daughter, so of course they're going to listen to her."

The lies came out of Allasta's mouth so fluently that she almost believed them herself.

"Well, that isn't a real reason; do they have any legitimate cause to consider her over you?" he asked.

Why was she talking to this man?

"No, they don't," she answered.

This time, her words were honest, but she didn't like how she was sharing them with him.

"Are you okay with that?" Misha asked, looking disturbingly sympathetic.

"No, I'm not, but what can I do about it?" she retorted, feeling that the conversation was pointless.

"That's what I am trying to find out: how to bring true equality to all societies," he answered, sounding a bit high and mighty.

"Setting some lofty goals, aren't we?" she asked, muffling a laugh.

"No," he answered, seeming amused as well. "Just trying to make a difference."

He then walked away in some random direction. Allasta stood in place for a moment, not sure whether to laugh or be worried or even to seriously consider what he said. Soon enough, she decided to just shrug it off and continue her search for Malachi, hoping that he would be willing to tell her what really happened with those three deaths.

*   *   *

Myla didn't know why everyone was staring at her when she entered Eli's café that morning. She kept checking to make sure her hair wasn't sticking up straight above her head or her clothes were on backwards. As far as she could tell, everything was normal, but people kept looking at her and whispering. She even saw someone point. She didn't let it bother her though and found a table to sit down. Eli brought her some tea, which she sipped silently, averting her eyes to all the glares.

Luckily the awkwardness didn't last too long, as Neph and Zira came into the café pretty soon after. Myla didn't even hide her relief to see them and waved them over to her table. They hurriedly walked over, and the looks on their faces confirmed her fear: that everything was not normal.

"What's going on?" she asked them nervously as they sat down.

"It looks like everyone is going to have to call you Mel again," said Neph, trying to look somewhat amused.

"What?" she asked, confused.

"Myla, about thirty men from Mertana arrived yesterday afternoon while you were on the hunt," explained Zira.

"Zira just told me this morning," added Neph.

"What? Why? I am going to need more details," responded Myla, completely stunned.

This was too random. She couldn't see how it was related to Amos, but there was nothing normal about thirty Tarran men managing to enter the village with their lives.

"They arrived while Allasta and I were teaching a class," explained Zira. "I escorted them to Malachi. They say they want peace, but they haven't really explained their position in great detail. They did say that they had united all of the known Tarran villages already. Needless to say dinner was slightly awkward last night."

"They want peace? Why?" asked Myla. "We don't even interact with each other."

"That's what the council was curious about," Zira answered.

"Did they give any reason for coming now?"

"They said that there was a mysterious death in their village," Zira responded.

Myla froze as she felt her heart was about to stop.

"But it's a lie, Mel," continued Zira. "I overheard Dansten and Misha talking this morning."

"Misha's here?" Myla asked distressed. "And what were you doing to overhear them?"

"I couldn't sleep so I got up and decided to walk to the school ground to plan my classes," answered Zira. "As I was going there, I overheard voices in the town hall so I sneaked into a room in the top floor."

"The top floor? You practicing self-levitation?" asked Neph.

He looked confused, but then again Myla was a little taken aback by Zira's boldness herself.

"No, I just climbed up," answered Zira, shrugging off Neph's surprise. "Anyway they came into the room, so I hid and heard them talking..."

"Where did you hide?" asked Neph.

"Under a wardrobe, and what does that has to do with anything?"

Zira was looking annoyed.

"Under a wardrobe? Really?" he asked, looking astonished.

"What's so shocking about that?" Myla asked, being more amused than anything.

"Zira doesn't do well in small places," he answered as if Zira wasn't even in the same room.

"Really? How did I not know that?" Myla asked.

"Would you guys just pay attention?" asked Zira. "It's a trap – they're trying to overthrow our government. Dansten isn't even in charge; it's all Misha. He thinks he can convince enough of the Caldar to support him. He even has certain people already in mind."

"Who?" asked Myla, much more seriously.

"I don't know," Zira answered.

How could Misha be doing this? He was an inn manager! Her inn manager! This is the same man who would yell at her because she didn't make the eggs correctly. It didn't make any sense.

Yet the look on Zira's face told Myla that this was real. It was yet another piece of trouble that would be connected to her. Her hometown was trying to conquer the village. Just what she needed... Just what anyone needed...

Myla stared across the room past her friends hoping to find something of significance, something that she could say to bring a quick and easy solution to this all. Her gaze was interrupted, however, as Amos appeared right in front of her.

Myla dropped her cup of tea on the table. It splashed up causing Zira and Neph to quickly turn and stare at Myla, then in the direction she was staring and then back to her. She could see them in the corner of her eye. They couldn't see him. Only her.

He beckoned to her, smiling his usual sickly grin. She could hear Zira and Neph ask her if she was okay. She turned and nodded and apologized for spilling her tea. Then she made up some story about how she forgot that she left a pot of water boiling on the fire and that she better move it before it destroys the pot. Quickly she stood up and followed Amos out the door.

Silently, she tailed him away from Eli's and towards the edge of the village, towards the library. Myla didn't know why she was following him or what he could possibly want, but there was too much going on for her to ignore anything he had to say. She hated leaving Zira and Neph so confused. She never told them about her visits with Amos, about how not a day would go by when he didn't appear to her.

The conversations were always endless and typically pointless. They spent more time spouting philosophical ideals to each than actually discuss anything important, yet Myla kept talking to him, hoping – wishing – for the day that he would give her back his hostages: Kalina, Paul, her mother. She wished so greatly for resolution, to be free of his constant presence, but as time went on, she became more and more convinced that it would never be.

He stopped at the door to the library, turned to her and beckoned her inside. His silence was aggravating as nobody was going to hear them out here, but she followed him inside anyway. There she found him sitting at a table. She sat down on the opposite end.

"Did you have to pull me out of breakfast?" Myla asked, displaying the frustration in her voice.

"Yes, why?" he laughed.

Myla rolled her eyes.

"I'm hungry," she answered, trying to make it sound obvious. "Unlike you, I actually need to eat."

"I eat..." Amos answered a bit defensively.

"I don't want to know what you eat," Myla quickly retorted.

"I thought I'd fill you in on this whole Mertana thing," he answered smiling.

"What, are we co-conspirators now?" she asked, a bit disturbed at this new information sharing session.

"Of course," he answered with a soft laugh, making the whole thing more disturbing.

"One problem," she noted. "I don't like you, and I certainly don't agree with anything you are doing."

"True, but this isn't my doing," he answered.

"You're not involved?" she asked skeptically.

"Not me, no... but I will tell you that it seems quite fishy."

"Thanks for informing me of the obvious."

This conversation was already a dead end.

"Their cause, however, is a noble one," he added.

"One that doesn't involve you, however," she noted.

"Oh, that can be fixed," Amos answered with a smile.

"And what is their cause?" Myla asked.

"To unite the world in peace and equality, of course."

She already saw where this was going.

"Under one government, preferably a Tarran one," she added.

"Well, of course," he answered.

"Of course for that to work..." Myla said with a pause. She knew she was drawing the right conclusion, but she didn't like it.

"Yes?" Amos asked.

"They'd have to do something about those annoying Caldar gifts..." she finished, glaring back at him.

"They do interfere with that whole equality thing," he answered, clearly finding this all amusing.

"Except how do you get rid of Caldar gifts?" asked Myla. "You could make using them illegal, but humanity was born to break laws."

"You create a Tarran government with a very powerful Caldar at the head," answered Amos. "Any Caldar that uses his powers is punished by the leader appropriately."

"Sounds like a dictatorship to me," said Myla, disgusted at the idea.

"A necessary measure for equality," answered Amos.

"So to create equality, you just strip everyone of their rights?" she asked.

"Why not?" he asked.

"I'm not going to humor that question," she answered.

"Why?" Amos asked. "It's a legitimate one."

"You can't make everyone the same; people are born different," Myla answered. "No one is that powerful. People will rebel, and rightly so."

"Like the Tarrans rebelled against the Caldar a thousand years ago?" Amos asked. "Yet I thought that was a bad thing."

Myla silently groaned as she stared at the man across the table from her.

"Let me guess," she said. "In this government plan of yours, you see yourself as the dictator."

"Somebody's got to do it," he answered, smiling. "Though I wouldn't object to having a partner..."

"Is this a new plan or the old one?" she asked.

"This has always been the plan."

"And the Tarrans just happened to make this very convenient offer," said Myla, not believing a word he said.

"They've had good influences," said Amos with a shrug.

"How very thoughtful of you," said Myla disgusted.

"So are you interested?"

How could he ask her that?

"I already told you," she answered. "I don't work with murderers."

Amos smiled in response.

"I haven't murdered anyone… this millennium," he said slyly.

Myla got up and walked away disgusted, but she stopped at the door and turned around glaring at him.

"How can you think that depriving people of their talents and gifts is bringing equality?" she asked, raising her voice.

She had lost it. He was too infuriating to stay calm.

"Because the Tarrans don't have those gifts!" he answered in a loud voice that still somehow sounded reasonable. "Why should they suffer because of something they can't change?"

"They aren't suffering," argued Myla angrily. "We have two different societies and two different ways of life. How can they suffer from our gifts if most of them don't even acknowledge our existence?"

"And what about the Tarrans that do acknowledge your existence?" he asked. "What about the ones that come into this forest searching for you? What happens to them?"

Myla did not like where he was going with this.

"Do you think the trees have always murdered the Tarrans who enter the forest?" he asked. "Who do you think placed the magic on them so that they do that?"

"I'm going to guess that Caldar that fled from Caldaria after you murdered everyone else they knew," she answered. "And I suspect it was designed to protect them from you."

Amos stood up from the table, clearly irritated.

"Look at this forest, Myla!" he yelled. "Look at your village! Look at what you and your little friends have that they never will! How can you think that is okay?"

"You know what?" she answered. "I can see this forest and my village and what me and my *little* friends have and you taking it away from us doesn't give it to the Tarrans. All it means is that everyone suffers. I would rather have this beauty enjoyed by some than never enjoyed by anyone."

"I could give it to them, Myla," he answered, almost pleading with her. "I could keep all of this for everybody, so that everyone can enjoy it, but no one can create it. This forest could stay alive and beautiful for everyone."

"Like Caldaria did?" she asked coldly.

Amos shot her a slightly vulnerable look. She walked towards him.

"You know I have seen your *great* city, Amos. I have seen what you did to it. It is cold and wet and black, with the sky replaced by clouds and the ground made of soot. The magic would not stay, here, Amos, with you in charge. All that would remain would be depression and despair under your throne embedded with evil."

For several seconds, Myla and Amos stood there staring at each other waiting for the other one to speak, but Myla didn't need to speak. For once she had won. He had no response, so she turned around and left him there. There was no point in asking him for his prisoners now. His prisoners... the only reason she stayed alive. This Mertana mess was not for her because she had another goal. She could only hope that Zira and Neph could put an end to this plan of "peace" and expose Misha as the incompetent bastard that she had always known him to be.

*　　*　　*

Zira didn't like lying to Neph and Myla, but she didn't know how to say "it's all Allasta's fault" without them rolling their eyes at her. Why can't a girl have a pointless feud without it coming back to bite her? She didn't even hate Allasta; she just thought she was one of the most annoying human beings to have ever been given life. That wasn't a crime. It was a statement of fact.

Zira took her time to finish breakfast after Myla made her early dramatic exit. The girl kept getting stranger, even though Zira still did have an awesome amount of respect for her, carrying the weight of the world on her shoulders and all. She knew that Myla left for some important reason, and Zira just didn't want to deal with it right then. Now she had her own stress to deal with.

Neph didn't seem to have much to say on the subject either so they ate in mostly silence. Once they finished, they decided to head over to the town hall. With that decision, Neph suddenly had difficulty containing his conversational skills.

"So do they talk like us?" he randomly asked.

"Myla and Paul did when they arrived," she answered wanting to slap him. "Why would these guys be any different?"

"These people aren't Caldar," he explained.

"Being a Caldar doesn't affect your speech pattern, Neph," answered Zira.

"Yeah… I guess," he said.

Then after a pause he was at it again.

"So do they dress like us?" he asked.

"Are you two?"

207

"And twenty," he answered laughing. "Now answer the damn question."

"Yes, they dress quite similarly except their clothes are a little more... decorative," she answered.

"Well, do they eat the same things as us?" he asked.

Zira started to laugh.

"No," she answered. "They only eat tree bark and rubble."

Neph didn't get an opportunity to make a real comeback to this. He only was able to make a disgusted face as Malachi walked up behind them.

"Hello, my young friends," he said in his usual sophisticated tone.

"Hello, Malachi," they answered simultaneously.

"Going to pay our guests a visit?" he asked.

"Actually, I was planning on finding you," Zira explained.

"I wanted to see the Tarrans," added Neph being his usual blunt self.

"Do you know they all have to wear hats to block out the sun?" Malachi asked turning to Neph. "Apparently if they spend too much time in it, their skin turns bright red."

"Really? Why would they let it do that?" Neph asked.

"Apparently they never made peace with it," Malachi said shaking his head.

What was this? Were Neph and Malachi having some sort of bonding conversation? Zira couldn't take this.

"Whatever they wear on their heads, Malachi, doesn't change the fact that they are lying to us," she interrupted.

"I can't judge them on speculation, Zira," he said, turning to her.

"How about a witness?" she asked, crossing her arms in front of her chest.

208

It was kind of fun, trumping Malachi. She didn't understand why Myla didn't take more pleasure out of it.

"I was wondering why Zira's sense of humor had vanished so quickly," he said, clearly impressed. "Perhaps we shouldn't discuss this in the open. Would you two care to join me for a cup of tea at my home? Neph, I am afraid you may have to put off seeing our very unusual guests for a bit longer this morning."

Neph nodded his head in agreement and the three made their way to Malachi's house. Zira and Neph had some difficulty containing their amusement at the whole situation. They were the ones involved. This was Zira's development, and not Myla's. They felt strangely important, as if they were finally proving that they hadn't just been tagging along this entire time. It was a nice feeling.

Apparently Malachi meant it when he mentioned tea, for as soon as they arrived, he started making some, beckoning for the two to sit down at his table. They both did, awkwardly. Neither of them had ever thought of Malachi as the hospitable type.

"Well, I guess we should get started," he said as he brought the last of the tea over to the table. "Zira, explain to me what happened."

Zira awkwardly told the story, leaving out Allasta and Markus's names yet again. She justified her choice in her head because, in reality, she had no idea whether or not Misha was telling the truth. He could have just been using them as random names to get Dansten to agree to follow him.

At first, Malachi didn't say anything after Zira finished speaking. He just sat there, looking at her and Neph, tapping his fingers on the table. Finally, he took a breath and spoke.

209

"Thank you for bringing this to my attention Zira," he said softly, though he looked very helpless. "Unfortunately, I find it very difficult to use this information."

"Why?" Neph asked, unable to hide his surprise.

"Because Zira obtained it in the most dishonest of methods," he answered simply.

"Because she hid from them?"

"And sneaked into our town hall," Malachi answered, sounding very practical.

"It doesn't change what she heard," Neph argued. "These people are trying to bring down our society as we know it, and you aren't going to do anything because she had to eavesdrop to find out about it?"

"What do you expect me to do?" Malachi asked. "Turn them down on their request for *peace* because of a gut feeling?"

"Yes!" answered Neph, standing up as if he was threatening to leave the room.

Zira sat still. She was feeling extremely guilty and didn't want to bring any more attention to herself.

"And how would our people react to that?" Malachi asked, staying in place.

"They would accept it. You're Malachi; they think you know everything," Neph argued fervently.

"No, I am afraid they don't," Malachi disputed. "Thanks to my granddaughter, they have doubted my sole authority."

"She knows about this, and she would support you," Neph responded.

"Even if the entire council agreed with my decision, it would not change the opinion of the people," said Malachi. "They have doubted the entire council and all those in power, including Myla and the two of you for that matter. Misha couldn't have picked a better time to try to convert our village to his plan. With the deaths of Paul, Kalina, and my daughter, the people of our village no longer feel safe. They will make many compromises to return to that feeling."

"And you'll just let them," said Zira, finally confident enough to speak. "You'll just let them throw away the world they love for a better feeling of security. As they bring equality, we'll lose our identity as Caldar. And yet you'll just let them."

"My arm is twisted," Malachi said calmly as he took a sip of tea.

"I'm starting to really believe that Myla was right all along to not trust you," said Zira stunned. "Well, Malachi, my arm is not twisted, and I will not stand idly by and let this happen."

With that she and Neph left Malachi's house, bumping into Allasta at the doorstep. Part of Zira wanted to yell at her, but she didn't have the energy. Her anger was too focused on Malachi right now.

"Unbelievable! It's like he wants them to win!" exclaimed Neph as he paced around the main room of his house.

Zira sat in silence. She knew Malachi didn't *want* them to win, but he also didn't want to bring the council under fire, which was a significant concern. If the people truly doubted his power, then making an abrasive and most likely very unpopular move such as turning down an offer of peace would only alienate them more. They were looking for reasons to blame the council for the deaths of their people. As much as Zira hated to admit it, perhaps Malachi's hands were tied.

Yet then again, he could at least have started working on some sort of plan to expose the Tarrans for what they were truly trying to do. In fact, that was all she had really expected him to do. Even if it weren't a public gesture, doing something would have been better than nothing.

Which is why Zira had to do something, yet how could she stop thirty Tarrans and most likely many Caldar from toppling a government that was already so unstable that it couldn't defend itself on its own? What could she, Zira, do against so many people?

Of course, Myla and Neph would help her; that was for sure. But Myla wasn't herself these days, and that was also for sure. As powerful as she was, could Zira rely on her if she couldn't even survive a breakfast without being distracted?

And then there was Neph. He was probably one of the most powerful people in the village behind Myla and one of the few Caldar in history to have successfully self-levitated, yet his personality was so undisciplined that he never learned how to properly control his powers. He had passion about the issue, as Zira saw from his constant muttering and pacing, but what if he got bored? Where would he be then?

Yet then again, Zira knew she hadn't always taken things seriously herself. And when Neph was needed, he was always there. So was Myla. Perhaps things were not so hopeless. Perhaps it was possible to fix this mess.

But how?

Chapter 13

Myla woke up in what she knew was her room. She climbed out of her four-poster bed and her feet hit the cold marble floor beneath her. Cold, she ran and grabbed her robe from its hook on the wall. Quietly, she walked out of the room and into the hallway... her hallway. She turned to the right and made her way down the white spiral staircase.

She was in a room lit by firelight. It was a study of some sorts. Myla knew it for she had spent many hours here, talking and laughing with him. This was a warm home to her. She walked up to the coffee table and sat down on the velvet sofa behind her. On the table's glass surface lay a book, a diary. She began to read it. She could relate to everything in it, but it was not hers. Suddenly, she felt overwhelmingly guilty and ran outside.

It was a courtyard, completely empty of any other sign of life. In the center, there was a fountain with a crystal figurine of a man, perhaps a king, in the middle. Myla realized then that she was very thirsty, overwhelmingly so. She ran up to the cool refreshing water of the fountain and knelt down to drink.

Yet she stopped, for as she was looking into the water, she didn't see her face, but the face of Amos, still young and innocent. He was pure, yet as she kept staring, he changed into the Amos she knew. She fell back on to the ground. Suddenly, the fountain was no longer crystal but black, and the water was like mud. Myla scrambled to her feet as she watched the statue change form into the shape of a man, one she did not know. It pointed to her and hundreds of snakes began to slither out of the fountain towards her.

She ran for her life. Out of the courtyard, out of the city. She ran to the woods, to safety. Yet once she entered the forest, the vibrant trees around her suddenly withered and died, as if all the life had been sucked right from them. Further into the woods she ran, only bringing death with her. As everything around her saw its end, she didn't care. There was nothing she could do. This was not her fault. What had she done? Up ahead, she saw a cave and she knew what it signified: safety, away from everything living. She ran towards it.

Myla awoke in her own bed in her own village. Sweat trickled down her face and her arm shook in pain. She looked down at it. The wound that Amos had given her eight months before had reopened and was bleeding down her arm. Calmly she stood up and walked to the cupboard and pulled down a towel, which she proceeded to tie around the wound tightly to stop the bleeding. Then she poured herself a glass of water and sat down at the table, waiting for him to arrive.

He appeared next to the fire, probably for some sort of dramatic effect; Myla didn't really care. It had been a long time since she had dreamed about that city, and her dreams of that nature had never been so terrifying, or real. That dream was so vivid it was as if it had really happened. Why would he give that to her?

"Did you call?" he asked, looking amused.

Myla just stared at him.

"I see you're not in a very talkative mood," he continued, walking over to where she was sitting and leaning against the table.

He placed his hand on her wound.

"Now, Myla," he said softly. "You really should stop getting into fights."

She stood up and looked at him right into his eyes.

"You know perfectly well how I got this wound," she answered coldly. "Now what the hell do you want?"

"What everyone wants," he said, smiling as he sat down and leaned back into one of the chairs. "Love, acceptance… power."

"Typically the first two and the last don't go together," she said, walking away from him and over to the fire.

"Such is the dilemma of the life we lead, isn't it?" he asked. "Too powerful to ever be able to give it up, and too separated to ever really belong."

"Speak for yourself, Amos," she lied as she stared at the fire. "I have friends and a community."

"That you can never really be a part of," he added. "You are too far above them; you think differently. They may care about you, but they don't *understand* you."

"Comprehension is overrated," Myla answered shortly.

"Speaks the girl that must understand everything."

Amos walked over to her and stood next to her as she watched the fire.

"With you, there will always be a warning next to your face: that this woman is capable of too much and can never truly be trusted," he said softly.

"Is that why they trust me?" she argued.

"Do they?" he asked. "Or do they just tell you things because they have to? Remember how long it took Malachi to tell you about me?"

"You know," said Myla with a pause. "You were much creepier in the ghost form."

"I doubt you would talk to me if I looked like that," he answered with a small laugh.

"That doesn't mean I forget what you really are, Amos," she said much more forcefully. "Now if you don't mind, I think I am going to go to bed. Unlike some people, I have things to do in the morning."

With those words, she turned away from him and started walking towards her bed. By the time she turned back around, he was gone, or at least that's what she believed, for once her head hit the pillow, she fell into a dreamless sleep.

*   *   *

"I just don't really see what we are doing right now," said Dansten, as he stared at the pen in front of him, fixated.

"Deliberations are not always easy, my friend," said Misha, not even turning to look at him. Instead, he stood in front of the desk, staring out the window.

"But that's exactly my point," said Dansten, still staring at the pen, his chin resting on his hands. "We've been here three days, and we haven't deliberated anything. All you do is say a bunch of nonsense to the council about peace, and treaties, and constitutions. Then you split at the first moment and go to try to talk up the citizens. They are going to kick us out of their village soon if we don't do something."

"We are gaining supporters," said Misha, still not turning around.

"They don't even know the cause," responded Dansten.

He reached out and tapped the pen. Then he retrieved his hand and kept staring.

"Of course, they know the cause," stated Misha.

"Oh, right... equality. Except, what does that mean?" asked Dansten, his eyes still not leaving the pen. "Do any of them know what they are actually supporting? Saying they are willing to give up?"

Misha finally turned around slightly and looked at Dansten.

"That pen's not going to move," he said bluntly.

216

"I just don't get how they do it," Dansten said, finally letting his eyes leave the pen as he looked up at Misha.

"They do it in a way that you will never be able to imitate," answered Misha, walking over to the desk and leaning against it. "That's exactly why we have to do what we are doing. If you can't move that pen, why should they get to?"

"It's just a pen," said Dansten, looking quite skeptical.

"It's the principle of the matter, Dansten," said Misha, getting up and walking about the room. "How are you supposed to receive the respect and honor that you deserve as a human being if you can't even move a simple pen with your mind?"

"Yeah, but we don't really know what we're asking them to give up," argued Dansten. "I just don't think they will do it."

Suddenly the pen flew off the table and into Misha's hand. Dansten stared at him, dumbfounded.

"I know exactly what they are giving up," said Misha firmly, leaning toward a frightened Dansten. "And I want it gone."

Misha then handed him the pen and walked out of the room, leaving the shaking Dansten alone.

*   *   *

Markus hesitated as he was about to knock on Myla's door. He didn't really know where to begin and once he knocked on that door, and she answered, he would have to say something. He knew that he had questions for her, but he didn't know how to ask them. Eventually he found the nerve and knocked on her door. Within a few seconds, she was at the door.

"Markus!" she said smiling. "How's it going?"

"I was wondering, Myla, if I could talk to you," he said cautiously.

217

She always had intimidated him, from the moment he first met her when she was just a child. She was too powerful... so far from him.

"Come on in," she said, beckoning him in through the door to her small home. "Take a seat. Do you want some tea?"

"I'm good, thanks," he answered, sitting down at one of the chairs only as she did. He was unsure of how to act.

"What's up, Markus?" she asked, clearly aware of his nerves. "You seem a little distracted."

"Mel, I was wondering if you were ever planning on actually meeting our visitors and taking some sort of involvement in the issue," he asked, staring down at the table and only looking up at the end.

"Ah, so you're here to confront me about my lack of involvement," she said smiling, as she leaned back in her chair.

"Well, yes," he said, a little more confidently. "This is a big deal, and you have ignored it completely."

"I've been keeping informed," she said simply.

"But that's not enough," he said strongly now.

"Why do I have to be involved? I don't recall ever being elected to a leadership position in this village, Markus," she argued.

"You didn't have to be," he responded. "You're as much of a leader in this village as the council, if not more of one, and you're our one connection to Mertana. You know a lot of those people, and you haven't even said 'hello'."

"I wasn't a fan of those people when I was there, you know," Myla answered defensively, but Markus knew that she didn't have an argument.

"You were ten," he answered simply.

"Doesn't mean I was stupid," she answered, clearly not expecting that kind of logic.

"No, you were brilliant, but you were also so bitter, and against everyone," Markus answered.

"And you think that's changed?" Myla asked, looking a bit surprised.

"Yes, actually. At some point in your time here, you stopped fighting for yourself and started fighting for others," he answered.

She looked at him thoughtfully.

"So what do you want me to do with this whole Mertana thing anyway?" she asked.

"You have a way of seeing things ten steps ahead everyone else," he explained. "These Tarrans... They have some good ideas. I think your insight would be valuable."

"You mean my support," she said, suddenly looking very skeptical of him.

Markus started feeling uneasy.

"Well, yes, I guess," he said cautiously.

"You know these Tarrans have some very bad ideas as well," Myla said calmly, looking at him.

Markus felt a twinge of guilt. What was she getting at?

"What's wrong with peace and equality?" he asked, trying to remain confident in his argument.

"That depends on the cost," she answered, pausing. "What side are you playing for Markus?"

Markus' head started to hurt. It had never occurred to him that there were "sides" on this issue. He always thought it was a very cut and dry matter. How could Myla not want this?

"Shouldn't we do everything possible for peace and equality?" he asked.

"If I were you I would check with Misha – I mean Dansten – about what he thinks should be done for it," Myla said calmly.

How did she know it was Misha that had talked to him? It was such a blatantly obvious slip that it was sickening.

"Clearly this is a conversation that should be left for another time," he said, very much wanting to get out of that room. "Thank you for speaking with me, Myla. Hopefully you will decide that involvement on your part is a good thing, and not necessarily a bad one."

"Perhaps, Markus," she said calmly, suddenly looking very sad. "Have a good day."

He nodded his head and walked out of her house. It was the closest to a storming off that he had ever managed and it didn't exactly feel good. He felt betrayed. Myla was an image of wisdom and knowledge to him, and if she didn't support this, he didn't know what to do. How could she be against this?

Then it hit him: it would take away power from her.

*   *   *

Myla sat very calmly in her chair after Markus left. Her mind was racing too fast for her to move. Markus. She shouldn't have been surprised. He was one of the few Caldar that was born without many gifts. In fact, Myla wasn't entirely sure if Markus had ever displayed any gifts at all. The only sign that he was a Caldar was his ability to remain in the village, yet then again, the Tarrans weren't doing a bad job themselves.

Myla ran her fingers along the lines in the wood of her table. Some things weren't so perfectly clear. Shouldn't they do everything possible for peace and equality? At what point did it become okay for them to sacrifice certain freedoms for that? Maybe Markus had a point.

Maybe Amos had a point. Maybe he isn't all bad.

Myla shuddered at that thought. She couldn't let him get to her. He was evil. His plan for peace was costing the Caldar the very essence of what they were. That was an unacceptable price. She knew it. She couldn't let him change that with his clever wording and impenetrable presence. Markus was right about one thing, though: this was an issue she had to be involved in. She couldn't let Misha get away with leading her people into the service of a devil.

"How's life in village land?" said a voice behind her.

Amos. Would he ever go away?

"You know I can't remember the last time you allowed me to think by myself," she said, turning to glare at him.

"You're too much of a multi-tasker for that," he answered.

"Oh, now you're being funny?" she asked, standing up and walking over to her bag that was sitting on the counter.

"I've always been funny; you've just always been too dense for it," he answered, smiling his usual sickening grin. "Going somewhere?"

"Unlike you, I have things to do," she said.

She felt his eyes piercing through her as she turned away from him and knelt down at the chest that she had against the wall.

"And what are you up to, my friend?" he said, walking over behind her.

"You are not my friend," she responded, as she opened up the chest.

"I said you were my friend; I didn't say I was yours," he answered.

"What a disturbingly sad little distinction you have working there."

Myla reached down into the chest and pulled out a small shirt and pair of pants.

"I don't believe you'll fit those," Amos said, clearly a bit confused.

221

"I wore these the day the Caldar came and rescued me from Mertana," she said softly.

"And… you just felt reminiscent?" Amos asked, but she didn't respond. "What's the story, Myla?"

"I have a lot of memories in these clothes," she said slowly and softly. "These holes and patches, they were there when I was ten. These, and a ratted old nightgown, were the only clothes I had as a girl. The only clothes Misha ever bothered to let me have."

"What? Am I supposed to feel sorry for you now?" Amos asked, sitting down leaning his back against the wall that the chest was against. "You know I didn't exactly have an easy childhood either."

"And I'm sure you really care about that now," Myla said under her breath as she blankly stared at the clothes in her hands.

"I've had a few years to work past it," he answered, looking very unconcerned with her.

"You know the first time I met my mother, I was wearing these clothes," she said softly. "My first conversation with Paul…"

Amos didn't respond.

"We had to do a history project together, and he talked to me as if I was normal. He was the only child in Mertana to ever do that…"

"Why in hell would I ever want to know about your first conversation with Paul?" Amos asked, visibly bothered.

"Because *we are* in hell," she answered in a quiet anger. "You've been dragging me there with you for the past four months."

Myla dropped the clothes back into the chest, stood up and started to head out of the room.

"Where are you going?" Amos asked.

222

"To say 'hello' to an old friend," she answered and then walked out the door.

*　　　*　　　*

We are uprooting their government and way of life without their permission. Dansten's words rang in Zira's ears as she listened to Misha and him lay out some more political garbage to the council and a large group of ignorant Caldar in the town hall. As the days passed by, Zira had expected Caldar interest in their visitors to wane, but the opposite had occurred. Today showed an enormous increase in people. They could barely fit everyone in. As she stood in the back of the hall, she watched the clueless people eat up everything they said. Peace, safety, security. This was one hell of a revolution they were planting seeds for. Uniting the world... Like that could ever happen. This would only bring unnecessary chaos and destruction. Why couldn't they see that?

Yet more and more people kept coming to listen to the ideas and "plans" of Misha and Dansten. Every time one of them said something that was slightly bold or controversial whispering would spread throughout the room, and after that the people only took them more seriously. Even some of the council members were nodding their heads along with what Misha and Dansten were saying. Not Zechariah though. And not Malachi.

Neph sat down on the floor next to where Zira stood. She looked down at him. He was hanging his head in his hands, shaking his head in disbelief. This turnout was too depressing.

"We as people – as a community – can do so much more if we work together equally," preached Misha to the crowd. "We can create a system where all people will be represented and given their proper chance. No more distrust, and no more fear. We can raise our families in safety and hope."

The crowd cheered as applause filled the hall.

"Why should we treat each other with hatred and fear when at heart we are all people and all the same?" Misha continued. "The treaty we propose will do more than create an artificial agreement to not attack each other. What we propose is unity, as friends and neighbors. There is no need for a distinction between Caldar and Tarran. Let us live as friends in safety, where we don't fear the loss of our friends and family at a second's notice."

Applause filled the room as the memories of Kalina, Malika and Paul clearly jumped to everyone's mind. It was too much for Zira. Misha knew about their village's loss, and he was exploiting those deaths. Zira found herself pushing through the clapping crowd and reaching the front of the room, face to face with Misha.

"Misha, tell me," she said.

Her voice echoed into everyone's ears above the deafening sound of applause. Silence filled the room as they all stared at her.

"Yes?" he asked, smiling awkwardly and clearly trying to look amused at her defiant tone.

"At what sacrifice comes your plan of *peace*?" Zira asked. "What are you asking the Caldar to give up?"

"Well, naturally, it will require some sacrifice and hard work on everyone's part," Misha answered, in an attempt to evade the question.

"Sacrificing what? Our culture? Our way of life? Who we are as a people?" Zira asked. "You don't want unity. You want everyone to be just like you."

"We will need to embrace our similarities for true success as a unified people," he answered with a fake laugh, but the crowd did not echo his attempt. "But who you are as people will remain the same. How am I supposed to change that?"

224

"By forcing us to give up our gifts," said a loud voice from the back of the room.

Zira turned around. It was Myla, standing still as the crowd separated around her. Misha only stared. The look on his face indicated he didn't know she was here.

"Why hello, Misha. What a pleasure it is to see you again," said Myla, in a cynically monotone voice.

Misha paused, looking for a way to handle this surprise.

"Is this how you welcome your guests?" he said loudly to the crowd. "Parade the child you kidnapped right in front of us? It is exactly these kinds of actions that we hope peace will prevent!"

The crowd started laughing.

"My friends," Malachi called over the crowd. "Myla is my granddaughter and one of the most respected members of our village."

"So your fantasies were true," he said turning back to Myla.

"Clearly your presence here indicates that you already knew I got at least part of it right," answered Myla. "I hardly believe that you would still assume that I got the rest wrong. Yes, Misha... I am a Caldar and this is my home."

"So then you are a sign of our hopeful future," he claimed, clearly now speaking to the crowd instead of Myla. "We can live together as the same people."

"I will not be privy to the development of any government that denies the Caldar the use of their natural gifts," stated Myla, showing more anger than Zira expected to see from her.

"My old friend, don't be so dramatic..." he answered, clearly trying his best to not appear stressed, but Zira could see the sweat trickling down from his forehead.

"Friend?" Myla asked angrily. "You are not my friend."

225

"Misha, why don't you tell these people what your real plan is?" interjected Zira, hoping to steer the conversation back to the original focus. She hadn't really expected such a strong clash between the two.

"Why, young lady," he said in a condescending tone. "I, of course, would never dream of asking the Caldar give up what makes them who they are. I wouldn't think of instilling such a tragedy upon the world. Now, naturally, there will be some tricks you have that will be illegal, but only the most dangerous ones. Some of us can't defend ourselves as well as you do."

"How curious that you refer to yourself as the one asking these things," spoke Neph from the back of the room. "In fact, I don't think I have heard a single word from Dansten this entire time."

Zira smiled. Neph had come through at just the right moment. The crowd started whispering among themselves feverishly. Dansten froze in his chair as everyone turned and stared at him.

"Who's in charge here, Dansten?" Zira asked, quite casually.

"I am!" Dansten said, trying to sound more confident than he was. "Misha is simply my chief advisor. When he used 'I', it was simply a slip of the tongue. He speaks for both of us."

"I would never dream of infringing on the authority of our elected leader," added Misha, hurriedly.

"Like you wouldn't dream of infringing on the rights of the Caldar?" asked Myla coldly. "This whole *movement* reeks of foul play. I would strongly advise anyone from listening to this disgusting attempt at a man."

Misha just stared at her blankly. Myla paused a few seconds before she turned and walked out of the hall. Zira smiled to herself. Misha would not get to continue his speech today. The crowd had taken Myla's queue and started moving to the door.

Noise filled the room as everyone immediately started to discuss what just happened all at the same time. Misha turned and walked toward the dumbfounded Dansten.

"Well, that was unpleasant," he said quietly to Dansten so that Zira could barely hear him. She looked around. No one else was paying attention to them. Malachi was talking with Zechariah and the rest of the council had dispersed. Zira walked to the side of the hall and placed herself conveniently behind one of the columns near them.

"Was that really Myla?" Dansten asked. "She used to be so odd. Now she actually seems kind of normal."

"That's because here she is normal, which makes her even more of a problem."

Misha sounded worried. He didn't even know how powerful Myla was, and he was already worried. Zira couldn't help but be amused.

"What do you mean? Didn't you say that she represented possible unity of our peoples?"

"Dansten, are you really that much of an idiot?" Misha asked, whispering a slight bit louder and then quieting down. "Myla wasn't kidnapped from our village. She ran away…"

"But I thought…"

"She doesn't want to have anything to do with us, Dansten. She hates me. She hates all of us. We lied to her as a child and made her an outcast to keep her identity a secret. And those people out there, the way they looked at her showed that they respect her, a lot. They'll listen. That little uproar is going to take a lot more damage control than you realize."

The hall had entirely cleared except for the three of them. Zira suddenly felt very vulnerable. She had no excuse for being behind that column, and unlike the wardrobe, she was much more visible. All they would have to do as walk a few feet to the left, and she would be right in front of them. Of course, they hadn't exactly said anything too incriminating. They only expressed fear of Myla, and who wasn't afraid of Myla?

Zira could hear footsteps walk up behind her.

"That was a successful endeavor," said a female voice.

Zira knew it immediately. It was Allasta. What an idiot! How could she have turned so quickly?

"Yes, nice job warning me that Myla was here," Misha said coldly.

"I did tell you about her!" answered Allasta defensively. "She's the psychotic powerful one that could make or break this operation."

"Myla can't be the most powerful of them," argued Dansten in disbelief. "She's from Mertana!"

"Of course, she is the most powerful," said Misha. "How could she not be?"

"Don't expect me to buy that ridiculous notion that you didn't know she was here or was a Caldar, Misha," said Allasta coldly. "You knew perfectly well who she was, even when she was working in your inn."

"And what makes you say that?" Misha asked angrily.

"Because everything you said out there was a performance," she answered practically. "There was no actual surprise in your voice."

How was Allasta this observant?

"You assume so much for knowing me so little," Misha answered firmly.

"You're a natural liar. I know the type."

Her confidence surprised Zira.

"Then why are you helping me?" he asked.

"I believe in your cause," she answered simply. "And I'm tired of getting passed over. It's about time there was some equality around here."

"Well, my cause isn't going to get very far if you don't tell me everything," Misha answered coldly.

"Misha, don't act like an idiot when you aren't one," answered Allasta. "And certainly don't treat me like I am one. There are more people than the three of us involved in this. You have more sources of information."

"What are you talking about, Allasta?" asked Dansten. "The entire Tarran people are involved in this."

"The entire Tarran people know nothing about Myla," responded Allasta. "Misha, however, clearly has someone else involved who does."

What? Zira was confused. Who was Allasta talking about? Another Caldar? A Tarran? Maybe Amos?

"Who is this other?" asked Dansten, clearly also confused. "How do you know this?"

"Yes, tell me Allasta," asked Misha. "Who is this other?"

"That I don't know," she answered. "But you had way too much knowledge of us coming into our village than any Tarran should have. Dansten asked questions about everything. You saw it all without the slightest hint of surprise. Quite odd for a first time witness."

Of course... How had Allasta noticed this and Zira didn't even register it? Misha was way too confident here. He didn't act like a man out of his own territory. He always acted like a politician with the goal to win over the Caldar. Shouldn't a normal Tarran have been at least somewhat taken aback by the reality of their existence?

Zira, however, didn't have much time to examine it all for once she turned her head away from the floor she was staring at, she looked up and saw Dansten standing in front of her, staring at her. She froze and didn't say a word. She only stared back at him. This was not going to be good.

229

"Misha, I think you should get over here," he said loudly, never taking his eyes off her.

Zira briefly considered making herself invisible, but she knew Allasta would be able to spot her. Instead she just stood there like a dumbfounded idiot. Misha and Allasta walked over in front of her.

"What are you doing here?" asked Allasta, angrily.

"To the best of my knowledge, it was an open meeting," Zira responded.

They weren't amused.

"And you just felt like standing behind this column?" Allasta asked.

"I was trying to figure out what to have for dinner. Soup or salad? It's the ultimate question…"

Zira's voice trailed off as she became very aware of the "I'm going to kill you" look on Misha's face.

"So what do we do with her?" asked Dansten, shaking nervously in place.

"We take her upstairs," answered Misha.

Allasta then grabbed one of her arms and Misha grabbed the other. Zira tried to phase away from them, but she couldn't. Allasta must have been stopping her. Zira had never realized before that Allasta was that strong of a Caldar.

*   *   *

"Well, that was dramatic," said Amos as Myla walked in the door. She looked at him sitting at her table and rolled her eyes.

"I see you were able to make it," she said calmly as she put her bag down on the counter.

230

"What? Like I would miss the great confrontation between Myla and that old man that gave her a slightly tougher childhood?" Amos asked sarcastically. "That's the kind of material that songs are written about."

Myla turned around and just stared at him.

"How is it that you wonder why I hate you?" asked Myla frustrated. "You kidnap my friends, stalk me every day and on top of that you still find time to ridicule me. Really, Amos... do you honestly think that I am going to choose to join you after all of this?"

"And what makes you think that you are so much better?" he asked quietly.

"Do you want a list?"

"You disrespect everything about this society as you try so hard to maintain it," he answered standing up and walking towards her. "You tell the rightfully elected elders what to do. Your very presence endangers those around you, and yet you still find more ways to put them at risk. You have even attacked your own flesh and blood for a reason fueled only by anger and distrust. Really Myla, at least there is a cause behind what I do."

Myla could feel her eyes tearing up, but she used all of her strength to stifle them.

"And what cause is yours?" she asked. "World domination?"

"We are no different, Myla," he said softly.

"We are everything different."

"Is that why you keep talking to me everyday?" he asked, looking somewhat amused.

"I want Paul back..." she answered, her voice trailing off.

"No, not really," he answered, walking closer to her. "He's so simple – a good guy I'm sure – but he's far too elementary for you. I bet even these arguments with me have

231

been more of a thrill to you than any conversation ever was with him."

"Talking with you has never been anything more than a nasty chore," she answered defensively, but she could tell he wasn't buying it.

"I don't think I believe you," he answered.

He then moved toward her and before she could even think, he kissed her. For a moment she didn't react, then she pushed him away. Tears streamed down her face as she stood there staring at him, knowing that hesitation would cost her.

"Tell me where they are!" she yelled at him in a broken voice.

"Why should I?" he asked coldly, unsympathetic to Myla's tears.

"Because I can't do this anymore!" she answered hopelessly fighting back tears. "I can't keep playing this game. Why must you make me? I mean… are you really this evil? This hateful?"

"When are you going to realize, Myla, that you can do anything?" he asked, almost in disbelief. "The only reason you haven't found them is because you haven't wanted to."

Amos then disappeared, leaving Myla standing there alone in her room.

Chapter 14

Zira wasn't exactly in the most comfortable position. She had been sitting in a hard wooden chair for far too long, her hands tied with a rope that was clearly strengthened by magic. Allasta sat on the other side of the room, staring at her. She looked angry and hurt, but Zira couldn't believe that she was this evil.

"Allasta, what are you doing?" she asked, hopelessly trying to wiggle out of her restraints.

"What's best for our people," she answered. "The only reason you can't see that is because you are too wrapped up in the power that you have."

Zira rolled her eyes and sunk her head down. Did Allasta really hate her this much?

"And what's the point of keeping me captive?" Zira asked. "Will this really help your cause? Endangering another Caldar?"

"You are not in danger," Allasta responded mildly as she turned and looked at the wall.

"Seriously, though," Zira insisted. "What's the point?"

Allasta smiled. Then she walked over to where Zira was seated and kneeled down.

"Don't worry, we'll let you go once it's done," she said in falsely sweet voice. "Right now, however, you need to be another mysterious disappearance for us. The first three proved to be so accidentally advantageous to us that we thought we would create a fourth."

"Once what's done?" asked Zira nervously.

"The creation of the new unified government, of course," Allasta answered. "It shouldn't be too long."

233

"You have a lot more work to do before you get that far," Zira snapped back.

Allasta started to laugh.

"Zira, do you really think this is the only Caldar village being courted?" she asked. "Don't be silly. It's only a matter of days before the entire known world is under our rule."

Zira wanted to be sick.

"You know you should take a trip to Caldaria some time," she said disgusted. "I think you'd have a lot in common with its current residents."

Allasta shot an offended look at her.

"What?" Zira asked. "It makes sense with you working for them and all."

Allasta didn't humor Zira with a response. Instead, she stormed out of the room in a fury. Zira couldn't help but slightly laugh at the response. She, however, was too angry and too driven to dwell on it. She immediately started working on a way to get out of the room. There were no windows, which wasn't a good thing. Of course, a window wasn't all that useful at that moment, considering that she was still very much trapped in her chair.

Zira sat there for what seemed to be forever. It was still dark, however, when she finally figured out how to free herself. Allasta had held her in the chair assuming one thing: that Zira couldn't transport herself out of the room. This, of course, wasn't that bad of an assumption, since Zira had yet to prove herself able to transport anything, and transporting oneself was a rare gift. Like self-levitation, no Caldar in history had successfully accomplished it. Of course, Zira wasn't entirely sure if Myla had done it. Yet, right there at that moment, Zira knew she had to try to be the next.

She stared at the door and started focusing. She imagined herself breaking into millions of different pieces flying

234

past it, but it only freaked her out. She tried to picture herself on the other side. That didn't work. Then she started to laugh.

She didn't need to transport herself out of there. All she needed to do was transport the rope off her hands and feet. She couldn't see it, but she could imagine what it looked like. Once she had a picture in her head, she started to visualize it breaking up into millions of pieces floating to the other side of the room. Suddenly Zira found herself free from her restraints and the coiled rope was sitting neatly in the corner.

Zira jumped to her feet and ran to the door. Quietly she tried to open it for fear of someone on the other side. It was locked, as expected. Without a window her successful transport lost much of its merit. Then Zira had an idea. She took her outer cloak and draped it over the chair. Then she took the rope and placed it below, where her hands and feet had been.

"Move!" she yelled, stretching out her hand to make an echoing cracking sound.

Sure enough, Dansten and Allasta came barging into the room, only to find the chair, cloak and rope.

"She couldn't have," Allasta said, in shock. "She wasn't that good."

Depends on your definition, Allasta, Zira thought as she slid down from above the doorframe and quietly sneaked out the door. She immediately started to run silently. Deciding that exiting through the front door would be too dangerous, she threw herself out the window, falling the two stories and landing softly on her feet. She hadn't made a sound. With her luck, they were still standing in the room trying to figure out what happened.

Zira bolted to the stables. If Allasta was telling the truth and other Caldar villages were also converting to this cause, they needed to be warned. There was too much corruption in this new "government", and Zira needed to stop it. She would simply have to trust Neph and Myla to finish the work here by preventing this catastrophe.

One of the sleek black horses, Libby, trotted up to her. Zira patted her nose, threw a blanket on her back and mounted. She steered Libby out of the stable, but not straight out of the village. She first swung by Allasta's place. Stretching out her hand, she shot a flame burning a *verradere*, the symbol for traitor, on her door. It faded to being invisible to the regular eye, but Zira had hope that Neph would find it. He would have to expose Allasta for who she was.

Zira then steered her horse around and made quickly for the forest. As she rode out of the village, she wondered what Allasta and Misha were thinking. Would they follow her or let her leave? Whatever they were thinking, one thing had come to light in the past twenty-four hours: their village and home was no longer a safe haven. As Zira sped for the Dalesian Woods, she could only hope that there was some place in this world still free from such corruption.

*   *   *

Neph stared at his soup with great intensity. Not that he was really focusing on the soup albeit, but anyone who wasn't aware of recent events may have thought so. Neph, instead, was counting everything that had gone wrong in his life in the past four months. It was becoming a disturbingly large list. Paul died, Myla went crazy, and now to cap it off, Zira had gone missing three days ago. He couldn't help but feel a little bit abandoned.

Most of the people in the village had jumped to the conclusion that Zira was dead. It was just another notch in the list of strange losses for their people. Neph, however, didn't believe it. He didn't think she was dead nor a victim of some plot by Amos. He simply noted what everyone else chose to ignore:

236

that one of the horses had disappeared that night too. Zira had left (why he didn't know), but he sure didn't believe that she was dead. It wasn't how Amos liked to kill people, and no one else in this village had the guts to go through with it.

Neph scooped up a spoonful of soup only to let it splatter back down into his bowl. Abruptly, he put down the spoon and moved to stand up. He wasn't hungry. He didn't like thinking about the loss of Zira. It was sickening. He quickly walked toward the door of Eli's to only bump right into Nora. She looked at him vulnerably and then immediately switched to the "poor boy" look. As if she was one to talk. Zira was her daughter. Paul was her nephew, and they actually knew he was dead! Neph tried to keep walking, but Nora grabbed his arm and whispered to him: "Come with me." Neph looked around at first to make sure that she wasn't talking to anybody else, then proceeded to follow her out the door.

The sky was cloudy. It had been since Zira left. Neph couldn't remember the last time the clouds had just lingered in the sky without raining. For some time, Neph walked three paces behind Nora in silence, as she proceeded to make for the edges of the village. Soon enough they passed all the remaining houses and were at the edge of the forest. Neph sprinted up to Nora's side.

"What's going on?" he asked, as she finally stopped.

"Do you remember that year when my family was not in the village?" she asked turning toward him.

"Yeah, you got back around the time Myla arrived, and then the duo began," he answered with a smile.

"It became a trio over time," she returned.

"And for a while a quartet," he added with a smile.

"But only a short while," she returned sadly. "Neph, I'm talking to you because there are only two people in this world that Zira trusts, and neither of them are her parents."

237

"She trusts you," he insisted, not quite as confidently as he would have liked.

"No, we lost Zira the moment Myla entered her life," Nora answered.

"Well, I guess Myla isn't known for being the most trusting person," he confessed. "But what's your point?"

"Zira trusts you," she responded.

"Which is odd, don't you think?" he asked, trying to lighten the conversation.

Nora was striking him as a bit too sullen. She, however, didn't respond. Instead, she beckoned him to follow her into the woods. Neph questioned how sane this woman was briefly and then followed her again.

Eventually, they reached a brook that Neph wasn't quite sure he previously knew existed. Nora knelt down at the ground and beckoned Neph over. He looked down, and suddenly was able to spot a trail of hoof prints heading away from the village.

"I take it these belong to Libby," he said slowly.

"That's what I'm thinking," she answered.

"So she ran," Neph said. "Why?"

"That is what I am asking you to find out," she answered. "But I can tell you this: these prints head in the direction of the Dalesian woods."

"Which is where your family lived for the year before Myla arrived," Neph added. "Well, don't worry, Nora. You don't have to ask me to find out what happened to your daughter. I'd do that anyway."

"I know," she answered. "That's why I asked you."

*   *   *

238

"You're not going to find your answer in the book," Amos said, sounding very bored. "But then again, why believe me?"

His words fell on deaf ears. Myla hadn't spoke to him in three days and she sure wasn't planning to now. She didn't think he was responsible for Zira's disappearance. It didn't fit his pattern, but that wasn't why she was ignoring him. He was only a distraction from the answer to where his prisoners were. He only meant to deter her.

Three days ago, Myla didn't wait in her home for very long after her encounter with Amos. Once she regained her composure, she ran to the library and started scouring through the books. She found books on everything imaginable, yet nothing with the magic "here is where to find your kidnapped people" title. Instead, she found herself skimming through books upon books hoping to catch one little clue to their location. So far, her luck had been absent at best.

It didn't help that Amos was always there, watching her and examining her every move. Most of the time he was silent, yet every now and then he would offer up some discouraging advice. Yet he was not her friend. He didn't want to help her. Myla knew this and used every inch of her will to completely ignore him. Anger boiled in her as she sifted through page after page praying that the answer would be on the next one.

"Do you really think I would hide them in some place recorded in literature?" he asked, seeming amused at her plight.

Myla continued to stare at the book, trying to ignore his words, however logical they may have seemed. Why would he hide them in a known place? Wherever they were, it was somewhere far from any knowledge. It would be the only way to ensure that she would not find them. Unless, of course, the place was so well protected nobody could rescue them.

Myla started to flip through the pages at a hurried rate, until her eyes fell upon the words she wanted. She looked up at Amos. He stared back at her curiously.

"Nefarisis," she said smiling. Amos didn't react, but Myla didn't care. She closed the book and walked out of the library.

*   *   *

Zira woke up on the back of her horse still riding through the woods. She looked up at the stars. Libby had kept moving in the right direction. Zira hadn't realized how tired she was. She had barely slept in the past three days. It didn't feel like there was enough time to waste on sleep. Her horse was tired, but drew strength from the trees. Zira was not so successful in that endeavor. She brought Libby to a halt and then walked her over to a stream that she spotted a few yards over. Libby knelt down to drink, and Zira walked over and leaned against a tree.

It was lonely, out there in the woods. The only words she spoke were in encouragement to Libby, but her communication with the horse could only go so far. She couldn't help the fear growing in her stomach, that her effort would be a waste, and that she would return home to a village under Tarran rule. Her lack of presence wouldn't help the situation either, but she doubted it would be enough to make a difference. She alone could not save that village. She needed help. The Caldar needed to unite.

Zira pulled Libby towards her and mounted. They were in the Dalesian woods. They would arrive at the village within the hour. Now she feared what she would find.

*   *   *

It was starting to get really annoying how insane everyone was. Myla was nowhere to be found, and now Allasta was preaching to him some mindless nonsense about how immediately dismissing the Tarrans was a stupid thing to do. In Neph's opinion, she was being stupid, but it wouldn't have been the first time.

"You really think we should consider this?" he asked in partial disbelief, though it was hard to be too surprised by anything these days.

"Well, why not?" she asked. "Four people are dead now, Neph…"

"Three," he interrupted. "Three people are dead. Zira must have ran, and she wouldn't have without good cause."

"Don't be silly, Neph," Allasta said, trying to talk down to him. "What would she have been running from?"

"That's what I have been trying to figure out," he answered.

"Well, even if she ran, it was probably from the same thing that killed the other three so my point remains the same," she responded. "We need to start considering what is best for everybody, and maybe the Tarrans have a good point."

"You're insane," he answered stunned. "You have all gone insane."

Neph couldn't wait around for a response. Instead he walked out the door and made his way over to Malachi's. Not that he had any faith in Malachi, but at least the old man acknowledged there was a problem, even if inaction was his preferable solution.

As he walked past the town hall, he noticed how packed it was again. Misha must have been making some sort of speech. There wasn't even a pretense that Dansten was in charge anymore. Somehow this creepy old man was winning the people over without his little puppet. It was unbelievable.

241

Malachi was sitting on his front porch staring at the trees. A rather boring pastime, but Neph still couldn't help but feel like he was interrupting him. Perhaps it was Malachi's lack of reaction to his presence that gave him that impression.

"Um, sir…" he said awkwardly.

Malachi looked over to him.

"I just thought I'd let you know that Allasta has gone insane," he said bluntly. "This entire village is turning toward the Tarrans. Allasta seems to think that Zira's disappearance is a good enough reason."

"How curious that it is the disappearance of Zira that Allasta carries so deeply," noted Malachi.

Neph hadn't really thought of the connection.

"She must be scared that she is next," answered Neph.

"Allasta has been known to display her fear quite visibly," Malachi responded, standing up and walking inside his house.

What was this? Some dramatic exit in order to make Neph think for himself? He really wasn't in the mood, so he proceeded to open the door and walk in after Malachi. The old man turned around and looked at him.

"I believe this could be considered trespassing," he said calmly.

"I don't really think we're done yet," answered Neph, more annoyed than anything.

"Oh?" he asked, appearing surprised.

"Okay, I am through with all the mysteries and secrets and stuff. It's fine when you're messing around with Myla, but don't pull that stuff with me. I'm not a mystery solver, and I'm not going to learn a lesson, so you might as well do something extremely unusual and tell me what you're thinking."

242

"Neph, do you remember from your lessons what the two rules are for a Caldar that must go into hiding?" Malachi asked.

Neph searched his brain, wishing he had paid better attention in classes.

"Never leave a trail for your enemies to follow..." he answered, unsure of himself.

"And?" Neph searched his brain.

"Always leave a trail for a friend to," he answered suddenly remembering. Why hadn't he thought of this before?

"No Caldar would leave a note that anyone could read," Malachi explained. "We leave our notes for specific people and only they can read them. Neph, I assure you that I am not that specific person, nor are her parents."

"Myla..." Neph pointed out.

"Zira stopped relying on her some time ago, and not without good reason."

Neph suddenly felt very stupid. If Zira had left him some sort of note, then why hadn't he found it? Why hadn't he realized that she would have? And where was it?

Then something dawned on him.

"Wait a second..." Neph said cautiously. "What does this all have to do with Allasta?"

"That I am not entirely sure, but I would find that a person's nemesis always finds a way to be involved somehow."

"Allasta and Zira didn't like each other, but I wouldn't qualify them as nemeses," Neph argued. "They competed; that's all."

"And who was winning the competition?" Malachi asked. "Perhaps the loser has found the upper hand."

"What's your basis for this?"

"Allasta's never once involved herself in the Tarran issue since the morning after the first day. She completely ignores everything."

"So?" Neph asked, skeptical. "She's never been much into politics."

"But she has always wanted to be involved. She was one of the first to meet them. This is rightfully her issue."

Neph didn't like what Malachi was telling him. Allasta was his friend, and he couldn't possibly believe that she was capable of doing something to Zira, let alone supporting these Tarrans. Yet this is what the week had done. It had created a divider among their people. No longer were they a unified community. Neph wondered how long it would take them to recover.

How swiftly had the Tarrans shaken their village to the point of near collapse! Every day a new person arrived at the town hall curious as to what everyone was talking about. And with each day more and more people seemed to mention how much they liked Misha's words and dreams. They had been given a new cause, a mission separate from the tired goal of waiting for Caldaria, and they readily accepted it. And now, Malachi was forcing Neph to question those closest to him, a task that he had no desire to take on.

*   *   *

At first, Zira was excited to spot the outskirts of the village, but her excitement quickly turned to despair as she came a little closer. The buildings had been burned, and it was some time ago. All that was left was a few partial houses and some stripped trees. Tears rushed down her face as she feared for their lives. She brought Libby into a gallop and raced for the edge.

She slowed as she reached the village. The devastation was incredible. Just the frames of most of the houses remained and rubble was spread throughout the streets, yet there was no sign of life.

Nothing changed as Zira reached the center of the village. It had been completely abandoned. No one was here anymore. Zira had known this Tarran government was misguided, but she had no idea they were capable of such destruction. Up until this point, she had assumed that they had good intentions, but if they were responsible for this, who knew what evil they had let into their homes? As she stared at these scorched buildings, Zira felt herself shrinking in fear. The future that she had expected would not be. She would not grow old in her safe happy village. Instead, destruction and devastation lay before her. The Dalesian village was a signal of her own future.

"Hello!" she yelled to the empty village. Her words were only absorbed by the trees. Further in she walked, calling out as she went, hoping for some sort of answer. Unfortunately, only silence echoed back to her.

Then she saw a shadow dart behind a tree. Zira didn't even hesitate as she ran after it into the woods.

"Stop!" she yelled. "I just want to talk to you!"

For quite a distance, Zira followed, unsure of whether or not this was a good idea. She could be wandering into a trap, but she didn't know for sure.

"Please stop – I'm a Caldar here to help!"

She could feel the presence halt. Whoever it was, was terrified, but good. Zira walked a few steps forward and then collapsed on the ground in shock.

Kalina was sitting there, shivering as she stared back at Zira.

*   *   *

Neph walked swiftly back to Allasta's house. He didn't want to confront her, but he felt that he had no choice. If Allasta had done something wrong, he thought it was better he found out versus someone else. At least he could try to steer her in the right direction before someone went crazy on her.

There were no lights in her windows and no sound from inside. He ran up to her door and started banging it with his fist. No response.

"Allasta, if you're in there, can you open up?" he shouted.

She clearly wasn't there. Neph stepped back and stared at her door lost in thought. As the moonlight filtered down through the trees, he noticed something glimmer on her door... something that wasn't originally in the wood. Could it be his note? He lifted his hand and let a warm yellow light shine on her door. A diamond shaped symbol appeared, with a circle fit inside. A *verradere* – traitor. That was his message from Zira. Allasta had betrayed them. Neph froze in disbelief.

"Apparently some don't leave quietly," said a voice behind him.

Neph turned around and faced Allasta.

"I take it then that this speaks the truth about you," he said softly.

"Neph, I'm not a traitor," Allasta said with a fake smile that made him shudder. "Zira and I just have different opinions on what is best for the village."

"So what?" Neph asked angrily. "You threw her out? Did you hurt her?"

"We didn't throw her out of the village. She escaped and left on her own accord," Allasta answered, her voice full of spite. "If she so valued this village as you seem to think, wouldn't she have stayed and said something?"

246

"Not if she feared her life," he answered. "Maybe she thought she could get help."

Allasta walked up to Neph and stared him straight in the face.

"I've got some bad news for you, there is no one left to help your cause," she answered coldly. "Every Caldar village has already submitted to our new government."

Neph wanted to be sick.

"And let me guess, they are so much better for it."

"Of course."

"How could you do this, Allasta?" he asked, still in disbelief.

"Do what?" she asked. "The intelligent thing? Neph, face the facts. You have already lost."

"I have more faith in our village than that," he answered confidently.

"Really?" she asked. "Our entire village is at the town hall right now voting in our new government."

"What?" Neph asked stunned. "And why didn't I hear about this?"

"We couldn't have any uprisings," she answered. "The detractors will be asked to exit the village by sunrise."

"What?" he asked. "That's half the village!"

"Actually it's roughly under fifty," Allasta corrected.

Neph stepped back. The village consisted of six hundred people. Was it at all possible that so many of them had voted this government through?

"Sunrise, huh?" Neph asked, trying to hide his shock. "And how do you plan on making us leave? The strongest Caldar are all in the group of detractors."

"That I concede," she answered. "But right now more than two thousand soldiers are marching on our village's

247

borders, supporters of the new Tarran government, Tarran and Caldar alike. Can fifty really challenge that?"

"Mel can," he answered, not sure why he was even bothering.

"Neph, you fool," Allasta said shaking her head. "Misha may be even more powerful than her."

"Allasta, what have you done?" he asked, losing hope.

"Inserted myself into the top of the new Tarran government," she answered simply, walking past him toward her door. "Your followers will be informed of their departure shortly. I suggest you gather them and leave."

Allasta proceeded to walk inside, shutting the door behind her. Neph didn't know how to react. Who was left that he could trust? He didn't even know anymore, but he immediately ran toward the town hall to hear the verdict.

*   *   *

Nefarisis: the prison of the forgotten. Long ago when Amos and Sherah set on their quests for power, it was where they placed their captives. It was the one cell that no one knew how to break into or out of. Many myths circulated through old literature about people approaching its gates and not returning until years later, when only a day had passed to them. No one understood its power.

Myla didn't think Amos' three hostages were in Nefarisis, however. She had no idea where that prison was, and as far as she knew, Amos didn't even know how to let someone out of the prison. He only knew how to put them in. But no one entered Nefarisis through the front door. She knew that. According to the myth, prisoners were placed into Nefarisis from a secret location far away from everything. It was that location where Myla expected to find her people, in a cave she saw in a dream.

She entered her house in a fury and immediately started putting together a bag of food and supplies. She could feel Amos' watchful eyes, but he did not make himself visible. She feared what he would do to stop her. How to rescue them safely was beyond her knowledge, but she knew she had to try.

Myla finished packing her bag and started walking to the door when she heard a knock on the other side of it. It was Neph. He didn't even say 'hello' as she opened it. He just plowed inside.

"We lost, Mel," he said, sounding very upset.

"Lost what?" she asked, confused and a little bothered at his timing.

"Everything," he said hopelessly. "The Tarrans... they won."

"That's impossible," she said bluntly.

"Our stupid village just passed a referendum moving us under their government ten minutes ago!" he answered, unable to hide his frustration.

"What?" Myla asked, completely bewildered.

"And you haven't even heard the best part!" he continued. "All the detractors – which number fewer than fifty – must be out of the village by sunrise!"

"*What?*" she asked, even more stunned. "How are they going to enforce that?"

"Two thousand Tarrans and Caldar are marching on our village as we speak," he answered, his voice dropping to a more hopeless sound.

Myla stared at him, unsure of how to answer.

"And there's more Myla," Neph continued. "Misha... he's a Caldar, and according to Allasta, a powerful one."

"That's insane. He's an innkeeper!" she answered confused.

"An innkeeper that got past the trees and conquered our village," he answered.

Suddenly, Myla felt very stupid that the idea had never dawned on her before.

"How would Allasta know this?" Myla asked, feeling herself start to shake.

"Because she's been working with them," he answered sadly. "She's the reason Zira left. Zira was escaping from her, from them."

Myla sat down in a chair and hung her head in her hands.

"I don't have time for this," she said quietly. "I have to leave."

"What?" Neph asked surprised. "Myla, I need your help. We have to be out of this village before the sun comes up."

"Then you'll have to lead them, Neph," Myla said looking up at him. "Out of the people in this village, you're probably the one they trust the most right now anyway."

"And why can't you help?" he asked, looking very upset.

"I'm too close to finding them, Neph, to bringing them back," she said, pleading with him.

"Too close to finding who?" Neph asked, confused.

"Paul, my mother, Kalina..." her voice trailed off as she looked at Neph guiltily.

He looked back at her, suddenly very sad.

"Myla, they're dead..." he said softly.

"Maybe not!" she answered, realizing she looked ridiculous. "He says he has them alive. It's an old trick he used when he took over. I know there's a good chance they're gone, Neph, but I have to try."

"Amos said this?" Neph asked. "You've been talking to him?"

"I've had to. If they're alive, I have to rescue them," she explained. "This is my fault."

"No, it's not," he argued. "How many times have you talked to him?"

Myla got up and walked to the corner of the room, facing away from Neph.

"Too many times," she answered quietly.

"What's too many?" he asked, very suspicious.

"Every day since Paul died," she answered looking back at him with such guilt. She could feel his disappointment.

"Myla, no..." he said, shocked. "He's evil. He'll fill your head with lies and most likely already has."

"But they aren't here because of me..." she responded, starting to fight back tears. "Paul... my mother... gone because of me."

Neph walked over to her and hugged her. Then he looked at her straight in the face.

"Do you really want to do this?" he asked, gently.

"I have to, Neph. If they are alive, I can't leave them without help," she answered, much more confidently. "I know you can lead our people. You're a strong leader. You don't need me."

"Not as strong as you, but I'll do my best," he answered. "Just promise me that you'll come back to us when the day is done."

"Without a doubt, I promise," she answered, then she picked up her bag and walked out the door.

Chapter 15

Zira wasn't sure if she was still alive as the trembling child jumped up and hugged her. This child was dead. She had seen the body at the funeral. What kind of spectacular lie had been displayed before her eyes? Or perhaps this was a lie now?

The figure of someone else stepped into view in front of her. Zira looked up to see a young woman that she did not recognize. She let go of Kalina and brought her to her side as she stood up.

"Who are you?" she asked cautiously.

"I should ask you the same, but it appears that our friend knows you, so I shall give you the benefit of the doubt," the woman answered in a friendly voice. "My name is Nabeeha, and that is my village you just were in."

Zira searched her memory; she knew this woman. They knew each other as children.

"Well, then that is news I welcome because I am Zira," she answered. "We were friends long ago."

"Then still are," Nabeeha responded, smiling. "What brings you here? Was your village attacked as well?"

"Only by a herd of dishonest politicians, but I fear the worst," Zira explained.

"And you should because that's how it started with my village as well," Nabeeha answered. "They mean to destroy all Caldar. The few of us detractors left were driven out of the village by a great army. We later returned to find it destroyed."

"Do you know what happened to the rest of your people?" Zira asked.

"Only fifteen of us left before the army attacked," Nabeeha explained. "We hid in the woods for a week. That's

252

where we found Kalina. No one was left when we returned. We don't know what happened to the others, though we believe most of them joined the Tarrans."

Zira felt herself getting sick, but she was able to control herself. Fifteen people escaped! Of a village of five hundred! It was too devastating, and too much to comprehend.

Zira knelt down and stared at Kalina. The girl looked back at her with eyes that were not as naive as they once had been.

"How is it that you are alive?" she asked quietly.

"He let me go," the child answered.

"Who?"

"He didn't seem alive," Kalina said quietly.

It wasn't a detailed answer, but it was enough for Zira.

"Why would he let you go?" she asked.

"Paul and Malika went days without food or water until he did," she answered. "I didn't know where I was so I just started walking until Nabeeha found me."

"How could a hunger strike defeat Amos?" Zira asked, confused. "Did he really value their lives that much?"

"He didn't kill them," Nabeeha noted. "Who is this Amos?"

Zira felt herself starting to lie, until she remembered that there wasn't much of a point anymore. Their world was being destroyed anyway.

"He's the second sorcerer," she answered. "Still alive and ready to finish the job."

Nabeeha stepped back in disbelief.

"How do you know this?" she asked cautiously.

"Because my best friend is the one that's supposed to beat him," responded Zira, standing up and grabbing Kalina's hand.

253

"Talk about pressure," Nabeeha said, looking overwhelmed.

Zira laughed. It was good to find another ally, considering that lately she had been losing so many.

Zira had never felt so welcome as she did when she entered Nabeeha's camp. They were all clearly glad to find another person against the Tarrans and especially thankful to hear that there was still one village intact (though probably not for long). Zira was quick to notice that there were more than fifteen people at the camp; there were thirty-four to be exact. Apparently one of the men in their group, Abhinav, had ridden to the three other villages, but he only found nineteen Caldar that were still free. He was set to ride to Zira's village the next day.

"If your village is still intact, we may have a chance preventing this tragedy from occurring there as well," Abhinav said.

"If only you had come to us first," Zira answered. "My knowledge is three days old. My village may no longer exist."

"Then we should at least go bring the survivors here," concluded Nabeeha.

Zira looked around at the camp that was at the verge of falling apart. Blankets were hung on the branches of the trees attempting to create some sort of roof and the tree were too close together for comfort. There wasn't a convenient water source either.

"I think we should bring this camp to them," Zira argued. "My village contains the most powerful Caldar in history, with exception only to the two sorcerers. There are people in my village that will follow her anywhere, and she clearly is against this Tarran government. It may not be by much, but there will be more detractors than there are here."

"Is she the head of council in your village?" Abhinav asked.

"No, that would be Malachi, her grandfather," Zira answered. "And he is also equally against this movement."

"Really?" Nabeeha asked. "All of our councils readily accepted the new Tarran government despite our protests."

This surprised Zira. Then again, all of the other councils didn't know that Amos was back in the business while Malachi did. He probably swayed the council's opinion because of this.

"Why would your councils accept a Tarran government?" Zira asked surprised.

"All of our crops were destroyed," said Abhinav. "People will do anything to satisfy their hunger."

"Our crops were never touched," said Zira.

Why was that? Because the Tarrans knew about Amos. They knew he was killing people. They didn't have to destroy the crops because the people in her village were already afraid and doubting their government. It was the proof they needed. Amos was definitely behind this.

"Then why would your people give into this?" Nabeeha asked.

"Three of our people were found dead and they promised us safety," Zira answered. "Quite ironic when you consider that one of the dead people is sleeping next to that tree happily."

Nabeeha and Abhinav stared over at Kalina.

"Then this is the work of the second sorcerer," Nabeeha said slowly. "And we are all doomed."

"No," Zira comforted. "There is someone who can save us, and she is with my people as we speak."

"Then it is settled," Nabeeha answered. "We will go to them. Your people clearly have some sort of upper hand in this mess, and I think we all would like to share in that."

Abhinav nodded his head in agreement.

"We will leave tomorrow," he said.

255

*　　*　　*

Myla walked down the lonely path to the map room and Amos was with her every step of the way. He tried to dissuade her with magical trickery, but she refuted every attempt. For once, they were evenly matched. Somehow, over time she had caught up to him. Maybe it was her more practiced skills or simply her determination. Either way, she could feel his frustration. He couldn't stop her, yet could she stop him?

The door to the map room never felt so cold as she opened it. She could hear noise from the village behind her. Her home was collapsing, but she couldn't let it distract her. That was exactly what he wanted. Quickly she walked to the center of the room and stood on the small round platform. The walls and floors melted away around her, and suddenly she was flying above the trees of the forest. But Amos was there. She could see him, watching her. She flew high above the trees to where Caldaria was in sight. She recognized the clearing between the city and the forest. It was dark and dismal, the ground was black and a heavy mist settled on the plain. Myla, however, knew it from a dream where she once ran from a fountain. She could see where she escaped to a cave in the woods, and she could get there.

The map melted around her and she was back in the room. Amos stared at her coldly.

"If you go there, you'll never be able to take it back," he said, a warning in his eyes.

"Is that supposed to be some sort of threat?" she asked, holding back a small laugh. "Amos, I have no choice. You know that."

"That I do," he said, nodding his head.

256

Myla stared at him, amazed. There was a small part of him, however miniscule, that wasn't arguing with her. It was pleading with her. She wasn't about to listen to him nonetheless.

Through crowded roads, Myla ran. She could hear angry voices all around her, and others crying. A man plowed into her side pushing her over. He didn't even turn to see if she was okay. He just kept moving. The whole village was in a complete state of chaos. She couldn't let it distract her however. Instead, she ran for the stables and brought out a horse. She mounted and galloped for the forest. At the edge, she turned around and looked back for one final glance. A warm glow was coming from the village as a cloud of smoke circled into the sky. It was burning. The village was burning.

Please, Neph... take care of them.

*   *   *

Three families stood huddled in Eli's café. When the insanity began, they quickly found each other, but didn't really know what to do or where to go. Neph and Zechariah entered the café to find them frightened and confused.

"What's going on?" Eli asked, stepping forward in front of the others.

"The Tarrans have taken over the village," said Neph. "All who are against this decision have been asked to leave. If you are in this group, I ask that you join us. We may be forced to leave our home, but we don't have to stop being a united Caldar people."

They all looked between each other, in a silent decision.

"Of course, we are with you," said Eli, confidently.

The others nodded their heads in agreement.

"Good, then we all must gather everyone who is against this new government," Neph responded. "We have gathered outside in the old schoolyard. Malachi and others are already there waiting. Zechariah will lead you there, but be careful because the village has lost all reason. I think this building burning is only going to lead to more fatal actions."

Zechariah quietly led the people out Eli's café. Many of the children clung to their parents in fear, but they all were silent as they moved. Neph didn't join them. There was still someone that he wasn't quite sure that he could give up on.

She sat on her porch staring at the destruction in front of her. As Neph approached, she turned and gave him a sly smile. He hesitated and then kept moving forward. Allasta had been one of his closest friends since they were both orphaned as children. He couldn't give up on her.

"You know I thought you were more intelligent than this," she said, forcing a laugh.

"Wisdom has never been one of my strong points," he answered, pausing on her porch steps.

Allasta leaned back and looked up at him. Then she brought herself to her feet and looked straight at him.

"This isn't something you can win, Neph," she said, her voice suddenly displaying more sadness. "I'm not going to change my mind. This is where I belong."

"Allasta, they're criminals," he pleaded with her.

"They are cleansing us from the past, from our hypocritical ways," she argued.

"This is death and destruction, not cleanliness!"

He was now choking back tears, and he could tell that she was as well.

"Why won't you leave?" she asked, showing more of her humanity than Neph had seen in a while. The burning village was affecting her.

"Why must you stay?" he responded.

258

"Because there's no place for me with you," she answered. "You chose them. You chose her. I don't fit."

Her emotions were getting the best of her now too. Neph stared at her helplessly. She leaned over and hugged him.

"Go with your people, Neph," she said quietly in his ear. "I promise I won't let them follow."

Neph looked behind Allasta and saw Misha standing at her doorstep. He then turned back to Allasta, not knowing exactly what to do, but knowing that he had lost his friend some time ago. Eventually, he found the energy in his feet to move, turned around and ran to his people, leaving Allasta to her chosen fate.

*　　*　　*

Forty-seven people stood in the schoolyard, gathering their bags. Some debated an appropriate destination, others just stood around waiting for the final decision. Many waited for Malachi to say it was time to go, but the majority waited for Neph's return.

Malachi knew that Neph had become his people's chosen leader in this time of crisis. It wasn't because of his wisdom, or past record, but only for his connection to Myla. They would follow him because he followed her. Myla, Neph and Zira were their new elders, and Malachi realized as they prepared to embark on a new way of life, that his role in that society would be well diminished. It didn't bother him, though, for it was a fate he had long expected.

Neph ran through the trees and into the sight of the Caldar. Immediately they all stood up and lifted their bags. They were ready to go, to follow him. To follow Myla. They didn't have to ask to know that she would meet up with them in the future. They knew they were on her side. That was where they felt safe, comfortable.

Neph walked up to Malachi and Zechariah, who both nodded their heads in acknowledgement.

"What way?" Zechariah asked.

"North... toward the other villages," Neph suggested.

"You don't think they are still intact, do you?" Zechariah questioned skeptically.

"No, I don't, but they don't need to be," he responded.

"If there are any other detractors to this movement, we need to find them," explained Malachi. "I believe Neph's suggestion is a strong one. We can set up camp halfway between here and the Dalesian woods."

"Agreed," said Neph. "After we are settled, we can set out scouts to search for other survivors."

"Okay," Zechariah consented. "What about Myla?"

"She'll have to find us," said Neph with a sigh. "I wouldn't worry too much though. That girl could track an ant."

The other two men both laughed and then started to gather all the people. After much confusion, they were able to gain some sort of organization, and Neph led them into the woods with Zechariah in the middle and Malachi bringing up the rear. Silence fell over the crowd as they left their home. Many of them were carrying sleeping children and were exhausted themselves. A general wave of sadness fell over the Caldar as they realized that they were leaving everything they knew. Once again the Caldar would be nomads without a home. Nothing about it felt normal. Nothing about it felt right, but as they felt their village burning behind them, they could only hope for a safer future.

*   *   *

As Myla raced through the forest, the trees moved out of her way. Instead of dodging around them, she sped down one straight path. She knew he was with her. He wasn't as limited by physical constraints as she was, but she felt that the faster she moved, the less he could prepare for her. She could not lose this battle now.

Myla...

His words meant nothing to her. She brushed it off as if it never was. She kept moving, her heart beating faster and faster. She could feel them now. She was getting closer. They were still far off, but she knew where she was going. Perhaps it was the speed at which she was moving, or simply pent up rage at Amos, but she had never felt so powerful as she did right then.

Myla...

She thought back to the first time that she heard his voice in her head, that day on the woods. She would not be so easily swayed now. Nothing could pull her from her path. She would not give up now.

Eventually her horse grew tired, so she dismounted it at a stream and tied its reins loosely to a tree. She didn't want it to be impossible for the horse to escape, in case she didn't come back. She would make the rest of the trek on foot. She was close now anyway.

As she ran through the forest, she did not get tired. Instead she felt herself gain energy. The trees were feeding into her. Instead of being surrounded by death as in her dream, she was surrounded by life, but she recognized it all. She was there. The place in her mind was real. She could see the cave just ahead, and she could feel them inside, still alive.

Myla sprinted toward the cave and then slowed to a walk. A ghostly chill came from it as she stood in its entrance. Suddenly, every nerve in her body wanted to turn around, but she wouldn't. Instead, she stepped forward and into the cave. A

261

dark narrow tunnel lay before her. Myla could see no end, or a sign of light. The ground was damp and the air was thick, as if it was pushing her back outside, but it did not sway her. She kept walking. She could feel them, closer than ever.

Myla...

The voice was stronger and not just in her head. It echoed down the cave walls sending chills down her spine. Shaking, she continued to place one foot in front of the other. Eventually she saw light and an end to this tunnel. She picked up her pace and moved toward it. Gradually, it got bigger, and soon enough, she found herself standing in a room, gasping at what she saw before her.

A silver flame centered above a pedestal on the opposite end of the room. Dangling from chains above it lay the very conscious Paul and Malika. She started to run toward them but between them appeared a table, which she immediately bumped into. She looked forward. In front of the flame and between the two prisoners, Amos had appeared, staring at her.

"So here we are then," he said coldly. "Enemies once again."

"I don't recall us ever being anything else," she responded, to which Amos just smiled in return.

Myla quickly started to circle around the table, but Amos quickly spoke up.

"If you come any closer, they will fall into the flame of Nefarisis," he stated. "From there, you will not be able to rescue them."

"How very convenient for you," said Myla, disgusted. She looked around the room for some unexplored means to rescue them, but her mind was dry of ideas.

"Perhaps I could offer you a bargain," Amos said.

On the table, a goblet of water appeared. She stared at it with a new worry.

"Water from the fountain," he said practically. "Drink, and your people walk free."

Myla stared at the cup in disgust. So this was always going to be it. She could not stop him here, and she could not rescue them. This is why he kept them alive – not to know more about her, but to win her, and she had played perfectly into his hands.

"So this was your plan from the beginning, wasn't it?" she asked.

"Everyone does what they have to do," Amos answered, sounding very practical.

"Then why bother waiting all these months?" She asked angrily. "Why didn't you set this up before?"

"It's not my fault that it took you so long to figure out where they were," he answered. "Anyway, now you don't just care about them, you also care about me."

Myla felt sick to her stomach.

"I'll never care about you," she said with fury growing inside of her.

"You do, and you will more soon," he answered with a smile.

"And you really think that this water could make a difference?" she asked. Even while drugged, I'd believe the same thing. I, unlike you, wouldn't let some spell change me like that."

Amos, walked toward the table and leaned in toward her.

"Then why don't you show me?" he asked quietly.

"Don't do it, Mel," shouted Paul from his restraints.

Myla looked at him. His voice counteracted his words. He was alive. How could she end that? Her society was ended anyway; what harm could it possibly do? She felt her arm reach for the cup in front of her, yet her other hand was throbbing. Slowly, she touched the glass and lifted the goblet into the air.

"Myla, don't! We aren't worth this!" shouted Malika.

Her words were meaningless, however, for as Myla stared at Amos, she knew exactly what she had to do. She lifted the cup to her lips and watched her hand start to turn gray, lifeless in front of her. Even through the glass, whatever water this was, it was powerful. If she drank, it would be over, but what harm would she be capable of then? She looked up at Paul and Malika. Their faces were pleading with her. Then she looked at Amos, into his cold dark eyes. She could not become him. She placed the cup back down on the table.

"Interesting choice," Amos answered. He then waved his hand and Malika dropped into the fire, disappearing from the room.

Myla felt her heart hit her stomach, and she couldn't control the pain. How could she come so far, just to lose her again? She had never had the chance to know her mother for who she was. For a moment, she had hope that she would get another opportunity, and he just threw it away. She felt her knees bend as she held onto the table for support. The pain, the devastation, it was too much for her.

"You bastard," she whispered, her anger over-boiling. She felt her hands, her feet, her heart all pounding. There was too much magic pulsing through her. She couldn't control it.

She threw the cup against the wall and pointed her hand toward Amos. A blinding blue light came pouring out of her hand onto him. Immediately, Amos shot back with a blue light of his own, and Myla fell backwards in shock. She didn't know what this blue light was within her, but it was a gift he shared as well. She should have known. He was so strong. What did she have to defeat him?

"Oh, Myla, you are still so very young," said Amos, with his voice seething. "I could have taught you so much, but instead, you've chosen to let your life end so early. Such a loss of potential."

For a moment, she contemplated giving up. His power was too great, and she couldn't overcome it. Painfully, she held up her hand and let the blue light spiral out of her hand. It danced with the light from Amos's hand in between them, but neither of them were able to reach the other. At first, she couldn't quite comprehend what was happening. She wasn't defeating him, but somehow, she was matching him. He wasn't able to defeat her, and she realized that at this point, he was actually trying to. He was trying to kill her, for the first time ever, and he couldn't. This was the prophecy. It was true. She was his equal.

And she was stuck. She was locked into a battle that she couldn't win. They were perfectly matched. Nothing set them apart from each other. She could tell Amos was surprised by the development, but he didn't lose his focus.

"What do you hope to accomplish here, Myla?" he asked. "Just what is it that you think you are going to do?"

She didn't answer him. Instead, she thought about Paul, hanging there helplessly, and then she thought about Malika, lost to Nefarisis. Her devastation consumed her, but instead of it weakening her, she found strength in it. This was what set her apart from Amos: her anger was too great. Her emotion was too strong, and he couldn't stop her.

She looked into his eyes and saw the acknowledgement in them. He had waited too long. She was more powerful. For once, she was more powerful. He collapsed in pain. A thick black liquid seeped out of his pores, and soon he began to change colors and fade in and out of visibility. After what seemed to be an eternity, his body relaxed and whatever form of life that was in him left. Then suddenly an explosion of black smoke and fire in his place threw Myla back against the wall.

After the dust settled and Myla came to her senses, she jumped to her feet and ran to where Paul was dangling. She looked up at him and he smiled down at her. Without the magic of Amos holding him, it was relatively easy to free him from his chains. For several seconds, the two of them just stood there, a little overwhelmed at what had just occurred. Then Myla threw herself into his arms.

"I never thought I'd see you again," she whispered.

"And I never doubted you would," he said.

However, the joy of finding each other was masked by the devastation of losing Malika. Both Myla and Paul looked into the flame, unsure of what to say or how to react. Nefarisis. The place from which there was no escape. Was it hopeless?

Eventually, Myla looked toward the corner where Amos had been. She was expecting an empty corner, but instead she was stunned to see that he was still there, or at least someone was. A young man, probably no more than twenty, lay there on his back on the ground. His skin had a warm color, not the old pasty look of Amos. He resembled him, but it was not the Amos that Myla knew. Myla could feel this man's presence, and it was pure.

"Okay, I'm kind of confused right now," said Paul, clearly not knowing how to react. "What did you do?"

Myla looked at the wall where she threw the glass. The same black liquid that seeped out of Amos' skin was splattered on the wall where the water hit. She looked back at Paul. Of course, it was what she had been intending to do the entire time.

"He is no longer under the influence of the fountain," she said simply.

"So you freed him from a thousand year old curse," said Paul. "That was some crazy magic you just did there. Myla, you were glowing."

Myla didn't really listen to him. She walked to where Amos lay and knelt down by his side. She rested her hand on his head.

"He's alive," she said, unsure of what to do.

266

Paul walked over to where she was and began to examine him.

"He's definitely alive and will wake up at some point," he said. "So do we just leave him and run?"

"No, we may need him," she said strongly. "My mother is in Nefarisis right now, and I plan on doing something about it."

"Do you think it's possible to save someone from there?" Paul asked.

"Probably not, but I thought it was impossible to find you as well," she answered, before suddenly pausing. "Where's Kalina?"

"Amos let her go a few weeks ago after Malika and I stopped eating or drinking," Paul explained. "I guess he wanted us alive."

"To trap me," Myla concluded. "Do you know where she went?"

"Myla, I don't know where we are," Paul said sadly. "I was hoping she found her way back to the village, but I'm guessing that didn't happen."

"Well, there isn't even a village to find anymore," Myla answered depressingly. "But that's something I'll explain on the way back. First, let's see if we can carry this guy."

"Are you sure this is a good idea?" Paul asked. "What if he wakes up?"

"Then he better behave himself," she said grabbing Amos' arm. Paul looked at her amazed.

"Clearly you're not deathly terrified of him anymore," he said smiling.

"Winning does that to a person."

Myla and Paul carried the unconscious Amos between them. It was a slow walk out of the cave and back to Myla's horse. The entire time, Myla filled in Paul with news about the village and the truth about Misha. She was pleased to hear that Paul had never guessed Misha's secret either.

"Misha was definitely always a creepy guy, but he struck me as a clueless weird, not political madman weird," he said trying to comprehend it. "I always knew Dansten was a pushover though."

Myla looked back at Paul. She couldn't believe it. He was alive and talking to her. His eyes were sad, his face a little more worn, but he was still Paul. She couldn't imagine what he had gone through in the past four months, yet somehow he was there, and okay. It was astonishing.

Yet there was someone they were carrying, someone Myla hoped for a brief second that she would never have to see again. And now, he was no longer under the influence of the fountain. Was he good? Was he evil? Was he even the same person that she knew? She didn't know if he would wake up as they dragged him toward their horse and then lifted him onto it. Perhaps they were saving the one man in the world that deserved death the most. Perhaps they were saving an innocent victim of a crippling spell.

And Malika was gone, locked in a prison outside of time where no one could find her. Would she ever be saved?

As they left the cave in the direction Myla hoped she would find the others, she wondered what she was heading to, and what she was bringing with her. However, as she looked toward Paul, she couldn't help but feel a small part of happiness.

Chapter 16

Amos sat shivering in the cold damp cave. He didn't dare move for fear that Sherah would return, or notice him leaving. He ran his hands through the dirt next to him. This ground was lifeless, abandoned. The comforting warm fire that once lured him inside was now a small silver flame, which instead of releasing heat, seemed to steal it away. Amos leaned his head back against the rocky wall. Slowly his eyes began to close but his dreams were far from comforting.

Screams. Terror. It shook him awake. He saw people crying at loved ones lost. They were in pain, suffering for things far from their own control. He wanted to reach out and help them, but he couldn't. There was a wall between them that was separating them from each other.

Amos opened his eyes and looked at his hands. He couldn't tell if it was the lighting in the cave, or reality, but his hands were pure white. He clenched them together and wondered if he was still alive.

He heard footsteps from the opposite end of the tunnel. Someone was coming. It was him. Amos knew it. Sherah was here. He walked into the room and looked at Amos, who recoiled in fear. Sherah's hair and skin were white, and his eyes were almost hollow. Amos couldn't decide if he was looking a skeleton or a man, but he stood up in obedience. He quietly followed the emaciated man out of the cave.

At the entrance of the cave, Amos stood in shock. Hundreds of people stood there, staring back at him. Slowly every one of them of knelt to their knees with their faces to the ground. Amos looked back to Sherah amazed.

"Who are they?" he asked, overwhelmed by what he saw.

269

"Tarrans," Sherah answered quietly. "Most abandoned by their Caldar parents. They are here to serve you. They are your people."

"Why me?" asked Amos, unsure of how to react.

"Because you will lead them to greatness," Sherah responded. "To a society composed not of one kind of person, but of everyone. To a place where someone is not discriminated against because they can't light a fire with the snap of their fingers."

"What was in that water I drank?" Amos asked, kneeling down, overwhelmed.

"Knowledge, wisdom, perspective," Sherah answered. "I gave you the ability to look past the crippling limitations of the Caldar mind."

Amos looked out at the many faces. They were filled with hope, almost excitement, and trust. They believed he could save them.

"I am not worthy of this responsibility," he said softly.

"You are the only who is," Sherah answered. "Now speak to them and lead them. They will listen."

Sherah was correct in his assessment of the people. They followed Amos with full loyalty, and they followed him well. Amos had no idea how Sherah expected him to conquer the Caldar world with a few hundred Tarrans, but he worked with them nonetheless. Sherah watched on, as if he was always ten steps ahead of Amos and just letting him lead them to boost his confidence.

As the days went by, Amos' confidence did grow, as did their numbers. More and more Tarrans wandered into the forest to find them, in hope of creating an equal world where they could live in acceptance.

Still, Amos didn't know how to conquer the Caldar, or at least that was the case until one random day when he was walking through the forest. Tired from many hours of hard work, he leaned against a tree. However, the trunk that he thought had been strong sank in. Amos jumped up and looked at the hole his back had created. Termites had eaten through the insides of the tree to the point that it just a hollow shell. Amos immediately made the connection in his mind. This was his Caldaria.

It wasn't uncommon for Tarrans to be servants in Caldaria. In fact, every servant in Caldaria was a Tarran, so when Amos' army began applying for jobs, they were readily accepted. Quickly, they were able to spread the word of their movement throughout the city's servants. This was how Amos had access to every room in the city.

Of course, he never came near those walls himself. His face was too likely to be recognized. This didn't matter, however. He would enter when the time came, only he would enter as their ruler.

The death of Caldaria's king and his family was an unfortunate sacrifice. It happened in the middle of the night, where the only ones that heard were servants in the palace, and that was far from a concern. The council was also kidnapped that night and banished into Nefarisis. Many of the most powerful Caldar put up a fight, but Amos was easily able to squander them. Thousands upon thousands of Tarrans sacked every small surrounding village and then stormed into the city, killing anyone that got in their way. That evening Amos took the throne, having conquered the city in a day.

At first, the Tarrans tried to live with the Caldarians peacefully, as long as none of them used their powers. However, the Caldar were not used to living without their gifts. Soon hundreds were banished to Nefarisis as a punishment. Amos was quickly fed up with the Caldar interfering with his rule, so he exiled the rest to the forest. Many resisted and many died, and the few who were left hid in the forest, ashamed and in despair. Amos did not rest with that, though. He ransacked every city and village in the known world, including his own, killing every Caldar that still lived inside.

Finally, Amos' mission was complete. True equality had been achieved. The Caldar would experience the life the Tarrans had led, and the Tarrans would rule the world. He would rule for thousands of years. Sherah was pleased.

Chapter 17

Neph stared at the ground impatiently. Malachi and Zechariah wouldn't stop arguing about the place that they had chosen to reside. Neph thought it was perfect. It was a small clearing right off of a river. There were enough trees for them to find shelter, yet enough space for them to move. The water was fresh, and it was far enough from the Tarrans for them not be a concern.

Malachi, however, wanted to go further away towards the other border of the forest, away from the Tarrans and closer to Caldaria. Zechariah thought that idea was foolish and that they should stay where they were. Neph didn't entirely agree. He would have described the idea as insane. Luckily the people seemed content with their current resting spot so the argument eventually subsided.

Everyone was exhausted. They quickly threw together tents and went to bed even though it was afternoon. A few chose to stay awake and keep watch. Neph was happy to be one of them. He quietly walked around the camp looking out into the woods, hoping to maybe spot one of his friends, finally returning to them. He worried that Zira and Myla wouldn't be able to find them, if they were so lucky as to still be alive. He feared that Zira had been captured by the Tarrans in a neighboring village, and he couldn't even fathom what Myla's encounter with Amos had been like.

Eventually, he sat down on a log facing to the river.

"It's amazing how different the forest can seem from a new location," said a voice. Nora sat down next to him.

"The river makes a lot of the difference," he answered, not looking over.

"So do the people you're with," she added. "Why do you think we lost?"

"We were privileged," he answered, unsure of what to make of his response.

"No, not really," she answered. "Look at the people here. Eli was never a gifted Caldar, but he joined us without question. Yet there are members of the council that surprisingly aren't among us."

"So, why did we lose?" he asked, realizing for the first time that Anala and Ratel were not among their numbers.

"Because the majority of people strive to be normal, while we have always strived to be different," she answered.

"Myla never wanted to be anything but normal," he pointed out.

Nora smiled.

"And then there are those of us who could never be anything but different," she answered, pointing to behind him.

Neph turned around to see Myla and Paul walking toward him. In between them was a horse carrying a man he had never seen before. He feared who it might be, but he didn't care. He jumped to his feet and ran to greet his friends.

*   *   *

Myla knew when Amos had woken up. In fact, she could feel him immediately. His presence was overwhelming. Quickly, she stretched out her hand and surrounded him in a globe of light. He stood up and stared at her, but it was different. He had changed. The man that stood there was not the evil one she had once known. She could tell that almost immediately, but she did not trust him.

Paul had been in the process of telling a group of Caldar about how Myla had saved him. Once Myla imprisoned Amos

274

though, no one was focusing on Paul. One child screamed as she saw him standing there, but everyone else just stared. This was him: the sorcerer of legend, the man who conquered the world; and he was trapped under the power of Myla. She completely controlled him. It was a shocking realization for many of them.

"Hello, Myla," he said softly, sounding weak in his words.

"I see your memory isn't damaged," she answered coldly.

"Myla, I am so sorry."

His voice sounded genuinely sad, but Myla didn't let it get to her.

"Save your apologies," she said unsympathetically. "With so many to make, you will never have time to reach us all."

Quickly, she motioned to the others. All of them gathered around Amos and used their joint powers to bind his hands and feet together and hold him to a tree. Once he was securely held, Malachi pulled Myla away from the rest of the group.

"Myla, he is not the man he used to be," he said quietly. "A presence has lifted from him. He is not the evil that once followed you around."

Myla shot Malachi a look of distrust. So he had known. He had been aware of her situation and never once mentioned that he too could feel Amos' presence.

"Malachi, I know he is different," she answered. "That spell has clearly been lifted. I can tell that just by looking at him. This man is actually human."

"Then why do we hold him captive?" he asked.

"Because I don't know how much of his actions were due to a spell or logical reasoning," she answered. "And I wouldn't dare let him go free without the consent of the people."

"Then I will have to take it up with them," he answered. Then he paused and looked at his granddaughter.

"Myla," he said softly. "I am very proud of you."

She looked back at him a little unsure of how to react. She never knew how to take compliments from the man.

"Malika and Kalina are still both lost," she answered. "I will take no credit until I find them."

*   *   *

That night was anything but restful. For hours, the adult Caldar debated what should be done with Amos, and they came to no resolution. Myla knew that if she offered any opinion, they would decide to go with her choice, but she didn't know what opinion to offer. She didn't know who this Amos was.

She wandered over to where he was sitting captive, and she sat down a good six feet away facing him. He looked at her, but did not speak.

"How much of a difference can a drink of water make?" she asked.

He didn't answer. Instead, he just stared at the ground, motionless. Myla could feel nothing but despair and horrendous guilt coming from him. After several minutes of just sitting there, he spoke, almost inaudibly.

"Kill me," he whispered.

Myla sat up straight and stared at him.

"What?" she asked.

"Kill me," he said barely louder, but looking at her straight in the face. "Why haven't you killed me?"

"It's not my style," she answered, a little disturbed.

"I don't want to live anymore," he insisted.

"Because of what you did or because you failed?" she asked, disgusted.

"Because of what I did, Myla," he answered, his voice stronger. "And because he won't stop haunting me, and I won't follow him anymore."

"Who?" she asked, both confused and scared by his words.

"Who do you think?" he asked. "Sherah. He's not dead, Myla. In fact, he's stronger than ever. Who did you think I was getting my orders from?"

"You," she answered practically, though his words terrified her. If Amos was always bowing to someone else, how powerful was Sherah?

"No, a drink of water can't make you turn evil with a plan," he answered. "What that water did was bind me to the will of another, and I could not disobey."

"So what now?" she asked.

"Kill me and free me from this pain," he pleaded with her.

"So that Sherah can do what?" she asked. "Haunt me? No, thanks."

"Please, Myla," he asked.

"If you knew me at all, you would know that there is no way that I am going to kill you," she said.

"And if you acknowledged anything at all, you would know that no one in this world deserves death more than I do," he argued.

"No, it sounds to me like Sherah does," she answered.

Myla didn't feel like talking with Amos anymore. She had done too much of that as it was. She looked to the rest of their group. Neph and Paul had been watching her for some time. She realized that neither she nor Amos had been speaking loudly. They interacted as if they knew each other, and they did.

277

There wasn't much doubt that Neph had informed Paul of Myla's interaction with Amos since his kidnapping. Myla couldn't regret it though. It was that interaction that saved Paul.

She stood up, walked over and sat down next to Paul. They both looked at her with a certain level of amazement, but neither said anything.

"Were you all able to make it out of the village okay?" she asked Neph, trying to change attention focus, though the village wasn't exactly a lighter subject matter.

"Yes, but I wasn't able to convince Allasta to change her mind," Neph answered. "She is very involved in this new Tarran government."

"If you can call it that. I have a feeling it's going to be more like a dictatorship," she answered.

"With Misha at the top," Neph finished, but Myla shook her head in disagreement.

"Misha is a pawn, in what sounds to me like a long line of them," she corrected.

"A pawn to whom?" asked Paul, confused.

"Sherah," answered Myla. "Apparently he's been pulling the strings the entire time."

"Did Amos tell you this?" Neph asked.

Myla nodded her head.

"He wants me to kill him," she said. "Begged me to."

"Are you going to give him his wish?" asked Paul.

"No, I believe that he feels genuinely regretful of his actions and could be of great use to us," she answered.

"Why do you think that?" Neph asked. "He could also be a great danger to us."

"Because he is still one of the most powerful Caldar in history, and he needs someone to take orders from," she answered. "I'm just volunteering to be that person."

278

"What makes you think he'll listen to you?" asked Paul. Neph nodded his head in agreement.

"Because I know him," Myla answered.

Myla knew it bothered Neph and Paul that she had been in communication with Amos for so long, but she wasn't about to let it get to her. It angered her that Amos was still alive, and that she still wasn't free of his presence, but it was different. She was in control. He was no longer the one pulling the strings. Their fight wasn't over at all. The village was taken and they were small in numbers. The world was under the leadership of Sherah, and Myla had no idea how powerful he was or how to find him. Until then, however, she would comfort herself in her much smaller victory. Amos was defeated, and Paul had been returned to them. That was a spectacular feeling.

*   *   *

Allasta stared at her village, or what was left of it. Only a few buildings were left standing, the rest in burned from the fire. Out of all of the Caldar who chose to join the Tarrans, only about fifteen were still in the village. The rest had departed for the Tarran villages. There they would start their lives over as giftless Tarrans, their magic only being a part of their memory.

Allasta would not be one of them, however. She had been chosen to join Misha's private council. There, she would use her gifts to prevent uprisings among the people and to punish those who strayed from the anti-magic laws. It was an amazing opportunity. Who would have thought that she, not Myla, Zira or Neph, would be the one to help rule the world? It was unbelievable.

Yet it still felt strange, leaving her village. She had purposely loitered around so that she would be in the last group to leave. It did make some sense to stay. Misha and Dansten were still there, so she wasn't disobeying anything. Still, the village had never seemed so lifeless. It wasn't just the lack of people. It was the trees. They had lost their color. No longer did the branches move out of her way when she was walking by. In fact, they didn't move at all, except in the wind. Something had been lost.

"Allasta, are you ready?" Markus asked.

She turned around and smiled at him.

"Yes, just about," she answered. "Markus, where do you think you will live now?"

He shrugged and looked back at her.

"I guess I figured I'd live in Mertana," he said after a pause. "I mean, with knowing Myla and Paul, they might be welcoming to us."

"Or accuse us for causing their demise," Allasta pointed out.

"Do you really think she's dead?" he asked softly.

"She wasn't among the group that left and no one's seen her," she said quietly.

She didn't want to seem too worried, but it did bother her some. Myla was crazy and all, but it didn't seem right for her to die. Then again, it didn't seem right for her to live life as a Tarran too. Maybe she was better off wherever she was, away from everything.

"Let's not let this distract us from the amazing future we have ahead of us," Allasta said to Markus.

Markus nodded his head in agreement, and then walked toward the market square, where everyone left was gathering in preparation to leave. Allasta lingered at her house for a few minutes longer. It was difficult saying goodbye, but it was time to go. She knelt down to pick up her stuff and looked ahead of her. Misha was walking toward her. He stopped and beckoned to her. She nodded her head, picked up her things, and followed him.

*   *   *

That baby would not stop crying. It was really beginning to annoy Zira. They had been traveling for almost two days now, but it seemed a lot longer because no one had been able to sleep. Zira understood that the baby was young, and probably hungry, but in reality, he was the only person there that wasn't going through the most traumatizing experience of his life. It seemed unfair that he was the only one that was allowed to cry and scream.

Zira suddenly stopped her horse. Had she really become this bitter and grumpy? What was wrong with her? It was probably the fear that she didn't have a village to return to and that all the people she cared about were lost. She tried to not think about it though. There were too many logical people in that village for them all to fall victim to the same disaster. They had to be okay. She just knew it.

Eventually, they stopped for water at a river. Everyone plopped down on the ground, too tired to really move. Zira could tell many of them wished they could just stay here. She wasn't about to give up, and she could tell that Nabeeha and Abhinav supported her in that decision. Wherever Myla was, she was sure that would be safer, despite the whole evil sorcerer situation.

"Zira, you should get some water," said Nabeeha to her. "You look exhausted. Even Kalina has mentioned how weak you look."

Zira managed a small laugh.

"I'm fine, just tired," she answered. "I'll be better once I am assured that friends and family are safe."

281

They had to be safe. She refused to believe otherwise. Nabeeha certainly didn't offer an objection. It was strange how these people looked at her. They saw in her a leader, yet she couldn't fathom what she had done to deserve such responsibility. In fact, she probably hadn't done anything. They were simply that desperate for someone to lead them.

Zira pulled herself up onto her feet and started to wander down the river. This water was a useful discovery. The trees were too thick where they were, but she wondered if there was a better spot further down to put up camp. As she walked along the river, the trees began to be less compacted. Eventually the river turned and she was able to see far down the riverbank. Then she saw it: tents and people. They were there.

Zira quickly turned around and bolted back to the others. Hurriedly, she convinced everyone to get on their feet and follow her. They readily did, and she led them quickly down the riverbank. Once they were able to see the others up ahead, excited whispers circulated throughout the group. They would no longer be alone. They had found their friends.

*   *   *

Zechariah didn't know what to think when he saw his daughter leading a group of over thirty people toward him. He was beginning to lose hope of seeing her again, yet there she was, leading more Caldar to them. Nora walked up next to him, but once she spotted Zira, she ran to her daughter and hugged to so hard that they both almost fell over. Zechariah laughed as he walked up to Zira and hugged her. Her brothers and sister also ran up to greet her. Then the twins started to squeal with glee as they spotted Kalina, a friend of both of them. Zechariah turned and stared at the child and then back at his daughter.

"So Myla brings home Paul and a former sorcerer, and you bring home Kalina and more than thirty other people," he said, in amazement.

"Myla did *what*?" she asked, but she didn't wait for an answer because Myla, Neph, and Paul were jogging towards her. She quickly ran to them and greeted them completely overjoyed. She then turned back to her father and the Caldar she had brought with her.

"Father, these are the survivors of the four other villages," she said to Zechariah.

He looked at her stunned.

"All of them?" he asked. "What happened to the others?"

"They chose to follow the Tarrans," explained a woman who was about Zira's age.

"Father, this is Nabeeha," noted Zira. "She and Abhinav have been leading these people since their villages were taken over. They hope to join us."

"You are more than welcome," Zechariah said, to all of them. "Our numbers are by no means great, forty-nine to be exact, but if we all work together we may be able to survive this great tragedy."

*   *   *

The other Caldar were welcomed quickly into the camp. Finding friends seemed to lift everyone's spirits. In no time, the children began to play together happily. Myla couldn't help but feel a little sad, though, as she watched Kalina play with the other children. As happy as she was that Kalina was alive and safe, her parents were not there to learn of this. They had chosen to join the Tarrans. It was understandable. If anyone had a cause to want a safer environment, it was them. Kalina was now parentless in their group.

"So she's alive and Paul's alive. Who would have thought?" asked Neph, as he sat down next to Myla on the grass.

"I did," she said, turning to him and smiling.

"Well, I think that's the most of an 'I told you so' that I've heard from you yet," he answered, laughing. "I'm impressed."

Zira walked up and sat down on the other side of Neph.

"What are you two talking about?" she asked, acting very suspicious.

"The fact that I'm always right," Myla said with a smile.

"Um, no... the fact that we are having an amazing love affair," Neph corrected. "Myla, you have to stay up with these things."

"Oh sorry, did I miss a joke opportunity?" she asked, laughing.

Zira just rolled her eyes and started to laugh as well. A weight had been lifted between the friends with the defeat of Amos. Myla knew, though, that their troubles weren't over yet.

As their laughter died down, Myla looked to Kalina playing.

"Seriously, though," she said. "What do we do with her?"

"What would happen to us if we brought her to her parents?" Neph asked.

"You mean if we knew where her parents were?" Myla asked in return. "We would probably be killed for venturing onto Tarran territory. And even if we weren't, she would be forced to live a life in denial of all that she is."

"Versus a life in exile," Zira pointed out. "To be honest, I don't know. I don't know what she wants, and I don't know what the morally correct thing to do would be."

284

"Are we having some sort of deep conversation?" asked Paul from behind them.

He walked up and sat down next Myla, completing the circle.

"What is this?" Myla asked. "I sit down and you all have to come to?"

"I was eating!" defended Paul, shoving the remains of an orange into his mouth. "I forgot how good food could be."

"We were just discussing what to do with Kalina," explained Zira.

"I could take her to Mertana," he said. "As far as I know, I'm still a Tarran in their eyes. They could point me in the right direction of her parents."

"That may be a viable option," noted Myla.

"What if she doesn't want to go?" asked Neph.

"She's eleven and hasn't seen her parents in months," said Zira. "Is she really qualified to make an appropriate decision in this case?"

"I would have been," said Myla.

"Actually, you did," said Zira. "But then again, you were going home, not leaving it."

"She didn't know that," responded Paul. "Not to mention that we didn't either. For half my life, I thought she was dead."

"Well, she thought you were dead for almost five months," said Zira.

"No, I didn't," corrected Myla.

"I think I need to get this full story," said Zira.

"Amos told her that he had them prisoner," explained Neph. "He was stalking her every day, and she was keeping it from us."

Zira gave Myla a look that made it clear she didn't approve. She didn't dwell on the subject, however, which Myla was grateful for.

285

"Out of curiosity," Zira asked. "How long are you going to leave Amos tied to that tree?"

Myla shrugged.

"Until I figure out what to do with him, and I'm in no hurry."

"Okay, just curious…" Zira answered, standing up in a rather frustrated manner. "Well, I hate to be the antisocial one here, but I really should go see my family."

Zira started to walk away. Neph looked over to her, and then back at Myla and Paul. He smiled and then jumped up and followed her, to the minor amusement of the other two.

"It's nice being with you all again, even if it is under these conditions," said Paul quietly.

Myla turned to him and laughed.

"You mean you like us more than you liked the cave?" she asked. "Shocking!"

"I was asleep for most of it," he said smiling.

"Why? Did he make you guys unconscious?" Myla asked.

"No, we were just really bored," he answered. "There's only so much you can talk about with a person. Oh, by the way, I know your mother really well."

"Did she tell you how she and my father got together?" Myla asked hopefully.

"She said she lived in Mertana for a while and met him there," he said. "But to be honest, I never thought to ask her how that happened."

"Paul!" she exclaimed. "This is my life-long mystery, and you didn't ask?"

"Sorry… I hope this doesn't mean you're regretting saving me," he said smiling.

"Just a little frustrated, that's all," she answered, with a laugh. "So, how well do you know him?"

286

"Who? Amos?" he asked. "I don't know him. He was almost never there. Every now and then he would come in angrily and tell me that he should just kill me now. He never said it to Malika. I was feeling a little picked on."

"Oh..." said Myla slowly.

Paul looked at her skeptically.

"Is he in love with you?" he asked.

"What?" Myla asked surprised. "No... he's just a sick freak."

Her words didn't sound too confident, and Paul could tell, but he didn't question further. Myla wondered if he realized how much time she had spent with Amos and what she had gone through to save him. She didn't feel the need to inform him of it now. That was a path that she had to follow. It was her destiny. She was just glad it was over...mostly.

Later that night, Myla walked around the camp by herself. She couldn't stop thinking about Malika, falling into that fire. The image was burned into her memory. How could she let him drop her into it like that? The guilt was almost unbearable. Nefarisis... where was this place? Was it even possible to save someone from it?

"There are over four hundred Caldar inside," said Amos from behind her.

She hadn't realized that she had walked right by his tree.

"What, are you reading my mind now?" she asked turning around.

"Versus before?" he asked. "And no, if you're curious. You were talking to yourself."

Had she been? Thinking back, she realized she was. How out of it was she?

"Four hundred Caldar were banished to Nefarisis, but that was a thousand years ago," she argued.

287

"Oh, you mean when I was ruling the world?" Amos asked. "Don't humor me, Myla. You know perfectly well that time is relative and therefore can be modified, if you know how."

"And you know how?" she asked, looking at him skeptically.

"Me? No. I never cared much to learn," he answered shrugging. "But Sherah does, and so do you."

"What makes you think that?" she asked, feeling a little vulnerable.

"You're far too studious to not have learned," he answered laughing.

Then he nodded, and a log slid along the ground to behind her.

"Have a seat," he said.

Myla sat down and looked at him disapprovingly.

"Should I tell the others that you aren't as much of a prisoner as they hoped?" she asked.

"What?" he asked. "I have not left this tree once – I can't. But I can still do things from here, you know."

"I figured that would be the case," she answered.

"And you didn't tell anyone?" he asked. "How sweet."

"What do you want from me, Amos? The game is over. I won," she asked angrily.

"Exactly!" he exclaimed. "The game is over and yet you are keeping me here. What am I still doing here on this world? I have been alive too long, Myla, and I don't want to be. I want to be rid of this world, and the guilt that comes with it. I hate knowing that my only honest memories were as a twelve year old boy running through the woods scared and deathly thirsty."

"So?" she asked, trying to seem unsympathetic.

288

"So it wasn't me! I hate what I did, and I want nothing to do with it," he answered. "Anyway I am being too loud, and I should stop talking before I wake up your people."

"They can't hear us," Myla said practically.

Amos looked at her surprised.

"How considerate of you. Do they know you can do that to them?" he asked.

"As if you're one to talk," she answered, getting up and starting to walk away.

"Myla, I know how to break out of Nefarisis," he called after her.

She stopped and turned around, staring at him.

"What?" she asked.

"You can't break in; no one knows where it is," he said. "You'd have to break out. I know how, but I can't myself."

"Why can't you?" she asked.

"I wasn't as studious as you," he answered giving her a frustrated look.

"So I can then?" she asked.

"Yes. You'll probably need help from your friends, but I bet you could," he said.

"And how do I know that this isn't all part of your plan to still defeat me?" she asked skeptically.

"That I can't help you with, but I can tell you it's possible and how to do it," he answered.

"Unless…" she said pausing as she looked at him. "You go with me."

"Not a chance," he answered. "I'm trying to die, remember? Not get stuck here for eternity."

"So what if we struck up a bargain?" she asked. "You help and I let you go free."

"How about I help and you agree to kill me after?" he answered.

"That's not exactly a normal bargaining chip," she said, a little disturbed.

"No, but it's one I like," he answered.

"You can't kill yourself once you're free?"

"No, I'm not that powerful," he answered shrugging.

"You're not powerful enough to kill yourself?" she asked. "That's pathetic."

"So do we have a deal?" he asked.

"Let me think about it," she answered. "Goodnight, Amos."

Myla turned and walked back to her tent, leaving Amos alone to his tree. She didn't sleep much that night though, as she couldn't stop wondering the entire time if she should trust him and if that was even possible.

Myla tracked down Malachi the next morning and pulled him away from the rest of the crowd. She knew it was strange going to him for advice, especially now when his control over the Caldar was only in name at this point. Myla, Zira and Neph were the ones the people looked to for leadership. It was probably only a matter of time before Paul took on a similar role due to association. Even still, Malachi was the official leader of the surviving Caldar community and in these trying times, she decided she wanted his approval before she did anything too drastic.

"What is on your mind, my granddaughter?" Malachi asked as they walked through an area of the woods away from the camp.

"Fears for my mother's safety," she answered, stopping to look at him.

"Two out of three isn't a success in this world, is it?" he asked with a saddened smile. "I too fear for her safety, but not even you, Myla, know the secrets of Nefarisis."

"True," she answered. "But I know someone who does."

Malachi shook his head disapprovingly.

"You cannot trust him, Myla," he said. "He will only betray you."

"And if he knows how to save Malika?" Myla asked.

"And if he doesn't?" Malachi argued. "And he uses this opportunity to gain his freedom?"

"You yourself just said yesterday that he had been freed from the spell that held him," Myla said. "He is no longer a slave to Sherah. He doesn't have to do his will."

"Sherah is dead," stated Malachi flatly.

"Sherah lives and breathes as we do," refuted Myla. "Think about it Malachi. It makes sense. What kind of spell forces someone to do another's bidding for a thousand years, when the controller is already dead?"

"There wouldn't be one," Malachi conceded. "The controller would have to be alive."

"We always assumed that Amos had taken over on his own this whole time," Myla continued. "But if this weight has been released from him, we know that someone else is involved in this."

Malachi looked back toward the camp and sighed. After a long pause he looked back to Myla.

"If Sherah is still alive, then he is certainly behind this Tarran movement," he said, almost to himself.

"Misha was always too dimwitted to do this himself," added Myla. "Believe me: he is definitely taking orders from someone else."

Malachi looked up to the sky without saying anything. Myla could tell he was feeling overwhelmed.

"Four hundred of the most powerful Caldar are trapped in the cells of Nefarisis," she said. "It may seem small, but I believe with them, we could have enough to take back our people and our world."

291

"You plan on bringing hope to the Caldar people," he said, looking a bit amazed.

"Even more than that," she added with a smile. "I plan to take back Caldaria."

"Then I shall not just give you my support, Myla," Malachi said. "I shall join you on this quest."

Myla looked at her grandfather stunned. At first, she refused his help, but he insisted. In the end, she let him win. She didn't know what it would be like working with him, but she was grateful for his support and encouragement. It was an unusual feeling, having him back her up.

After Myla was able to convince Malachi to agree to her plan, she tracked down Zira, Neph and Paul. She found them with ease, only to discover that they had been taking care of another issue themselves.

"Kalina wants to stay, but the remaining elders from all of the villages decided almost unanimously that she needed to return home if at all possible," explained Zira.

"Well, actually the only reason that she said almost unanimously was because Malachi wasn't around for the vote," added Neph.

Myla was surprised by this news. She herself conceded that it was best for Kalina to be with her parents, but these were not normal times. She didn't expect them to decide so easily to send Kalina to a life of hardship.

"We don't know that it will be hard for her there," added Paul, as if he was reading Myla's mind. "We grew up in Mertana, remember? It wasn't a bad life."

"For you…" she retorted softly.

"Oh Myla, you know it's best," insisted Zira. "Kalina should be with her parents. I'm sure she will be fine there."

"Under Sherah's rule?" asked Myla.

"We don't know that," argued Neph.

"Amos just told me. Can you really think of a better witness than him?" Myla asked.

They all looked at her skeptically.

"How do we believe him?" asked Zira.

Myla suddenly realized that her plan was going to take a lot more convincing than she realized. She knew it was strange that she trusted Amos as much as she did, but trusting him hadn't been the driving factor in her decision. Getting her mother back was.

"I am going to take Kalina back myself," said Paul, trying to break the silence. "My plan is to leave by the end of the week."

Myla breathed a heavy sigh.

"All right, then I'd like to ask Zira and Neph something," she said slowly.

They looked at her in disbelief as she proceed to explain to them that Amos had offered to show her how to break out of Nefarisis, and that with his help, she would try to free Malika along with four hundred other Caldar. Both of them stared at her blankly.

"Basically, I wanted to be sure you two could watch our people while Malachi and I are gone," she ended, trying to avoid their stunned stares.

"You're insane," Neph said bluntly. "He's still just trying to win."

"Maybe, but that is my mother in there," Myla answered practically.

"What if he isn't trying to win, Neph?" asked Zira. "This could be our one chance to take back our home. Four hundred supporters is not something we want to pass up."

"Not to mention those people have been stuck in there for a thousand years," Paul added quietly.

Myla looked at him surprised by his help, and he just shook his head in surrender.

"Mel, I have to take Kalina back to a world that I know will not be safe, but I'd feel a lot better about it knowing that there is a chance that it won't be permanent," he explained.

Myla looked at Neph, hoping for his consent.

"Whatever, Myla," he answered with a sigh.

"Cool," said Zira. "When are we leaving?"

Myla was stunned by the newfound confidence of her friend.

"Just me, Amos and Malachi, Zira," she answered. "I am not about to risk any more of the Caldar leaders."

"Well, too bad for you," answered Neph. "You go, we go. End of story."

"Anyway, we're not about to let Paul go off on his adventure into the Tarran world and then let you find Nefarisis as we just sit here and do nothing, are we?" asked Zira. "This camp is way too boring for me to agree to that."

*   *   *

Malachi told the Caldar that they were leaving for a hunt, but not even the most gullible person believed them. It was a bit too hard to dismiss that Malachi, Myla, Zira and Neph were all going on this hunt, and taking the sorcerer with them. Despite the disbelief, no one questioned them either. The people had enough confidence in them to trust them, and enough trust in Zechariah to follow him as a leader.

Planning the operation turned out to be a much more challenging task, especially since everything Amos told them was met with a "how do we know you are telling the truth" type of a remark. Amos showed remarkable patience though. Gradually his courteous attitude surprised not only Myla but the

294

others as well. No one trusted him much still, but even Neph was finding it hard to hate him.

The plan was simple. They would attach themselves to a certain moment in time before jumping into the flame. Then, by combining all of their powers together, they would orient Nefarisis to that moment in time. Once the prison existed at the same speed of time, they would be able to leave it. The entire plan was based on the assumption that time could be altered to that great of a degree. It was a heavy risk, but as Amos pointed out to them when they questioned him, someone had to put Nefarisis on an off-speed to begin with.

Anything that was created can be destroyed. This is what Myla kept telling herself as she packed her small sack in preparation for the upcoming evening. They would leave shortly after nightfall. Paul and Kalina would depart at the same time for Mertana. The coordination was not a coincidence. Malachi hoped that if the Caldar were focused on Kalina's well-being, they would not give as much thought to the others leaving. Myla didn't exactly believe it was working. She sensed much fear and anxiety from the people. They were feeling abandoned, but sure enough, they didn't know who to blame, so they kept quiet.

Kalina certainly didn't want to leave. She had been crying on and off all afternoon. Paul would not have an easy journey ahead of him. Myla couldn't help but feel terrible for the girl. She knew that this was the choice her parents made, but she kept out hope that once they saw Kalina, they would choose to return to the Caldar with Paul. It was a foolish hope, and Myla knew it.

Myla looked inside her almost empty bag. She had no idea what to bring with her. A few vegetables and some bread were all that she had decided on so far. Water would be helpful. She picked up a small bottle and walked out of her tent and toward the river. The sun was just setting on the horizon as she knelt down by the water's edge. They would be leaving soon. As she leaned over to fill up her bottle, she noticed another reflection behind her own in the water. It was Paul.

"You ready?" she asked, not turning around.

"Not really," he answered, coming over and sitting down next to her. "I feel way too horrible for taking that girl back."

"At least it's you," Myla suggested. "She knows you a lot better than she knows most of us."

"They are not exactly the most pleasant memories that she has associated with me," Paul answered, shrugging off her optimism.

"You were hope in a time of trouble," Myla said. "You let her know she wasn't alone, which is a reminder she could use now."

"Maybe, but I still don't want to go back to Mertana," Paul said smiling.

"Now that is something I can't imagine doing," Myla conceded.

Paul laughed and then looked back out to the horizon. The sun had set. He looked back to Myla.

"Come on," said a smiling Myla after a pause. "We have things to do."

The others were already with the horses when Myla and Paul arrived. Neph, Malachi and a newly freed Amos were readying the horses as Zira was sitting on an overgrown tree root with a very somber Kalina on her lap. Not many words were exchanged as Paul picked her up and brought her over to their horse. Each of them, with the exception of Amos, came by and hugged the girl goodbye. He then proceeded to lift her onto the horse and mounted after. He circled around and the waved goodbye. Myla looked at Paul. They were saying goodbye once again, only this time it was by choice.

After Paul and Kalina were out of sight, they all mounted their horses and left in a different direction: towards a cave that Myla, and perhaps Amos, had hoped never to see again. Wordlessly, the five rode into the night, moving so swiftly that they could barely feel the ground beneath their horses' feet. After a short period of time, they reached the entrance to the cave. Myla hadn't realized it was so close, since they had walked to the camp when she had been there before. They quickly dismounted and walked inside.

The cave was just as she had remembered; it was cold, damp and lifeless. As they lit their torches, she looked over to Amos. No reaction to their return showed on his face. He simply walked forward determinedly. The others followed single file, with Myla right behind him and Malachi bringing up the rear. Eventually, they reached the end. The room was dimly lit by the small flame on the opposite end. The table Amos had hoped to blackmail Myla with still sat in the center, with the broken pieces of the cup lying against the wall.

Neph and Zira immediately walked toward the flame in awe, though neither of them went too close for fear of falling into its gateway.

"I can't believe something this small is the only entrance to Nefarisis," said Neph, but no one responded.

Amos and Myla had walked to the table. She pulled out a small candle from her sack and placed it on the table. Amos motioned to everyone and they all gathered around. He waved his hand over it and the candle lit. Then the five of them held hands, forming a circle around the table. Intensely, they all stared at the candle's yellow flame until it turned silver, mimicking the other silver flame on the opposite side of the room.

"All right," Amos said after he was assured it had worked. "This flame will tie us to our time; as long as it burns, we can return home."

"That simple, huh?" asked Zira, a little skeptical.

297

"Hopefully," answered Amos. "Okay, shall we?"

"After you," said Myla, motioning him toward the flame.

He looked at her with understanding. She wasn't about to let him be the last to enter. He looked to them and then walked confidently toward the flame, vanishing before their eyes. Zira went through next, followed by Neph and Malachi. Myla looked at the flame, wondering if these moments would be her last. However, she took a deep breath and followed them in, vanishing into another world.

Chapter 18

Kalina tried to sleep as she and Paul rode through the forest, but Paul could tell that her attempts were unsuccessful. She kept being jolted awake by the movement of the horse. Paul, however, didn't want to stop in unfamiliar territory. He was not an experienced enough Caldar to feel comfortable sleeping in any spot in the forest, especially after the trees had closed in on him his first time there.

It was morning by the time they reached the outskirts of their old village. Paul didn't know if he should expect to find anyone inside, but if by chance Kalina's parents were there, it would make the experience much easier. His hopes were soon crushed, however, as he quickly discovered that the village had been abandoned as expected. Few of the houses were still standing, and those that were had clearly been ransacked. It was strange that the Tarrans had kicked them out of the village to only abandon it themselves, but Paul wasn't about to examine the logic of the situation. Instead, he hoped to find a comfortable place for them to sleep.

Paul steered the horse in the direction of his old house. Sure enough, it was still standing, though the door was broken in and the windows had been smashed. It was strange seeing his old home. It had been so long since he had been in this village. The vibrant lively place he once knew had been replaced by a ghost town. He figured the creepy familiarity would bother Kalina, but considering where both of them had spent the last few months, it was still a striking improvement. Paul led the horse up to the tree and tied him outside. Then they climbed up the familiar ladder to his house in the trees.

His furniture was all still inside. Rocks were scattered around the floor, but the damage was surprisingly minimal. Paul

299

quickly gathered a few remaining blankets together and made Kalina a place to sleep on Neph's old bed. She gladly accepted the place, and within seconds she was fast asleep. Paul didn't have such an easy time. His mind was racing through the last few days in this place, when there was fear of this evil sorcerer, but his presence hadn't so penetrated their lives. It was hard thinking back to then. It was so different. He had changed, and so had Myla. He could tell that too.

Paul stepped out of the house onto the wood bridge that he once spent so much time on. He could see Myla's house up ahead. The pathway was still there, but the damage to her small place was far more than his. A black verradere was painted over her door. So that is how they viewed her: the traitor that chose to keep her gifts over a Tarran government. They thought she was selfish.

Paul walked back to his house. Kalina lay fast asleep on Neph's bed. He felt sick to his stomach knowing that he was taking her to the people that would do this to their village, but it was what the Caldar decided, and he would honor that. He turned around and walked to his old room, and fell fast asleep on his old bed.

*   *   *

Paul woke up to crashing noises outside the house. Quickly he jumped up and looked out the window. The trees were moving. Slowly they were circling in together and carrying the remaining houses with them. Paul saw what looked to be Malachi's old house get crushed to pieces between two trees. They were demolishing what remained of the village; there would be no ghost town in this forest. It was far too alive too allow that.

300

Paul heard a scream. He ran to Neph's room and found a frightened Kalina sitting up on the bed. She looked at him, her eyes filled with tears.

"The trees!" she screamed. "They're destroying the village!"

She sobbed as Paul lifted her off the bed and into his arms. Hastily, he carried her out to the bridge, but it was no longer stable. The wooden planks began to crack and break around him as it swung through the air. Paul grabbed onto the rail in hope of keeping his balance, but he could feel it breaking as he held it. There was no way down. The bridge had broken on both sides of him. He searched his brain for some kind of Caldar magic to save them, but nothing came to mind. He didn't know enough! Four trees were closing in on them. He didn't have the time to make a decision, so he took a deep breath and jumped.

Paul could feel the air catch them as they fell. By the time they reached the ground, they were slowly floating. Somehow, he had broken their fall. He didn't think about it too much, however, as the trees were still closing in on them, and large pieces of wood were falling all around them. He whistled, and his horse trotted up to them. He lifted Kalina onto the horse's back and jumped up after her. They galloped out of the village in the direction of Mertana, dodging the rubble and racing between the trees till they were safe.

So much for returning home. Paul and Kalina would be the last people to see their village. All that remained of it now would be the memory. The Caldar were, once again, a truly homeless people.

*   *   *

301

Myla landed on her back in a dark and dusty room. A piercing pain penetrated through her head as she unsuccessfully tried to sit up.

"Hello?" she asked loudly amidst coughs.

There was no response. In fact, there was no sound at all with the exception of her own breath. She pulled herself off of the cold stone floor and stood up. At first, she couldn't see a thing, but her eyes gradually adjusted to the darkness. The room she was in was completely empty. She felt the stone walls for any sign of a door, and as her fingers ran over the cold rock, they fell upon a crack in the shape of a door. Unsure of what to do with this, she simply tried to push. At first there was no movement, but as her mind became more involved in the task, the stones began to move.

She pushed it about a foot deep, until a crack of light began to appear. Once she realized her success, she moved at a quicker pace until she was freed from the room. She found herself in a dimly lit hall. She could see the shapes of doors all the way down it. At the end, she saw a man pushing open the doors. She quickly recognized him to be Amos.

"I think all of these are empty," he said to her, showing no surprise at her presence.

"Probably because they figured out how to get out of them," she answered, shrugging off his statement.

"True," he said as he leaned against one, forcing it in. Then he looked back at Myla, with a smile.

"Well, apparently they're not all empty," he said, as Malachi walked out of the cell.

Malachi nodded to them indicating that he was okay, and Myla and Amos immediately started pushing in every door left in their hall. Myla was convinced that Zira and Neph would each be in one, but they couldn't find either of them. Eventually every door had been opened, yet Zira and Neph were nowhere to be found.

"Maybe they already escaped," suggested Amos. "We have no idea how long we were laying on the ground before we came to our senses."

Myla shook her head in disagreement. Zira and Neph had been placed somewhere else in the prison. Of course, they were. It was perfectly logical that the entrance wouldn't put them all in the same place. Whoever designed this fortress didn't want people getting out, and allowing them to band together would counteract that goal.

Myla started walking down the hall toward the doorway at the end. It was locked by some form of magic, but that didn't stop her. She waved her arms, and the door fell completely over. It was too easy. No one really tried to prevent them from getting this far, which was good because she needed to find everyone in that prison and free them all.

"Amos," she said turning to him. "How many people were in Nefarisis before you sent the Caldar in here?"

"You're wondering if anyone actually deserves to stay?" he asked. "Sherah claims that he killed everyone inside before I took power, but you can never know for sure."

"So Sherah could enter Nefarisis," Malachi said, speaking for the first time.

"He didn't build it, or at least I don't think that he did," answered Amos. "But he was the one that found it, and learned its secrets. That's how I know how to get out."

"You'd think if it was as simple as creating something in time to hold onto, someone would have figured that out by now," noted Myla.

"Yeah, but how would they know that?" asked Malachi. "Didn't you once think that time was unbendable?"

Myla rolled her eyes and kept walking through the dark damp path they were on. Amos had created a small flame to light their way. It kind of worried Myla though since it was sitting midair and not actually burning anything. Just moving where they moved. The thought of Amos controlling fire so well was a bit unnerving.

Eventually they saw a light that was provided by something else besides Amos's fire. They were reaching the end of the tunnel. The light lined the edge of a door. Unlike every other one, Myla didn't have to knock this door down. Instead she reached out and pushed it open with ease.

Inside was a massive corridor filled with barred cells, though none of the doors were locked. The room was also occupied by at least two hundred very rough looking people, in the halls and the cells, and each one of them turned and stared at the three when they walked inside.

*   *   *

Paul and Kalina shared few words as they raced to Mertana. Paul could tell that the child wasn't handling the image of her home getting smashed to pieces too well. He felt bad but didn't know what to say. He wasn't even taking her where she wanted to go, which was a fact that didn't help anything.

Gradually the trees thinned out. They had reached the edge of the forest. Paul could see Mertana up ahead. Paul slowed his horse down to a trot. He was in no hurry. Mertana wasn't the most welcomed sight. He didn't know how they would react to seeing him there, but he tried not to address that.

"Is that it?" asked Kalina, speaking up for the first time since the village.

"Yes, that's Mertana," said Paul.

Kalina shielded the sun from her eyes to get a better look. She didn't look too impressed.

"You and Myla grew up there?" she asked, sounding very confused.

"Why is that hard to believe?" he asked in return.

"It's just looks so boring," she answered. "The houses are shaped funny, and there aren't any trees."

"Oh, it's not so bad," Paul responded, trying to not crush any hope Kalina had. "Myla and I did grow up there."

"Yeah… and you left," Kalina added.

Paul nodded his head in agreement. He couldn't argue that point. He never had the intention of returning.

"Give it a try, Kalina," he finally said after a pause. "You may like it more than you expect."

Kalina shrugged as they approached the border of the town. Paul steered the horse toward the main street. Most of the houses were empty, with everyone at work or school. However, as he came down the main street, he passed by the old blacksmith, who proceeded to drop his hammer at the sight of Paul. Paul wasn't exactly sure where to take Kalina, especially since he didn't know whom to trust. Eventually he decided that a former friend was better than no friend, so he turned his horse in the direction of the house of a girl who once used to make a hobby of aggravating the odd child in town.

*   *   *

It took Zira a few moments to realize that the reason she had no feeling in her hands was because they were tied up above her. She looked across the torch-lit room and saw Neph, also sitting down with his hands tied up against the opposite wall.

"You okay?" he asked.

305

"Yeah, I guess I just blacked out," she said, trying to ponder her predicament. "Do you know how we got like this?"

Neph shook his head and started to feverishly try to free his hands from the rope holding them. Zira could tell he was not encountering much success.

"They've been bonded with some sort of magic," he said after giving up.

"No surprise there," Zira answered. "Everyone in this place is a Caldar."

"Are we sure we want to free them if they would do something like this?" Neph asked.

Zira tried to shrug, but it didn't quite work with her arms above her. Her head hurt. There was a piercing pain right above her right eyebrow. She looked over to Neph. He had a huge bruise on his cheekbone. There must have been a struggle, but she couldn't remember one. Her mind was a blur.

There was a sudden sound next to Zira. The stones were moving. Someone was coming. She could see Neph pull himself up to a standing position. She echoed his actions. In walked a very pale rough-looking man, who clearly hadn't seen the sun in a long time. He looked at them with untrusting eyes and walked to the center of the room.

"What are you doing here?" he asked with a raspy yet strong voice.

"Oh, just looking around," said Neph, clearly not sure if he should mention the whole prison-break part of the plan. Zira agreed with his caution.

"You came with *him*," he returned.

Amos. They recognized him. It had been a fear, but Zira hoped his face would have been forgotten. However, this seemed to not be the case.

"He's not the same," Zira insisted.

"No, apparently he's only damned five Caldar since he put us all in here," the man said. "Yet then again, all five of you are here."

"And thank you for welcoming us so kindly," said Neph.

The man rolled his eyes and turned to Zira. Neph gave an innocent look that Zira tried not to laugh at.

"Now, why are you really here?" he asked her.

"We came to free the Caldar that were wrongly imprisoned here," she answered confidently. "Yet by your treatment of us, I'm not so sure you are one of them."

"Why would you do this?" the man asked. "Why would *he* do this?"

"Because he has been defeated," Zira answered. "And we're making him."

"And why should I believe that?" he asked, looking at her skeptically.

"What's there to lose?" she asked in return.

The man made no response. Instead he turned around and walked out of the room. Zira looked at Neph. He looked just as concerned as she felt.

"I take it they have the others locked up as well," Zira said.

"Or they're hoping to hold us for ransom," Neph pointed out. "We aren't who they want. Why would they bother interrogating us?"

"It's not like they are short on time," Zira pointed out.

Neph nodded his head in agreement. Whatever was going on, both of them realized that their current predicament was probably not the best one. Right now, though, the only thing they could do was try to come up with a way to escape.

Zira examined the knots that were tying her hands together. She couldn't figure out why she wasn't able to undo them. Whatever magic was being used was surprisingly efficient.

Neph didn't seem to have any more luck either. He had taken to biting the rope, which looked more painful than effective. Zira leaned against the wall and stared at him. It would have been such a funny sight if it hadn't been so frustrating. Neph finally gave up and leaned against the wall.

"Why are we here again?" he asked with a frustrated sigh. He gave Zira a disgusted look, which she could only smile at.

"To help," she answered simply, not really knowing what else to say.

"Yeah, we're doing a great job at that," he pointed out, not really buying her explanation.

"Well, maybe we are helping," she argued. "We don't know what situation the others are in, and even if they are fine, there's no way our captors are going to follow them out of this place without a bit of convincing."

"So how do we convince them?" Neph asked. "They aren't even in the room."

Zira looked around the room, searching for an idea.

"So let's bring them in here," she answered after a pause.

"How?" Neph asked, clearly not following, nor trying to.

"Well, we can't go get them, so let's make it very easy for them to come in," she answered. "Let's break down the door."

Neph looked at her skeptically.

"I'm sorry, Zira," he said. "I didn't learn how to destroy solid rock in school."

"The same as transporting things, Neph," she answered. "Break it down in your mind, and it will move."

"Zira, you don't know how to transport things," Neph pointed out.

Zira knew he was right. She had only once successfully transported something without the help of Myla, but now was a better time than any. She turned away from Neph and stared at the door. For a few moments, nothing happened. She could feel Neph looking at her skeptically, but she blocked it out of her mind.

"Do you want me to help?" he asked, but as he spoke, a small piece of rock crumbled off of the door.

He walked as close to the door as his tied hands would let him and started staring at it as well. Another piece of rock crumbled off of the door. Then a large piece crashed to the ground. It was working. Soon they could see light from the other end. Eventually, the whole door was a pile of rubble on the ground. The sound of it crashing was so loud that it echoed throughout the room and down the hall. They could hear shouts. They would have visitors momentarily.

"Well, it wasn't transporting, but it worked," said Neph, clearly impressed with their result.

Zira didn't have much time to respond as six not-so-friendly looking people appeared at the doorway. Behind them walked up the man that they had talked to before. He walked up to Zira, looking more confused than anything.

"What's the point of breaking down the door, if you can't leave?" he asked Zira, who just stared back at him. Neph looked a little bothered.

"Why do you ask her?" he asked.

The man glanced over to Neph briefly and then looked back at Zira.

"Just wanted to talk," said Zira after a pause. "How's life here? Is your living area comfortable? I mean I'm sure it's more comfortable than ours right now, being that your hands aren't tied to a wall, but do you like it here?"

The man looked at her angrily.

"Do you mock us?" he asked. "It was your friend that put us here."

"As we said before," she answered. "He's not our friend. In fact, one of our friends is a prisoner here because of him. He is our prisoner and is here helping us out of force."

"I hate to rain on your parade lady, but we are all prisoners here."

"What's your name?" she asked him.

"Sudhakar," he answered. "I was the chief advisor to the king and the only survivor of the high council destroyed by Amos."

"Well, Sudhakar," she answered. "My name is Zira and this is Neph, and we are two of the few Caldar left loyal to our heritage."

"The Caldar were destroyed when Amos put us in here," he said, his voice depressingly believable.

"As recently as a year ago, almost two thousand were living in peace in the forest," argued Neph.

"And now?" Sudhakar asked.

"Almost all have fallen victim to a new Tarran government," Zira answered. "Less than one hundred remain free."

"A new Tarran government?" Sudhakar asked with a bit of a smile. "I've heard that line before. It destroyed our society."

"And yet it happens again," Zira responded.

"But you have Amos as your prisoner which you so valiantly defend," Sudhakar pointed out. "How do you explain this movement since this clearly resembles his work?"

"Perhaps Amos was always working for the original sorcerer," said Neph.

Sudhakar was silent for a second. The other Caldar in the room backed up at that statement and quickly started to glance at each other with worried looks.

"It was five hundred years after Sherah that Amos rose to power," Sudhakar tried to argue.

"It's been a thousand years since Amos did, yet he is here now, is he not?" Zira asked.

Sudhakar stepped back, clearly trying to comprehend the timeline. Up to this moment, Zira had assumed that they were aware of how much time had passed, but now she realized that they were not privy to this information.

"I apologize," he said quietly. "But we were not aware that so much time had passed. We knew we had been here years, but…"

"This prison is outside of time," said Neph. "It would make sense that it only seemed within a normal lifetime to you."

"And the battle has not ended?" Sudhakar asked. "Within a thousand years?"

"It was dormant for most of the time," said Zira. "The Caldar lived in the forest, the Tarrans lived on the other side, and Caldaria remained abandoned."

"And now?"

"Our people are further away from their home than they have ever been," said Neph.

"We have the strongest Caldar in history within our camps," Zira explained. "Our numbers may be small, but we are not weak. If you join us, we can break out of this place and take back Caldaria, bringing hope to our people once again."

Sudhakar paused, staring at the two strangers under his authority. Then he walked over to Zira and then to Neph, and removed their restraints. They both immediately walked to each other and then looked at Sudhakar.

"I, and every other Caldar in this prison, live for the day that we will return home to our great city, and live in peace once again," Sudhakar said slowly. "If you say that you can help bring this to be, we have no choice but to believe you."

* * *

"Hello, Serena," he said, as he stood in front of her.

Serena stared in disbelief at the sight of Paul standing at her doorstep. He couldn't really blame her. He had left with no assurance of his safety the previous year. He figured she would be angry. Now, however, was not the time to discuss his past decisions. He only hoped that Serena would recognize that it was for Kalina that he was even there.

"We need your help," he said cautiously to the dumbfounded woman in front of him. "Kalina is from one of the Caldar villages, but was separated from her parents. Can you help us find them?"

"What?" she asked while still trying to process his presence. "I'm sorry... Aren't you dead?"

"No. Actually it turns out I'm a Caldar," he answered cautiously. "So I just stayed with them."

"Yeah, so is Myla!" inserted Kalina, which a stressed-out Paul quickly squeezed her hand for.

The child looked up at him perplexed.

"Myla, huh?" she asked. "Yeah, Dansten mentioned something about her leading some sort of rebellion. He didn't mention *you,* however. So, you two have been hanging out together in your little forest. How nice for you."

"Oh, yeah," said Kalina. "He totally loves her."

Paul stared at the child. How is that she picked this time out of any to stop being shy?

"Does he now?" Serena asked. "How special."

"Serena, can you help us, please?" he asked, stopping this side conversation.

"Come inside," she said with a sigh. "I'll see what I can do."

312

Serena's house wasn't in the best condition that Paul had seen it in. Muddy tracks of all different sizes circled her living room. Laundry was strewn about the furniture, and three bags of trash were sitting in her kitchen, along with a washing basin full of dirty dishes. Serena initially tried to pick up some things, but quickly decided it was a lost cause, so she dropped it on the floor.

"Been busy?" he asked, trying unsuccessfully to not crack a smile.

Serena looked at him clearly not amused with her arms crossed in front of her.

"Difficult times," she said. "You've missed out on a lot since you've been gone."

She then turned around and started searching through some papers on her desk. Paul breathed in, hoping for some sort of calming effect. It didn't work.

"You know I've had some adventures of my own," he said to her.

"Yes, I'm sure it's been difficult for you having fun out in the forest as we've had to take in fifteen-hundred of your refugees," she answered angrily. "And yet your very presence here indicates that you have been associating with the very Caldar that caused this mess."

"Excuse me?" Paul asked, shocked by her outburst.

"Oh, please!" she said, frustrated. "You set up a society that only caters to the privileged, and you expect everyone to be sympathetic that it didn't work."

"It did work," answered Paul forcefully. "They were living happily in peace for hundreds of years, until you came along and disrupted their society because you couldn't do any of their tricks. I lived there, Serena. I know what it was like. I had absolutely no ability when I entered that village, and those people you blame are the very ones who accepted me and welcomed me into their world."

"Oh, really?" she asked. "Then why did your people accept our ways so quickly? I hear your people had gotten so corrupted, there had been three vicious murders right before my people arrived!"

"Well, you're looking at two of the three people murdered, Serena, and we don't seem that dead to me."

"Well, whatever happened, we had nothing to do with it," she said, a little confused.

"Maybe you didn't," Paul consented. "But Misha is working for the guy who did have something to do with it. This was all a set-up."

Serena threw her papers down on her desk.

"Did you really come here to try and convert me?" she asked. "I don't know if you noticed Paul, but I'm not a Caldar."

"I came here to bring Kalina home to her parents," he answered.

"Please leave me out of this," inserted Kalina so forcefully that Paul and Serena bust up laughing. They had both forgotten she was in the room. She looked so overwhelmed that Paul felt horrible for debating such things in her presence. It seemed that Serena did as well, who immediately walked up to the child, apologized for their rudeness, and offered her something to eat. Kalina readily accepted.

Serena made her guest bedroom ready for Kalina as she ate. The child was quite tired from their restless trip, so once she was done eating, she went to bed quite willingly. Paul led her upstairs and tucked her into her bed.

"Paul?" she asked as he was walking out of the room.

"Yes?" he answered turning around.

"When we find my parents, can we all go back to the forest?" she asked.

314

Paul smiled at her sadly.

"I will certainly make the offer," he answered. "But your parents will do whatever they feel is best for you."

"And staying here is best?" Kalina asked.

"Maybe it is," he answered. "These days, it may be a lot safer here than it is in the forest."

"I know that isn't true," Kalina argued.

"But it is," he said. "Kalina, we are fighting something much larger than ourselves. We don't know how it will turn out."

"When I am old enough, can I return to the forest and to you all again?" she asked.

"Absolutely," Paul answered.

"Paul?"

"Yes?"

"Thank you," she said softly, and then closed her eyes.

Paul smiled, walked out of the room and closed the door behind him. As he made his way down the stairs to the living room, he saw Serena sitting on her couch, staring out the window. He walked over and sat down on the chair next to her.

"So when you find this girl's parents," she asked, not looking in his direction. "Do you go back to the forest? Back to Myla?"

"Yes," he answered.

"What's she like now?" Serena asked.

"She's amazing," he answered. "The most powerful Caldar ever, a leader to our people, and a great person."

"High praise," Serena noted.

Paul nodded his head in agreement.

"I'm getting married," she said.

"Really?" Paul said, suddenly very glad there was still good in her life. "Who's the lucky guy?"

315

"Dansten," she answered bluntly.

Paul sat up in his chair, shocked and a bit disgusted.

"That's gross," he said, before he could stop himself.

"Thanks for your support," Serena said, sounding a bit annoyed.

"Why?" asked Paul, not sure how he should react.

"It's the practical thing to do," she answered. "Sometimes you have to realize that you're not going to have your perfect magical life and understand that you will need food on the table."

"Serena, are the Caldar allowed to use their skills?" he asked suddenly.

"No, it's forbidden by law in order to enforce equality," she answered, a bit surprised by his question.

"Too bad," he said. "Because if there was truly unity, there would always be food on the table with the Caldar around."

"Stop trying to convert me," she said, as she stood up and walked over to her desk. "A week ago, Dansten mentioned to me that there was a Caldar couple that had lost a young child to the murders. Apparently many of their neighbors have expressed concern because they never seem to have the energy to do anything. I can only guess that these are the parents that you are talking about."

"Sounds like it," he said. "What are their names?"

"Samson and Kaila," she answered, holding out a small sheet of paper. "Here is their address."

"That's them," he said, taking the sheet. "We can leave in the morning and be out of your way."

Serena smiled and shook her head in a hopeless way. Then she turned and walked up the stairs as Paul proceeded to stretch out on the couch and fall fast asleep.

He woke up early the next morning. The sun was barely cracking above the horizon. He didn't hesitate. Quickly he

316

jumped up and walked up the stairs to Kalina's room. She was fast asleep, not surprisingly. He quietly whispered her name, and she opened her eyes and glared at him. Clearly she did not want to wake up yet. She didn't argue, however, and slowly pulled herself out of bed. Once she was up, they gathered their things and headed for the door.

"Paul," said Serena, as they were walking out the door.

He turned around and looked at her.

"Despite all of this stuff," she said. "You have a friend in Mertana. Don't forget that."

Paul smiled and nodded at her. Then he grabbed Kalina's hand and led her out the door.

*   *   *

Myla stared at the hundreds of people staring back at her, Malachi and Amos. She didn't really know how to react to them. They all looked so confused, and some were backing up to the farthest parts of their cells. Myla glanced over at Amos. The look on his face said it all. They recognized him. This was not going to be easy.

In Myla's head, she was frozen, but her feet started to move forward despite herself. Soon, she was several steps ahead of the two men behind her and very much in the spotlight of the murderous stares from all the people around her. She didn't know what to say, but she found herself speaking.

"He is our prisoner," she said loudly. "There is nothing to fear. He is here to help us save you."

"And why would you want us saved?" asked one woman from the far end of the cells.

"One thousand years have passed since Amos conquered the Caldar world, but some of us survived," she answered.

317

"Sherah now has risen again. With your help, we can defeat him together."

The room echoed with laughter from many voices.

"No one can beat Sherah, little girl," said the same woman as she walked toward the insulted Myla. "He is unstoppable."

"I can," answered Myla, a bit too confidently.

"Oh, and why do you say that?" she asked. "Because you have your little friend here? How do we even know he is your prisoner? How do you even know? You don't... And yet somehow you still think you can beat Sherah."

Myla walked up to the woman and stared at her right in the face.

"I can," she said firmly.

The woman shook her head hopelessly, but the ears of many of the residents had perked at Myla's words.

"What's your name, little girl?" asked the woman.

"Myla," she answered firmly. "And yours?"

"Novia," she responded. "I suggest you learn it well because no one breaks out of this place, and you will want me on your side."

"Novia, we have some friends here," Malachi spoke up. "Two that arrived at the same time as, and one that arrived prior to us. Have you seen them?"

"No one new has entered this part of the prison in a decade," said Novia. "They must have appeared somewhere else."

She was lying. Myla could tell, and the look on Amos' face indicated that he could tell as well. He rolled his eyes when Myla glanced at him. She could only agree with his assessment.

"There are some empty cells a few floors down. I suggest you find one and make yourselves comfortable, as you are going to be here for a while," said Novia, who proceeded to turn back to her cell.

All of the prisoners went back to their previous business, so the three just looked at each other and started to head down the stairs. Sure enough, two floors down, they found an empty cell. Myla was glad. It was a lot emptier of an area, so they could discuss their situation with more ease. Of course, none of them knew exactly what to say. Instead they mostly looked around the prison, trying to mentally assess their situation. Nothing looked promising.

"There aren't four hundred people here, Amos," said Myla after a pause.

He nodded his head in agreement.

"There must be two sections to the prison," he said thoughtfully.

"Ah... the kink in the plan," said Malachi.

"So how do we get to the other side?" asked Myla.

"Well, any part of these walls could be a door, so we look until we find one," answered Amos.

Myla didn't like that answer, but she knew it was probably the truth. She could still feel the flame in the cave, paused momentarily in time, but she wondered how long she would be able to find it and how much time they actually had. These people had all been in this prison for what seemed to be a decade, but in reality, it had been a thousand years. If they were to somehow lose their lock to that one space in time, how much would they miss? Would a thousand years go by for them as well?

Amos and Malachi lay down on their cots to sleep, but Myla wasn't feeling any desire to. She sat there until they drifted off and walked out of the cell. Most of the prisoners were asleep as well. It was the perfect opportunity to take a look around and figure out where these other two hundred prisoners were, as well as their friends.

Myla climbed down the ladder to the very bottom floor of the room. There were no cells down there, which was primarily the reason that Myla was curious. It was entirely empty and unused. She walked around the various poles scattered around to hold up the floor above them. It was dark, but not enough so that she wasn't able to see anything. She walked to one of the stone walls and started feeling it for cracks. Slowly she circled around the room, hoping to find something different. As her hands felt the walls, suddenly one of them went right through it. There was a doorway here. The wall was an illusion. Myla found the edges, took a breath, and walked through.

It was pitch black. Myla held up a glowing light from her hand and looked around. She was in a tunnel. Cautiously she walked down it, but she didn't get very far because there were footsteps behind her. Myla paused and then flipped around. Novia was standing there staring at her.

"And what brings you to this part of our dear prison?" she asked Myla, who was beginning to feel she had cause to fear.

"Just looking around," she said, trying desperately to seem casual.

"There isn't anything down here," Novia answered coldly. Myla rolled her eyes.

"You're down here," she responded. "What's your big concern?"

Novia didn't respond with words. Instead she flipped around and kicked Myla in the stomach throwing her backwards onto the ground. Myla coughed as she tried to breathe in and stand up, but Novia was right there to punch her in the head. Myla tried to stop her with her mind, but her magic was muddled there. She couldn't feel anything.

Her face hit the dirty floor, but she flipped around on her back and kicked Novia. It was too little too late, however, as her vision was tunneling in. Up above her, she could see Amos appear behind Novia, pushing her against the wall with a blue light. Novia froze for a few seconds in a face of remembrance, and then she disappeared from sight.

Amos knelt down beside Myla and placed his hand on her head. She could feel her vision clearing and the pain leaving. Then he lifted her up off the ground.

"You okay?" he asked. She nodded.

"What made you come down here?" she asked.

"I heard you leave, and when I saw Novia follow you down, I figured I might want to check up on you," he answered.

"I'm glad you did," she answered.

Amos, however, shook his head.

"Maybe you shouldn't be," he said. "That doorway back into the room disappeared when I came through it. I don't know how to get back."

Myla looked around. Sure enough, there were walls on both ends. There was no entrance back into the main part of the prison. She ran to each side to try and find some sort of secret door, but there was none

"It gets worse," Amos added. "Myla, I lost all connection to the flame when I came through that wall. I can no longer feel it."

Myla sighed and leaned back against the tunnel wall. This was no good, for she too could no longer feel the presence of the flame, which was their only way home.

Chapter 19

When Malachi was a boy, he wanted three things in life: to become a great warrior, to explore the world outside the village, and to be the one who brought his people home. The first two goals were easily accomplished. Even as a child, he was recognized as the most skilled Caldar in generations. Often he would hear the adults whispering about him as he passed by. His strength only gave him more hope that he would be the one to lead his people home.

When he was fourteen, he left on a hunting trip alone. He was the youngest to do so, but that was no surprise to the other Caldar. Their confidence didn't calm his nerves, however, as the trip was three days long, and while in his head he knew he was ready, he wasn't so sure in his heart. There was much fear weighing on him. It would be his first venture outside of the boundaries of the village, and he planned for it to be a significant one. He planned to venture as close as possible to the eastern border of the forest in the direction of Caldaria. No one seemed to know how far away it was, so he planned to find out. It would be his first step toward coming home.

Malachi could tell his mother was worried about him as he packed his things and readied his horse. She stood still in the doorway the entire time, staring at him. She always had a calmness to her, a sense of serenity even at times of trial. Malachi wondered if this was one of those times for her. He would not come back to her a child. He would be a respected adult in the village. He would still be a student, yes, but an equal. If all went as planned, he would also come back with a clue toward their journey home. This, however, was information he chose to not divulge with her.

The first day of Malachi's journey was uneventful. He was successful in his hunt, but his true mission had not come to pass. It seemed there was no end to the forest. The further east he journeyed, the thicker the woods would become. Eventually the trees did become less dense. However, the more open space there was, the darker it became. Soon he was surrounded by a thick fog, and he could no longer see where he was going. It was far from what he expected to find.

In the darkness, his horse stepped in mud and reared up to throw Malachi off his back. Stunned, his body slapped down on a muddy black surface. He couldn't see his horse. He couldn't even hear him. Instead he heard whispers in the wind. There was no light, and only black fog and death. He would die here, at only fourteen years old. He could not find his way home.

Malachi lay down in the mud, looking into the fog toward what he knew was the sky. Gradually he started to whisper the words of the forgotten prophets. He had never heard them, but they were burned into his mind. *Alle cunsin sandri no meiri. Alle cunsin sandri no meiri.* Be still and believe in hope. He whispered the words over and over again, until someone answered back.

You will not die here.

The voice was clear, and warm. It startled Malachi, causing him to jump on to his feet. Who could be speaking? There was no one.

"And what would you have me do?" he asked, his voice quivering in the air.

Return home, and rest assured that someday your people will return to Caldaria, though it will not be by your hand.

Malachi felt his heart hit his knees. He did not realize how deep his desire to be the savior of his people was. He felt himself sink back onto the ground.

Get up Malachi. Return home. The chosen one will come, and at that time, your life will be necessary.

The fog didn't clear up, but Malachi suddenly knew which way to walk. He found his horse and led him back in the direction of the forest. He buried his experience deep inside, never to speak of it, and quickly returned home.

*   *   *

Paul knew that Mertana was fully inhabited, but it had never seemed more like a ghost town. Few people were outdoors, and the ones who were looked at him with faces so sullen. The reaction confused Paul at first, since most of these were people that were Tarrans to begin with. Then it occurred to him: the town that seemed abandoned was actually too full. They didn't have enough food. There were too many people, and the Caldar couldn't use their magic. It had already gotten so bad that someone like Serena would marry someone like Dansten to ensure a meal on the table.

Paul pulled his horse to a halt in front of the house that Kalina's parents were staying at. He had never felt so guilty in his life, wondering if Kalina would survive staying in such a place. Of course he would offer to take them all back to the forest, but he already knew that there would be no such luck. He dismounted and lifted Kalina off the horse. She held his hand so tightly that it made him want to turn around and take her back to the Caldar in the forest, but he did not hesitate. Trying to convey confidence in every inch of him, he led her up to the door and proceeded to knock.

Kaila, Kalina's mother, answered the door. She didn't say anything. Instead she gasped in shock, knelt down and held her child in joyous tears. Samson walked up behind her and also sank to the ground in shock of seeing his daughter alive. He quickly recovered and walked over to Paul, proceeding to shake his hand whispering "thank you, thank you" over and over again. It eased Paul's guilt to see them so overjoyed. With such love in her family, perhaps Kalina was not in such danger.

Once Samson and Kaila regained their composure, they quickly invited Paul inside. The place wasn't a far sight from Serena's home. The two parents quickly tried to pick up some of the mess, but were too overwhelmed with the presence of their daughter to do much.

"How is she alive?" Samson asked, still in shock. "How are you?"

"It was a trick, by the second sorcerer himself," said Paul. "We both were kidnapped until Myla was able to save us."

"The second sorcerer?" asked Kaila, clearly confused. "That isn't possible…"

"It is, though," argued Paul hurriedly. "Please, you must believe me. He didn't die. Sherah didn't die. We were able to defeat the second one, but Sherah is behind everything, including this new Tarran government."

Looks of complete fear came over their faces, however they weren't given much time to react, for Paul heard footsteps behind him at the front door.

"That is a lie," said Misha coldly walking toward him. "Where have you heard such foul nonsense, Paul?"

Paul turned around and looked at Misha.

"I see you remember me," Paul noted. "Yet there is no surprise in you at my very existence. Quite interesting since I was presumed dead."

"I always knew you were up to something," said Misha shrugging off Paul's comments.

"Now that is a lie," answered Paul strongly. "You knew perfectly well that Sherah was behind my disappearance since you have been in league with him since the beginning."

"I don't know any Sherah," answered Misha simply before turning to a stunned Kaila and Samson.

"My dear friends," Misha said softly. "I do suggest you keep your family away from Caldar as loathsome as this one."

"Paul, I suggest you leave," said Samson sadly.

Paul looked at him shocked.

"You don't have to listen to this man!" he argued pointing at Misha.

"Yes, we do," answered Samson. "Don't worry; we will keep Kalina safe. I thank you for bringing her home to us."

Paul couldn't believe what he was hearing. At a complete loss of words, he turned around and walked out the door. As he made his way down the porch steps, he saw Allasta across the street. He started to grab her attention, but hesitated. She, like everyone else here, was a friend no more. Instead, he walked to his horse, mounted, and left in the direction of the forest.

*   *   *

Malachi sat up in his cot. He had been aware that Myla and Amos left, but chose not to say anything. That choice wasn't due to his confidence in their abilities. He feared they had too much of that between the two of them. No, the reason he chose to not say anything is because he too planned to do some exploring. He was just waiting for the right opportunity. That opportunity came with a short little man, who clearly had as much curiosity as he did.

"How do you like your new cell?" he asked, as he stood in Malachi's doorway, playing with a small stone in his fingers and chewing on some sort of weed.

"It's quite exciting," answered Malachi, almost sounding sincere. "Now tell me – I'm sorry I didn't catch your name – where would you find a plant in a place like this?"

"The name's Ash, Ashutosh to be exact," he answered. "I got it from the courtyard. There are all sorts of plants in there. That's where we get all our food."

"A courtyard?" Malachi asked, trying to not seem surprised. "Where is that?"

"Between the two prisons of course," Ash answered, surprised by Malachi's question. "What? Were you that put off by Novia? She does have a way with people."

"I could tell," Malachi agreed.

"Well, I wouldn't go getting your hopes up about getting into the courtyard," added Ash. "Novia has the entrance guarded, and none of her people would let you through."

Malachi smiled at that.

"Why do I suspect that you know how to get through that obstacle?" asked Malachi.

Ash perked up at that comment.

"Now that you mention it," he said, walking over to Malachi's cot. "I do."

Malachi laughed at Ash's blatant display of an ulterior motive.

"And what is it that you need in order to share this information?" asked Malachi.

Ash smiled.

"Just that you will, in fact, free us from this place," he answered. "I'm sick of the food, the living arrangement and the lack of fresh air, water or anything for that matter."

"You have my word," said Malachi.

"Then let's get you to that courtyard."

327

It turned out that Sudhakar wasn't such a bad guy after all. In fact, Zira and Neph kind of liked him, once he calmed down a bit and started talking to them like they were real people. He listened intently to their stories of the villages, the Tarrans, and Myla and Amos. The more they talked, the more Neph and Zira could see his skepticism die.

"So why would you risk coming to a place like this, knowing that you may never leave?" he asked.

"Less than a hundred Caldar remain in the forest, but I believe that many more will turn to our cause once they see the evil exposed in this Tarran government," answered Zira. "However, we cannot accomplish such a thing with our small numbers."

"So you free us, and in return we have to help you?" asked Sudhakar.

"No, it's not like that," said Neph. "You will be free to do whatever you choose. However, we hope that you will remember the greatness that once was Caldaria, and do whatever is in your power to help us restore it."

Sudhakar paused and breathed a deep sigh, nodding his head.

"If there is any cause we can rally around, it is the restoration of Caldaria," he answered.

"Well, we will need to find our friends, the rest of the prisoners, and a woman who was sent here recently," said Zira.

"We've been informed that your friends appeared on the light side of the prison. That's how we knew that he was with you. As for the woman, she is here, but I doubt you will be able to reach her or your friends," stated Sudhakar. "There is a woman here, Novia, who basically controls the entire prison. I held you captive under her orders. Most everyone hates her, but she is the only one who controls the passageways between sides, and nobody dares to challenge her."

"Why?" asked Zira.

"She was here before – before the sorcerers, before anything. Many believe her to be an agent of Amos and Sherah. Others suggest that she serves an evil predating even him. She has that woman prisoner. She won't let her go willingly."

"Well, Sudhakar," said Neph. "I think you've met the first two people willing to challenge her, because where we come from, if someone holds one of our friends prisoner, they get what's coming to them."

"Way to state it, Neph."

"Why thank you, Zira."

*　　*　　*

Amos and Myla sat on opposite walls of the tunnel staring at each other wordlessly. The situation was too depressing for words. They were stuck in a tunnel, with no way out, and no way home. If they couldn't figure out how to escape, they would die there, and Caldaria would be lost. Unfortunately neither of them were coming up with any ideas.

"What's your favorite food?" asked Amos.

Myla was more bothered by the question than anything.

"What's yours?" she asked, too frustrated to think about it herself.

"Mashed potatoes," he answered. "My mom used to make them: really lumpy, salty and with tons of gravy."

"I'm not sure your mom knew how to make mashed potatoes," noted Myla.

"No, she didn't," Amos answered with a smile. "But we lived in a village north of Mertana with tons of potato farms, so we ate them all the time. It made me want to be a farmer, so I could grow different types of vegetables besides potatoes."

"Tarran village or Caldar village?" asked Myla.

"They weren't separated then," answered Amos. "My father was this really powerful Caldar who scowled upon all things without magic."

"But wasn't your mother…"

"A Tarran?" he asked. "Yeah. It was the great shame of his life. I hated him for how he looked down on her, so I chose to not use my gifts. I kept them a secret. He thought I was giftless and threw me out of the house. I wandered alone through the forest until I found Caldaria."

It was the most human Myla had ever seen him.

"Why are you telling me this, Amos?" she asked.

"I don't think we are going to die here, Myla," he answered. "And when we do break out and win this thing, I want to make sure that for once, we are doing it for the right reasons. I don't want a Caldar superiority any more than I want a Tarran one. Promise me that you won't let that happen."

Myla paused and looked back at him. He was sincere.

"I promise," she said.

*   *   *

According to Sudhakar, Malika was being held in a small room on the bottom floor of the main prison cell. No one was allowed down there. It was always well guarded and a giant iron door blocked the room. Neph seemed intimidated as Sudhakar explained this but Zira wasn't about to let it sway her. They were way too close to finding Malika.

Neph and Zira smiled at each other awkwardly as Sudhakar was binding up their hands and feet. It was strange to be willingly subjecting themselves to this. Once he was done, he put a knife in his belt and led them out of the room in which they were residing.

"You ready?" asked Neph quietly.

"As ready as I'll ever be," answered Zira.

Sudhakar led them out to the main prison center. It was the first time they had been there. They looked around at the couple hundred faces looking back at them from the many different cells. *They think we are criminals*, thought Zira. *They think we must have done something exceptionally evil.* She looked down at her feet as she passed them by, unsure of where else to look

They followed Sudhakar down a small metal staircase to the ground floor. A few empty cells lined the walls. There were four guards, rough looking men who had clearly been in more fights than they would liked to have to their name. They were guarding a giant iron door with a very large wheel at the front of it holding it shut. The guards stared at the three of them as they walked toward them.

Then Neph started coughing, uncontrollably. Zira looked over at him. His face was turning purple. Quickly she shouted at the guards and Sudhakar for help, but no one seemed to know what to do. They all stood around him awkwardly, not really sure how to help. After several seconds, one of them bent down to the choking Neph on the floor to try to help him. Immediately Neph's leg shot up in the air and kicked him in the stomach. Before the others could react, Zira broke her bindings. She then approached two of them from behind, grabbed their arms and flipped them on the ground. The three of them then dragged the guards into one of the empty cells. Neph let out a large fire blast at the cell door, melting it shut. Zira had always hated learning the warrior tactics in school, but surprisingly, they had turned out to be quite useful.

331

Zira ran to the large door shutting off the room where Malika was inside. With all her strength she tried to turn the wheel but couldn't.

"It's stuck!" she shouted at her two companions, who were still admiring their work on the opposite end of the room. Neph ran over to her.

"What?" he asked. "Turn it the other way."

Zira rolled her eyes, and tried.

"It won't go that way either!"

"Let me try," said Neph, who then proceeded to pour all of his strength into moving the wheel, but it wouldn't budge.

"Try it the other way," said Zira.

"Well, obviously I am going to!" answered Neph, but he too could not move it.

"Novia is the only one who has ever opened this door," said Sudhakar softly.

The three of them stared at each other silently, unsure of what to say. Then Zira had an idea.

"*Malika!*" she shouted at the top of her lungs.

Neph immediately jumped over to her and tried to quiet her, but Zira only shouted it again.

"What are you doing?" he whispered. "If you shout out loud, she isn't going to hear you, but the couple hundred prisoners above us might."

"So? Don't they want to be rescued?" she asked him. "*Malika!*"

"Zira, stop!" asked Neph almost as loudly himself.

"Look," Zira said. "Novia is the only one who can get in, but maybe Malika can get out."

"Then why wouldn't she have already?" asked Neph.

"There were four guards; maybe she was scared to," answered Zira. "Now there aren't, so I am trying to let her know it's safe."

"Maybe she's tied up," added Sudhakar. "The restrictions on the door may only go one way, but if she can't move, she can't open it."

Zira looked at them and then back at the door. She wasn't about to run into this Novia down here, so she had to do something.

"I'll transport in," she said resolutely.

"What?" said Neph. "I can't transport you in there. I don't have the control for that."

"I couldn't transport a book," said Sudhakar shaking his head.

"Then I'll transport myself," answered Zira.

"Zira, you couldn't transport me in there let alone yourself," said Neph. "It's like self-levitation. It can't be done. No one is that powerful."

"*You* self-levitated," argued Zira. "And that's precisely why I'm not sending you in there. I'm sending me in there so no one else is in danger."

"You self-levitated?" asked Sudhakar turning to Neph.

"Yeah, but I lost control," answered Neph, staring at Zira. "Myla had to bring out her blue light to get me down remember?"

"Okay, well then you better figure out how to break out a blue light because I am going in there," she answered.

Then Zira raised an eyebrow and disappeared.

*   *   *

Ash led Malachi up to the very top of the prison. With each level, people started to pay attention, wondering what they were up to. They all came out of their cells and stood on the edges of the walkways looking up at them. Eventually, they

333

reached the top. A small vent was above them on the ceiling. Malachi looked at Ash skeptically.

"I'm an old man, Ash," said Malachi.

"Apparently not as old as any of us, and that's our path," Ash responded.

Ash jumped up and pulled open the vent cover. A ladder dropped down. Malachi looked over at Ash and laughed. This was all quite the ordeal to get past a few guards. He didn't argue, however; instead, he followed Ash up the ladder and then down a small but long corridor. Eventually, they reached a door that they were able to open and climb through, finding themselves on the roof of the prison.

"Welcome to the top of the world," said Ash, as Malachi climbed out. It was white all around the prison, no sky or ground, just a fog. Malachi walked to the edge of the roof and looked down. Sure enough, there was a courtyard and another identical tower to the prison.

"That's the dark side," said Ash. "I'm not sure if it's actually any darker. Only Novia goes between the two. No one has ever been able to find an alternate means of entering it besides the courtyard. Some have gone through the opening on the ground floor where your friends went, but they never returned."

"How do we get down there?" asked Malachi, looking over the edge.

"Jump," answered Ash.

"Okay," said Malachi, taking a deep breath.

"Wait!" said Ash. "You're not actually going to jump down there are you?"

"Of course I am," said Malachi, who proceeded to jump down the many stories and landed safely on his feet.

The courtyard was empty, and clearly not that well attended. Malachi didn't immediately walk to the other side.

Instead, he started to circle the courtyard. Ash had mentioned that Myla and Amos had gone somewhere that no one had ever returned from. Was it the dark side? Malachi couldn't be sure, so he examined the courtyard thoroughly for openings. At first it seemed normal, but as he was walking through the center, he stepped on something hard. He knelt down to the ground. It was a pipe, in the center of the courtyard. Malachi laid his ear against the opening. There were voices. He couldn't differentiate the words, but it was Myla and Amos. They were below him.

Malachi looked around for some sort of tool to help him get down there, but there wasn't one. Unbothered, he stood up and placed his hands together with his palms down to the ground. The ground all around him started to shake and dirt started to fly up and spiral into the air. A hole was forming. Soon he had broken through to the tunnel underneath him. However, his feat was definitely not unnoticed.

"Congratulations," said Novia from behind him. "You've destroyed my garden, and now you will never leave it."

*   *   *

"Zira!" shouted Neph over and over again.

"You realize you're doing exactly what you told her to not do?" asked Sudhakar. "She's not here, so she's probably in the room."

"Or dissolved into a million pieces never to appear again," added Neph, his voice laden with worry.

He couldn't believe Zira actually did that. What was she thinking?

"Look, all we can do is wait and hope she walks out of there," said Sudhakar.

Neph nodded his head in agreement and leaned against the wall. However, as his back hit the wall, he could feel it shake. The whole room was shaking, more and more vigorously. Dust started falling on their heads.

"What's going on?" asked Neph.

"I don't know. This has never happened before," Sudhakar responded.

Neph lifted his hand toward the cell with the guards and sent the door flying off the hook. Sudhakar looked at him in shock.

"If this place collapses, I don't want to be responsible for their deaths," he explained.

"You people are unnaturally powerful," he said softly.

Neph was surprised by his words but immediately ran over to the guards and helped them out of the cell and the room. He turned to Sudhakar.

"Make sure they don't help this Novia person," he said. "I have to wait for Zira."

Sudhakar nodded and followed the guards out of the room. Neph started pacing around. He couldn't stand not knowing what had happened to Zira or if she was okay. Then the ground stopped shaking, and the wheel on the front of the door began to turn.

"Zira!" he shouted.

A muffled sound came from inside. He grabbed the wheel and found he could help turn it. Out of the door walked Zira leading Malika. Neph immediately ran over and hugged Zira.

"Don't ever do that again," he said, which Zira only laughed at. Then he turned to Malika. She smiled back at them.

"Thank you both so much," she said with tears in her eyes.

Zira and Neph smiled back at her and each took an arm and led her up the stairs to witness an entirely unpredictable sight, for before them part of the prison wall had collapsed and they, along with hundreds of other prisoners, were looking outside into a courtyard.

*   *   *

Myla shook the dirt off her head, completely confused as to what just happened. Immediately she pulled herself over to Amos. He was lying still covered in dirt, but he turned over and looked at her, nodding that he was okay. Myla looked up. There was an opening out now, and they were no longer trapped. She was able to climb up a hill of dirt up to the courtyard. There she saw Malachi and Novia staring at each other. Neither of them acknowledged her presence.

"What is your intention here?" asked Malachi.

"This prison is mine," she answered, her voice filled with anger.

"You're the guard of Nefarisis," said Malachi thoughtfully.

"I am Nefarisis," she responded.

Then Novia lifted up her hand, and Malachi began to collapse. Myla looked over at him, and she saw blood coming from his chest. He was dying. Novia was killing him. Quietly, she watched the life leave him as he stared helplessly at his killer. Myla didn't know what to do, but she had to do something. She could feel it, throbbing inside of her. She knew what she had to do.

"*Stop!*" she shouted at the top of her lungs.

And all that was around her froze: Malachi, the prisoners, even Amos below. She could see everything. She could see her home, Mertana, and everyone from her village. She had time in her hands, just as before. She could feel the flame. It was burning strong. She could bring them there. She could control it.

Novia, however, moved.

"So it is you," she said, turning to Myla.

Myla looked away from the frozen Malachi and stared back at her.

"I will free these people," Myla said in response.

"You free these people, and you will have an army," Novia answered. "But the road will only get harder for you."

Myla looked at Malachi. She had a newfound confidence that she didn't have before. An aim. A destiny. And for the first time in her life, she accepted it. She walked forward and stared straight at Novia with complete conviction.

"I will free these people."

And then everything moved again, except in her own time... in their own time. Novia had disappeared. The fog surrounding the prison rolled away to a blue sky and the prison walls began to collapse. Prisoners everywhere started to pour out of their cells and out to the courtyard where they could see straight out into a large valley. They could see the forest up ahead, but no one ran for it. Instead they all paused and watched as Myla knelt down by the side of her grandfather. She tried desperately to heal him, but she couldn't. The magic Novia used was too great. With tears streaming down her face, she grabbed his hand as he lay there. He squeezed it back, and for once, he had tears in his eyes as well.

"You did it," he said.

"No," Myla argued shaking her head. "I would have been stuck in that tunnel if it wasn't for you."

Malachi smiled back at her, and Myla knew what was going to happen.

"I can't lose you," she said, unable to fight her tears. "I am not ready."

Malachi squeezed her hand even harder.

"You are the greatest thing that ever came out of my life," he said softly. "I love you, my granddaughter, and I am so proud of you."

"I love you too, Grandfather," she said, in almost a whisper, as Malachi let go of her hand and took his last breath.

Zira walked up to Myla and placed her hand on her shoulder. Myla then stood up and hugged both Zira and Neph, as Malika knelt down by the side of Malachi and cried.

Quietly, Amos climbed out of the tunnel and also walked over to Myla. Some of the prisoners looked scared at his presence, but she held out her hand and clenched his. He gave her a nod of understanding. The pact that they once made for her to kill him was no longer in play. He would help her because they were friends. Somehow, they were friends.

Eventually, they were able to gather all of the prisoners together and leave Nefarisis. Once everyone was out into the valley, the prison disappeared from sight. Novia had taken it back. Myla looked out at the more than four hundred prisoners in disbelief, and they all stared at her with awe. She didn't feel worthy of the attention.

"You're their hero now," said Zira to her quietly. "They will follow you."

"And yet, I wonder how it is that they will," Myla answered, looking to her friend. "Do we really have a chance to take back our home?"

"We have that chance now, Myla," Zira answered. "And we will."

Myla looked to Malika, her mother, and in that moment, she felt a sense of peace. Finally, her mother would return home with her safely. Finally, the evil of Amos in her life was resolved.

The journey home through the forest turned out to be quite easy. They were a good deal south of their old village, but it wasn't as confusing as she expected to find the way home.

It took them four days to reach the camp of the Caldar, and their greeting was a joyous one. The people had begun to build a new village by the river and with the addition of four hundred new people it was starting to feel a bit more like a home instead of a refugee camp.

Paul was there when they arrived home. He didn't hesitate to go up to Myla and give her a giant hug.

"You survived," he said with a smile.

"As did you," she answered simply, but it was all they needed to say.

There was finally hope in their lives. She would spend her life with Paul. She knew that now. And the two of them and Zira, Neph, Amos, along with every other Caldar would accomplish that dormant goal of a thousand years. Caldaria would no longer be a myth. Myla would lead her people home.

Epilogue

Amos patted the ground with his hands. The seeds would grow well in this soil. He breathed in the fresh air of the forest and smiled at the small garden he had created. The village would be pleased with the vegetables he would provide them.

Several weeks had passed since they returned home from the prison, and in that time, the people had accepted him into their village. He was thankful for them, but there were also times, such as this one, where spending time alone was most fulfilling. He, however, was not alone.

"I see that your little insurrection has served you well," said a voice behind him. "It will not last."

Amos turned around to see Misha standing before him.

"I am no longer your servant, Sherah," Amos answered. "I no longer bend to your will."

Misha looked at him angrily.

"You cannot defeat me," he said. "You are not strong enough. This world is mine."

Amos stood up and stared at Misha in the face.

"You're right," Amos said. "I am not strong enough, but with Myla I am, and we will beat you."

"Yet you are not the one she turns to," Misha said slowly. "You are not the one she trusts. You served me too long for that."

"She will trust me, Sherah," Amos answered confidently. "And she and I together will have victory."

Misha paused a second before disappearing and leaving Amos be. Amos then knelt to the ground and continued to tend to his garden.

The adventure continues in

The Quest for Caldaria
Book 2 in the Caldaria Trilogy

A novel by Julia Faye

Acknowledgments

Thank you to my husband, Andrew Slade, for reading, editing, supporting, encouraging and in all ways simply being awesome while I've been working on these novels.

Thank you to Alden King, who voluntarily donated so much of his time towards helping me edit my novels.

And lastly, thank you to Kelsea Schmidt for drawing such an excellent map.

About the Author

Julia Faye is the author of the Caldaria Trilogy, including The Vision of Caldaria, The Quest for Caldaria and The Waking of Caldaria. She was raised in the San Francisco Bay Area in California and then in Seattle, Washington. She attended the University of Washington and majored in both French and Journalism, where she initially developed her love of writing. She now lives in Orange County, California, with her husband and son, where she is a teacher and writes part-time.

Made in the USA
San Bernardino, CA
23 March 2016